MATRICIDE

THE TRAGEDY
ON
PROSPECT HILL

Vincent L. Lombardi

MATRICIDE
The Tragedy on Prospect Hill

ISBN: 1-892590-31-X

Fifth Way Press
4686 Meridian Rd.
Williamston, MI 48895
jp@outyourbackdoor.com
outyourbackdoor.com

Cover Art: Original clay mono prints by Peg Lombardi

Printed in the U.S.A. by PrintTech, Ann Arbor, Michigan

10 9 8 7 6 5 4 3 2 1

To my students: More than a generation of
M.S.U. undergraduates

In memory of Jeff Oberlee,
no longer Caught in the Rye

Thanks to Charles P. Silas for his encouragement

Thanks to the late G. Marian Kinget
for her enthusiastic support of the project

Thanks to Katherine McCracken
for her keen criticism of every word

Love and thanks to
Margaret Petrarca Lombardi
for her help in every way

There are buildings or metal structures so made
that if they are struck at a certain point
or if a certain stone is moved,
the whole thing collapses.

—Raniero Cantalamessa

It is not for you to know times or seasons. . . .
But you shall receive power when the
Holy Spirit has come upon you;
and you shall be my witnesses . . .

—Acts 1: 7 - 8

MATRICIDE

THE TRAGEDY
ON
PROSPECT HILL

Vincent L. Lombardi

1
Discovery

Home for Easter break from the university a few months back, I was lonely. All my friends were away, and Prospect Hill was deserted.

But houses were sprouting everywhere—the place was like a garden gone to weed—cluttering the slopes and blemishing the landscape. I walked to the edge of the woods on the mountaintop overlooking Sacred Heart and was sad to see it too being eaten away. It pleased me to roam through a vestige of village woodland standing since the Pilgrims settled here.

It was a cool crisp morning and the chilly breeze made me feel refreshed. Resting on a rock beside the stream, I stared at the tip of the church steeple stretching up from the valley below. A shaft of sunlight filtering through the budding trees lit up the other side of the stream. In the blink of an eye, I caught sight of something sparkling. At first I didn't make anything of it; then curiosity got the better of me. I jumped from rock to rock across the shallow stream and started to move a few stones around—looking for I didn't know what. A sharp bit of metal stuck out from under one of them, and I picked away at the heavy clay covering it. Soon the outline of a square metal container emerged. The sunlight must have reflected on its exposed edge.

The old rumors burst into my mind—the rumors about Lena Penta, the crippled dwarf who'd lived on Prospect Hill. People said she often walked alone howling in the woods at night. For years they gossiped about her: supposedly she'd left a legacy, a manuscript shaming them. People around town laughed at and ridiculed her. But people stopped talking about Lena long ago.

Fern roots had wrapped themselves around the container like heavy ropes. Could I pry them free without tools? I found a sharp stone and began to hack away at them, one by one. It seemed like an eternity of unsnarling and tugging, of scraping and breaking before they gave up their hold. The job was only half done and already I was worn out. The container—a lockbox—still needed to be dislodged from the caked clay clutching it. Banging it with the stone and kicking with all my might, I finally jarred it free.

I struck at the rusted lock until the hinge came loose. A branch used as a lever helped me rip the lock and hinge off. Sweat poured out of me and stung my eyes.

I turned the container upside down and shook it so the contents would jar the lid loose. Little by little a crack appeared and my fingernails could grip the lid and jimmy it till I got the opening wide enough to force a stick into. At long last I got the lid up and yanked the rusted thing off.

In it was a thick manuscript wrapped in wax paper and, around that, sections of old newspapers. The writing was in uniform, perfect letters and looked like a woman's. My heart nearly jumped out of my chest when my eyes lit on the title page.

Matricide: The Tragedy on Prospect Hill

The paper was almost perfectly preserved, and it was Lena's manuscript.

My excitement during the next few days is hard to put into words. I was carried back in time to the tragic events on Prospect Hill—bewildered, yet heartened. Feelings of belonging and of pride filled me. I felt bonded to the older generation as I never had before, and I was surprised to learn of those folks' ethnic backgrounds, their joys and sorrows, their simpler ways in those days long past.

With Easter vacation past, I haven't been able to keep those feelings or to delight in village history so much. Once I went back to school, fear and loneliness began creeping up on me again. But when they do, I turn to my roots and, delving deep down inside myself, enter into the hearts and minds of the people of our town who were filled with a yearning for the goodness of life.

Here's this story as I found it, with Lena's comments splicing together the various parts and with its inconsistencies and irrelevancies. For instance, she tells us we'll hear no more about her, she wants to be dispassionate. But every now and then she slips back into the story passionately. Then there's her nostalgic lingering over the children—did she want to show us life in olden days? But some of the children we lose sight of. Most likely she was working against time and intended to fill in the gaps and smooth out the bumps later. It took her years to gather information and she didn't begin writing till 1967. She died a few months after finishing the manuscript.

She had to be much more intelligent and educated than people gave her credit for. Yet there's lots I find strange. Her obsession with matricide for one thing—the mother who was killed on Prospect Hill. And her far-fetched views that our village was the first to commit matricide and that killing the mother is likely to spread around the world. And the way she hid her manuscript—hiding a light under a bushel.

Often I find myself thinking about Lena. Some say she was not all there. My father told me how people about town often taunted her. But why were so many drawn to her, seeking her out to talk to and listen to as she rocked in a tiny rocker on her porch?

Michael Santangelo
Journalism, Class of 2001
Prospect Hill
July 1999

Matricide
The Tragedy On Prospect Hill

This is a story about a murder that runs deeper, far deeper, than fact. Take it from Pasqualina, or Lena as the townsfolk call me.

To be deformed, to be detached, to be afflicted, to be alone— somehow you enter the inside track of reality. You see with the eyes of an eagle. Little escapes your sight.

Like a magnet drawing both crude and refined metal to itself, I, a misfit, drew to my porch the beautiful and the ugly, the good and the bad, the righteous and the self-righteous. Like people disrobing shamelessly before an animal, our townsfolk thoughtlessly bared their souls to me. Yes, dear folk, I saw through you—all.

To be sure, there's a vast chasm between the virtuous and the vicious. From the one I felt the beneficial presence of the good; from the other I felt the contempt of the base.

Many say I howl in the woods on the mountaintop above Sacred Heart. They are liars. My heart howls and, yes, I go and have always gone to the woods alone to pray for love, for help to soothe my savage breast, for forgiveness for my anger, and for the lessening of my torment—the thorn in my side I know will stick with me all the days of my life.

Of course, I had my darlings, too. When Anna or Paul dropped by, my heart would sing. Then after the murder, when Anna was taken away, no day passed that I didn't think about her.

Years before Anna began coming to me, her mother Felicia and her grandmother Assunta brought me great comfort. They'd bring sunshine into my life, melting away the cold misery of loneliness. And I could not have gone on without the warmth and friendship of our beloved priest, Fr. DiSanto.

Then there were the likes of Lillian, the gossip whose groaning mouth smeared so many: the morally feeble who darkened the lives of others.

But I get ahead of myself. I must start at the beginning. I know now that we are all maimed beings: all disconnected from ourselves—all prisoners of the world. Every one of us is seeking salvation, is seeking goodness, even though we often lose our way.

My soul is no longer in agony: my rage and enmity have given way to grace that flows through me now and then, nourishing me. I now feel more compassionate. It's my tormentors who are the cripples, the ones howling like animals at night in the woods. It's for them too that I now pray, hoping and trusting they'll be born to their true humanity.

When you read my story, you'll be skeptical: How could I, a deformed dwarf scorned and sought out by the townsfolk, penetrate their minds and hearts? Some will no doubt accuse me of making it all up. Think what you will. I know it's the truth. And truth defies proof. It must be lived through and understood. All we see is simply the reflection and shadow of what is invisible to the eye.

When the murder took place my heart nearly broke. For days on end I went alone to the forest on the mountaintop overlooking Sacred Heart, grieving and hoping that light would be shed on the darkness visited us on Prospect Hill.

For years I agonized over what had happened before and after the murder. To tell the whole story is not possible—too many details are lost forever. Yet I will tell you as best I can about the events leading up to the crime, and after—to the unique upheaval of the twentieth century. To do that, I must go back to Rome and to that unfortunate noblewoman who came to dwell among us.

Much that we'd like to know about her and her family and about the changing times of the 1940s and 1950s is buried in the souls of our townsfolk. Even though they confided much about their inner thoughts and feelings, I still fail to make sense of the crime and the criminal. This tale of love and death came to me bit by bit over many years: reading personal journals, listening to wives, children, and husbands. Of course, pouring out their hearts to a dwarf—there was no shame in that. I always lent a listening ear despite their mockery: secretly jotting down every trifle, scrutinizing every shard, and fitting them into a mosaic. In the course of time and from the sludge of passing events the truth gradually surrendered itself.

In moments when the sun shines in my life I like to think that the tragedy is an omen of new prospects, a turning point—an opening of new vistas on our planet. Maybe the mother killing did not happen in vain.

I now take leave of you. You'll hear no more about the dwarf of Prospect Hill, the afflicted soul. I withdraw into myself to reveal to you the tragedy that will pass from our village to towns, from towns to cities, from cities to nations and to the world—matricide that promises to wrack and ruin the twentieth century or to give birth to the spiritual evolution of mankind.

Knowing what I now know, I sleep better. I've passed through the night of darkness. I wish only that my story help you, dear folk, in finding eternal joy.

Many people helped make telling this story possible, during the past year. Count and Countess Petrarca made Felicia's journals available to me and visited at my home to confirm many facts about their daughter and grandchildren; Assunta and Piero Benedicta helped me piece together the happenings in Rome and on Prospect Hill; a cadre of social workers and psychiatrists opened my eyes to the contradictions they found in trying to evaluate Anna's mental condition after the murder; Father DiSanto shared his library as well as his knowledge of the changing times we are living in and the changing nature of community life; and some townsfolk put their trust in me.

As soon as I started writing in 1967, it became clear to me that public disclosure of intimate details might embarrass Anna and Paul, and not only them. Why not bury the manuscript then? Recalling many delightful stories of buried treasures read during my youth, I rushed headlong throughout the winter, spring, and summer of 1967 penning this manuscript. Let fate determine whether or not it will surface as testimony from this generation to the next.

> Pasqualina Penta
> Prospect Hill
> September 1967

THE CRIME THAT SHOOK PROSPECT HILL

Providence Journal, Sunday, March 26, 1950

OBITUARY

Mrs. Felicia Margarita Benedicta, 35, found dead, 9 a.m. yesterday morning in her home at 12 Wakefield Lane, Natick. She is survived by two children: a daughter, Anna Maria, and a son, Alessandro Luigi . . .

Providence Journal, Sunday, March 26, 1950

DEATH OF ITALIAN NOBLEWOMAN

Mrs. Felicia Margarita Petrarca Benedicta was found dead yesterday morning at her home at 12 Wakefield Lane, Natick.

The West Warwick Police are investigating the circumstances of her death. At this time the police do not rule out foul play. The medical examiner's report has yet to be issued . . .

Mrs. Benedicta was the only daughter of the Countess Clara Orsini and Count Luigi Colonna Petrarca of Rome. The count and countess have been notified of their daughter's death and are expected to arrive at Logan Airport tomorrow.

Mrs. Benedicta is survived by two children, Anna Maria, 12, and Alessandro Luigi, 10; her mother-in-law, Mrs. Assunta Benedicta; and her brother-in-law, Piero Benedicta.

Pawtuxet Valley Times, Saturday, May 13, 1950

ITALIAN NOBLEWOMAN SLAIN ON PROSPECT HILL: HEARING BY JUVENILE COURT

A court hearing for the juvenile suspected of the murder of Mrs. Felicia Benedicta of 12 Wakefield Lane, Prospect Hill, Natick, concluded yesterday.

It could not be learned what its findings were because the hearing was closed to the public. Rhode Island law prohibits public disclosure of court actions involving juveniles.

Mrs. Benedicta, the 35-year-old daughter of the Count and Countess Luigi Petrarca of Rome, was stabbed to death in her home on March 25. Her death has baffled the West Warwick police in the weeks since. Investigators found no evidence of forced entry into the house.

Mrs. Benedicta emigrated from Rome in 1936 with her husband, Marco, now deceased. The couple lived on Prospect Hill.

2
Events Leading to the Crime

Anguish in Rome, 1936

In many of the forty-seven rooms of the fifteenth-century palazzo, servants scurried frantically—gathering, folding, pleating, ironing, packing, hauling. For days, the palazzo had been a beehive bustling with work. All this, only days after the count and countess had entertained the American ambassador. All this, for something the servants just didn't believe would come to pass.

There was no shortage of speculation passing from servant to servant, from ground keepers to kitchen cleaners, from the count's social secretary, Francesca, to the chauffeur, Antonio. "I'll believe it when it happens!" . . . "We're getting down to the wire, there's no turning back!" . . . "Damn shame, if you ask me—Marco's a fine chap!" . . . "The poor countess—a real saint, to put up with it!" . . . "You'll see, the count will relent!" . . . "My bet's on Felicia giving in!" . . . "Never happen! The date's already set!" . . . "All the count's dealings with the snobby

uppercrust. Let Felicia make her own choice—that's what I say."
. . . "Time for the count to loosen up!" On and on the chatter
went—mouth, feet, and hands in perpetual motion.

In her suite of rooms on the third floor, west end of the
palazzo, Felicia looked out her window and stared at the familiar
skyline. The early morning haze over the Tiber was slowly lifting.
She paused sadly and took in the towering dome of St. Peter's.
Getting married, she thought, is no simple matter; her world
had come crashing down. She turned and glanced down at the
bustling traffic on the Lungotevere, astride the river.

Not that she had cold feet or any qualms about Marco. Not
at all. But he was a commoner and this, above all, outraged her
parents. It didn't matter that Marco Benedicta was trustworthy,
of good family, well educated, and fairly well off, not to mention
handsome. All this was lost to sight, hidden or screened out, as
it filtered through the prism of her parents' minds.

They had put up with her courtship for well over a year.
They believed that she would come to her senses one day, view
Marco through the same prism, and see him as they did—
unsuitable. After all, wasn't there an impenetrable wall between
the nobility and the commonfolk? Yes, let's bear him; let's put
up with him. It's simply a matter of time.

They had not counted on Felicia's strong convictions or her
willfulness. She held dear that her heart and head should work
together, not be split apart—one chosen over the other for social
gain. Even if her head advised, she'd refuse to silence her heart.
As for Marco, her reason got on very well with her emotions,
thank you. Her father insisted she surrender her heart to the
welfare of her family and class and become wise in the ways of
the world. Wasn't that what nobility was all about?

Dressed in a dark blue suit, she'd been waiting anxiously in
her study on the third floor, ready to leave at a moment's notice.
Her fate hung in the balance and her heart—yes the very same
heart—was torn in two because her parents still claimed part of
it. Her ears were tuned to the clamor coming from her father's
rooms. She reached over to her bookshelf and straightened out
her journals, some she'd packed away to take with her. She looked
sadly at her stubby ceramic vase crammed with pencils and passed

her hand over her oak-top desk, tenderly dusting it as if she'd soon be parting from an old friend.

Her body ached from top to toe after a fitful night's sleep. Nightmares, incited by her inner turmoil, gave her little rest. Over and over she'd find herself lost in a dark dreary woods filled with dread. No matter which way she turned, she could find no way out. She woke up with an undeniable feeling of betrayal.

From the first her father had held his ground: under no condition would he consent to this misbegotten marriage. Descended from the Colonna of Rome (and her mother from the Orsini), he deemed the union unthinkable and promised to use every means to prevent it. Having discounted the seriousness of his threat till he refused to see her again, she now began to own up to the fact that she'd misjudged him and that he'd decided to abandon her—unless he got his way.

All morning in a last-ditch effort on her behalf an entourage trooped into and out of her father's rooms. Many in her family and among the long-time staff had taken up her cause, pleading with him, for her well-being and the family's, to honor her wishes.

In a note sent by way of his social secretary, Francesca—a woman held high in the count's esteem—Felicia begged to see him again:

> *Dearest Papa,*
>   *In my anger I threatened to leave home today for good. Forgive my willfulness. Please, Papa, don't desert me. I know we can work out our differences. I need to see you.*
>   *I wait trembling.*
>   *Your loving daughter,*
>   *Felicia*

Actually, when she'd told her parents she intended to run out on them, it was simply a bluff to force her father's hand. Her father, unlike her mother, who'd taken it to heart, refused to budge. Now the reality she so feared, breaking with her family, faced her like an impending storm.

Yes, she was partly to blame. At least the cavalier way she'd handled it. It all began with her defiance: her refusal to bend to her father's will and to submit to a dynastic marriage. She had no intention of giving up Marco and, in a rash act to bring the conflict to a head, announced a wedding date, counting on her parents to give in. It would put an end to their bitter conflict, she had hoped. Feelings no doubt would be bruised, but then love and affection were bound to bring them back together, with her parents' agreeing to the marriage—grudgingly, to be sure. Marco, she was sure, would win their hearts and be welcomed into the family.

The one person she had put her faith in was her father. Till now he'd not only been father to her but a friend cherished beyond words. Youthful in his ways, he was more comfortable with her generation than his own. Open to new ideas and critical of those who failed to keep their fingers on the pulse of history, he'd gained a certain reputation among his peers as a reformer, an intellectual of sorts. But for all his bravado he refused to act upon reforms he'd championed (like accepting a husband from the middle class), now that the reforms had come home to roost. The nobility was too strongly rooted in his blood, she thought. To her dismay, their arguments had skirted reason and took place in an abyss of entangled emotions.

Worst yet, what had been a family affair had mushroomed into a well-publicized and intriguing social scandal throughout Roman society. Just turned twenty-two and sole heir to a vast fortune, she was sought after by some of Europe's oldest, noblest families. The fate of many, she now saw, hinged on the outcome. The great wealth at stake caused ripples throughout the privileged class: not only did it arouse the appetite of uncles, aunts, and cousins, who stood to gain the most; it also turned the heads of others who coveted her inheritance. Only her mother, Clara, foresaw the storm brewing—the tragedy in the making, as Clara put it.

So by the spring of 1936 Felicia found herself at loggerheads with her father while her mother, like the proverbial ass torn between two bundles of hay, pleaded—turning first to one then to the other, frazzled. "There's something more to this, believe me," Clara had told Felicia. "It's more than defiance on your part or reprisal on Papa's." Countess Clara saw all too clearly the mutual betrayal of the love and trust forged between father and daughter. "If you don't watch out, you'll end up wounding each other," Clara said, flustered. "Then where will we be? You're so bent on having your own way there's nothing Papa can do that'll please you. And he's as stubborn as a mule. Short of a miracle, our family will be ripped apart forever."

Over the years, the countess had seen her daughter become her father's child. Felicia was daughter-son-pupil-friend-historian-philosopher to her father—all rolled into one. There was so much of Luigi in Felicia and so much of Felicia in Luigi that in heart and mind they were like siamese twins. "Any split," Clara had cautioned Felicia, "will leave me with two cripples." Felicia had put little stock in her mother's words.

But now, staring out the window, she thought of all the suffering she'd put her mother through—a woman who'd borne four children. Only she, Felicia Margarita Colonna Orsini Petrarca, survived. Her Christian, confirmation, ancestral, and family names, her parents explained, each had its significance. She smiled as she recalled how they'd boastfully tease her as a child:

> *First you were happy, then a real pearl—*
> *   that's Felicia Margarita;*
> *The nobility of antiquity gave you a mighty soul—*
> *   that's Colonna and Orsini;*
> *At bottom there's the freedom of the Renaissance—*
> *   that's Petrarca, the father of it all.*

Startled by the bang of the door to her father's rooms, she stiffened. Only one person—her mother—dared show him such contempt.

Seconds later she heard her mother rush past her study, sobbing.

Still she waited. She picked up the short, quick footsteps of the count's secretary, Francesca, going in. Minutes later she heard the same quick footsteps coming toward her rooms. No doubt he had rebuffed Francesca's appeal. Shaking, Felicia got up, put on her hat, and braced herself for the ordeal ahead.

"I'm sorry . . . the count refuses—has nothing more to say," Francesca announced as she entered Felicia's study.

Felicia saw tears in Francesca's eyes and looked away. "Thank you, Francesca . . . for all . . . thanks—"

Francesca rushed toward Felicia, embraced her, and whispered, "God be with you!"

Gripping the banister of the high curving stairway and feeling queasy, Felicia slowly descended to the foyer of the great hall. She felt herself being severed from the womb that had for so long protected and nourished her. Can anyone escape the taint of family life, she thought, a taint that stems from love itself— a love that suffocates? But where would we be without the nurturing of our parents? A terrible conflict churned within— love for Marco vied with the need of her parents' blessing.

Clara, anticipating her daughter's departure and cringing like a shrunken figure before the sixteenth-century fresco depicting Dante's *Purgatorio,* had posted herself at the bottom of the stairs. She sighed and cupped her temples as if to stay herself from madness.

"Mia cara," she stammered, "how can you leave like this? For the love of God—you're breaking our hearts. Yes, yes, his heart too." Tears trickled down Clara's cheeks. Given the count's tirade minutes earlier, she could hardly speak. She'd failed to bring her husband and daughter around to reason.

"I never thought it would come to this," Felicia said. Glancing toward the stairway, she hoped to see her father trailing after her. "Think of Marco—*povero* Marco!—you've been so unkind to him."

Clara saw her own and her husband's youth mirrored in Felicia's face—bright brown eyes and full red lips. With her handkerchief Clara wiped away Felicia's tears and patted her lustrous hair. "Can't you see, once you leave, the chasm widens— the crisis comes to a head. But . . . but with it, separation—an end for us all." Her mournful voice begged Felicia not to leave.

Clara lamented her earlier attacks on Marco; even more, she regretted the threats against Felicia to get her to call off the wedding. What a tempest was set off once the date had been set.

She now wanted so much to comfort Felicia, but anger rose up in her. "Papa's stubborn . . . hopeless." Looking straight into Felicia's eyes, she said, "You . . . you too, you're just like him."

Her mother in her mid-forties looked old and frail. Her large brown almond-shaped eyes, wide mouth, and high cheekbones gave her an unusual beauty. But her face from days of weeping was covered by taut creased skin, and her light brown hair was dry and brittle.

"You and Papa have looked on Marco as 'a man without a title.' What a farce, Mamma, to put the title before the man and to dismiss our love." After all, Marco, an artist of twenty-five, would please the most devoted parents. "What good's a title, can you *please* tell me, Mamma, if not backed up by goodness?" Hadn't Marco borne her parents' contempt long enough?

At first, Clara had failed to support Felicia against her husband's outbursts, had been cold to Marco, had looked on their courtship as a passing fancy. Clara's efforts to help Felicia were too little and too late. Now she couldn't shake Luigi's obstinacy and wanted to fight him tooth and nail, to claw into his stupidity. Yet Clara amazed herself when she heard herself mouthing Luigi's words—"My love, a loss of title will come home to haunt you." Clara blushed and her heart sank.

"Not again! Please, Mamma." Felicia was torn between rage and heartache. Her eyes darted from her mother to the stairwell, still hoping, still waiting. If her father made the slightest gesture, she'd fall at his feet and beg forgiveness.

Antonio, the chauffeur, waited at the front door ready to take Felicia to the Benedictas'. She'd be staying with one of her future sisters-in-law till the wedding. Servants, who'd been collecting and carting her belongings for the better part of the morning, came round to the front of the palazzo to wish her well.

Felicia hugged and thanked each in turn. She turned to her mother. "I'm sorry, Mamma. Forgive me, Mamma. You've done your best. I'll always love you—Papa, too."

The countess strained every sinew in her body to keep from ranting. She mumbled as if death had already claimed her, "May

God watch over you, my love!" In tears, they embraced for the last time.

As Antonio shut the iron gate between the high walls encircling the grounds, Felicia took a last look at the gardens, the fountains, the old grand palazzo. She saw her mother, still as a statue, shrinking in the background as Antonio drove off down the Via Giulia toward the Tiber, passing ancient houses and artisan shops.

How did such a misfortune befall her and her family? Her thoughts fled back in time. Even the European war of 1914 had not disturbed them much. Aunts, uncles, cousins, servants, and her British nanny—all took refuge at Castello Petrarca, their summer home, a villa that looked like a small castle in Rignano sull'Arno. Perched high up on a Tuscan hill, it overlooked valleys blanketed in vineyards and olive groves. Felicia, born on the eve of the war, had spent her first four years there, shielded from the violence ravaging Europe. On returning to Rome, the count's wealth and stature intact, she began her formal schooling, having a liking for the arts and humanities. Brought up trilingually, she was fluent in English and French. Recalling her childhood she smiled—her doting parents had always praised her.

Her courtship with Marco was an agony to them. She pulled a handkerchief from her purse to dry her eyes. Reluctantly Papa had called off his efforts to unite their family with one of Europe's noble houses. His heart had been set on a dynastic marriage.

Oblivious to Antonio inching the car through the early afternoon crowds on the Via Arenula, she thought of the Benedictas. She as well as Marco saw the world through different eyes. They dreamed of a humanity valuing virtue and justice above class standing.

The warmth she had been brought up to believe abided in those of high birth and breeding she now found lacking. The feuding of the old families over etiquette, lineage, and prestige— in a world striving to find its soul—sickened her. In her journals she had taken to writing things like, "Unless privileges are extended to all mankind, raising all to the level of nobility, modern civilization threatened by anarchy will rip itself apart."

Antonio drove in silence. The passing sights churned up long-shelved memories. This one reminded her of Josephine, that one of her professors. Yes, many she counted among those who helped her see the failings of her class. Did it start with Papa's cousin, Josephine? Outraged by the pettiness of the nobles, Josephine, a countess herself, often mocked them.

Then there were her professors. Many of the old aristocrats in league with Mussolini didn't escape the condemnation of the intellectuals at the university. Safe among select students, professors exposed Mussolini's ignorance to ridicule. She and Marco would open their ears and eyes to the truth that Mussolini's brutal Ministry of Culture and Propaganda tried to stifle.

Yes, Papa too was her first and true teacher. How much truth had come from his lips before their falling-out! In pain she pictured his handsome face, bashful smile, short brown hair parted on the left, and his svelte body wearing his years—forty-five—like a man in his mid-thirties.

Finally Antonio parked the car beside the large block of flats at the north entrance to the Piazza Navona.

The Benedicta family had gathered together to greet her. Marco's married sisters, Carla and Ida, in their late twenties, and single brother Piero, five years Marco's junior, welcomed her into the family with open arms. Her mother-in-law-to-be, Assunta, ten years a widow, had treated Felicia as one of her own.

A well-educated woman of fifty, Assunta Benedicta had a youthful figure and thick dark hair pulled back into a bun. Her lively green-blue eyes and saucy smile signaled spunk: a woman tender yet upright, wise yet cheerful.

Fleeing Rome

The Benedicta family, middle class and *nouveau riche*, had spared nothing in schooling their children, giving them an education second to none. The count and countess, had they not turned a deaf ear to Felicia's praise of the Benedictas, would have found them refined and honorable.

The wedding took place with two Petrarcas present—Felicia's cousins secure enough to defy the count's authority. Count Luigi forbade that Felicia's name be spoken in his presence; Countess Clara, foregoing this special and sacred event in her daughter's life, fell into despair.

Felicia and Marco accepted Assunta's invitation to move into her spacious flat on the Piazza Navona. Cut off from her parents, Felicia teetered between happiness and hopelessness. The honeymoon was strained. Marco grew more and more fearful as Europe's dictators rushing toward war were sending out signals as obvious as the rumbling of a volcano about to erupt.

A few weeks after the wedding, Mussolini captured Abyssinia and, savoring his triumph, spoke from the balcony of the Palazzo Venezia to crowds drunk with victory. The King of Italy had taken the title of Emperor of Abyssinia.

"Abyssinia today—where will Mussolini strike tomorrow?" Marco asked Felicia one morning. He was convinced the Benedictas should leave Italy. Word was spreading that General Franco was on the move to overthrow the Spanish Republic. "Mussolini, you'll see, will soon be sending troops to aid General Franco," Marco charged. "Europe's getting ready for another bloodbath. We've got to get away before it's too late, Felicia."

"Easier said than done." This was not the first time he'd sounded her out. He seemed bent on emigrating to America. Looking out the window at the statues bathed in the early morning sunlight, she was drawn to the statue of Neptune spearing an octopus. She felt the tentacles of destiny entrapping her.

Marco got up, walked over to the window, and put his arm around her. Standing in the same spot a few days earlier, they'd heard the screaming hordes at the Palazzo Venezia—little more than a half mile away—where Mussolini spoke from the balcony, loud speakers blaring. His victory in Abyssinia shattered their hope for peace.

"It's too late for us now," Marco said, "we're trapped by Mussolini's lust for power. God help anyone who stands in his way."

"He's a wolf preying on the sheep now. But, believe me, he'll be cut to shreds," she said.

Looking out at the piazza in silence, Felicia felt Marco press against her affectionately. He was tall and muscular. A few months of marriage and already they could communicate by a touch, a movement of an eye, a grin. Occasionally she'd catch a glimpse of her mother's face in his expression. Not the almond-shaped eyes or high cheekbones—was it his smile, his gentility? He, like Piero, had inherited Assunta's green-blue eyes; Piero's were real green, offset by wavy auburn hair. Marco's dark hair and moustache complemented his fair complexion.

"I wouldn't bet on it," Marco said. "You have to agree—people are taken in by Mussolini. He's displaced the monarchy and got rid of democracy. Italy's in for no end of trouble. You know—you've said as much yourself—by supporting the Abyssinian war, the king is in thick with the fascists. Who'll be able to hold back the bully now?"

"It's the other side of the ocean that scares me. What'll we find there? Besides, America's in a depression."

This was not the full truth of what was on her mind. She had for some time come to see that the power of Mussolini, Hitler, and Stalin was an upshot of the terrible disorder bred by the war of 1914: everywhere chaos, suffering, and killing. These dictators, playing on the fears of the people and glorifying hatred and violence, she thought, incited greater anarchy, and this increased their power. Divide and conquer, that was their game. Yet, her fears of being uprooted from Rome outweighed her anxiety over the looming European war.

Hearing Assunta and Piero come into the living room, they turned to greet them.

"Marco, did I tell you Mr. Cecere's son Paolo is doing pretty well in America?" Piero asked, as if he had been privy to Felicia's and Marco's conversation.

Felicia looked up at Marco. "You've really made up your mind to leave?"

"We've talked about it for some time."

"No doubt the fascists are out of control," Assunta said. "Il Duce, like a dragon full of rage, has come to be offended by democracies—the one sprouting in Spain affronts him. Too bad!" Her own words seemed to anger and spur her on. "His delusions of power will soon land us all in the middle of another nightmare.

And that monster to the north—God only knows how soon that mad Hun will set Europe aflame." Having lived through the world war, Assunta saw it all happening again: Europe bathed in its people's blood and without a thought of what these dictators, like the emperors before them, were really after.

A servant's steps heard in the hallway silenced them at once. Who could you trust nowadays? Felicia thought. Debate had been cursed in the régime as families and friends turned against one another. Even an indiscreet remark to those you trusted, if repeated, could land you in serious trouble with the blackshirts. Felicia knew of good, loyal people beaten within an inch of their lives without legal charges or court action restraining the arm of power. Servants long in your employ—you never knew their political leanings. So at breakfast, the family limited themselves to chitchat and saved serious talk for their morning stroll.

Listening to Marco and her in-laws, Felicia was a bit put out as they walked in the piazza. Already they'd weighed options and found possible means. This was news to her; she felt excluded. It soon became obvious—they didn't want to worsen her anxieties till they'd formed some plans based on real prospects. Not having made peace with her parents, she found herself in a fix. What would she do if the Benedictas decided to leave Italy? She was cut to the quick and tightened her grip on Marco.

"Don't worry, *tesoro mio,*" he said to reassure her. "At the moment we're biding our time. Mamma will be in touch with the Ceceres. Let's see what conditions are like over there."

They sat on the low wall surrounding the Fountain of the Four Rivers for a bit, then got up and set out for the Campo.

"I hear houses can be bought for a song . . . in New England, anyhow," Piero said. "Many émigrés are doing well despite the depression. Paolo Cecere's been living in a small town in Rhode Island since he left Rome in '22—has got his own house."

Piero didn't have to say more. After all, they knew he was bound to be called up for military service soon. Marco, too, at the age of twenty-five was unlikely to escape it. And then they'd find themselves embroiled in a mess that, as Assunta put it, "looked as if it's going to be worse than the bloodletting of 1914 that gobbled up millions of Europeans. To what end!"

"Mamma has already started to settle accounts with her family," Marco said.

"What do you mean?" Felicia asked troubled.

"Well, we must begin slowly." Marco put his arm around her waist and drew her close. "No, we must begin in secret. We've got to decide whether to flee or not to flee—if to flee, how to finance it. We'll need to get enough together to weather a few years there if Piero and I can't find work."

"We've got more than enough," Assunta said. "But transferring assets is no simple matter. And then . . ."

"Then?" Felicia asked, distressed by her mother-in-law's tone of voice.

"Your parents . . ." Marco said.

Felicia did not answer.

"Felicia," Assunta said, "you must patch things up. Please don't let matters fester."

By this time they found themselves in the bustling marketplace of the Campo dei Fiori. They sat outside at a bar and ordered espressos. Facing the statue of Giordano Bruno in its solemn stance at the center of the square, they planned their flight from Rome. Felicia no longer sustained any illusion; plans had been long in the making.

At first she opposed the move; then she thought better of it; finally she gave in. She felt both frightened and elated.

Settling in on Prospect Hill

Time passed quickly till the eve of their departure, and still Felicia agonized over leaving her parents and homeland.

The deep wound from her parents' rejection hadn't healed. Every desire to rush to them was opposed by a feeling of resentment. Rancor stiffened her will against giving in, as if to punish them for her loss. She was caught in a vicious cycle: love and anger alternated in an inner brew of shame and guilt. All this she kept bottled up, not talking about it to Marco and her in-laws.

For months she'd been in contact with cousins well informed of her plans to emigrate. Surely her parents knew. She waited them out, hoping they'd make the first move. Hurt by their silence and crippled by resentment, she left Rome without so much as a goodbye. With her sisters-in-law and their husbands soon to follow, she, Marco, Assunta, and Piero set sail for the New World from the Bay of Naples in the sweltering August heat of 1936.

After less than a day at sea, a fire got started and raged in the ship's kitchen, gray-black smoke seeping from the lower to the upper decks, the ship a floating pyre, the passengers panicking. The top deck, thronged with people scrambling in fear from the stifling fumes, was in pandemonium. The crew soon got the fire under control and put it out, with little damage. In soothing words the steadfast captain apprised the alarmed passengers that he needed to return to Naples, assuring them the repairs were a mere precaution. No one would be allowed off the ship.

Back in port, the brilliant sun shone down from the cloudless sky on a listless sea—not a breeze stirred. For two days they lived on top of an oven, drenched in sweat and dried out. For three days Felicia felt the fluttering wings of death, and her thoughts lingered on her parents. Not a word, not a message— her heart sank. Her frightful start to the New World was a bad omen!

As the ship set sail again, Marco, with his arm around her, tried to cheer her up. Assunta and Piero, standing beside Marco and Felicia, clapped with the cheering passengers and waving crowds on the dock. The beautiful Bay of Naples receded in the background.

"*Vedi Napoli e poi muori!*" Marco said, hugging Felicia. She smiled.

"Well, I've seen Naples, and I'm not ready to die," Piero joked. "The Neapolitans are much too taken with their city. As if Rome didn't exist! Then, they haven't been to America, have they!" He looked at Felicia and winked.

"What a magnificent sight—Naples overlooking the bay," Assunta said, happy that they were on their way again. "What a spectacle!" As the ship pulled out to sea, Assunta felt, as did the noisy Neapolitans aboard, gaiety and sadness.

For a few moments Felicia was overcome by the bay's beauty. "It's truly lovely," she said. "Ischia, Procida, and Capri look like jewels floating in the dark blue sea."

"Yes," Assunta said. "No doubt one of the most magnificent gulfs in Europe. Too bad we had to stay on board, roasting in this scorching heat!"

Once on the open sea, Felicia's thoughts slid back to her parents. Every wave of the ocean deepened her feeling of separation from them. The infinite horizon encircling the monotonous expanse of water magnified her longing. Her anguish nearly asphyxiated her. She fought to stifle her unhappiness behind a mask of serenity.

Crossing the ocean, painful as it now was, did not fully thwart her dream of a new life in the New World. The small milltown where they'd be settling—indeed a small village within it—she began to imagine as an idyllic place to settle. Such thoughts eased her pain momentarily. More and more she bestowed on it the beauty she yearned for. But mournful thoughts about her parents would suddenly creep to mind, and the confidence she'd mustered would seep away like air out of a balloon. Then she'd sink back into anguish. Her voyage was a long see-sawing between hope and despair.

Plans for settling on Prospect Hill had been arranged by Paolo Cecere, an old family friend in his forties who, with wife and two children, had left Rome in 1922 after the fascists came to power. His help proved crucial in transferring assets and bargaining over the purchase of a house.

After eighteen miserable days of seasickness in the rolling and pitching of the ship and what seemed like an eternity filing through customs, they arrived in East Natick, Rhode Island. Despite all her disappointments up to this point, Felicia was able to keep her emotions in check. But when she got off the train and walked down a wooden platform next to a granary that shook and creaked as gusts of wind blew dust in her face, despair engulfed her. She felt as if she was drowning and gasping for air. An enclave of ramshackle buildings with utility poles leaning every which way made her dizzy. The train station, with its dirty oiled floorboards, had a flimsy broken door flapping in the wind. It looked like a place animals might be corralled in before they were sent off to the stockyards. The approach to the station was a rutty dirt road leading to a dirt parking lot full of potholes.

"My God, it's so ugly," she said heartbroken. "This can't be the right place. Paolo Cecere would never have brought us here!"

"There he is," Assunta said, pointing out the waiting-room window covered with cobwebs and grain dust. "There—in that black car."

Marco went out and waved to him, and Paolo Cecere came running in to meet them. All four stood stunned.

Paolo Cecere with a big smile and shining eyes was happy to see them. He hugged them one by one. His eyes misted over. His gaiety and good humor lessened their fear. They soon wedged themselves into his car and off he drove, jostling and bouncing over the hard clay ruts onto the paved road.

Prospect Hill, not far from the train station, was six miles from the Atlantic shore and about ten miles from Providence. Appalled by the crudeness of what she'd seen already, Felicia dreaded what she'd find on Prospect Hill in a milltown established in 1913, only a year before her birth. Horrors! Marco's words about its being ethnically tolerant and playing a big role in the industrial revolution gave her little comfort.

"Mamma mia!" she blurted, as they turned onto Providence Street in Natick, a sort of village in the town of West Warwick. Though the buildings were more solid and squared than the rickety ones at the train station, she was shocked by the vastness— "everything spread out . . . barren!" Alarm resonated through them all.

"You'll take to it," Paolo Cecere said as he drove up the main road through the village. "We were shocked too when we came. It's home to us now. You'll see—Natick's got real charm. Its rocky hills and valleys form the banks of a winding river."

Marco stared at the buildings blemishing the hilly, rocky terrain and thought of Rome's sturdy blocks of apartments, centuries-old villas, churches, palaces, and communal squares with fountains, marketplaces, restaurants, and bakeries. Yet he felt a spirit of openness, of lightness, and felt thankfully free of fascism. You could breathe freedom in the air, he thought.

Paolo Cecere pointed out Sacred Heart church with its broad

steps and high spire standing before a stone ledge hundreds of feet high. Across the street, like a poor cousin, stood the clapboard elementary school, Providence Street Grammar, humble and unadorned. As they climbed to the center of Natick, he showed them the long, garrisonlike Natick Mills beside the riverbank. In silence they stared out at the provincial surroundings.

He turned up a steep hill—Prospect Hill—that gave the road its name. They gripped the door handles for dear life. Loaded to capacity, the four-door Chevy sputtered as it slowly heaved its way up. They crested onto a half-mile plateau that abruptly halted before a second steep hill.

"There!" Paolo Cecere pointed. Kids were playing in the street and, honking his horn, he swerved the car around them. The Benedictas all turned looking for their new house. "See it? The white, two-story one—there . . . that one, with black shutters . . . look!—up the next lane."

On the half-mile stretch, they saw lanes crisscrossing Prospect Hill, running north and south—cul-de-sacs abruptly ending before massive rock formations as though fearing to descend the treacherous terrain to the river. Their lane, one of the cross streets, served two houses. The first, facing the road, had a white picket fence around it. Behind on a small knoll, a two-story rectangular clapboard structure stood like a sentry guarding the valley to the south.

Across the street a young woman sat on her front steps giving the breast to her baby. Children played about, some chatting with her. Others played on the sidewalks and in the road. Here and there women stood in clusters chatting. As the car turned and made its way up the short lane, the kids in the street and the woman nursing her child turned to stare. Felicia felt the eyes of the townsfolk on her.

"This is your private lane, almost—Wakefield Lane—you share it with the family in the front house," Paolo Cecere told them, as they hastened to get out of the car.

"The panorama—it's magnificent," Felicia said stepping down from the car. "The backyard opens to the valley."

From their knoll they saw the land sloping down to the river, patches of goldenrods swaying in the breeze. Felicia forgot her pain as she studied the nearby village slumbering in the distance. About a mile away, the river arced gradually, snaking its way through villages below.

Assunta took in the view with its cascade of flowers and shrubbery fluttering in the soft breeze. "Ah, the freshness of the air—what a smell!" They stood gazing in wonder at the glossy foliage of native shrubs. "Mountain laurels, aren't they?" Assunta asked.

"Rhododendrons, no?" Felicia wondered. "And the house— it is really prettily adorned by forsythias and lilacs, but now they're past their spring bloom."

"What's that huge stone building?" Marco asked, pointing down the valley to a massive structure over a mile away. "It seems to be growing out of the river with a railway bridge running in front."

"That's a soap factory—the Bradford Soap Works. And there, to the southwest diagonally across from it, that's a cloth factory— the Royal Mill."

They saw a long six-story stone building that sat like a fortress on the river bank, its tall turret shooting up above the roof. On a knoll across a lawned boulevard—Royal Square—stood West Warwick Junior High.

"How far down does our land go?" Piero asked. Little could be said about the clapboard house.

"See the hedgerow—about two hundred meters south and west," Paolo Cecere pointed. "Your property ends there. It's about half a hectare, all told." The L-shaped lot stretched all the way to the road—a long narrow strip passed beside the lane and the house in front.

The house had two flats—the lower larger one taken by Piero and Assunta, who prayed that her two daughters would soon join them. They'd need a place before moving into their own homes. From the upstairs flat Marco and Felicia looked out onto a view of the south slope. Trees, bushes, and wild flowers trailed down to the river, and crags sprang randomly out of the ground.

The west windows opened onto a lane winding its way up a hill to the second plateau. "Look, Marco," Felicia called. "The road curves around rocks."

He came and stood beside her, putting his arm around her shoulders. "We'll get used to it," he said, looking into her tearful eyes.

She relaxed in his arms and together they studied the houses springing up beside massive, jagged rocks rising sporadically out of the earth. The lane curled back onto the main road—Prospect Hill—and wound its way northwest for nearly a mile, losing itself in the farmland beyond. A massive barefaced rock—Indian Rock—towered in the distance.

Soon they'd discover the town of West Warwick, situated in the Pawtuxet Valley made up of nine villages hugging hills and valleys—Natick, Wescott, Riverpoint, Arctic, Centerville, Crompton, Phenix, Clyde, Lippitt. The Pawtuxet River served as the major source of energy and supply of water for the mills. Along the riverbanks, the hamlets, hatched around huge stone or brick textile mills—some unsightly, some grand—gave a quaint but picturesque air to the town.

In time the Benedictas spruced up their house, gracing it with flowerbeds and a veranda on the east side. Fruit trees, grapevines, and a vegetable garden on the south slope supplied them with fresh produce.

Despite the depression, Marco found work as a jewelry designer in Providence. Felicia, after some time, found work as a seamstress, altering clothes in a department store in Arctic, the town's business district. Piero found work in a wholesale patent medicine business in Phenix, a village about four miles away. Assunta kept house.

In 1938 Felicia's and Marco's first child, Anna Maria, was born; two years later, a son, Alessandro Luigi—named after both grandparents, the preference given to the paternal side.

The four immigrants, struggling together, survived the first phase of their exodus from Rome.

As I write, I remember as if it were yesterday the day the Benedictas came to live on Prospect Hill thirty-one years ago. Shortly after, I met them at Sacred Heart and they visited me on my porch.

Little did we know then, in 1936, that our village would, like a storm center, give rise to a crime that would shatter the complacent life of our times. And Felicia would be at the center of it.

At first everyone marveled at this seamstress talented in so many ways: in her dress, cooking, learning, fashion design. Felicia was always an enigma, always a fascination for us. Her cultured ways, her perfect English, her British accent, her working-class status—they didn't add up. It rankled some.

The Benedictas all spoke English. Assunta and Piero had a pronounced Italian accent when they came. Piero's gradually faded. Marco, having studied English for many years, was practically bilingual from the first.

As the years passed, the disparity between Felicia's working-class status and her cultured ways made her suspect. Some wives took her to be a phony—a snob putting on airs. Not a word had been dropped about her high birth. We learned about it after the tragedy when we read it in the newspapers. It was a bolt out of the blue.

Assunta and Felicia had confided much to me through the years and so did Anna when she got older. Why didn't they ever mention what kind of family Felicia had sprung from? Gradually I came to understand, or thought I did. Felicia did not want to trade on anything like that. She wanted simply to live among her neighbors without calling attention to herself. As if this were possible—she stood out like a swan among a flock of ducks.

These were hard years for the Benedictas. They had to work hard to keep the family afloat during the depression. Then war broke out in Europe, cutting them off from their families.

An unfortunate event further cast the Benedictas in a bad light—the division that took place at Sacred Heart. In 1939, the bishop of the diocese ordered the old pastor, Fr. D'Annunzio, much beloved by the parishioners, to take a post at another parish. A young priest in his late twenties, Fr. DiSanto, was appointed to replace him. A vexing problem preceded the new pastor.

At first, many in the church opposed the bishop and rallied around Fr. D'Annunzio, thought to be a true man of God. But the bishop, sticking to his guns, soon got his way, and Fr. DiSanto came to Sacred Heart to take over a divided parish. Naturally, most of us submitted to the diocesan decree, accepted Fr. DiSanto, and soon came to love and respect him.

A small minority felt short-changed by the bishop's decision. They thought he was imprudent to replace a seasoned priest by a young man who had just taken his vows. Some, among them the Benedictas, left Sacred Heart in something of a huff, for another parish. These rebels, as the townsfolk came to call them, were treated as traitors by many families on the hill.

After the rebellion, it took nearly five years for the parish to settle down. Some of the rebels, including the Benedictas, were seen as apostates for years to come, having taken their stand against the bishop.

I met Fr. DiSanto shortly after he came and I learned that he was wise beyond his years. Or so it seemed to me. It was then that he told me that a terrible darkness was descending on the world, a darkness that might oppress mankind for decades to come. "Your words frighten me," I told him.

"You know, Pasqualina, there are buildings so made that if a certain stone is removed the whole thing collapses," he said with a gentleness I'll never forget. "The foundation stone is gradually being pulled from our civilization. It's the children we must work on, the new generation, if we're to reverse this truly frightening trend."

His words and demeanor were those of a serene and gracious man. From the first his love of people touched me. He saw that I had calmed down somewhat.

"Can anyone enter a strong man's house to plunder his goods unless he first ties up the strong man?" he asked. "Of course not. We must help our children become strong, able to resist having their souls plundered and colonized by the spirit of the times." He explained his theory that just as toxins can pervade the air we breathe, misinformation can infest the atmosphere of the mind and poison the souls of our children, turning them into slaves manipulated by invisible forces.

His ideas alarmed me. But he radiated a confidence that gladdened me. I felt sure that, like a good shepherd protecting his flock, he'd never abandon us.

Cut off from Rome, 1943

"Who knows when they'll come!" Assunta said about her
daughters and their families as she carried a tray of coffee and
biscotti onto the porch. "Putting it off . . . procrastinating—
now stuck in Rome ready for another bloodbath!"

Felicia and Marco, relaxing after dinner on a September
evening, hurried to clear a spot on the coffee table.

"Every autumn—I repeat myself—forgive an old lady,"
Assunta went on, "the valley puts on such a spectacle. Its beauty
tugs at my heart for my loved ones." Seeing Felicia's sadness,
she stopped herself. "How dense the wildflowers on the slope
this year—ah! it's like heaven."

"We've got much to be thankful for here—and we can hope
that the fall of Mussolini's government spares Rome," Felicia
said.

"Marshal Badolgio's government declared Rome an open city.
You'll see, Rome will escape bombing," Marco said.

"Word is that the Allies have already bombed Rome . . .
rumor, no doubt," Felicia caught herself.

"The Germans have pledged an open city, all right!" Assunta
fumed. "What open city? Romans are living in fear for their
lives—both from the Germans and the Allies. Where will it all
end?"

In their grief they fell silent.

Felicia listened to Piero's telling an oft-repeated story to Anna
and Alessandro in the next room. The kids lay on each side of
him on the living-room floor.

". . . one night your father and I sneaked out. After Nonna
and Nonno fell fast asleep, we went to see the statue in the
Campo. You remember, I told you, the statue in the piazza where
we used to hang out after school—"

"Giordano Bruno!" the children yelled. They'd heard many
stories about it.

"It had gotten pretty dark and we were scared. There wasn't a
peep in all of Rome. Trembling and holding onto each other
tightly, we tiptoed slowly into the Campo. We wanted to know:
did Giordano cry at night? Many said the statue wept. We

stared up at his blank face lit up by the moon and stars. Then a noise scared us and we dashed home like frightened mice. The next day the kids at school said a baby bird nesting on Giordano's hat had fallen from its nest."

"What happened to it?" Anna asked.

"Luckily it fell into straw the farmers left in the marketplace. The kids rescued and nursed it till it could fly away."

"Piero, *vieni*, come—coffee's ready," Felicia called.

"Mamma, Mamma," Anna barged in, "can Alex and I go watch the kids playing in the street?"

"Yes, dear. Put on some playclothes first."

"Please, Mamma, I won't get my dress dirty. I promise."

Every Friday to mark the end of the work week the children dressed in their Sunday best for dinner. Marco sat in a brown jacket and tie, stroking his dark, trimmed mustache. Felicia had on a pair of beige slacks, a matching jersey, and a red scarf tied around her waist.

"Okay, but mind, stay inside the yard."

Anna flew back into the living room to collect Alex and off they scampered. Piero joined the grown-ups on the porch.

"What, no date tonight?" Marco asked.

"What girl'd have me!" Piero joked, turning to Felicia and smiling playfully. Piero saw her as a fish out of water, isolated from her family. "Things pretty bad at Sennetts'?"

"It's Lillian," she said. Was it really her work getting her down? she wondered. Being a seamstress brought her in contact with the town's uppercrust—wives of judges, businessmen, and the privileged. Most of them treated her as an inferior. They praised her work and often confided in her; yet she found little joy in trying to satisfy them. With no friends outside the family—except for the Ceceres—she felt she was losing her grip on reality.

"Lillian's not worth thinking about," Marco advised.

"An irony," Assunta said shaking her head. "Florence Lambert—such a good soul; her daughter Lillian—such a *stronza*, such a pain in the neck. Goes to show—you never know how your children are going to turn out."

"Take Piero. A lady's man," Marco teased. They laughed.

"He sure impresses the girls on the hill," Felicia said. "'How's

Piero doing?' 'Say hello to your handsome brother-in-law.'
'Piero's done all right for himself in America.' We've got a
celebrity among us."

"What do you want from me? Some of us got it, I guess,"
Piero said. He ran his fingers through his dense wavy hair. "From
what I hear, Lillian's getting out of hand."

At work Felicia had gotten wind of Lillian's malicious gossip.
Living across the street with a birds-eye view of Felicia's goings
and comings, Lillian took on the role of eyewitness for the local
wives confined to homemaking.

"The way I see it, Felicia," Assunta said, "gallivanting from
house to house, Lillian takes the edge off the drudgery of wives,
with her tattletaling. Believe me, these women long for gossip
the way an alcoholic longs for a drink."

"Besides, Lillian's life's no bed of roses," Marco added. "What
with three kids—Eddy alone counts for several. It's a shame
they don't find some school for him. And Frank's not much
help—a boozing skirt chaser. No wonder she's got a mouth and
a half. She's stumbled onto a gold mine with you—there's a
ready-made audience craving to know about you."

"Why?" Felicia asked. After all, she'd had little to do with
Lillian.

"Lillian's a windbag with a husband stepping out on her—
uneducated, tied to her home and children," Marco said. "You're
free as a bird, talented. Is it any wonder?"

"Free? As a bird? Ah, would I had wings—I miss the Old
World. You know, I thought the other day—it's an intellectual
desert here. We Romans, cursed with big mouths, too, were
forever arguing about life and politics. Remember how I used to
rush to get it all down in my journals?"

"Too bad you left most of them behind. Your idealism,
endearing as it was, might be a source of amusement to us now."

Felicia pinched his cheek. "What a critic you were—"

"All those ideas sprang from your head like dreams. What a
future you imagined. Yeah, Mamma, even in the throes of fascism
Felicia imagined the coming of a new age."

"A spark of idealism goes a long way, believe me," Assunta
said. "It's seeping into her beautiful designs. Ah, Felicia, be

thankful for the gift. Now you're to give a course in fashion design."

"What course?" Piero asked. "Am I always the last to hear?"

"Sennetts' Department Store is taking Felicia off alterations and sponsoring a course for seamstresses, using her own method," Assunta said proudly.

"By the way, Felicia," Marco remembered, "I turned your jewelry design portfolio over to my boss. It made quite a stir among the bigwigs. I think they'll be coming up with an offer soon."

He'd been encouraging her for some time to get her away from long hours of drudgery at Sennetts'. Artists were little valued these days when even the jewelry industry had been enlisted to produce military goods to aid the war effort.

"Thanks, Marco," she said, kissing his cheek.

"Felicia's quite the intellectual, Mamma," Marco said, chuckling. "'Out of the chaos facing Europe would come a transformation to a new epoch,' she wrote. Do you remember, *tesoro?*"

"Transformation?" Piero asked.

Felicia flushed. Marco's arm around her shoulder comforted her. She adored the Benedictas, their interest in history, and their love of literature. Assunta was an intellectual in her own right, reading everything for the sheer joy of it, kindled by her father, a self-taught man. He championed women's rights long before it became fashionable.

"Who knows what Marco's babbling about," Felicia said slyly.

"What, you no longer hold to your old views: a world where the dignity, the value, and the liberty of every individual will be honored?"

"Well," Felicia said sheepishly, "I still hope for it—yearn for it." Since living on Prospect Hill among the working class, she could see that she didn't fit in. There was a gulf between the classes, and only God knew how it might be bridged.

"So, Marco," Piero came to Felicia's rescue, "when did you become such a cynic? I recall you preaching—wasn't it the divine image in all men you believed would be respected: whether noble, middle, or working class? Now there's a bit of youthful optimism, for you."

"You've got a hell of a memory. Goodness, you were just a kid when I spouted that bit of idealism," Marco said.

"Perhaps he's become a broken-hearted idealist himself," Felicia said, smiling at Piero.

"I think you've hit the nail on the head, Felicia," Assunta said. "What an idealist. One would have to scour the halls of academe to top him. Count on the academic, my father used to say—there's no idea so insane you won't find some professor hawking it."

As they went on talking, Felicia's thoughts flew back to Rome—the last talk she'd had with her father.

"A man's patrimony is in question here, Felicia," Papa had said calmly, trying to reason with her. "The passage of the estate to you is not assured unless you marry within the fold. Without primogeniture—with no son born from noble stock to continue our line—you'll lose it all. Our estate will go over to my oldest nephew, your cousin. Is that what you want?"

"I've heard it all before," she said indifferently.

"Get it into your head—it's a question of losing the Petrarca stemline stretching from the Colonna back to antiquity. What's to happen to our estate? Think about it."

Anger was getting the better of him. "Please, Papa, don't fret. Families do manage to pass their titles through the female line. The monarchy, you'll see, will come around. Things are changing."

"Damn you, Felicia, you understand nothing. Suppose the monarchy can grant you the title 'Countess,' do you think this will be possible? You, a descendant of Ghibelines *and* Guelfs! Married to a nobody. For the love of God, remember who you are before you go off half cocked." He paused to collect himself. "Since the fourteenth century, when the Colonna adopted the son of Francesco Petrarca, the great poet, opening a line of Petrarcas through intermarriage—"

"Papa! God only knows how the Petrarca branch evolved." She felt defiant, listening to the same irrelevant facts. As if Rome's history could sap her love for Marco.

"I beg your pardon, my daughter." His lips twitched in anger.

"The Colonna go all the way back to Julius Caesar. Have you forgotten? Or has your education been for nothing? Yes! Don't smile in ignorance." His dark, bushy eyebrows bristled. "The lands of the Colonna correspond exactly to the property of Caesar's family. The emperor's own villa on the Via Labicana belonged to the Colonna in the Middle Ages, and the site is still part of their land. Some claim that the Colonna reached back even further—to the Egyptian Osiris, the builder of Cairo."

"What are you telling me, Papa? Fantasies are getting the better of the facts here!" Her faint smile of amusement was not lost on the count. "That's a pretty piece of propaganda if the Colonna can pull it off. Even Julius Caesar isn't enough for them. Now they've got to drag in the Egyptians."

"Think with pride of your lineage, Felicia. Don't be a modern bigot scoffing at the service we render the state—its stability. Yes, its stability. You're laughing, are you? Gripped by passion, well might you think a nobody worthy today, but . . . but I tell you, my love, you'll live to regret it."

"Please, Papa, enough!"

"Lacking the will and character of the nobility, you'll see: Europe will splinter, slip into pettiness, succumb to massocracy. After enough suffering, people will beg the nobility to come back. Fascism and communism, you'll see, are like tumors on the annals of time."

"You mistake history, Papa," she said passionately. Righteous indignation swelled in her, displacing the good humor and affection called for at the moment. "No, no! Not the old aristocracy, so parasitic on society . . . professionals and technocrats will steer us into the future." She recalled the folly of the nobility: two French monarchs, one in 1830 and the other in 1848, fled to England for their dear lives, after short reigns. Then the slaughter of the impudent Russian czar, as well as the czarina and their children in 1918. To survive, King Victor Emmanuel II, their own monarch, sold out to the fascists in 1922. Not a pretty picture—history had passed judgment on European monarchies.

"Parasitic! Parasitic! You say. What a betrayal of your upbringing—your family and class," he thundered. "Professionals and technocrats, all right. But they'll fail; they're doomed to fail. Let me tell you, the nobility alone has the authority to inspire the masses. Unlike the fascists and communists, we alone possess wisdom. Don't turn up your nose, Felicia. Scorn is unbecoming. Yes, whether you want to believe it or not, we are the true leaven of humanity. The nobility alone can lift the commonfolk to justice and freedom."

"Nonsense, Papa. Be realistic. The nobility inspire citizens to lofty ideals! Really, now." Pride overpowered her. "History records another, more tragic story, I'm sorry to say. The nobility has enslaved the masses, abusing its power. I tell you, Papa, fascism and communism will be replaced not by the monarchy but by bureaucrats, professionals, technocrats capable of managing the chaos breaking out."

"What are you saying, Felicia? Use your head, will you! Do you believe in some blind fate? Is that what you're telling me? Some inflexible Providence?"

"Inflexible Providence . . . fate . . . destiny?! All I know is that history doesn't evolve tidily. It has twists and turns not yet visible. But I doubt the degenerate nobility can harness the social forces—"

"There's no use arguing with you." The count's face reddened. "Your mind's polluted by bourgeois nonsense. You'll live to see who'll raise men's souls to acts of heroism and freedom—"

"Come now, Papa, do you really believe history is moving in your direction? Lord only knows, I wish it so—it might sidestep the fascists. But remember, King Victor Emmanuel sold us down the river to that blackguard Mussolini." She flung in his face the sellout that, in her mind, severed the bond between the monarchy and the people forever.

Now, thinking back, she regretted her arrogance and pride. She failed to appreciate her father's wounded heart, his fear of losing her, his fervent love for her, and his loneliness without her. These were at the root of his stubbornness. And her own pain and stubbornness were a mirror image of his. Her mother had been right: Felicia and her father were like siamese twins. Had she for a moment felt his terrible torment, she would have been filled with shame. Admitting their fear of separation from one another would have aroused sympathy in them instead of obstinacy, and their sympathy would have led to compassion. Then, putting their heads together they would have worked out a solution. Humility, much needed to tap the wellspring of their love for each other, evaded them. The count had stamped out of her rooms, and a wall of silence stretched between them ever since.

She fought back tears.

Seeing Felicia lost in thought, Marco put his arm around her and drew her near. "Get a load of Anna and Alessandro at the edge of the lawn." They looked toward the road alive with neighbors. "Cecilia and Anna talk all the time about first grade next year. Poor Alex—bored silly trying to make sense of it."

"The whole hill's out tonight," Piero said. They glanced at the kids roller skating not too far from Anna and Alex. "There's Norman. That kid's bound for trouble."

"I remember when we came here," Assunta said. "Whoever locked their doors? Can it be? He's got such crooked fingers. His family seems decent enough."

"Who knows," Piero said. "Don't forget the beating he gave Guido, Mrs. Sassi's boy."

"Poor woman, her husband not yet cold in the grave." Assunta was well acquainted with a widow's grief. Unlike Mrs. Sassi, who was alone in the States, she'd had her relatives in Rome helping out. "Thank God Mrs. Sassi's the housekeeper at Sacred Heart—living with the rectory roof over her head and food on the table."

They watched the kids playing tag, running from one utility pole to the next; others played hide-and-seek. Junior high and high school youngsters huddled here and there. Still others in the middle of the road threw a baseball back and forth, competing for the same space with those that played kick-the-can.

With the doors flung open at Louie's Tavern a block away, the smell of sour beer, peanuts, and wild game wafted outside with the raucous voices of men seeking relief in camaraderie and booze after a week of work. From Petrella's Bakery up the street came the smell of pizza baking in big wood ovens. In a distant pasture on the Lamberts' farm a cow mooed. The eight-o'clock church bells rang at Sacred Heart.

Assunta looked over at Lillian's steps. "I see Lillian's got her crowd around her. "Ah, how that woman loves to embroider nonsense."

Friday Night on Prospect Hill

"My oh my oh my!" Lillian exclaimed to the girls gathered on her front steps. "Where does that woman get those outlandish outfits?" The girls turned to look at Anna and Alex across the street.

"Lillian!" Alberta protested. She stood at the bottom of the steps with her arm around Lillian's shoulder. Alberta, a pretty brunette in junior high, shook the short robust woman in her early thirties affectionately. "I think they're so cute. That's a darling dress Anna's got on. Isn't Alex cute in his little sailor suit?"

Crammed together on the top step, Nancy, Phyllis, Gloria, and Mildred thumbed through a stack of fan magazines—*Hollywood, Motion Picture,* and *Screenland*—one of their favorite pastimes. Phyllis glanced from the page to the two children. "Look at this!" she said. "Look familiar?" She practically pushed the issue of *Screenland* in Mildred's face.

"Imagine! Look, Nance."

Nancy grabbed the magazine from Mildred. "Wow! Who would've believed?"

Gloria craned her neck over Nancy's shoulders to see.

"Well, what's all the commotion about up there?" Lillian Pastori asked. She presided over one of several clusters of neighbors on the hill. The wide steps leading up to her front door offered a roosting place for youngsters who loved to hang out and catch up on small talk. She had a knack for amusing and being amused by the kids. Some moved from one cluster to another, up and down the street, getting their fill of village gossip.

Phyllis took back the magazine and brought it down to Lillian. "How do you like this, Lillian?" smirked Phyllis, a brunette, doe-eyed and slightly buck-toothed. The younger boys playing nearby with sticks and peg got interested.

"My word. I do say!" Lillian did say. She passed the magazine to Alberta as if it were contaminated. Lillian fidgeted with her hair, trying to entwine the loose strands around her "rat." "So, Anna's got another perfect copy of a Shirley Temple dress!" Her words dripped sarcasm. "Imagine, dressing a child in a frilly dress just to play in. Never allowed to play with other kids. Look at those two lost souls," she went on, shaking her head in righteous disbelief.

"You've got to admit Felicia's quite a seamstress," Alberta said, smiling slyly behind Lillian's back.

The boys came over to take a look at a picture of Shirley Temple in a dress Anna had on—an exact replica of it. The kids gawked in awe. To them, Anna and Alex gained celebrity status vicariously wearing clothes seen only in the movies or in magazines.

"Really, Alberta. You do miss my point. Really you do. Of course those are dazzling clothes. The Rita Hayworth and Katherine Hepburn dresses Her Highness wears—on Prospect Hill!" Lillian rolled her eyes and shook her head to drive home the point. "You've got to be out of touch—among the uppercrust of New York City or Newport—okay. But here?" she sneered. "It's silly—such a waste. Miss hoity-toity with her uppity airs has to work all those hours to pay for it all. Doesn't make sense. Poor little Alex. Three years old and never had a haircut—with banana curls like a little girl. Really!"

"Oh, Lillian, let me fix that for you," Mildred said coming down the steps. In her excitement, Lillian's hair-do had unraveled. One of two sisters living on the second hill, Mildred Bergman, a bright chubby high school freshman, loved to play with people's hair. Hers frizzed out like a rat's nest. Using her fingers as a comb, she smoothed out and refastened Lillian's dark thick hair with hairpins around the soft flexible tube that served as a form to shape the roll around her head. "Don't you think Alex's adorable in his long curly locks? Surely Felicia'll get his hair cut before he goes off to school."

"Cecilia, get up off the sidewalk," Lillian yelled at her five-year-old daughter, who was lying down on the sidewalk bordering the Benedicta property. Cecilia ignored her mother. "Nobody's allowed to go into the Benedicta yard, and the poor kids are not allowed to leave. Gosh, that's a nice shade of lipstick you've got, Phyllis," Lillian said, taking hold of herself. She complimented Phyllis, who started smearing her lips. "Does your ma approve?"

"Yeah, my ma don't mind so long as I don't put too much on," Phyllis mumbled. She puckered and pressed her lips together to spread the lipstick evenly while holding a compact close in the meager light from the utility pole in front of the house. She handed the tube and compact to Nancy, who was also eager to doll herself up.

Reddened lips altered Nancy's boyish, angelic face. They all looked on, fascinated at Nancy's transformation. "Wow, Nance, lipstick sure likes you. Gone is Miss Plain Jane—born is Miss West Warwick," Mildred said, enviously.

Down next to Louie's Tavern, high school boys hung out on Dante Giorgio's front steps.

"Come on Pete, tell 'em!" Billy nudged his friend, egging him on.

"Tell 'em what?" Pete asked slyly.

"You know—Helen. Come on," Billy pleaded, putting his arm around his friend's shoulders and shaking him.

"You got a big mouth," Pete said, smiling.

"Helen Butler locked Pete up in her old man's outhouse," Billy said, dying to let the cat out of the bag.

"No shit, Pete!" Nick said. The boys laughed, huddling closer to get the scoop. Butler had two daughters: Helen, sixteen, and Lucy, fourteen. They loved to tease the boys.

"Come on Pete, let's have it," Freddie said, grinning from ear to ear. The antics of the Butler girls fed the rumor mill among the high school crowd.

"What's to tell," Pete said. He liked kindling their interest. Knowing Pete, they expected him to cough up the facts boastfully.

"Helluva place to get your first piece," Dante baited him. Smiling in anticipation, the boys glanced at one another.

"Says you, my *first.*"

"Yeah, sure, we know, Pete's bagged a few in his day," Dante jeered. "I gotta tell you, Miss Rose's got the most fantastic legs. Pete can't wait to get to algebra class these days; he's becoming a real scholar—loves Miss Rose's praise."

Pete smiled as if to confirm Dante's claim.

Miss Rose, West Warwick High's new algebra teacher, had wowed the boys in her class. They couldn't get enough algebra. Every day she'd put a word problem on the board and the first to get the answer got extra credit. The guys soon gained a love for algebra—each trying to outdo the other. They got to take their paper up to Miss Rose and stand next to her while she looked to see whether they had it right and the others watched enviously. The boys beat the girls out nearly every day. Ruth Rose, it turned out, had sat in the same room five years earlier. This, her first teaching job—she had full command of the class.

"Well, Pete, you gonna spill the beans or not?" Freddie taunted.

"Pete was necking with Helen behind the old barn—" Billy said.

"I'll tell it if you don't mind," Pete broke in. "Well, you know what a tease Helen is? I met her behind the old barn next to the outhouse and she let me . . . well, she liked me feeling her up all over."

"Wow!" the boys let out in unison, drawing nearer to Pete to get the details.

"We were necking pretty heavy. I had to go, so I went to use her old man's outhouse. She followed me and pushed her way in behind me and locked the door. Her back was up against the lock. The stench damn near knocked me out. I lost the urge. All I could think was to get the hell out of there. The bitch blocked the way. 'Well, Pete,' she says, pressing herself against me, 'take it out and let's have a look.' Of course it was as limp as a piece of wet rope. The smell was making me sick. *Let me out,*' I yelled. She laughed and started to rub me all over. 'My, ain't much there to brag about, is there?' 'Yeah,' I said, 'let's go back behind the old barn and I'll give you something you won't soon forget.' 'Better keep it so it can grow some more,' she told me. She grabbed it and squeezed it hard and turned and opened the door and ran out. She better not meet me behind the old barn again!"

The guys howled and rolled around on the pavement, laughing their heads off. The girls sitting on the steps at Lillian's a few houses up the street wondered what happened. The laughter pierced the quiet on the Benedictas' porch.

Next to Lillian's house and across from Anna and Alex and Cecilia some kids stopped playing peg-and-stick and sat on the curb beneath the light of the utility pole.

"I heard there are boats—submarines the Germans have. They go under water," Tony said, sitting with his friends from grammar school.

"That must be something—wow, to float underwater," Paul said. He made undulating motions with his hand, trying to depict this incredible thing. "Do you believe the Germans have such things?"

Norman piped up. "My ma says, 'Lord only knows what those Krauts are up to.' She says, 'I'll die before I'll be put under water!' And those Japs—"

"Yeah, there ain't no messing around them animals," Pasco said. "Man, if they ever catched ya, they'd put bamboo shoots under your fingernails and slice out your tongue. They're sneaky little beasts. I heard they got secret powers and can beat up the biggest Yanks."

"Don't believe everything you hear," Paul put in. He'd heard such stories, but his parents told him not everything said about the enemy was true.

"Yeah, Paul, it's true," Tony said. "Did you see the new posters of those huge Krauts and mean little Japs in Louie's?"

"Yeah!" Paul said, his eyes dilated and his voice cracked. "Eddy let me in yesterday when he was cleaning up the place."

"Boy, those Krauts must be ten feet tall—real giants," Tony said. "And those Japs—I sure wouldn't want to mess with them. Disgusting."

"One of my grandfathers is German," Paul let slip. Astonished, Norman, Pasco, Dom, and Tony stared at Paul Risch. The boys from second- and third-generation Italian, French, and Irish families had never seen a German before. They'd never seen an oriental either. They knew Paul's mother was Italian and thought his father was Irish.

"No kidding!" Tony exclaimed, pained by his best friend's secret. "Is he a giant like on those posters?"

"Heck no. He's no taller than my dad," Paul said, fearing ostracism.

"Heck, you just a runt, Paul," Ralph said. The kids turned around to see Ralph and Eddy joining them.

"Whata you know? Ralph, the idiot. You ain't got past third grade," Norman mocked. A second-grader, Norman tried to distance himself from Ralph and Eddy—both turned out of school. Ralph Mullen had always been not quite right; he managed to learn to read but left school in the third grade. More and more he had fallen behind, became a comic in the classroom and got the kids to laugh at his antics. Norman had trouble himself in first grade. He had to be tied down in his seat nearly every day to keep him from getting up and disrupting the class.

"Shut your mouth, Norman!" Ralph defended himself. "I see your pa beats you up a lot. You're always beating up Guido, Mrs. Sassi's boy."

"If I was twelve and couldn't hardly read, Ralph, I'd shove my head down Sam Butler's outhouse." Norman guffawed. The boys looked down, embarrassed. Norman was nearly a head taller and much stronger than all of them.

"Come on, Ralph," Eddy said. "We don't hafta put up with this crap. Norman, your mouth's smellier than Butler's and Louie's outhouses put together." Eddy, a few years older than Norman, didn't fear him.

"Yeah, dummy number two on Prospect Hill. When you gonna learn to read? Eddy lame brain."

"Hey, that's enough!" Tony warned, encouraged by the presence of Eddy, his older brother. Both of them could take Norman on. Eddy Pastori had not done well in the first grade. After a few weeks, the principal, thinking that Eddy was retarded, urged his parents to take him out of school and to get the advice of the family physician about a fitting school.

"You know, Eddy, someday I'm gonna get you alone and fix you good," Norman threatened.

"Yeah, you and who else?"

All this time, Ralph Mullen just listened. He was prone to deep feelings, and many on the hill began to recognize something uncanny about him. Though in school subjects he did not fare well, he often had visions and seemed able to foresee events in people's lives. All of a sudden he said without bitterness or anger, "Norman, you're gonna come to a bad end."

"You're full of shit, Ralph," Norman said.

Ralph laughed and clapped his hands. "I know," he said good naturedly. "I'm full of it . . . that I am," he said and took off with Eddy.

Norman and the boys couldn't help laughing. Ralph had a knack for dissipating hostility.

"I wonder when Butler's gonna get rid of his outhouse?" Tony asked, shriveling up his nose.

"What about Louie's? He's already put in a toilet in his tavern," Dom noted.

"Hey, you know what Louie's servin' tonight?" Norman asked. He stuck out his tongue in disgust. "Turtle soup . . . Sam Butler caught the turtle, and 'coon . . . Louie trapped them on his farm up near Indian Rock."

"Yuck," they all said, mimicking one another pretending to be puking.

Louie Boucher cooked all sorts of wild game and served them free to his patrons. According to the scuttlebutt that drew many to the hill, Louie cooked fantastic raccoon, fox, squirrel, turtle, and snake.

"Here comes Her Highness to get her dressed-up dolls," Lillian announced. All eyes turned toward Felicia who had come down the lane to get Anna and Alex. All this time the children stood at the edge of the lawn, talking to Cecilia over the hedges. "Come on home now, Cecilia!" Lillian yelled. "Get a load of Felicia!"

Tall and slender, Felicia had on her beige slacks with a matching scooped-neck blouse. Her chestnut hair parted on the left and, pulled back, fell to her shoulders in deep soft waves.

"Really, Lillian," Alberta ribbed her, "you're a card. I wouldn't mind having an outfit like that. It's like one Katharine Hepburn

wore in a movie I saw. And I wouldn't mind Piero Benedicta—
he's some dish. I'd like to run my hands through his waves."
Alberta fluffed up her hair behind her neck with the back of her
hands and wiggled her hips, pretending to be glamorous. The
girls all giggled.

Phyllis whistled. "Hubba hubba, zing zing! Piero's got
everything! He's some dish all right. I sure wish I was older."

"I'm surprised at you two," Lillian said smiling. They were
all in accord about Piero Benedicta's good looks. Lillian, not
much older than Piero, couldn't keep her eyes off him.

"Surprised or not, you've got to admit, Lillian, Piero's got
it—plenty of it," Mildred, who practically swooned when she
heard his name, backed Alberta up. "He's not stuck up like his
sister-in-law either."

Felicia handed Anna, Alex, and Cecilia each a bag of biscotti
and told them to share them with the kids. All four ran across
the road to Lillian's steps. Anna and Cecilia climbed up the steps,
sat down next to the girls, and passed the cookies around. Alex
went to sit on the curb between Paul and Tony and handed the
bag to Paul.

Felicia greeted Lillian and the girls cheerily, spoke to each of
them in turn, and asked after their parents and family, as they
munched on the cookies.

"I just love your outfit, Felicia," Phyllis said, "did you make
it?"

"Thanks, Phyllis. Can you tell where I got the design?"

"A movie star?" Phyllis asked.

"Yeah. Which one?"

"I think . . . wasn't it Katharine Hepburn in *The Philadelphia
Story?*" Alberta replied.

Felicia nodded, amused. "Actually, I had to copy the design
for one of Sennetts' customers who wanted one made just like
it."

"I saw a lovely gown in Sennetts' window yesterday. Is it your
design?" Alberta asked.

"A copy of a gown Ginger Rogers wore in a film with Fred
Astaire. Lena DeCiantis did the sewing—she's a very good
seamstress."

On and on the girls gushed, wanting to know how she had learned to design clothes.

Felicia smiled at their enthusiasm. "Fashion design . . . if it's something you take to—it takes a bit of patience learning. No matter how good you get at it, designs you make need to be tested before Sennetts' farms them out to seamstresses. To make sure I've got them right, I've got to try them out on Anna or my mother-in-law or me."

"Did you make Anna's dress? Isn't it one of Shirley Temple's?" Nancy asked.

"Sennetts' got a lot of requests for that one. My, Nancy, I didn't recognize you. You've grown up since I saw you last," Felicia said, seeing Nancy all made up. "By the way, I'll be giving a sewing class next month. Anyone over sixteen is welcome to join. You'll need a sewing machine at home. It won't cost you anything—Sennetts' is sponsoring it."

All this time Lillian had remained silent. Felicia grew uncomfortable as the girls' attention focused on her. "Lillian," Felicia said, trying to draw her into the conversation, "Anna enjoys playing with Cecilia so much. We all enjoy having her over. Do please send her over tomorrow, won't you? If she wants to come, of course."

Lillian smiled as gracefully as she could and said she would. The girls had ignored her after Felicia joined them. Envy surged in her. She didn't blame them; she blamed Felicia—putting on airs and leading the girls on.

"Come, children, it's time for bed. Papa, Zio, and Nonna are waiting for us." The children resisted at first. Felicia held out her hand and Anna came down; Alex gave in and followed.

Felicia's intrusion, ending as abruptly as it began, cast a pall over Lillian's circle. No one spoke. Lillian finally said, "Humph, those slacks! You know what kind of women wear slacks?"

"They're all the rage," Alberta put in. She grabbed a magazine lying on the steps and flipped through it. "Look here, Lillian. Some Newport socialites—here's Katharine Hepburn."

"Mark my words: no good will come of that woman. Do you see any women on the hill dressed so outrageously. Slacks, really! In all my years I've never seen the likes of it."

Lillian's views struck a chord in the girls who, attracted to Felicia's beauty and talent, felt some taint, something sinister about her. While they admired her unusual clothing and hair styles seen only in magazines, she fascinated and frightened them at the same time. Her life outside the home went against the grain of the solid family pattern of the women they knew. Lillian's words sank deep in them, mingling with their own dark doubts.

"I passed her a few days ago when I walked into Natick Grocery," Lillian said. The group had grown bigger as some of the boys joined them, darkness cutting short their games. "'Hi, Felicia,' I greeted her. Her Highness in her phony British accent said, 'Hullooo, Lillian, how dooo you dooo? It's sooo nice to see you.' As always, I asked her to drop by some time and visit with us or come over for coffee or tea some afternoon. 'Dear me,' she stooped to answer. 'How dooo you find the time? You must organize your life sooo efficiently—indeed, with three children. Cecilia is such a lovely child. Anna gets on so well with her.' She never gives an answer; too good for the likes of us." The kids burst out laughing at Lillian's impersonation.

"My ma says she's a professional woman—different from other women on the hill," Alberta threw in half-heartedly.

"A married woman's place is in the home! Sure, some women are working in factories . . . it's wartime. But does it make sense for a married woman to work outside the home? Look at Miss Markey: she married last year . . . left her teaching job to take care of her home and husband—she's got common sense. But this thing of running out on children—disgraceful! Pushing them off on their grandmother all day long."

A somber mood took hold of them. To the kids, Lillian's claims, though harsh, seemed just. Alberta tried to argue Felicia's case. "But she's so talented, Lillian. I hear she's a great fashion designer, and the clothes she designs for Sennetts'. *Wow!*"

"Yeah, you can say that again," chimed in the others.

Lillian, about to answer, heard Norman asking her something.

"Hey, Lillian, what's your favorite radio program? *The Lone Ranger*'s gotta be the best."

Lillian and the girls laughed at Norman's childish butting in.

"Mine's *The Shadow*," Paul said mimicking the solemn radio

voice. "What evil lurks in the hearts of men, only the Shadow knows. The Shadow can cloud men's minds—always saving Margot in the nick of time."

"But nothing beats *It Pays to Be Ignorant!*" Tony giggled. "I nearly flipped last week—they couldn't figure out how much milk is in a quart. The panel asked so many crazy questions." He got the giggles just talking about it. "You know, one guy asked, 'Was the milk in a bottle or a can?' Another one said, 'Was it cold or hot?' Somebody wanted to know, 'Was it chocolate or white milk?'" The boys were jumping on and off the steps laughing.

"That sure was funny," Lillian agreed, giggling with the kids. "Remember the professor saying there's no right answer because it depends on whether the milk is bought in a store or off a milkman's truck?"

Gloria had her favorite, *Fibber Magee and Molly*, and Nancy just loved *Baby Snooks*, the spoiled brat getting the better of her dad; Mildred talked on and on about *Henry Aldrich*, telling about her favorite episode. Lillian threw in her two cents' worth—*Blondie & Dagwood* just had to be the funniest. She saw it was nearly nine-thirty.

"Goodness," Nancy said jumping down from the top step, "I've got to get home—my curfew." She wiped off her lipstick and dashed off.

The older crowd remained on the steps, gabbing. Lillian went in to put her two younger kids to bed. She'd have to wait till the tavern closed at twelve for her husband, Frank. On Friday nights he usually came home drunk.

Mrs. Lambert's Visit

Anna stared out the living room window at the early morning dew on the grass. Alex sat near her on the floor, playing with building blocks. Nonna was in the kitchen talking to Mrs. Lambert.

A matriarch of a family of thirteen, Mrs. Florence Lambert had taken over the running of a large dairy farm after her husband's death. She lived at the top of Prospect Hill, about a mile from the Benedictas, in a three-story farmhouse overlooking the Pawtuxet River. Dressed up by mountain laurels, rock formations, and tall evergreens, the two hundred acres dropped down to the river's edge dotted with golden willows and red oaks.

She often stopped by after Saturday morning mass, pleased that the Benedictas had returned to Sacred Heart. Felicia and Marco had gone shopping and Piero was at work.

"The families on the hill," Mrs. Lambert was saying, "were torn apart by the division in the parish. Many of us, Assunta, took your view to heart—wanting to keep Fr. D'Annunzio. You so-called rebels went about it in the wrong way. Thank goodness it's all over. But, my dear, those who've reviled you . . . dear me, such hypocrites. To claim they are the 'faithful'! Faithful to what? But listen, Assunta, I must run. I'll call one of my boys to pick me up."

"Don't trouble yourself. Marco'll be along soon." Assunta refilled Mrs. Lambert's coffee cup without asking.

Mrs. Lambert's hazel eyes seemed sad behind her wire-rimmed glasses, but she rejoiced—Assunta had returned to Sacred Heart. A tall slender woman of keen mind, Mrs. Lambert had a compassionate face and a commanding presence. She had emigrated from Naples as a child of three with her parents and had lived for some time in New York City, one of eight children. Visiting relatives in the town of West Warwick when she was eighteen, she met a young man by the name of Vincent Lambert who had come to this country alone as a boy of ten, from Quebec. He found work, being taken for older than he was, and managed to save practically all his earnings to bring his whole family to the States. Both he and Florence were devout.

"Poor Marco. I'm always imposing on him," Mrs. Lambert said.

"For heaven's sake, Florence. Believe me, Marco—"

"Everyday I prayed for you and Mrs. Mansour. How are the Mansours, by the way?" Mrs. Lambert asked.

Assunta glanced out the window at the Mansours'—the house with the picket fence that stood between her house and Lillian Pastori's. "I should've listened to Felicia and Marco when they leaned toward the new priest at first and sided with the majority in favor of Fr. DiSanto," she said. "I convinced them to hold out for Fr. D'Annunzio. You know, he was loved by all. But most in the parish gave in to the diocese."

"Well, in the end, the bishop was right, I believe. We needed new blood: a younger priest with new ideas."

"Casting us as rebels—we've taken a good clobbering. Not treated in a Christian way. What else should we have expected after the fuss we kicked up? We meant to get our way. Did you hear? The Mansours have joined the Baptist Church."

"Converted to Protestantism! Poor Mansours." Mrs. Lambert made the sign of the cross. "People can be vicious, my dear." She crossed herself again. Thoughts of her daughter crept into her mind: Lillian had fanned the hatred against the rebels, especially against the Benedictas. This weighed heavily on her mother.

"When I threw my lot in with the minority, it wasn't a revolt against the church," Assunta said.

"Water over the dam, my dear. Now you're back. That's all that matters." Mrs. Lambert wanted to put the matter to rest.

"In the old country we used to say that 'God is known by many names.' The Mansours have taken another way. It might not be ours, but—"

"I understand. Mrs. Mansour's a dear—delights so much in life. Rachel and Mitri—lovely children. I haven't seen the older two in years. Hard keeping up friendships when we go our separate ways," Mrs. Lambert said.

"The new pastor, Fr. DiSanto, I'm happy to say, is every bit as inspiring—"Assunta admitted.

"Fr. DiSanto's every bit as devout as Fr. D'Annunzio. Fr. DiSanto's enlivened the parish, and his sermons, you know, Assunta, help renew our spirit. Most of all, he's able to touch the younger generation. The altar committee and sodality are happy you're back helping out at the church."

Assunta smiled in silence. Her mind turned to Felicia, to sorrow and suffering. Could it be that people react to suffering differently? Felicia suffers. Still not reconciled with the count and countess. Lillian Pastori, one of Florence Lambert's daughters, doesn't help. Mother and daughter, like day and night: one ready to cry at the word crucifixion; the other, a crucifier. Poor Florence—three sons in the war and she's enduring it bravely, Assunta thought. She thanked the Lord her sons, so far, had not been inducted. Her daughters and their families still in Rome under siege. The Allies had bombed Rome for the second time, trying to oust the Germans. In the first bombing, scores of Italians were killed—no word from her family.

"Already the hill's feeling the sting of this miserable war," Assunta blurted. "Two families have already lost sons." She wanted to bite her tongue.

Her friend crossed herself. "War, a scourge, a killing madness, I tell you. When it's over, Lord help us, we'll all wonder what it was about. Can suffering be for naught? I keep asking myself. Is it meant to be a trial? Sorrow and suffering flow over us like the raging waves of an ocean in a storm."

Assunta looked out at the south slope easing its way to the river. She heard birds chirping in the trees. Our nature is to recoil from pain, she thought. But Florence is different—she doesn't shrink . . . takes the knocks and masters them. "How do you do it, Florence?" Assunta asked.

"What's to do, my dear?" Mrs. Lambert thought of poor Assunta: months without any word from her daughters, and their families living in fear for their lives. Her own daughter Lillian with a vicious tongue; her son-in-law Frank hooked on more than the bottle; her grandson Eddy dumped out of school. Yet she couldn't give up her belief that human suffering has meaning. Doesn't it help us grow—spur us on to find goodness in life? No, we must delight in all things, in spite of suffering. She looked at Assunta: "We don't want to become indifferent to pleasures and pains and to joys and sorrows."

"What do you mean?"

"Well, my dear, we can become impassive—insensitive to life. Do you see what I mean? Fearing suffering, we pull back from life—to save ourselves pain. We try to escape pain by escaping life. We simply must have sympathy with all things in and through Christ," Mrs. Lambert said, crossing herself again.

"How do we make sense of this world? A slaughterhouse, I

tell you," Assunta said. "Sympathy with all things! What of the senseless killing going on in the world?"

"Dear me, Assunta, forgive my rambling. I express myself badly. I don't mean to be cold to the suffering sweeping over us. Without faith, my dear, I would simply not be able to go on. Faith helps renew me . . . lessens my pain . . . forgive me for saying—I don't mean to be . . ." she paused.

Assunta looked into her eyes. They were tearing over. Assunta turned away.

"Not to be immodest," Mrs. Lambert went on after a bit, "I want you to know I thank God. My pain is eased by prayer and His grace. The war will solve nothing. You'll see. Nothing. Absolutely nothing. It's another trial to set us right—to set the world on the right path. The last war solved nothing. We learned nothing after all the killing."

"What's to learn?" Assunta asked, baffled.

"We must love the world but escape its evil. We must love divine creation—all people. God will take care of the rest. If we try to live with others in harmony, to bear the burden of our tragic destiny."

Could it be possible—such idealism? Assunta thought. Europe had always been a madhouse plagued by wars and bloodletting. Nations seem to go insane more often than individuals do. She expected the young like Marco and Felicia to indulge such thoughts. But Florence?

"My dear Florence, you might as well ask people, the very people we see day in and day out, to turn into saints and ascetics."

"No solution is possible save in the love of Christ and in the fullness of love," Mrs. Lambert replied. "Not only love for God, but for man—yes, compassion even for one's enemy and for nature. This I believe with all my heart."

Anna slipped into the doorway unnoticed and took in their words.

Mrs. Lambert leaned over. "Assunta, the divine energy is released in us, penetrates and changes our heart, whenever we say the Jesus Prayer: 'O Lord Jesus Christ, Son of God, have mercy upon me a sinner.'" Mrs. Lambert recited it with such deep conviction that Anna felt a twinge of joy. "I repeat it many times daily and commend it to you, my dear."

Assunta, about to respond, heard the door open as Anna ran to greet her parents.

After dinner, Assunta brought up Felicia's long separation from her family. Felicia and Marco listened, taking her words to heart.

"You must get in touch with your dear father and mother, Felicia. They no doubt suffer terribly. Put an end to it, for God's sake. Listen, cara. Life's a gift. A continual struggle, too. Yes, for all of us, for as long as we live. But not for nothing. Much of our pain is of our own making. We have the duty to lessen it. We must try to build a good life for ourselves—working hard to do so. In the end, the earth waits to swallow us up, to take us back." She got a glimpse of herself as—what was the American word?—an old schoolmarm preaching to her children. She felt like laughing but rapture seized her.

"We need to fight two demons that never stop stalking us," she continued. "One that clamps onto us like the claws of a crab, never letting us go—life's daily struggle. It bites into our flesh every moment we live, every time we run into one another. Yes, every time we touch on God's creation—the world of nature that feeds and bathes us, that gives us home and shelter. The other is death—the end. Praise be to God." She got up and went to the cupboard.

Felicia and Marco listened in silence.

"The older I get," she said, fumbling around and filling a tray with *pizzelle* to have with their coffee, "the more I think our purpose here on earth is a continual struggle to the end." Setting the tray down, she looked into Felicia's tired eyes. "You are the younger, Felicia. You simply must take the first step. Make peace. Break the ice. Your family will bless you."

The words pierced Felicia. She resolved to get a letter off to her parents without delay. But mail to Rome, now under German occupation, was not likely to get through.

Marco, bogged down with work, had taken little notice of Felicia's anguish. He'd been promoted to head of sales and this increased his working hours. He found himself traveling out of state more often. Most of production at Supreme Gems had shifted over to war goods. Despite this, Felicia's design portfolio had been well received. She was to start shortly as a designer at Supreme Gems on a whole new line, as plans to shift back to peacetime production were in the works. She would stay on part time at Sennetts'.

That evening she wrote in her journal:

April 1943
Papa and Mamma were no doubt right: a loss of title does now and then haunt me. But not for the reasons they'd think of—not for privilege's sake. Lacking a title, you find it more difficult to make your efforts felt, harder to be a beneficial presence in the world. That's the way it is.

Would I want to change anything of my past? No. I see more clearly now the tendency of those in a position of privilege, terrible in its consequence, to trample underfoot those beneath them. And whether they realize it or not, those who command tend to wrench away the liberty and crush the dignity of those who obey. Titles that lend authority to rank can be worse than the plague when they diminish the dignity of man and sacrifice the human personality for the sake of the privileged.

Men of power scoff at such ideas. They talk of the impossibility of equality among people, of the inequality nature confers on themselves to be masters over others. For me, equality means securing the freedom and worth of every human being so that no single person will be treated as a thing—as a means to an end.

In the work I'm now doing, serving those who consider themselves superior, I'm thankful to be free of the temptation of the privileged. They delude themselves. The real aristocrat—I must be sure I become one—never pushes himself (or herself!) forward but is merciful. For the first (the strongest, according to the law of this world) will be last, and those who appear weak in the eyes of the world will (transfigured by spirit) be first.

We learn through our mistakes—they bring us pain. Siding against the appointment of Fr. DiSanto as new pastor at Sacred Heart was a mistake. Even here, my willfulness has taught me to be more humble—to take all points of view into account. Father D.

turned out to be a teacher and preacher for all seasons—spiritually nourishing our consciousness and conscience.

Often he warns that the end of scientific humanism is in sight. He sees man as a whole being—a spiritual center—losing his inner unity and quickly disappearing. In our technological civilization the whole man is dissolving into certain functions and is cared about only in terms of the function he performs. The image of man is being shaken: in making himself God, man has unmanned himself. Man no longer regards himself as a fallen being on the pathway to salvation—a creature both fallen and exalted.

Anguish in Rome, 1944

For some time Piero, through his sister Carla, had been trying to make contact with Felicia's father.

By September '43 things in Rome had taken a turn for the worse. Mussolini was thrown out of office and a new government formed under Marshal Badoglio, who signed an armistice with the Allies: Britain, France, and the U.S. This changed the status of Italy. Italy had now become an enemy of Germany while much of it was still under German rule. This spelled trouble for the Romans. Rome was no longer an 'open city' where Romans supposedly had free movement: it became a city under siege and the Romans a conquered people. Italy itself had become divided. The Nazis set up a puppet government and put Mussolini in command at Saló, in the north. This meant that Italians were now fighting on two sides—some under the fascist régime in the north, some with the Allies under the régime in Rome. Marshal Badoglio and the royal family were soon forced to flee Rome.

Not wanting to deepen his mother's fears, Piero sought to strike out on his own. He needed to keep in touch with his sister Carla in the hope of killing two birds with one stone—to get his sisters and their families under the count's protection, and to reconcile Felicia with her parents.

How to establish communications with Carla? She had, at the start of the war, lost her job at the American Embassy. She then took a position with the American Chargé d'Affaires at the

Vatican, which maintained neutrality with Germany.

Even before Italy signed the Armistice with the Allies, Carla was at risk. The British Ministry and American diplomatic offices at the Vatican had become a hotbed of covert activity. They helped prisoners of war escape the Germans by devising personal disguises and false identity cards, finding accommodations in Rome for them, and using the Vatican radio to send out secret messages to their families.

Carla was at the center of it. To keep her activities secret, as far as was possible, she was housed in the Convent of the Sisters of St. Vincent de Paul, in the Vatican. This was a dangerous business as German guns and field-glasses were pointed at the Vatican, though German soldiers, by mandate, were barred from the papal state.

To protect her identity, Piero wrote to Carla under the name Mario Buono (her married name being Buono) at the office of the American Chargé d'Affaires at the Vatican. Not to worry Assunta, he received Carla's mail at his office. He pleaded with Carla to get in contact with Count Petrarca, Felicia's father.

Carla kept watch for an occasion to comply with her brother's wishes. Despite the proximity of her family home and the Petrarcas', she could find no way to set up a meeting with the count. From the Piazza Navona to the Via Giulia was little more than a half mile. Carla reminded Piero that the highborn live secluded lives fenced in by cultural hurdles harder to jump than stone walls. How could she approach them? They ran in different circles and lived behind iron gates. Even if they were to meet, could she address Count Petrarca without being addressed? Then came the danger of alliances—would the Petrarcas be for or against the Allies?

Carla, involved in covert operations, kept her fingers on the pulse of the Roman aristocracy. Many Orsini and Colonna, putting their lives at risk, gave their time and money to the Resistance—those fighting against the Germans. She surmised that the count sided with the Resistance but could not be sure.

Cut off from their daughter, the Petrarcas had suffered no less than Felicia. They bore the guilt of having deserted their daughter. This took a toll on their marriage. The count had lost not only a daughter but a wife. Though she tried to conceal it, the countess never forgave her husband. Her bitterness soured their life together.

One day, while entering the Vatican precincts at the end of the Bernini colonnade to the left of St. Peter's and passing through the archways of the baroque sacristy, Carla by chance ran into the count. He was heading away from the diplomats' building in a large square on which stood the Convent of the Sisters of St. Vincent de Paul, where she worked.

"Count Petrarca," she addressed him on the spur of the moment.

Startled, he turned and faced her. "How do you do, Signora Buono?" He assumed a familiarity that practically struck Carla dumb.

"I'm . . . I work . . . with . . . at . . . the Sisters of St. Vincent . . ." she managed to say.

"Yes . . . yes, I know," he said cheerfully. "My pleasure." He extended his hand. They shook hands. He turned around to follow in her direction. He took her arm without saying another word and escorted her toward the convent as if two old friends had met.

At the entry of the convent he faced her. "Please, Signora Buono, come to visit us. The Countess would be delighted. Your sister? Would she visit, too?"

"We'd be delighted, Count."

"Tomorrow, then?"

"If—"

"Fine," he broke in. "Tomorrow at seven, shall we say? I'll send my chauffeur round."

"We're at—"

"Yes, Yes, I know."

Carla nodded as they shook hands. Their meeting took place as in a dream, leaving Carla baffled.

When the countess heard the news, she jumped for joy. The count, restored to her good graces, became a hero. She sighed with relief from years of yearning. At the same time she put much of the blame on herself. Yes, she was at fault. What a wall she should have put up between herself and Luigi at the time—

a wall of steel. Luigi would have thought twice before crossing her. Saving face in his tug of war with Felicia would have been nothing by comparison. In her rapture now she reproached herself on another count—she herself had misgivings about Felicia's marriage. She, too, thought Felicia unwise and immature and wanted to perpetuate the dynasty through her own line. She cringed at the thought of her own complicity in years of suffering. In the next moment, as if struck by amnesia, she delighted in Felicia's return to the bosom of the family.

Carla and Ida felt privileged. Driving from the Piazza Navona to the Via Giulia, Antonio, the chauffeur, accorded them the respect he accorded family members. The streets were deserted. Gasoline could only be bought on the black market by those of means. They drove down the Via Arenula toward the Tiber, taking the shortcut up the Via dei Giubbonari through the Campo. The marketplace was empty, its shops and restaurants sealed off behind metal gates. Going toward the Via Giulia, they passed the Palazzo Farnese.

The count and countess greeted them in the great hall and dropped all formality at once. Carla and Ida warmed to the Petrarcas and felt accepted as family. The palazzo, especially this particular room, had become famous in the 1920s when, on its social pages, the *Corriere della Sera* buzzed with rumors of the feud that had taken place between the two Roman dynasties— the Colonna and the Orsini.

"If I may be so bold as to ask, Countess," Ida said, a bit embarrassed, "is this the stairway that enchanted all Rome in the '20s?"

"Yes, my dear," the countess replied, reminded of the scandalous party Ida referred to. "Our cousin, Josephine Napoleon, you may have heard, sought to shock our families. Josephine handled our strong-willed cousins—the heads of the Colonna and Orsini—with humor. She came down the stairway smoking a cigar and dressed in a shameful outfit, to mock them. Let's leave that story for another time." Countess Clara smiled in spite of her tears. A picture of Felicia sitting at the top of the stairs that evening slipped into her mind.

To Carla's astonishment the count knew all about her work with the Resistance carried out at the office of the American Chargé d'Affaires and at the British Ministry. This established an intimacy between them and they spoke openly about it.

"Then you've heard," Carla said, "about Countess Josephine's run-in with the fascist?"

"Yes," the count replied, "I heard mention of it. No details."

The countess looked puzzled. The incident had happened some weeks before and the count had said nothing to her.

"Countess Josephine was on her way back to the city on her bike with the front basket full of bomb fragments," Carla told them. "She helps the Resistance collect them for making hand grenades." Carla looked up at them. Should she say more? she wondered. "Well," she went on, "Countess Josephine fell upon a road block where a fascist guard stopped everyone entering the city. 'Che cosa hai lì dentro? What have you in there?' he asked. Countess Josephine, well aware of an order for fascists to shoot on sight anybody caught carrying arms, let out a nervous laugh. 'Ha, ha!' Be careful. It's full of bombs,' she said. 'Fai la spiritosa. Aren't you the silly one,' replied the soldier sarcastically, and waved her on."

Countess Clara let out a sigh of relief. "Always the lioness, our cousin!"

"What have you heard about the incident at the Ardeatine Cave?" Count Petrarca asked.

"Three hundred thirty I'm told," Carla said in a hushed voice as if the walls had ears. "Hitler wanted many more killed. Poor Romans. Three hundred thirty Romans shot in a cave, as you may have heard. Massacred brutally! In retaliation for a bomb set off on the Via Rasella by members of the Resistance—Italian partisans who had killed thirty or more fascists, many of them Germans. The Resistance, I understand, wounded seventy all told near the Barberini Palace."

"How did the Germans select Italians—mark out the victims to be shot in the cave?" the count asked.

"What we've heard—how reliable I don't know—is that many came from prisons. A few rounded up off the street. Some seventy or eighty were Jews," Carla said. She and the count and countess fell silent for some time.

A breath of fresh air soon swept over them as they delighted in small talk about Anna and Alessandro. The countess came alive; her face sloughed off years of suffering. Her big almond-shaped eyes sparkled and her broad smile reflected her inner joy. "Luigi, what do you say? Let's plan a visit to America," she said, forgetting the war.

Carla and Ida were charmed by her *joie de vivre*. Luigi too came to life, hearing his wife laugh for the first time in years. He had forgotten just how beautiful she was.

"We've been tottering between emptiness and meaninglessness all these years," the countess confided. "We've not found a way of hardening our hearts against our pain." Bitterness crept into her voice. "Granted so much, we failed to resolve our impasse." In the next breath she was exuberant. "How happy I am that Felicia's sisters-in-law are with us tonight, Luigi." She stretched out her arms to touch Carla's and Ida's hands.

Luigi knew the war would prevent travel for years to come. Even now, unknown to the countess, he'd been planning to abandon the palazzo and take refuge in the villa in Rignano. Rome would soon become a battleground; bombing raids increased daily. The Allies' seizing and securing of the Anzio beachhead south of Rome had brought about scores of casualties. By late January the battle at Anzio, called the hell-hole of the Mediterranean, had set the stage for the beginning of the battle for Rome.

Thinking of Felicia lifted the count's spirit from his self-made prison—a prison lodged in his own heart. The Benedicta sisters would hold a special place in his family. They'd set him free from his own chains, giving him back his wife and daughter.

"So this is our granddaughter Anna Maria," Luigi said proudly. "Look at this, Clara." He passed the photos to his wife, one by one. "Anna's beautiful—curly dark hair, fair skin, sparkling eyes."

"Look at Alessandro Luigi, what a beautiful grandchild. Poor Alessandro Luigi, without any grandfathers." Tears blurred the countess's vision. Separation from her grandchildren stung her bitterly. "Alessandro looks like Anna Maria—what pretty curls, and his face so angelic. I'd say he favored his mother."

Luigi fished for tidbits of information about the life of the children and their parents. Carla and Ida supplied whatever came to mind, assuring the Petrarcas the children were being brought up speaking Italian as well as English. The count promised to aid the Benedictas in any way he could. Piero's wishes had been carried out, but it would be some time before he'd know what went on on the Roman front.

Death of the Father

Two months after Carla and Ida dined with the Petrarcas, Felicia's joy turned to stone. Late one evening Marco's car swerved off a road in Providence and rammed into a telephone pole. He did not survive the injuries.

At the age of twenty-nine Felicia became dependent on her in-laws once more for emotional and mental, if not economic, support. She thought of Assunta's crab that clamps onto life. Her joy in being reunited with her family was short lived. Marco's death sapped her strength.

She wrote in her journal:

The alternation of light and darkness, of life and death, has stumped moralists for centuries. Life continuously flows from life to death, from light to darkness, and back again. An eternal becoming and an eternal passing mock the stream of time. Life cannot escape the presence of its antagonist—death. Two eternal principles, creation and destruction, are not so much enemies as partners in life's struggle.

Explaining their father's death to Anna and Alex added to Felicia's grief. Anna refused to budge from her mother's or grandmother's side.

Sitting around the kitchen table upstairs, Felicia watched Anna cling to Piero.

"You won't die, will you Uncle Peter? Promise me. Will Papa come back? Why do people die, Mamma?"

"Don't worry, my love," Felicia said, taking Anna from Piero's lap and hugging her. "Papa has passed on to God's kingdom and rests in God's bosom. We must pray for him always and think of him in his new world."

"Has he gone to Rignano—to the castle—to be with Nonna Clara and Nonno Luigi?" Anna wondered aloud.

Over the years, Marco and Piero had depicted the life of the Roman grandparents in palaces and castles. In the minds of the children the life of the Petrarcas took on a perfection the children yearned for. Anna thought of the other side of the ocean as a radiant and heavenly domain. In moments playing around the flowerbeds or chasing butterflies and birds or lying in the grass with Alex, she felt the rays of the sun penetrate her. She asked her mother whether it was a visit from that other world. When Felicia dressed her after her Saturday bath or Marco snuggled her tightly in his arms or Nonna took her to the church full of incense and organ music, Anna felt the ecstasy of the other world she yearned for.

"Mamma, when will we go to Nonna and Nonno in Rome? Tell me, Mamma."

Lost in thought, Felicia didn't answer. Piero reached over and took Anna from her mother's lap. "Come here, you *scoiattolina*—you little squirrel!" Piero joked. He rocked her in his arms. "Wait till we surprise *i nonni* in Rignano. We'll tiptoe down that long arcade of cyprus trees lining the winding path to the castle. Then we'll bang on the *portoni*, so large it takes two servants to open. 'Ma chi bussa? Chi sta invadendo il nostro castello?' 'Who's knocking? Who's trying to invade our castle?' Nonno Luigi will yell. 'Send them away! Send the invaders away! We're waiting for Anna and Alex.'"

Alex, playing on the floor, clambered onto Piero's lap beside Anna. Piero hugged them. The children squealed in delight.

"When we go, Uncle Petah? Soon, peeese, tumowo?" Alex said, looking at Piero with his big brown eyes.

"Yes, Mamma," Anna turned to her mother, "let's go with Uncle Peter tomorrow."

"Anna, I told you we have to wait for the war to end. Travel across the ocean is impossible now." She thought about her parents, who by now had fled Rome. They managed to get a letter sent out through a liaison with the American military. She learned that Italians still lived in fear of bombing raids, with their countrymen divided—some fighting with the Germans, some fighting with the Americans and British. "Un bell'imbroglio! A bloody mess! This war is proving more risky to the nobility than the last. Papa wrote that the fascists, allied with the Germans, are vicious to those who don't lend support to their cause. He can't stomach their violence even though he stands to gain by them." Felicia feared for her parents' safety: the local fascists, operating outside the law in the small towns of Tuscany, preyed on the unsympathetic.

"Non ti preoccupare. Please, try to take things in stride," Piero said.

"When will the war be over, Mamma? Next week?" The word had little meaning to Anna. War touched her life only in the shortage of meat, sugar, fruits, and gasoline she heard her parents talk about.

Assunta kept up the garden, much expanded since the war. The trees now bore fruit. Vegetables and fruits, put up in Mason jars, lined the shelves in the basement storage room. Marco and Piero had built a chicken coop; chickens supplied them with eggs and meat. War made its tentacles felt everywhere. Busy with work, the family had plenty of money but few goods to buy. Save for the military, few durable goods were being produced. Scarcity of sugar, bananas, gasoline, tires, and meat kept them forever on the lookout for them. When it came to gasoline, their allotment always fell short of their need. Meat rationing through food stamps was a constant irritation. You often had to take whatever butchers handed out, happy to get it. And it could be awful cuts, sometimes nearly inedible.

Assunta came in with a tray of *pizzelle*—flat, crisp cookies the children loved—and put them on the table. The children helped themselves. She pulled up a chair and joined Felicia and Piero.

"A month ago Marco said to me: 'You know, Felicia, we've been Americanized!' 'What do you mean?' I asked. 'Well, all we do here is work—like Americans fixed on getting more wealth. We Italians have learned something over the centuries: for us, pleasure is connected to pain. Every pleasure either comes from pain or ends in pain. We know there's no such thing as pleasure without pain—as Americans seem to believe. But you know, Felicia' (how Marco loved to philosophize!), 'our awareness makes us more compassionate toward our countrymen than Americans are.'"

"Italians are compassionate all right!" Assunta shrieked. "What was he talking about? He must've forgotten those bloody blackshirts, *i fascisti*, brandishing their clubs in the streets of Rome. Compassion? Compassion! Sounds to me more like an attack of nostalgia for the Old World." Tears welled up in her eyes and a lump swelled in her throat. Marco now gone and Carla and Ida trying to hold on in the stink of war. She knew that Carla, having worked in the American Embassy, would always be suspect, and her life in danger.

Not to worry his mother, Piero still kept secret the letters he received from Carla at his office and said nothing about her position with the American Chargé d'Affaires at the Vatican. Carla of course did get letters through to her mother, carefully written not to upset her.

"No, Mamma," Piero said, "Marco's point is well taken. While Italians generally reject stoicism—not wanting to live like Puritans—they have no desire to give up pleasure altogether. But they embrace epicureanism. They know damn well there's got to be a limit to pleasure. We Romans believe pleasure is something good if limited and appreciated; but we also know pain is the mother of all pleasure." Piero hoped to keep them talking to help relieve their grief.

"Now another professor in the family! Epicureanism? Stoicism? We Romans have always been afflicted—oppressed since the breakdown of the empire. If we could harness all the suffering—"

"No, Mamma, listen. Marco's right. Americans have a simple-minded notion: Pleasure and pain have little to do with one another. So Americans can be fooled into thinking they can get rid of pain. They fail to see that suffering is a part of life to be endured and triumphed over, as the stoics believed. Americans think of suffering as something bad in itself—something to escape from. In America, everyone wants to escape pain: if you've got wealth, power, status, that's all you need—no more pain, only pleasure. Your life'll be a bed of roses."

"But compassion? Where does all this Italian compassion come from? How are the bitter dregs of pain whipped into this longed-for cream of compassion? Tell me this."

Listening to Piero and Assunta argue, Felicia forgot her grief for a few moments. "Marco said that we Romans, walking around and enjoying sights, sounds, smells, food, congeniality, knew pain to be hidden in it all. We sensed our countrymen's and our own sweat and blood at the root of our pleasures. Everything created by human beings has in it a hefty dose of suffering. Whether it's something we look at, drive in, live in, consume—all contain pain. This we knew when we lived in Rome. But here in America, we, too, began to imagine pleasure and pain to be strangers. Whether worker, businessman, or aristocrat, pain courses through everyone's life. Not just the pain of work, but of catastrophes, accidents, wars, famines, deaths . . ." Felicia thought of Marco.

"Yes, Italians see pleasure as an occasion to celebrate," Piero said. "We are born in pain and live in pain; pleasure is a reprieve. Knowledge of this fact makes us more humane—more compassionate."

Anna and Alex had become restless. Felicia reached over and tweaked Alex's nose and patted Anna's head. They had been speaking in Italian all the while, and Alex said: "Mamma, quando mi porti in Italia? When will you take me to Italy?"

"Yes, Mamma, when are we going to Rignano, to the castle?" Anna chimed in.

"Ah, yes, and to my favorite *trattoria* in Trastevere," Piero joked, as he tickled them.

"Really, Uncle?" Anna asked.

"E dal fornaio nel Campo dei Fiori," Assunta added.

"How about some *gelati* in the Piazza Navona," Felicia added.

"Sì! Sì! Mamma, tonight. Adesso! Now, some ice cweam," Alex entreated. They laughed.

Then they went around the table, each throwing out the name of a place as the children listened in wonder. La Piazza Farnese . . . il Vaticano . . . il Campidoglio . . . la via Arenula . . . il Campo dei Fiori . . . l'Isola Tiberina . . . il Bambinello di Ara Coeli—"

"E la via Giulia dove sono i miei nonni! and the Via Giulia where my grandma and grandpa live!" Anna put in. Alex followed suit—"e le mutandi di mio papa! and my father's underwear!"

"Time for bed, *andiamo!*" Felicia laughed, though she could have cried.

"How about a story, Uncle Peter?" Anna asked. Piero nodded.

The children jumped off his lap, hugged their mother and grandmother, and scurried off to get ready for bed.

"It occurs to me," Piero continued, "today's Italians, as epicureans, stand between the ancient stoics, who believed in denying themselves pleasure to save themselves pain, and American hedonists, who believe in increasing pleasure to escape pain. Italians say: '"Enjoy your pleasure when you can. But keep it in check. It's fleeting and rooted in pain.' But if pain is the shadow that accompanies pleasure, it can't be escaped. And to deny pleasure, as the stoics advise, is to deny life—"

"The kids are calling," Assunta said. "Va', va', Professore."

Assunta was full of grief. Marco had been taken from her in his prime. How to reconcile unmerited suffering with the existence of God? she thought. This disturbed her terribly. When she questioned her faith, Fr. DiSanto had told her that Christ changes the path of suffering into the path of salvation. "Unlike the stoics who do not accept suffering and who seek to flee it to secure relief from it," he told her, "Christianity accepts and triumphs over it." Her head could fathom Christ's counsel— take up your cross and follow me. But her heart failed to embrace it.

When Piero returned, Assunta, sitting close to Felicia with her head bent toward her daughter-in-law's, was saying: " . . . listen to me, an old woman of fifty-seven, get hold of yourself. Guilt is a double-edged sword. It cuts both ways: it can either help us grow or it can consume us. Marco's death cannot fall on your shoulders. Believe me: some dwell upon their wrongdoing, flaunt it openly as though it were a badge of honor. But I tell you, feelings are a tricky business—feelings of wrongdoing you must fight against. They can turn life rancid."

"Mamma mia! The ole lady's full of wisdom tonight." Piero

slipped in unnoticed, feigning good humor. Grief coiled up in them like a serpent ready to slither out and strike. He missed Marco profoundly and his anguish had deepened when he got his draft notice that day. He hid it from the household because he hoped the draft board just might grant him a deferment, since he was the only surviving son in the family. At twenty-seven he had managed to escape the military so far; at thirty-two, Marco had been too old to be called up.

"Do you remember the Campo, Mamma?" Piero asked, to divert them. His thoughts went back to the largest outdoor market in Rome where he had spent many hours with his friends after school.

"Ma come non mi ricordo. Credi che io sia scema? Do you think I've lost my mind?"

"Once Marco and I got up about three in the morning while you and Papa were sleeping, sneaked outside, and waited in the piazza for the *contadini*—those hard-working peasants. The statue of Giordano Bruno was standing in its eternal pose, a testament to free speech. With the pigeons still asleep, the silence scared us. The peasants soon filed into the Campo. Those wooden-wheeled carts of theirs, filled with fruits and vegetables, rumbled on the cobblestone streets radiating like spokes toward the piazza. We watched its magical metamorphosis into a noisy, bustling marketplace. The aromas like nowhere in the world: the smell of fresh-baked pastries and breads wafted out and mixed with the smells of flowers and freshly made coffee from the neighboring bars, and with fish and meat and fruits and vegetables. Heaven was coming alive."

"Ah, *figlio mio*, we must look forward, not backward," Assunta said. "Believe me, nostalgia can be a curse too."

Felicia's thoughts turned toward the Palazzo Farnese, a block from the Campo—not far from the palace on the Via Giulia. She and Marco often sat beside the fountains in front of the palazzo.

"Did you know, Mamma, the Campo was where Marco and I spent many hours when we were courting?" Her cheeks reddened. Assunta and Piero smiled. "Just up from the Torre Argentina, the little park on the Via Arenula, at the end of the

Via dei Giubbonari—we would sit on the benches, read, and feed the pigeons. One day after walking around the Jewish quarter, we followed the Via Porta Ottavia up to the Via Arenula. We retreated to our little park across the street at the end of the Via dei Giubbonari. You know how busy the Via Arenula is with traffic to and from the Trastevere? Marco sat reading on one bench and I lay resting on another across from him. One of our 'dear Roman boys' parked his bike and came up to me. He started flirting. I sat up and he sat beside me on the bench. He asked me to go out with him. So I thought I'd have some fun with Marco.

"I said to the boy, coquettishly, 'Don't be so impertinent! I don't know if I should answer you.' 'That's a sharp tongue for such a beautiful woman!' he shot back, thinking maybe he'd stumbled onto a conquest. 'Your presumption of familiarity is offensive,' I said. 'We haven't met. And what's one's tongue got to do with one's looks—or do I miss your point?' The young man couldn't tell whether I was interested or not. I could see Marco chuckling behind his book. 'How about a walk to the Trastevere—maybe a pizza, a glass of wine. How about it?' he asked. 'Well, I would if I could,' I said, making believe I was considering it. 'Why not then?' he persisted. 'Well, for one thing you'll need my papa's permission,' I told him. 'Mamma mia! A big girl like you. Come on, do you think we're living in the Stone Age?' he retorted warmly. 'Next, you'll need my husband's permission. What do you think, caro?' I said, looking over at Marco, who pretended he hadn't been listening. The boy looked from me to Marco, embarrassed. 'Yes? Is it time to go home and feed the kids?' Marco asked. 'Is that what you want to know? Well, come on, let's go!' He got up, took my arm, and off we went, leaving our Roman boy dumbfounded."

"To think how young you and Marco were then!" Assunta said. "Carissimi, this damn war can't go on forever. Like the ruins of Rome all things come to an end—good and bad. We'll go home soon and be on Roman soil that bears in it the blood, sweat, and tears of centuries. We'll go home. Count on it. And you, dear Felicia, will be reunited with your parents and I will embrace my two lost darling girls and their families. Andiamo a letto."

3
Week of Infamy

Years rolled by and things grew worse for Felicia on Prospect Hill. For some, she was a snob, contemptuous of the townsfolk, living in sin with her brother-in-law. Lillian Pastori continued to stir up trouble for her.

Yet Anna and Cecilia, Lillian's daughter, became best friends. The kids at Providence Street Grammar took to Anna. Who wouldn't? She was precocious and lovely, reserved and well brought up. She visited me often and I enjoyed our talks.

Paul Risch and Tony Pastori did well in sports at West Warwick Junior High and were looked up to by the kids on the hill. Paul finished at the top of his class. He came over often and told me funny stories about school events.

One I especially remember: In the seventh grade he insisted on knowing from his ancient history teacher whether the Neanderthals came before or after Adam and Eve. More than once he asked his teacher to clear this up. One day his teacher told him to report to the principal for being a wise guy. "Ah, Lena," he'd often say to tease me, "you don't know how hard we poor students have it nowadays."

Paul lived just to the east of the Benedictas. An only child, he took to Alex Benedicta, treated him as a little brother, and played catch with him.

Eddy Pastori and Ralph Mullen, unschooled and left out of much of the hill's social life, were rarely treated as misfits. The kids opened their hearts to the simple goodness in both of them, especially to Ralph.

Though behind his back many called Ralph "the idiot," often they said it with affection. Eddy Pastori's problem might have been dealt with through special education. This was not so with Ralph Mullen. Some deficiency of mind, some unique or unusual flaw, had given rise to a youngster who exhibited a purity of heart. Ralph seemed to live above the fray of deception, competitiveness, or the need of praise. Father D. said Ralph lived close to nature and to God—a person sent to us to make us see the faults in ourselves. Father D. took Ralph under his wing and gave him a job at the church several afternoons a week.

Whenever Ralph visited me, I sensed goodness in him. His views of the townsfolk revealed deep sensitivity, despite his mental limitations. Sometimes the kids even asked Ralph to settle a dispute. I remember one instance when the men at Louie's Tavern got into a tiff playing bocce—*a game in which the players throw balls, a bit smaller and lighter than those used in bowling, on a dirt court. The goal was to get closest to the queen ball. Thinking they'd have some fun with Ralph, Frank Pastori (Lillian's husband) and Edgar Risch (Paul's father) asked Ralph to call the play between two teams. To decide which of two balls came closest to the queen, Ralph ran off for a set of calipers. The men waited in wonder and then marveled at Ralph's keen sense of measure in declaring the winner. As usual when he felt happy, Ralph clapped his hands and, mimicking Father D., would say, "love each other as brothers."*

Ralph pried into everyone's business. He once told me that Anna was a goddess sent from heaven and that Cecilia loved Paul but Paul loved Anna. His list of kids who would "go away from Prospect Hill for better" included Anna, Paul, Tony, Alberta, and Dante. He saw trouble ahead for Norman, Pasco, and Jerry, who, he said, had big holes in their hearts.

Many still hung out at Lillian Pastori's steps on Friday and Saturday nights in idle chatter, amusing each other over the week's events.

School Kids and Catechism, Spring 1950

Crocuses and tulips, warming to the spring sun, poked their heads out of the soil on a mild Friday afternoon in March. Walking arm in arm and oblivious to them, Anna Benedicta and Cecilia Pastori puffed their way up Prospect Hill on their way home from school.

Their dream of entering West Warwick Junior High next fall preoccupied them. Their minds and hearts had already shifted to the new school and they talked of little else. They relished walking each morning and afternoon to Royal Square, meeting older kids who streamed into the town's junior high from all over the Pawtuxet Valley, and getting a look at those strict teachers they'd heard so much about.

They rested beside the picket fence at Wakefield Lane in front of the Mansours' house. The Mansours, like the Benedictas, had been "rebels" during the church upheaval, and a sinister air still clung to them. Even now, in the spring of 1950, children saw both the Benedictas and the Mansours as outcasts and misfits.

The reputation of the Benedictas did not carry over to Anna and Alex. It's as if the shadow hung over the older generation, seen as foreigners, and excluded the younger, seen as Americans. Anna and Alex could hold their own and were well accepted at school.

"I saw Paul run up the hill after you yesterday, Anna," Cecilia said, expecting to hear what took place. When Anna didn't say anything, she went on to prod. "He's pretty stuck on himself since he started junior high, don't you think?" As Anna was about to answer, Cecilia yelled across the street, "Hey, what're ya staring at, Rawolf?" She made a face at Ralph Mullen sitting on the wall in front of her house with her brother Eddy.

"Hi, Ralph! Hi, Eddy!" Anna yelled and waved to them. They smiled and waved back. The girls crossed the street to talk to them.

"Ralph can't keep his eyes off you, Anna," Cecilia said. "All the kids are talking about it. Eddy says he sits for hours spying with his binoculars—perching in a tree or looking out his bedroom window—watching everything you do."

Ralph Mullen and Eddy Pastori, bosom buddies at sixteen, did chores for neighbors and helped out at Louie's Tavern. Ralph was still spending a good deal of time working at Sacred Heart, too.

From the Mullen house, the goings-on in Anna's yard fascinated Ralph. The only other person living at the Mullens' was Ralph's aged mother. His brothers and sisters were married and, except for his sister Rose Golanski who lived on the hill, they had moved to other parts of the town. Ralph kept the house and barn in good condition.

At twelve, Anna, the brightest and prettiest in the sixth grade, was growing into a classic beauty, with dark hair, light skin, and bright-green eyes. Cecilia, with fine sandy-colored hair, closely set blue eyes, and angular face, could be called cute but not pretty. Friendly and flirtatious, she had a proud and free spirit. Anna, being reserved, the boys thought stuck up. Cecilia admired Anna's humility and thoughtfulness. Anna loved Cecilia's spontaneity and treasured her friendship.

Ralph jumped off the wall in front of the Pastori house as the girls approached. "It's nice to see you, Anna. You too, Cecilia. Paul's teachin' me math and helpin' me read better."

"That's good." Anna smiled.

"Yeah, Paul's real smart. Not like me. Father D. says I was born spiritu'ly perfect even if I can't read too good."

"Don't be a ninny, Ralph," Cecilia said. "He only wants you to feel good. Nobody's born perfect. That's silly."

"You think that, Anna? Nobody's born perfect?" Ralph turned to Anna, his big blue eyes sad at such a thought.

"Oh, Ralph. Cecilia's just pulling your leg. Aren't you Cecilia?"

"Yeah, sure. We're all born perfect."

"You don't believe it, Cecilia. I can see. Your sister don't believe Father D.," Ralph said, turning to Eddy who, looking off into space, seemed bored and uninterested. "What happened to me and Eddy, then?"

Anna wondered too. Ralph was almost as good looking as Paul. Tall, with smiling eyes and a well-formed face framed by dark wavy hair—all this conflicted with Ralph's mysterious deficiency. He baffled her: often she'd be taken by surprise at his keen intelligence. "All babies are born perfect, Ralph. Did you ever see a little baby? Every little finger and every little toe—perfect, beautiful. Father D.'s right—we're born spiritually pure. Father D.'s always saying that God loves every one of his children, Ralph. God doesn't care whether you can read well or not."

Ralph smiled. "You're so pretty and smart, Anna. Ain't she, Eddy?" He turned to Eddy and gave him a push; then he clapped his hands. He looked over at Cecilia. "You too, Cecilia. Yeah, Eddy, your sister's pretty and smart, too."

"Oh, Ralph!" Cecilia said. She nudged him gently. "You can be such a jerk sometimes."

Ralph laughed. "Yeah, sure. You know, Paul likes Anna. I know. You like Paul too, Anna," Ralph laughed heartily and clapped his hands again. The girls looked at one another and blushed.

"See, Eddy, I told you," Ralph said.

"Ralph, you're such a jerk," Cecilia said.

"I know," Ralph replied. "I won't say nothing to Paul. Honest, Anna, I won't."

"Oh, sure," Cecilia said, "you tell Paul everything. As if we didn't know."

"I like you too, Cecilia." Ralph laughed heartily. "But you like Paul, too, Cecilia."

"Shut up, Ralph, you talk too much."

"Cecilia loves Paul. Cecilia loves Paul. Paul loves Anna. Oh, look, Cecilia's getting mad!"

"You're a dope," Cecilia said, "and I'm not talking to you anymore if you don't stop it."

"I've got to go," Anna said. "Bye, Ralph. You too, Eddy."

Cecilia followed Anna across the street, where they talked for a few minutes in front of Mansours'.

"Don't forget the comic book trade tomorrow!" Cecilia shouted after Anna, as she started up the lane.

A series of comics put out for girls was all the rage. In countless versions, an ordinary-looking girl, neither popular nor happy, is instructed by her beautiful girlfriend to change her looks: her hair style, clothing, and manners. Overnight, the ordinary turns into an extraordinary beauty, surpassing her friend. The girls consumed the comics like candy, swapping them at recess.

"See you tomorrow," Anna yelled back, as she hurried home.

On Wednesday, a few days before, Paul had wanted to talk to Anna after their religious instruction. Catholics in the town, released from elementary and junior high school two hours early every Wednesday, went to their parish churches. Paul was in the same Confirmation class as Anna and Cecilia. First and second graders met for First Communion instruction in the front part of the basement; the third to fifth for catechism in the back; sixth through ninth for Confirmation in the front pews of the nave—boys on the right, girls on the left.

Paul waited to see where Anna sat, then squeezed his way into the aisle seat opposite her.

Fr. DiSanto, or Father D., as everyone called him, passed out a short story in comic-book form and selected a pupil to read it aloud. The story presented a moral dilemma: a builder, strapped for money, wanted to make a big profit on a house he was building for a wealthy landowner, who'd hired the builder to build many houses on the landowner's property. The builder cheated on the lumber and the quality of the materials, putting in flimsy walls and a substandard roof. The house looked splendid but it was unsafe. The landowner, impressed with it, gave it to the builder as a gift, in thanks for his long service. The builder, in distress, accepted but feared for his family's safety.

"What is the moral of this story?" Fr. DiSanto asked. The priest, dressed in a black cassock and white collar, shuffled between the pews waiting for a show of hands. He combed the pews for one of the brighter kids, when Jerry put his hand up.

"Yes, Jerry, what do you think?"

"The builder should sell the house to someone else, Father," he said.

"And make himself a bundle!" Norman quipped.

"Norman, I'm going to dub you 'my little grasshopper'." The priest smiled, rolling his dark protuberant eyes upward and cocking his head in a saintly pose. Norman has spunk, thought the priest. His answer sidestepped the moral issue but it was plausible. "You know why you're my little grasshopper, Norman?"

"No, Father," Norman said sheepishly.

"Your logic reminds me of the hop of a grasshopper; it goes here and there and where it lands nobody knows." There was warmth and humor in the priest's voice. The kids snickered.

Anna recalled an event in First Communion class. Norman, asked to name the seven sacraments, spieled off: "Baptism, Confirmation, Penance, Holy Eucharist, Extreme Unction, Holy Orders, and Macaroni." Bertha, the stout organist teaching the class, rewarded his cleverness with a stiff whack to the head. He thought twice about fooling around around Big Bertha after that.

Father D. scanned the pews for a victim and his eyes lit on Paul. "Paul, what do you think?"

"Well . . . I suppose it's trying to teach us—honesty's best. You cheat yourself when you cheat others," Paul said.

"Yes, Paul. God is all-knowing, and He sees into our hearts and knows our intentions. The storyteller is warning us to be careful . . ."

The hour dragged on. The kids showed little interest in the discussions, were restless, and mumbled to one another. The level of chatter escalated.

"Remember, children. You are in the House of God." The priest shuffled down the aisle and turned abruptly behind their backs. Not averse to pulling an ear or grabbing a tuft of hair here and there, he threatened the kids and managed to keep them quiet for a bit.

He did not fret unduly about their lack of attention. Children are not likely to be passionate about moral ideas. No, no! Rational debate is not what he was after. In a sacred setting the secret manna seeps into their souls and strikes a chord deep within— moral truths that slumber there till needed. In due course, they'll recognize them as their own. To introduce the manna he chose leaders to read the story and lead the discussion, gaining the attention of the less talented. This helped him pass on moral values.

Paul glanced over at Anna and Cecilia sitting side by side. His thoughts flitted to a shameful memory. One afternoon a few months back, Cecilia met him by chance as he was turning

down his lane. His house stood diagonally across the road from
hers, a few hundred yards away. They talked as she walked with
him. She wanted to see his electric trains. He invited her in. No
one was at home. They went down into the basement and lay
flat on the floor on their bellies, their chins resting on their arms
in front of the circle of train tracks.

Cecilia asked if he'd ever kissed "like in the movies." He
smiled, shook his head, and blushed. "Let's try it," she suggested.
As he rolled over, away from her, she pounced on top of him
and pressed her mouth hard on his, moving her head
rhythmically. He tried to tear away. Their lips were united as in
a scene in many movies he'd seen. His heartbeat quickened and
pleasant sensations pulsed through him. He began to respond
to her embrace as his hands found curves on her bony body—

"Let's kneel," the priest said. They knelt, made the sign of
the cross, and recited the Lord's Prayer.

"Nomina stultorum parietibus haerent: fools' names are stuck
upon the walls," he said, rotating his index finger on his temple
implying madness. "Please repeat."

"Nomina stultorum parietibus haerent: fools' names are stuck
upon the walls," the kids repeated. Their eyes darted here and
there in wonder every time they parroted Father D.'s Latin
quotations.

"What's the name of our Church?"

"SACRED HEART," they yelled.

"I can't hear!"

"SACRED HEART!" they shouted.

"Remember, in the Sacred Heart there are no limits. In the
Sacred Heart necessity is vanquished."

"IN THE SACRED HEART THERE ARE NO LIMITS.
IN THE SACRED HEART NECESSITY IS VANQUISHED,"
they roared.

"Within the Trinity there beats a human heart!"

"WITHIN THE TRINITY THERE BEATS A HUMAN
HEART!"

"Quidam spiritualis contactus esto: Be touched by spiritual
contact!"

"QUIDAM SPIRITUALIS CONTACTUS ESTO: BE

TOUCHED BY SPIRITUAL CONTACT." They stood up, raring to go.

"Dominus vobiscum—the Lord be with you."

"Deus vobiscum—God be with you," they answered, knowing the end was near.

"Remember, children," he continued, their patience wearing thin, "your life is written on the Heart of God. *Via crucis, via lucis*—the way of the cross, the way of light." He blessed them. "Go in peace!"

They gushed from the pews. As Paul genuflected and filed out, he wormed his way toward Anna, hoping to talk to her. Cecilia, pressing at her side, prevented him from cutting in. His eyes met Cecilia's. "Hi, Paul," she said, smiling.

"Hi." Paul slowed his pace, and let others surge in front of him. The kids stampeded out the front doors.

On Thursday, the next day, Paul hung out at Natick Drugstore hoping to see Anna alone. He caught sight of her turning up Prospect Hill and ran after her. "Hi, Anna!" he said, puffing.

"Hi, Paul. Where's Tony?" Tony, Cecilia's brother, and Paul, both eighth-graders and practically inseparable, played baseball for West Warwick Junior High.

"Still at school. How about coming out Friday night to Lillian's? Tony and the gang'll be there."

Anna smiled a small smile. Lillian's steps, for reasons that eluded her, were off limits. Her mother and grandmother talked about "the steps" as if the devil himself resided there. They welcomed Mrs. Lambert to their home but had little to do with her daughter. Lillian's husband Frank, they said, spent more time at the tavern than with his family.

Paul, seeing the look on Anna's face that said I wish I could you know I can't, didn't badger her. He knew her mother was strict, and he didn't push her.

Paul had sloughed off his ungainliness: a thin trunk sprouting lanky limbs, a huge head, and big feet. She laughed to herself, remembering his fear of being short. Now he topped her, nearly six feet tall. How handsome he's becoming, she thought—curly

blond hair, blue eyes, adorable dimple on his chin. It was no
secret that Father D. considered him an exceptional student and
hoped to recruit him for the priesthood.

"Did you tell your uncle Peter what we saw at Lamberts'
farm last week?" Paul asked.

"No. Did you?" Anna answered.

"I don't get to see much of Peter . . . he stopped going out
with my cousin Angela. Did you know?"

"Not really." Anna didn't know why she felt her answer called
for tact; she just knew. She had heard Nonna chide Uncle Peter
for hanging around the house so much and urged him to go out
more. Things had become more complicated at home since her
father died.

"Norman's a real problem, hanging out with Pasco and Jerry,"
Paul said. "They've been stealing things at Natick Drugstore
and Natick Grocery. We're missing lots of tools ourselves. My
dad says Norman's going to find himself behind bars one of
these days if he keeps it up. We've got to keep everything under
lock and key."

"We do, too. Quite a mess they made on that strawberry
patch," Anna said. Cecilia, Tony, Paul, Alex, and she had roamed
about the Lambert farm the week before and heard loud stomping
and thrashing in a field on the far side of a stone wall. When
they crept up and peered over, they saw Norman and his gang
smashing row upon row of strawberry plants with long clubs.

"He's a big bully—he must be darn near six-foot-four," Paul
said.

They walked in silence. A terrible scene crept back into his
mind. About a year ago while climbing the mountain behind
Sacred Heart, he heard a scream and turned to look down. He
could see Norman wrestling Guido Sassi to the ground. Guido
struggled to get free but Norman pulled down Guido's pants.
Shocked, Paul looked on from behind a tree—

"Did you ever notice the beautiful names in movies?" Anna
asked. "I mean . . . not only those of actors, but the characters
they play. You know, like Rhett Butler and Scarlet O'Hara in
Gone with the Wind. Even the actors' names are pretty—Clark
Gable and Vivien Leigh. Yours isn't that bad—Paul Justin Risch.

But Anna Maria Benedicta or Cecilia Florence Pastori . . . gosh!
Did you know Judy Garland's real name is Frances Gumm?
Almost as bad as mine."

"Seems your name suits you . . . I mean . . . anyway, it's real."
Paul blushed. To him, Anna lived in a different world from all
the other kids—a dream world. And her family was different
from all the others on the hill.

They approached Wakefield Lane. "I gotta go," Anna said.

"Yeah, I know. See you around. Think about Friday night."

"Bye!" She took leave of Paul in a happy mood.

Love and Pain

Anna got busy with her chores Friday after school. Alex was
feeding the chickens and gathering eggs.

Assunta and the children freed Felicia from much of the
housework because she often took work home. Sennetts' was
always pushing her to keep up the designs and patterns for their
exclusive collection. It farmed out her patterns to local
seamstresses, satisfying the town's elite eager to get up-to-date,
specially tailored fashions. Felicia had only to see clothes—dresses,
skirts, blouses, coats—and she could reproduce them or modify
the design, as well as make patterns for others to go by. If Lana
Turner, Rita Hayworth, or Shirley Temple wore a coat or dress
in a movie she and Anna liked, she'd make it. As some people
are able to play by ear a piano piece they've heard, Felicia learned
to fashion the pieces of the apparel she saw.

When Anna finished her work, she sat across from Assunta
at the kitchen table. Assunta was lost in thought as she cleaned
the dandelion greens she'd picked on the back slopes.

"Nonna, I had this crazy dream last night. It scared me, but
when I got up this morning it made me happy."

"Tell me about it."

"Well I dreamed that for no reason at all and by nobody I
know, I was shot through the heart. I was really scared. There
wasn't much pain, at first. I started falling into a black hole with
no bottom. I was sad to be leaving the world and I thought how
wonderful it would be to live. The fall seemed to go on forever.

I panicked. I was sure I was going to die. Suddenly I woke up with tears streaming down my face. I jumped out of bed. I was so glad to be alive and began hugging myself. I wanted to go outside to kiss the earth, to kiss Mamma, you, Alex, Uncle Peter, the whole world. I said to myself, Anna you better dry your eyes before Mamma calls the doctor. Does it mean anything, Nonna?"

A few moments passed. "Yes, Anna, life is dear to us." Assunta's eyes were fixed on her hands; she'd stopped working. She looked up at Anna, thoughtfully. "It shows you have deep feelings, mia cara. The understanding of your heart is ahead of your head. I'm proud of you. Marco your father, God rest his soul in peace, must be looking down on you with love. You have inherited your mother's and father's soul."

Anna delighted in her grandmother's words. But she sensed her sadness. Five years since the war ended, and Carla and Ida had not yet come to the States. So extensive was the devastation in Italy that Felicia and Piero still helped support their families in Rome. First Clara and Luigi planned to come, then they couldn't get away. Nineteen forty-six passed. Again in 1947 and 1948, it looked as if they'd come. Year by year, plans were made and cancelled—either Luigi couldn't get time off from work, or Clara was not well or something else turned up. So by the spring of 1950 the reunion across the Atlantic had still failed to come about.

"Have Zia Carla and Zia Ida decided to come this summer, Nonna?"

"Chissà? Who knows?"

Assunta had been dwelling on another matter lately, one intruding on their welfare. No one mentioned it. It hung over the family like a dark cloud. Two years after Marco's death, Assunta noticed that Piero had cut off his social life altogether. He stopped going out with Angela, Paul's cousin—one of the Risch twins. On the lane east of the Benedictas, two respected working-class families, the Risches, lived side-by-side in two-story houses with a driveway between. Risch brothers married sisters from a neighboring town—the women from Italian families, the men from Irish and German. One brother was Paul's father and the other the father of twins, Angela and Lenora, then about twenty-two.

Piero had always been a lady's man, Assunta thought, and many considered him quite a catch. She felt embarrassed whenever she was with Piero and they ran into Lillian. Lillian would gush when she talked to him. In his early twenties he'd dated many girls and kept in close touch with friends from all over the valley. Then his attention turned solely to the family. Mildred Bergman took it into her head to court him. What a pest she was, Assunta thought. She'd stalked him, often popping up in the lane when he went to work or loitering about on the lane when he came home. He ignored her, to no avail. Just when he thought he'd be shackled to this shadow for life, having become the butt of many a joke (Lillian dubbed her "the man-crazed blimp" and him "the Baron" for the crowd on the steps), Mildred spurned him and refused to talk to him again. Good that her parents finally put their foot down, Assunta thought.

He courted Angela Risch, and Assunta took it for granted they'd marry. Poor Angela felt betrayed when he broke off. She'd devoted two years to him. She loved him and wanted to marry him.

After that break-up, Assunta began to see a different relationship develop between Piero and Felicia. No one talked about the sparks that flew back and forth between them. Alex alone seemed oblivious to it.

Sitting beside Anna now, Assunta thought about Piero and Felicia and about the fact that they fooled no one but themselves. The pretense that they were nothing more than brother- and sister-in-law to each other was nothing but a . . . pretense. The whole world saw through it. How many years would pass, Assunta wondered, before they dared voice their mutual feelings? She knew she had to say something to them. Like a gentle breeze against a fortress made of playing cards, a slight nudge from one side or the other would knock down the props of their pretending. Prompted by Mrs. Lambert's not too subtle hints (no doubt issuing from her silly daughter across the street!), Assunta set her mind on giving Piero a nudge.

Before leaving work that Friday evening, Piero, having taken the gossip to heart, threw caution to the wind. In a trembling hand he scribbled down his rambling thoughts:

Cara Felicia,
    Half from anguish, half from apprehension, my heart is bursting. Could I but go on, I would wish for an eternity of tomorrows as we are rather than lose you. It is not as in-laws that we have lived these nearly seven years. What have we been to one another, in honesty? Tell me you care as I do, as your every smile makes me hope. Since Marco died I have loved you: I suppressed it and denied it to myself. My love only grew stronger, till it now consumes me. Only you can clear away this pain that mocks our short life on this enigmatic earth. What good can I be in such a fitful state, in this half-crazed craving? One word— a promise, let it be—would calm my yearning.
                                    Love,
                                        Piero

He was tired and put his head down on his desk to rest before going home. His life seemed to be in shambles. Seven years since Marco died. What had he accomplished? He was now thirty-three. He remembered a happy day a few weeks back when he, Felicia, Anna, Alex, and Paul had gone down the south slope for a picnic.

"Where's Mamma?" Felicia had asked. She had her picnic basket and Piero carried his.

"She's burning," Piero replied. "Carla and Ida can't get away— again."

Felicia poked her head through the kitchen door. "Mamma, *andiamo,* let's go. The spring flowers are beautiful near the river. We'll pick some dandelion greens on the way back."

"*Andate!* Go on! My heart's not in it."

"Let's plan a visit across—we'll go to the mountain if the mountain won't come to us. We'll talk about it later," Felicia said.

Spotting Anna, Alex, and Paul starting down the slope, Piero and Felicia followed behind. Paul and Alex played catch, maneuvering around the pink and white mountain laurels in bloom. The kids were happy. The bright blue sky and the warm breeze were perfect for a picnic.

Piero felt as if he was walking on air—his life complete with Felicia and the kids. He had no doubt Anna and Paul were sweet on each other. Alex loved Paul as a brother.

"Come, Sport," Paul said to Alex after they'd eaten, "let's throw a few." They walked a distance away where the land was flat, to play catch. Anna roamed around on her own, enjoying the spring flowers.

Piero and Felicia shook off the crumbs from the large beach towels they'd sat on, put the leftovers in their baskets, and folded the tablecloth. They then sat next to one another, looking at the rippling water a few yards away.

"I see you're still being pursued," Piero said out of the blue.

"Poor Paolo, won't take no for an answer." Felicia laughed.

Piero knew that Mr. Cecere's son Paolo Jr. had taken a fancy to Felicia. He was a year younger than she. His father, who had helped them buy the house and get settled in, often talked to Assunta about matching up his son Paolo with Felicia. The Ceceres had two sons. Paolo Jr. was the elder. Giuseppe was the younger and already married.

"A decent sort, no?" Piero said to make conversation. "An engineer doing well for himself." Piero wanted so much to break the silence of his feelings for her, but they'd lived so long as brother and sister he couldn't bring himself to it. It was this inhibition in him, this failure of nerve, that sapped his energy.

"You trying to get rid of me?" She blushed, then said, "So your old flame Angela has married Fred Flynn. Didn't take her long after you two split."

Piero's heart jumped for joy at her smile, but he let the lucky moment slip. He knew she was not interested in Paolo Jr. and had no reason to think she'd change her mind. She seemed happy with life as it was. They got on well together and he filled the role of father to her children.

"I'm happy for Angela." Piero said truthfully. "Fred Flynn's a good guy—has a law degree. I hope it works out."

They noticed that Anna, Paul, and Alex were talking to Cecilia and Alberta, who had been out walking on the river bank. Felicia went over to see them, and Piero lay down, his thoughts flew back to his last meeting with Angela.

"You've been toying with me, Peter," Angela had said, in tears. "I trusted you; I took you back after your flings." She took his photograph from the end table in her living room and flung it at him. He caught it as she charged him, entwined her arms around his neck, and clung tightly to him. The picture frame slipped from his hand onto the hardwood floor, the glass shattering. He grabbed her wrists and fought to free himself from her grasp. "I hate you, I hate you!" she screamed.

"Angela, what can I say? Forgive me. I'm not worth it . . . we had precious time together. Let's not end it like . . ." He searched for the right words, fearing another outburst.

"You bastard." She kicked the broken frame next to his feet. "Get out! Leave me!" she yelled, her lips quivering. She grabbed at his shirt and started shaking him.

"Please, Angela." He wanted to tell her that he couldn't control the dictates of his heart.

Looking at him, she sensed that it was no use. Her anger turned suddenly to tenderness. She pulled back. "I can't live without you, you know. I don't want to live without you."

He drew her head to his breast, responding to her pain. "I understand nothing, least of all myself. Since Marco died, my life's been a mess. Forgive me, Angela." He petted the back of her head. "Who's here, who's there, the family's all divided."

She drew back. "At least be honest with me. It's her—the snob," she said, unable to control her fury. "Haughty. Her Highness is too good for us. Say something . . ."

"I see Lillian's bad-mouthing Felicia has gotten to you," Piero said, downcast.

"Do you intend to take Marco's place? You owe me an explanation!"

He stared into Angela's sad brown eyes, speechless.

"You make me sick," she said.

Her anger stung him, but Piero refused to defend himself or his sister-in-law. He may have hidden his love for Felicia from himself, but he had not fooled Angela. Her outburst surprised him; Felicia had always treated Angela with respect. A terrible ambivalence began to gnaw at him: he saw now that he had wanted to break with Angela without admitting to himself that he was in love with Felicia. Angela's accusations helped him see his self-deception—he'd been hiding something from himself. Angela's hostility suffused him with remorse, and his remorse, like Angela's anger, turned to tenderness. He wanted to comfort her.

He looked her straight in the eyes. She didn't flinch. Rays of compassion penetrated her and soothed her anger. "I'll never forget you, Angela. Please forgive me," he said as he stooped to pick up the broken glass.

She stooped beside him. "Remember me, Peter. I'll be here for you," she whispered.

He was deeply moved and made futile attempts to conceal it.

She took the shards from him gently and then reached for the photograph.

A few months later Angela began dating Fred Flynn.

Piero got up from his desk, grabbed the letter to Felicia, and started for home. Having acknowledged his love for Felicia, he felt doomed. Life became a torment: fear of rejection alternated with the hope of conjugal bliss. Every act of kindness, every gesture, every smile from Felicia set his heart aflame. Hours on end in solitude he reflected on life with her. But he couldn't bring himself, till now, to voice his love. He felt he could break the ice only by expressing his feelings in a letter. Was he a coward or did he feel unworthy?

Love and Secrets

As Alex set the table for dinner, Felicia came in and hurried upstairs to change for Friday-night dinner. A few minutes later Piero stumbled in, paused in the entryway, then rushed upstairs. He shoved the sealed envelope under Felicia's kitchen door and came downstairs to change.

Assunta yelled up to Felicia: "Siamo pronti! vieni, vieni! Dinner's ready."

On her way down, Felicia, seeing the envelope, stuffed it into her dress pocket. Her pulse quickened at the sight of Piero's handwriting. She was sure she knew what the envelope held. For days now she'd been expecting Piero to put into words what was in both their hearts. She'd always loved him dearly as her brother-in-law. After Marco's death, she threw herself into work, to curb her grief. She and Piero were hardly apart, and his support in bringing up the children was a godsend. She looked forward to his return at night and felt relieved when he broke up with Angela.

During dinner, Felicia and Piero hardly spoke. Alex pleaded with Piero to play baseball later. Piero agreed half-heartedly. He talked about trivial happenings at work, eager to get away from the table. Felicia said she had a busy night ahead. Sennetts' wanted a wedding-gown as soon as possible. A shyness veiling their passion made them uncomfortable at dinner. They wanted to be alone with each other.

Lord, Assunta thought, something's got to give. Should she talk to Felicia?

Anna had similar thoughts. Tonight she'd ask her mother why she didn't marry Uncle Peter.

Wanting to talk to her mother, Anna stuck close by her side. Assunta shadowed Piero, hoping to get him alone. Alex tailed his uncle, waiting to play catch.

Walking arm in arm on the south slope, Felicia and Anna looked like two school chums. "I met Paul on my way home from school Thursday. Mamma, can I go over to Cecilia's tonight?"

Felicia stiffened and broke loose. "How many times have I told you, Anna, her mother is impossible. No. And no more about it." Cecilia could visit Anna, but Anna was forbidden to go to Cecilia's.

"You're unfair, Mamma. You want to control me too much. I've got to grow up, you know. I like being with the kids sometimes. If Papa were here, I'd have more freedom. I can't take his place."

"Anna, there are things you don't understand!" She thought to reason with Anna without touching on the reasons. "Later, we'll talk about it."

"I am going, Mamma!" Anna surprised even herself by her defiance. "I *am* going!" The thought of Paul being there crossed her mind.

Felicia needed time to be alone to read the letter and be assured of Piero's love. "Please, Anna, listen to me: I don't want to punish you."

"Why not, Mamma? Give me a reason." Anna felt she had to break free from her mother's clutches. If only her mother would marry Uncle Peter, she thought. No, she said to herself, this is not the time to bring it up.

"Let's drop the subject."

"Let's ask Uncle Peter what he thinks. Can we?"

Felicia's frustration boiled over and she slapped Anna's face. In an instant she felt she'd wronged a child so sensitive that the only scolding she ever needed was a change in tone of voice.

Felicia grabbed her in tears. "I'm sorry. Forgive me, cara." She hugged Anna.

"Don't cry, Mamma, it's my fault. I'm sorry. I won't disobey you."

Felicia couldn't stop her pent-up emotions as tears ran down her cheeks. She and Anna embraced and rocked back and forth, but Felicia couldn't be consoled.

"Please, Mamma, I didn't mean it. Please." With her fingers she wiped away her mother's tears and, looking into her eyes, suspected that her mother's anguish had a deeper source. "Come on, Mamma, show me the gown you're making." Putting her arms around her mother's shoulders, she guided her into the house.

Felicia felt both ecstasy and anguish. She longed to read the letter and to be assured. At the same time she thought about Lillian and how she'd hit on Felicia's love for Piero. Lillian's vicious slur—"the hussy on the hill"—pained. To be freed from such dismay—what happiness! No, Anna must have nothing to do with that woman!

"Anna, check to see whether I put the key back yesterday," Felicia said as they entered the entryway.

Anna checked the hiding place of their house key in the

flowerbed. In a ceramic sphere made to look like a stone, with a top that lifted off, they hid a key in case someone got locked out.

"It's here, Mamma."

They went straight to Felicia's workroom. Anna picked up a sketch Felicia had made of a gown. "It's lovely, Mamma."

Felicia sat at the table fumbling around for the measuring tape as Anna came from behind, bent down, and wrapped her arms around her mother's neck. Felicia took up her scissors and began to cut a length of silk.

"Listen, Anna." She took hold of Anna's wrists and tightened them around her neck. "I think you may not like what I'm going to tell you. Please listen and try to understand."

Responding to her mother's mood, Anna became cheerful. Her thoughts then dwelled on Uncle Peter. "Yes, Mamma."

"There are two types of people: those you can trust, real friends, and there are those you have to be careful of, not to be trusted. As you grow older you must learn to tell one from the other." She wondered whether she'd explained it well enough. But how could she tell Anna about Lillian's innuendoes and distortions?

Anna believed her mother meant her uncle, on whom her thoughts then dwelled. "Surely, Mamma, Uncle Peter can be trusted?"

Felicia laughed. "What are you saying? Our family? No, no, Anna. For the love of God, no. Oh, God forbid we couldn't trust those dearest to us." She drew Anna's arms tighter around her neck. "I'm referring to the *bocca aperta*—the big mouth across the street."

Anna pulled back and, facing her mother, cupped her chin in both hands, her elbows resting on the table. "What's Cecilia's mother got to do with us?"

The goings-on on the steps had filtered back to Felicia through a woman, a worker at Supreme Gems, who lived next door to Mildred Bergman. Mildred loved to blab about the Benedictas and gave her next-door neighbor a blow-by-blow rundown of the small talk that went on at Lillian's. Mildred's neighbor, wishing to warn Felicia, hinted at some of Lillian's slurs.

"It's Lillian's unkindness I was referring to."

"What's she been saying?"

"Never mind." She weighed her words carefully. Tender minds must not be tainted too soon with the bitter facts of life, she thought. "I'm trying to tell you why we forbid you to go there . . . and . . ."

"And?"

"Be careful what you say to Cecilia. Now I'm not accusing her of being careless, mind you. But understand, she may tell her mother things, and her mother likes to embellish—"

"Oh, Mamma. I'd never say anything bad about anybody to Cecilia. If you could only hear us—you'd laugh at our silliness. What do we talk about but the comics or school things?"

As she worked on the gown, Felicia's thoughts flew back to Rome. Marco and Felicia had chosen not to mention her family's social class to the children. And Assunta and Piero abided by their wishes. During Anna and Alex's early childhood, Marco and Piero had kindled their imagination with tales about the palazzo and the villa. The children never supposed that the villa or the palazzo was real. This safeguarded the facts and circumvented any wish the children might have, if they were to know, to boast to their friends. Secretly, Anna and Alex carried the ideal form of their inheritance within themselves, protected from the scrutiny of others. As they grew older Anna and Alex felt a little embarrassed even to mention the stories to one another. They had put away childish things.

"I'm proud of you, Anna. Nonna and Zio are, too. Your dear father has left me with two precious gifts—you and Alex."

"If Lillian's such a silly woman as Nonna says, why do people listen to her?" She moved behind her mother and rested her chin on her mother's shoulder as Felicia continued to work.

"Sometimes when we're empty, when we feel our lives are unimportant, it gives us comfort—false comfort, to be sure—in thinking ill of others. People spreading rumors feel important; others listen to them and take them seriously. Each feeds on the other, and back and forth it goes—hurting people."

"I don't get it."

"Well, malicious gossip's like a poison able to penetrate us when we're exposed to it. Healthy people leading good lives may have more resistance. Empty people with messy lives take in the poison as something satisfying—at first. You see, such a toxin, when it enters healthy people, has little effect on them. It evaporates through the soul like sweat through the pores of the body."

"If you're good and healthy, the bad things said about you can't hurt you, can they? Lillian's silly words can't hurt you, Mamma?"

"Lillian's lies about me are offensive. I can't and won't defend myself. How could I? There's a danger to those who listen—even if they're healthy."

"Really?"

"No matter how good you are, hearing something bad over and over again . . . well, you begin to be taken in by it. You begin to hate what you believe to be bad. You want the 'bad person' punished. Such talk can wear down the sense of a good person too. Slowly you get infected and begin to imagine things not there."

Anna's thoughts went back to Uncle Peter and her mother. She had no idea her mother's warning had anything to do with her mother's relation to her uncle. Nor could she imagine anything forbidden going on between them. Her mother's words had a hint of something bad. Since she had no idea what went on on Lillian's steps, and of course no one had ever told her, she could make no sense of what her mother was saying.

"Mamma, will you and Uncle Peter get married some day?"

Felicia's hands, measuring one of the panels of the gown, started shaking. Was it possible Anna had heard Lillian's lies? she asked herself. Remembering the envelope in her pocket, she froze. Is Anna's question an accusation?

When her mother didn't answer, Anna asked: "Why not, Mamma? Our uncle is so handsome and we love him so. He loves you too, Mamma."

Her innocence dispelled Felicia's fears and warmed her heart. "You're a little noseybody," she said.

Her ecstatic face told her daughter everything. Anna rejoiced at the prospect she'd longed for. "When, Mamma?"

"Enough, enough! Subject closed."

Overjoyed, Anna turned to the topic of her mother's work. "Can you teach me to design? Is it easy to learn?"

"If you knew the trouble I had learning from Countess Josephine! I must've been a few years older than you are now," Felicia said.

"Who's Countess Josephine?" Anna asked, baffled.

"My father's cousin. I was about twelve, about your age, when a conflict broke out between the two most powerful families in Rome—the Colonna and the Orsini. Our family was related to the Colonna, and so was Countess Josephine from France. My mother was an Orsini and also a distant cousin of Josephine. No host would ever invite the heads of these two families to a party together, so intensely did they rival one another for social standing. But Nonno did once—he invited them to a ball at the palazzo—"

"I remember Papa telling me about that story," Anna said. She thought her mother was trying to amuse her. Felicia smiled slyly and went on.

"Who'd go into the dining hall first? That became the big question. The first to enter would be thought to have more power and prestige in Rome. The two family heads bickered for nearly an hour and Josephine decided to do something outrageous. Nonno Luigi so liked the way Josephine handled her cousins that he packed me off once a week to Josephine's to learn about etiquette, whenever she was in Rome. Little did Nonno know that she was more interested in fashion design. That's how she sparked my love of sewing. Sometimes she'd tell me a little about etiquette. She had a very salty tongue, as Nonno used to say, and she spoke in English when we met. She was very wealthy and kept up estates in France and Italy and England—she lived some of the time in all three countries."

Anna laughed. She thought her mother was making up stories as her father used to do. Felicia laughed, too, recalling the social disaster that stirred all Rome.

"One day Josephine said: 'Forget those two old fools, they talk a lot of bloody rot!' That's how she talked about the heads of Rome's most famous families. 'Etiquette has its place, but fashion design is my love. Ah, to adorn the body and create garments to make even some of those noble cows look appealing,' she said, laughing and hitting me gently on the back. 'Don't you remember the stir I made at your dear father's ball when he was fool enough to invite the heads of both families? You were sitting at the top of that grand stairway. I designed a suit of rough blue wool, with a wide cape, and baggy pants. No woman ever wore pants. At a ball! Made of wool, mind you. That evening, decked out in spectacular gowns, Rome's uppercrust got a lesson they'll never forget. The heads of the Colonna and the Orsini spent an hour squabbling over who was to be led into the dining hall first. I felt like giving the two old goats a good boot in the behind—as useless as teats on a boar. Now's the time, I said, and I put on this wool getup.'

"We giggled like two high school chums as she dramatized what happened. Of course I remembered it. She said, 'Finally, I took out this cigar holder I managed to get for the occasion, to shock them. Remember: I lit a cigar, started puffing, and, in my homemade horror, strutted down the stairs like an actress making a grand entrance at a ball. Walking toward my cousin Antonio, with all the bluebloods aghast, I took his arm and we headed for the dining hall. Your dear mother, seeing me and fleet of foot, grabbed her cousin Giovanni, and together, four abreast, we broke the deadlock. The highborn—they talk a lot of rubbish. Their lives are a lot of useless rot. Then she started saying things I didn't then understand. She said that the nobles must learn not to be so pompous. They must learn to become real aristocrats, trying to serve mankind in the democratic world that's coming. She said they should teach their children to contribute to the arts, architecture, medicine, the professions. This she said would make our world more stable. She warned: if the nobles don't change with the times—'

"'Tell me about your driving?' I asked. 'I heard Papa say you shocked the whole of Roman society!'

"'Ah! That's after that demon Mussolini came to power,' Josephine answered. 'Must've been about '24. I decided to learn to drive my own car. Imagine: both the Colonna and the Orsini forbade it. No, definitely not! Out of the question. It would be a blow to the dignity of the family. It will not be done. For a nobleman to drive his own car—disgraceful. For a woman to drive—unthinkable . . . unforgivable. I did it anyhow. Little by little, my chauffeur took me out on the streets of Rome. Within weeks I mastered the beast and would go out for an occasional jaunt. One day I was spotted by a reporter and . . . well, you know the rest. When it broke in the *Corriere della Sera*—la Contessa Josephine Colonna Orsini Napoleon, "Blah, blah, blah—what a furor!'"

Anna laughed heartily. "But, Mamma, what you're telling me—is it like Papa's and Zio's stories?"

"Let me finish about learning design, then I'll explain. Being a perfectionist, the countess became pretty nasty. She was no longer the humorous 'salty tongue.' Up till she started teaching me fashion design, we got on fine. Foolish me! When she told me to pick out a picture of a dress I'd like to design, I chose a lace with appliqué around the bodice, if you can imagine. It was very hard to do, even for a seasoned seamstress. Goodness, I was a beginner at fourteen. I didn't know anything about design. She didn't try to talk me out of it. Let's get started at once, she said. We plunged in. The design was complicated. And the fabric was almost impossible to work with. She was after me to do it perfectly. Week after week I had to take it apart and redo it if some part didn't meet with her approval. I'd be in such stress that I'd go home crying. Every week I dreaded going back, afraid of her outbursts. Nonno told me how much Josephine loved me and was eager to help me learn to be a dress designer. Anyhow, her outbursts stopped the moment she came to think I had a talent. Then she became a most inspiring teacher. You can imagine how happy I was to get on with her again. She was so pleased that I took to it quickly that she never stopped praising me."

"Mamma, those stories about the palazzo and the castello are true then? I mean, there are such places?"

"Your father and uncle told a lot of stories. There's a secret I want to share with you tonight. I hope you're old enough. Now, we mustn't tell Alex till I think he's ready. D'accordo?"

"Yes, yes, Mamma, I won't breathe a word of it." Something

clicked in Anna's mind: She was not who she thought she was. She got very excited recalling how she often sensed that her parents were different from her friends'.

"This must be our secret. You mustn't talk about it to anyone outside the family either. Promise me?"

"Oh, Mamma, I promise."

"Well, Nonno has taken steps so that Alex can become a count one day. It's very complicated. In Italy the title normally passes down to the oldest son. You know Nonna Clara had four children, and three died when they were born. I was the only one that lived—they had no male heir. Now the title could pass on to a daughter who was married to a nobleman—she'd become a countess. But I chose your father, a commoner. With Nonno having no male heir, you see, the palazzo and the villa would pass on to the oldest son of Nonno's oldest brother, my uncle Alfonso's son. But in Italy nothing's for certain. Title and the passage of estates depend on power and prestige. There are exceptions to the way it's normally done."

"But what title, Mamma? What are you saying?"

"My father—he's a count—is related to the Colonna family, and my mother—she's a countess—from the Orsini. These titles—a right of distinction and privilege given to families— come down from feudal times, and some even earlier. You'll learn about them in your history classes. In the past, the Colonna and the Orsini had great influence on the laws and functioning of society."

"What about you, what's your title?"

"I don't have one. As it is now, my father has asked both the Colonna and the Orsini to approve Alex as his rightful heir. They've reviewed the request and decided in his favor. Alex will inherit the title and with it the estate—both the palazzo and villa will stay in our family."

Anna was speechless—an estate made up of a palazzo and a villa. She had had no idea of her birthright till then. "Is that why you have a British accent?"

Felicia laughed. "We—that is, my cousins and I—had nannies and governesses from England. The Italian nobility bring their children up to speak the King's English."

"Why have you kept this from us, Mamma?"

"Because, my love, Papa and I believed it's not the title or social position that's important in life but what you and Alex make of yourselves. We wanted you to become true aristocrats, humane and loving, not people thought so because of titles."

"Is that why Countess Josephine poked fun at the nobility, their titles were empty? Were many of them aristocrats just in title?"

Felicia reached over and patted her cheeks, smiling. "There's only one true aristocrat according to Papa: it's the person with a good heart. All titles, without this, are useless. With titles people can exercise too much power over others. Anna, it's time for bed, no? Go down and get Alex." Felicia turned her attention back to her design.

The Night of Infamy

While the kids played happily in the road, on the sidewalks, in the Pastori yard this Friday evening, Ralph Mullen and Eddy Pastori sat on the wall, talking to Lillian. She soon came into the possession of "facts": Felicia and Anna had a terrible fight outside the Benedicta house. When Ralph's story caught her ear, she badgered him for more details.

"Felicia whacked Anna. Felicia's bad. Whack!" Ralph repeated several times, as he swung his hand in an arc to show what he'd seen earlier through his binoculars.

Hearing about the tiff, Lillian promptly condemned Felicia. The sympathy Lillian said she had for Anna not only endeared Lillian to Ralph, it magnified Anna's danger in his mind.

Fascinated by what she'd heard, Lillian craved to know more. "What happened, Ralph?" She patted him on the back. "Come on. Tell me everything."

In his mind Anna got slapped and shaken badly. He took the mother and daughter's embrace of forgiving love—their rocking back and forth after the slap—to be a scuffle.

As Lillian drew him out, Ralph exaggerated what he'd seen. Then Eddy offered his version, embellishing it. "Felicia slapped Anna and shook her bad. She beat her bad." Ralph nodded.

"The poor child! Oh, the poor child! Never allowed to be with other children. It's not normal, I tell you. Such a shame— Anna being such a good girl and all."

Ralph kept nodding his head as Lillian talked. Lillian was good; Felicia, bad. In the past Ralph had sensed that Lillian was jealous of Felicia. Now he felt he had been wrong about Lillian.

As the news about Anna spread, others flocked to Lillian's steps. Gloria, Phyllis, Nancy, Cecilia, Mildred, among the girls; Ralph, Eddy, Tony, Norman, Pasco, Paul, Jerry, among the boys.

Soon Lillian drew all ears to her words: "Anna's been beaten by her mother. That woman! So intolerant. So strict with Anna."

"Mamma, please. Be quiet," Cecilia said.

"Be quiet, be quiet. Really. Should people just stand by and watch a mother hurt her own daughter?"

Mortified by her mother, Cecilia interrupted her again. "Mamma, Felicia's a nice lady—she loves Anna. Mamma, please. Stop it."

Paul and Tony, discussing the afternoon baseball game, now turned their attention to Lillian.

"Tell them what you saw, Ralph?"

Ralph got up and arced his arm in a motion to show a slap and then, with both arms, he made a shaking motion. "Felicia's bad. She whacked Anna. She hurt Anna bad."

"I don't believe it," Paul said. "Come on, Ralph. You can't be sure from way up the hill. You shouldn't be spreading stories like that."

"It's true, Paul." Yet, when Paul contradicted him, Ralph began to wonder whether maybe he'd made a mistake.

Lillian came to Ralph's defense. "'Her Highness' has a terrible temper."

"Somebody should take care of that bitch!" Norman yelled.

Ralph looked at Norman and shuddered. He began to worry that Norman might harm Anna. "You're crazy, Norman. Stay away from Anna."

"Ralph's got his nose stuck in everybody's business. Father D.'s little pet, aren't you, Ralphie?" Norman mocked.

"Lay off, Norman," Paul said, turning to Ralph. "You know, Ralph, sometimes when you're not sure of something, it's better to keep quiet."

Shouting, pushing, and shoving broke out all around, with Ralph caught in the middle. His account of what happened, like a match put to straw, set them off. Some sided with Lillian, giving vent to years of animosity and rancor toward Felicia, roused by jealousy and envy and nursed by slander about Felicia's way of life, her relationship with Piero, her visits from Paolo Cecere Jr., her flouting of social conventions.

Others sided with Paul and Cecilia, suggesting that, from such a distance, Ralph may have been mistaken. They said Felicia was a good mother, and the Benedictas good and decent people.

The cacophony of voices grew louder and louder. Tony finally yelled out: "Look, it's nobody's business what went on at the Benedictas'."

"Yeah, says who?" Jerry yelled back. "That snob. A phony with a British accent. Thinks she's hot stuff!"

Jerry's meanness was like a dagger piercing Ralph's heart. Ralph wanted to take it all back. But who'd listen to him now? Everyone talked at once. He looked into a sea of angry faces. "My God," he screamed out. They all turned to look at his contorted face. A vision of blood was flashing through his mind. He hated those visions that suddenly crept up on him. He began to whimper and to say he was sorry. "Please, forget everything. Please!"

"Well, I think 'Her Highness' is quite capable of cruelty—" Lillian began saying.

"Let's go in, Mamma. It's getting late." Cecilia grabbed her mother's arm and began pulling her up the steps.

"Go ahead. I'll be in in a moment, dear."

Cecilia went in, and her brother Tony walked Paul home.

Free of her children, Lillian began making fun of Felicia. She mocked her and Piero: "the hussy on the hill in her den of iniquity. The Lord looks badly on those who do not obey His laws. Some think they're above marriage—so high does a hussy fly over us common folk." She then painted a picture of Felicia and her secret lover, Paolo Cecere Jr.

Ralph didn't understand what Lillian meant, but he felt it was very bad. Lillian, he knew, had made fun of Felicia before.

But now Lillian was real mean. He stared at her, saw she was glad to put Felicia down, and saw the others glad to hear mean things about Felicia. He felt sorry for what he'd done. He saw Pasco laughing with Jerry and banging a stick against the wall as if he was hitting Felicia to make her suffer.

Ralph felt dizzy, hearing everyone talk at once. Felicia was always kind to everybody. He never heard her say nothing bad about anybody; not even Lillian. Then he heard Mildred say, "Let's hit the bitch."

He turned to Mildred and looked at her bloated face, her hateful smirk, her bushy hair. He remembered how Lillian used to make fun of Mildred, calling her a man-crazed blimp. This was bad of Lillian. Now she was friends with Mildred. He knew that Mildred and Lillian liked Piero a lot. Mildred used to stand at the corner of Mansours' yard, waiting for Piero to go to work. Many times on his way to work at Sacred Heart, Ralph would see Mildred waiting for Piero. "Hello, Piero," she'd yell, smile, and wave as he drove out of Wakefield Lane. Piero would wave back just to be nice.

When Lillian talked to Piero, she'd get all excited, the way little girls do with boys they like, flirting with him as if he was important. Ralph felt embarrassed to see Lillian act like a child, especially when she asked Piero silly questions about his girlfriends. Ralph could see that Piero wanted to get away from her. Then behind his back she'd talk about Piero and call him "the Baron of the Hill," and "too pretty for his own good, with all his lovers."

Mildred wanted to play a game Ralph didn't understand. They were going to "hit the bitch." Maybe Mildred hates Felicia because Piero and Felicia are in love, Ralph thought. Yes, Mildred was jealous of Felicia. Lillian too. Mildred's pa got real mad at her and told her if she didn't stop being man crazy about Piero, he was not going to let her go down the hill to Lillian's steps. So Mildred stopped chasing after Piero. It didn't make no difference to Mildred—she still wanted Piero to like her.

Mildred, Gloria, and Phyllis, the big girls in their twenties, and the younger girls now began to have fun with Mildred's game, laughing with Lillian and then putting their hands over their mouths like terrible things were coming out of them. Ralph and the boys listened, turning from one to the other as the girls made up songs about Felicia with words Ralph knew were bad—like hussy, whore, witch. Then the girls began whispering secrets about her, her boyfriends, and the terrible things she did. They even made fun of Assunta, who they said let Piero and Felicia do bad things in Assunta's house. They didn't care that Norman, Pasco, and Jerry and the other boys were listening to all these bad things.

Ralph was sad and afraid for Anna and Felicia. Ralph looked into Norman's, Pasco's, and Jerry's faces and saw hate and meanness shooting out of them. Ralph felt sick and was afraid for Anna. He was sorry he told Lillian what he saw. He was to blame for all this bad stuff about Felicia. He was mad with himself and wished Paul had not gone home. All at once he put his hands to his head, pushing against his temples, trying to turn off the picture in his head. But he couldn't stop the pool of blood running out of Felicia and onto Anna. He got real scared and wanted to go see Father D. to tell him bad things were going to happen.

As the girls whispered more and more, Norman jumped up and down. Jerry would laugh and say, "Let's scare the bitch. We should throw a big scare into her." Then he'd laugh so meanlike it sent a pain through Ralph's heart. Pasco kept beating a stick in his hand against the wall, breaking it into a dozen pieces.

Ralph heard Jerry say to Norman, "We ought to pay 'Her Highness' a visit—ha ha! Teach her a lesson or two."

Ralph suddenly felt sick and rushed home with the vision of blood raging through his head.

"You think Paul will ever play in the major leagues, Uncle Peter?" Impressed by Paul's athletic ability and friendliness, Alex looked up to Paul as a big brother. Before going to Lillian's steps that night, Paul, seeing Alex and Piero playing catch, stopped by for a few minutes to play.

"Who can tell? That's a long way off. One thing I do know, of all the kids on the hill, Paul's the most likely to make something of himself. He's got a good head on his shoulders."

"Alex, time for bed," Anna yelled, barging into the living

room, full of life and plopping herself down next to her uncle. "Mamma and I had a long talk . . . saw you playing ball with Paul."

"Are you interested in baseball or in Paul?" Alex asked. He and Piero smiled. Anna blushed.

"Neither, you little monster." She reached over and pinched him.

"Some people are good at pretending, wouldn't you say, Uncle?"

"What's gotten into him tonight? Help me out, Uncle Peter!" She pounced on top of Alex and began tickling him. Piero held Alex down as he screamed and squealed for mercy. Piero grabbed them as he did when they were little and gave them a peck on the cheek.

"Come, on, you two. Upstairs where you belong. Hey, brat," he said to Alex, "take it easy on your kid sister!"

Assunta, in the kitchen, waited for the children to leave. She had to give Piero "the nudge." Now. "*Figlio mio,* it's time we had a talk."

"About what?"

"About these sparks. If I'm allowed to speak frankly."

"You're allowed to say what you please, but I'm damned if I know what you're talking about." He held back, smiling. A great relief had come over him earlier while playing ball. Suddenly, the doubt about Felicia's love eased and he felt certain he and Felicia would marry. The thought of adopting the children gladdened his heart.

"Do you take me for a simpleton? The whole town's wagging, for the love of God!"

"Well, Mamma, the town's pleased to do what it damn well pleases. You love to talk in riddles. What's this town wagging about?"

"Sparks of love hidden in the darkness of night are bound to fly in the path of inflammable objects and ignite unholy fires." Try as she might, she could not come straight to the point. Suppose she was wrong? Could it be possible? No. Even a moron couldn't mistake their love.

"You missed your calling. You've got quite a way with words.

A novelist, I'd say. You've got the talent there—with the town wagging, sparks flying, and unholy fires! Lord, it sounds as if we're on the verge of an Inquisition. Where do I fit into this Inquisition?" He did everything he could not to chuckle.

She blurted out: "Are you going to marry Felicia or not, that's what I want to know?"

"Well, well, now we come to the heart of the matter. I thought you'd never ask." He laughed heartily. He went over and sat on the arm of her chair. "So the old lady's curious, is she? So am I."

"Be serious, for God's sake."

"I am. I asked her to marry me."

"And . . ."

"And what?"

"What's her answer?"

"None."

"None?"

"No word yet."

"Is this message going through heaven or what?" In her new-found joy she, too, could poke a little fun.

"Amusing yourself at my expense, are you? I wrote her a letter, left it under her kitchen door when I got home today. So far, no response. But she's been with Anna all night and I've been with Alex."

"Don't worry! Such chemistry, such sparks. I'm so happy for you two. It's about time. Marco must be smiling from above. Thank the Lord." She grabbed Piero and kissed him.

Midnight on Prospect Hill

Ralph checked on his mother when he got home. He found her asleep in the living room and helped her to bed.

In his room he pulled out a cigar box stashed under old magazines and newspapers in the back of his closet. He opened it and took out two pictures of Anna. He'd felt bad when she'd blamed Alex for taking the photos from her album. As Ralph fingered the photos, his mind went back to the day he'd snuck upstairs to Anna's house. The Benedictas were all away. He lay on her bed and delighted in seeing her room and smelling her presence. Looking through her school books, he came upon an album and took two of her photos.

His stomach was all knotted up. He thought of Norman and his friends. It'd be Ralph's fault if they hurt Anna and her mother. Had they really had a fight? Paul didn't believe him. And Paul was real smart; he knew everything. Ralph pulled out his binoculars and looked out his window to see if the light was still on at Anna's. It was too dark to see.

He remembered how Norman bullied and beat other kids. A few weeks back, removing storm windows at the Sacred Heart rectory and storing them in the church basement, he ran into Norman coming out of the bathroom, buckling his belt.

"What're you doing here?" Ralph asked.

"What's it to you?"

Ralph heard the bathroom door open and turned to see Guido. "You stay away from Guido. You hear? I'll tell your pa. He'll whip you. I'll tell Father D."

Norman opened the door into the foyer to go out. "You better talk to Guido about it. We've become *real* good friends." Norman laughed.

"You're bad—no friend of Guido."

"Shut up, dummy!" Norman slammed the foyer door in Ralph's face. Ralph turned to Guido.

"What're you staring at, Ralph?"

"Stay away from Norman. He's bad."

"What do you know? Screw you!" Guido's face turned beet red.

Ralph saw guilt all over Guido's face, and it entered into and pierced Ralph. He didn't want Guido to suffer more than he already did, and he wished Guido's pain could be taken away. Poor Guido—Norman had bullied him for years.

"Get off my back."

"Yeah, Guido," Ralph said clapping, "see, I'm off your back," he said, jumping.

Guido pretended to laugh at Ralph's antics, but Ralph saw tears in Guido's eyes as he turned away.

Ralph put out the light in his room and, taking up his binoculars, looked down at Anna's again. The night was pitch black. Why did he have to go and blab about Felicia? Lillian is really jealous of Felicia. That's why she was nice to him. His head was pounding and he felt short of breath. "Oh, no, no," he cried. "My head. Oh, my head," he said and shut his eyes and pressed his hands against his temples, trying to squeeze out the vision that sent pangs of terror through him. He began hitting his head. "Stop. Stop." But he couldn't black out the vision—a pool of blood was running out of Felicia's body. "Oh, my God, what've I done. No, no!" he screamed. He could see Anna with blood on her dress. "They're going to kill her!"

Should he go tell Father D.? He'd stop them from hurting Anna. Father D. says human beings are sick creatures and can only be healed by God. He began praying for Anna.

Frank, just in from Louie's Tavern, eyed Lillian going into the bathroom and slipped in behind her. His hands, like the tentacles of an octopus, ran up and down her body. She stiffened at the stench of booze and the lust oozing from him.

"Stop it, Frank," she said, trying to be stern without raising her voice. She pushed him away and pulled down her nightie.

"Don't be too long," he slurred.

Lillian lingered in the bathroom, wishing to God he'd fall asleep. Her face in the mirror reflected hate. What on earth made her turn so viciously against Felicia? Ralph, as Paul said, could get things wrong. Why did she make a mountain out of a mole hill?

"Lillian," Frank called, staggering into the bathroom. "Come on up." He stumbled and his body pinned her against the wall."

"Frank, stop! You'll wake the kids," she said fighting him off. "I'm coming."

"Hurry up!"

Self-loathing gripped her, and the ordeal awaiting her sickened her. Quietly, slowly, she climbed the stairs, fighting the force of gravity each step of the way. She slid under the covers; her body stiffened as she held her breath.

Primed and ready by the long wait, Frank pounced on her, his big muscular body sprawling on top and suffocating her. She felt like a toy being flung about by a reckless bully. His panting disgusted her and his penetration pained her reluctant flesh. Her thoughts shifted to Piero's handsome face. Envy of Felicia and her lovemaking with Piero—whom she often dreamed of— swelled in her, nearly choking her. Tears ran down her cheeks.

"Show some life, woman!" Frank said, heaving and grunting.

For a moment she imagined Piero smiling, speaking tenderly, taking her in his strong gentle arms, embracing her passionately. Her body began to stir and an intense yearning suffused her as she, against her will, gave in to the rhythm of the panting and heaving as though in a paradisal dream.

"That's better," Frank mumbled and, after a long loud sigh, turned over and began to snore.

Slipping out of bed, she tiptoed quietly downstairs to the living room. She looked out the window towards the Benedictas'. A light was coming from Felicia's sewing room. A dreadful shame tore through her.

Lanky Norman jostled skinny Jerry on one side and plump Pasco on the other as all three headed downhill. Norman's father owned a restaurant over the bridge next to a furniture store. For some time, Norman and his friends had found a way to break into it and steal small stuff. A ceiling panel, easily removed, gave access to the attic where another ceiling panel on the furniture side, also easily removed, gave them access to the furniture. Despite police help, the furniture-store owner remained puzzled by missing inventory and, crazed by the frequent theft, found all his efforts to catch the crook foiled. Easily removed and easily reinstalled, the panels served as the gateway to easy loot for Norman and his boys. They had no trouble fencing the stolen goods with the help of one of Pasco's uncles, who took the stuff out of town.

Norman and Jerry and Pasco giggled as they walked over the poorly lit bridge. The street by this hour was free of traffic.

"It's time to scare the bitch," Jerry said laughing. Norman and Pasco chuckled.

"Let's pick up a few items first," Norman said. "It's damn near two months since we did in the joint."

"Yeah," Pasco said laughing, "we're running out of dough."

Everybody was asleep at the Mansours' except Mitri. Unable to sleep, Mitri took up a floorboard under a large chest in his bedroom to retrieve his diary, hidden from his sister Rachel's prying eyes. Making several entries for Friday, March 24, he peered out the window as the moon peeked from behind the clouds, lighting up part of the valley. He lamented the location of the Benedicta house—it stood directly south of his and blocked the spectacular view of the valley from his upstairs windows.

After Anna and Alex went to bed, Felicia had time finally to sit down to read and reread Piero's letter. Her heart overflowed—his desires, feelings, and thoughts coincided with hers. Her life with Marco, though loving, was short and filled with pain.

Tomorrow would be a wonderful Saturday. She'd slip down early and put a note under Assunta's kitchen door, playing along with Piero. At breakfast the children would be told, and together they'd plan the wedding. Dead tired, she pulled out a piece of stationary and penned Piero a note, delighted with the new life that lie ahead.

Caro Piero,
  Yes, my love, my heart is yours—forever. With everything wonderful there is always a condition, so let this be mine: you must grant us all, Mamma and the children, a honeymoon at the villa in Rignano!
Yours forever,
Felicia

She put it in an envelope, addressed it—"Piero"—and sealed it. With both envelopes in her hand, she went to her bedroom. She'd completed most of the gown and, looking at her watch, saw that it was now after one in the morning. She turned the lights out and sat at the edge of the bed—exhausted.

It's time to return to Rome, she thought. We've been in exile long enough. Papa will give Piero a job administering the estates and I'll find work too. She thought of some of her old professors. Maybe she'd prepare to become a teacher.

She lay back on the bed to rest for a bit before getting ready for sleep.

A loud bang resounded through the downstairs flat. Assunta and Piero woke up, startled. In their separate rooms they listened, trying to discern what happened. Silence. Assunta got up and went to Piero's room. "Che é successo? What is it?" she asked.

"Sounds as if it came from outside. Probably a shutter loose upstairs—banged against the siding."

They listened. Hearing no more, Piero said, "I'll check in the morning."

They went back to bed.

About to turn off his lights, Mitri glanced outside. He thought he saw someone bending down in the flowerbed outside Assunta's door. He wondered what Assunta was doing out so late. A cloud obscuring the light of the moon made it too dark to see clearly. He stared for a few minutes and, as the moon reappeared from behind a cloud, saw someone walking away into the darkness. He rubbed his eyes, puzzled, thinking maybe the darkness was playing tricks on him.

He flopped into bed. Remembering his diary, he forced himself to get up and put it away. Seeing that he had stopped in the middle of a sentence, he took up his pen to write a few lines. He closed it, put it back beneath the floorboard with several other diaries he had, and dropped off to sleep at once.

Death of the Mother

By late Saturday morning, news of Felicia's death had spread throughout the town.

Sirens blew, horns honked, vehicles sped up Prospect Hill. Hordes trooped up—many on foot, some by car. People milled about everywhere. Prospect Hill, usually secluded from the valley, looked as if a swarm had descended on it.

Assunta's front yard became a parking lot: police cars, public officials from the medical examiner's office, Prata's funeral van to transfer the body to the morgue, reporters from the *Pawtuxet*

Valley Times and the *Providence Journal*.

Lillian posted Eddy, Tony, and Cecilia on the steps. All sorts of tall tales were being hatched.

Rose Golanski, Ralph Mullen's married sister and Lillian's neighbor, pooh-poohed the view Lillian put forth. The suspect, Lillian had it from a reliable source, was one of Felicia's lovers. Lillian scoffed at the mention of Norman and his gang as likely suspects. "It's too preposterous." Then Ralph's name was bandied about. Lillian thought it laughable. As the day wore on, many were fingered—even Lillian herself was not above suspicion.

Dying from curiosity, Lillian tried to wave down Dante Giorgio. Dante, who used to live next to Louie's Tavern and who was now on the West Warwick police force, waved back but refused to stop and talk. *"Who did it, Dante?"* she yelled as the police car careened off Wakefield Lane, passing a few yards in front of her. Dante shrugged his shoulders.

By midday, neighbors squatted on every inch of Lillian's steps. Her hangers-on encircled her and her rump court mulled over one rumor after another. Since not one shred of evidence surfaced, their minds, Paul said, were full of nonsense. How could anyone know at this point? When he heard Mildred refer to Felicia as "the hussy of Prospect Hill," he got up and left in disgust.

Lillian noticed the glee in Norman's eyes. When she asked him, as she asked the others, who might've done it, he shook his head. "She's the kind of bitch who thinks her shit don't stink! She had it coming, if you ask me."

"Why, Norman! That's awful," Lillian upbraided him. "Shame on you!"

Ralph Mullen did his Saturday chores as usual; no one thought to visit him. Even his friend Eddy, taken in by all the commotion going on at the Benedictas', forgot about Ralph, who worked around his yard—oblivious to the happenings at Anna's.

Another upheaval hit Prospect Hill on Sunday morning, again at Wakefield Lane. This time the procession was at the Mansours'. Word soon shocked the townsfolk. Mitri Mansour had died the night before in an auto accident.

The Sunday edition of the *Providence Journal*, March 26,

1950, ran the obituaries:

Mrs. Felicia Margarita Benedicta, 35, found dead, 9 a. m. yesterday morning in her home at 12 Wakefield Lane, Natick. She is survived by two children: a daughter, Anna Maria, and son, Alessandro Luigi. A memorial service will be held at the Prata Funeral Home, Riverpoint.

Mr. Mitri Mansour, 20, son of Samuel and Irma Mansour, died in an auto accident early this morning. His body was found at 1 a. m. in his car, which had plunged into the Pawtuxet River after midnight. Young Mansour lived at 10 Wakefield Lane. He is survived by his parents, two brothers, and a sister. He worked at the Henault Funeral Home and was in his last year of mortuary science. The memorial service will be held at Henault's . . .

On Monday, the *Pawtuxet Valley Times* carried two front-page stories—one of Mitri's untimely death and the other of Felicia's:

Mitri Mansour's body was pulled out of the Pawtuxet River at approximately 1 a.m. yesterday. Mansour, 20, of Natick was in his final year of mortuary science.

Mansour, who lived with his parents at 10 Wakefield Lane, was driving north on Providence Street toward his home. His car swerved off the road on the south side of the Natick Bridge, broke through the railing, and plunged into the river—a forty-five-foot drop. The car was not fully submersed. Mansour apparently suffered severe head injuries and was unable to get out of his car and drowned.

Police report mechanical failure combined with excessive speed as the probable cause. The medical examiner's report is pending.

Mrs. Felicia Margarita Petrarca Benedicta was found dead Saturday morning at her home at 12 Wakefield Lane, Natick.

The West Warwick Police are investigating the circumstances of her death. At this time the police have not ruled out foul play. A medical examiner's report has yet to be issued.

Mrs. Benedicta was the wife of the late Marco Benedicta, former head of sales for Supreme Gems Company of Providence, and herself a jewelry designer for Supreme Gems. She also did fashion design for Sennetts' Department Store in Arctic.

Mrs. Benedicta was the only daughter of the Countess Clara Orsini and Count Luigi Colonna Petrarca of Rome. The count and countess have been notified of their daughter's death and are expected to arrive at Logan Airport tomorrow.

Mrs. Benedicta is survived by two children, Anna Maria, 12, and Alessandro Luigi, 10; her mother-in-law, Mrs. Assunta Benedicta; and her brother-in-law, Mr. Piero Benedicta.

People from all over the valley began coming up the hill to get a glimpse of the Benedicta place. Dante Giorgio directed traffic to keep the street clear of sightseers.

Lillian was dumbfounded by the news of Felicia's noble birth. She began to wonder whether Felicia only seemed to be arrogant and aloof. Maybe it was good breeding and education after all.

As the day wore on, sadness and shame flared up in Lillian. She couldn't bring herself to go outdoors. Her telephone rang steadily, but she had little to say. Even in death, Felicia plagued her.

By Monday evening a rumor passed through the village of Natick, spread through the town of West Warwick, and reverberated throughout the Pawtuxet Valley—Anna had killed her mother. The name for the crime and for the doer of it sprang forth and attached itself to Anna Maria Benedicta—"Anna the matricide."

4
Grief and Torment

*I said you'd hear no more about Pasqualina. I wanted to tell this
story as dispassionately as possible. Now, years later, I find myself
grieving all over again as I think about Felicia's death.*

*She and I had been outcasts: she an object of fascination who
withdrew into her own circle, and I an object of ridicule who drew
many to my porch. A week before the murder a window on my
house had been broken. Piero came by to fix it and Felicia sent over
a colomba—an Easter bread made in the shape of a dove. With it,
a note.*

My Dearest Pasqualina,

Our chats always help me put things into perspective.
Anyhow, know that the best, the true aristocrat (and I count *you*
one), is not somebody who is proudly conscious of himself as a
privileged being. Nor is an aristocrat somebody who safeguards
his position as such. The true aristocrat is somebody who is able
to withstand and triumph over evil, loving life all the more.

I believe that the victory over evil is neither in birth nor in
death. It is in resurrection. The creative power of resurrection
conquers evil and death.

Enjoy the colomba!

Your friend,
Felicia

Had I known then that Felicia was of noble birth, I'd have cherished her message all the more. I hunted for other notes from her and found one she sent me after I almost died of appendicitis.

The Book of Job teaches that we should not be like Job's comforters who see suffering only as a punishment for sin. Suffering can be undeserved. Most obvious, to my mind, is suffering connected with the body, which sets limits to our infinite aspirations. Our bodies get sick, grow old, and die, and we carry on a painful struggle for existence—some of us more than others. Our prayers are with you, dear friend.

Poor Felicia, dead before her time. Once, when I was in despair about the children taunting me, she wrote:

Please keep in mind, dear Pasqualina, that Christ turned suffering into a way of salvation. I grieve when I think that what is true and good in our world is crucified. Yes, the one, sinless righteous man was crucified. Innocent suffering, guiltless suffering of the righteous, in my view, is a bright suffering that leads to salvation. Dark suffering leads to ruin. Isn't it St. Paul who tells us that no one knows the secrets of the human heart except the human spirit within?

Except for parents or guardians of the suspect, the Rhode Island Juvenile Court allowed no one in to its hearing. Anna, too ill to attend all but the first hearing, never heard the testimony against her and her family. She was kept in seclusion after the court hearing; Assunta, still grieving for her son Marco, now grieved for her daughter-in-law; and poor Piero was devastated by the loss of his wife-to-be. Anna, it was widely rumored, had killed her mother.

By sheer persistence, I was able to learn of bits and pieces of the testimony from people who came to trust me. Court proceedings and witness testimony were not available even to the town police. But many intimate details about the life of the Benedictas were shared with me when it became generally known that I intended to write as true as possible a story about the tragedy.

Anna in Seclusion

Paul Risch spent the whole summer thinking and talking about Anna—wondering, like the rest of us, what had happened at the Benedictas'. He saw her only once after the murder—the day she left Prospect Hill. No one visited or was welcomed at the Benedictas' except Mrs. Lambert. And she, it seemed, had taken a vow of silence about the goings-on there. Lillian begged her mother for news, to no avail.

Early one morning while walking his dog, Paul saw Piero's car pull off Wakefield Lane, headed downhill. As the car passed, Paul saw Alex in the front with Piero, and Assunta in the back with Anna. No one waved or let on they saw Paul. Anna, gaunt and ghostly, was hardly recognizable. Their eyes met for an instant—an instant pregnant with eternity—and Paul felt a final separation. Piero himself had changed: aloof, he looked like a stranger from another world.

Keeping the hearings from public view to protect Anna stirred up people's craving to know more. Sickening stories had circulated for months. Some said Anna had in a fit of rage stabbed her mother. Norman made her out to be a killer who bludgeoned her mother to death—a virtual Lizzie Borden. Everyone had a different version of the gruesome act.

Paul gave juvenile court his view of the Benedictas. He, like all those who testified, never learned what Anna was thought to have done or the court's finding. The Rhode Island Juvenile Court, by law, could not issue any formal, public judgment against a delinquent juvenile. Rumor persisted: Anna was charged with manslaughter. Despite the general consensus about Anna, Paul didn't waiver for a moment in his faith in her innocence.

Neither Anna nor Alex had returned to Providence Street Grammar to finish out the school year after Felicia's death; and now, only days before fall term was to begin, everyone at the school was wondering whether Anna would be joining them at West Warwick Junior High.

That night Paul dreamed he was standing alone in the Pawtuxet River, down the south slopes, waiting for Father D. The river was deep, dark, and disgusting. Nobody swam in it;

the mills used it for its water and for their waste. Anna, Felicia, and Paul's father stood on the bank waiting for some strange ceremony to begin. Paul was sinking in the muck and his heart pounded.

Father D. showed up at last, walked down into the water, and stood beside Paul. At that moment Paul noticed Anna fading away, evaporating before his eyes and disappearing into thin air. He felt as though a part of himself had left him.

Father D. scooped up a pail of water to throw over Paul's head. But when Father D. poured the water, it turned into millions of seeds. Several times Father D. repeated the ritual: each time the water was transformed into seeds that floated on the water like a film. The priest gave up in frustration.

Paul, sinking ever deeper, had one thought—to get out of the river as quickly as possible. Suddenly he found himself alone. The undertow was sucking him under.

His heart beat wildly and he could hear his mother screaming at him as she had screamed when he was a child: "Paul, never go into the water. People die in that river. It's got whirlpools in it, deep whirlpools that suck you down into the muck." He tried frantically to pull his feet out of the slime; the more he tried, the more the slime gripped him. He looked up just as he was going under and saw Felicia in the sky smiling down at him as she put her hands into a position of prayer. The floating seeds flew up to her and arranged themselves as a rosary.

A thought from Felicia penetrated him—"Anna's not to blame." As he was about to go under, the prayer beads in Felicia's hand swooped down. Frantic, he grabbed on to them and felt himself being lifted from the river.

He woke up wet with sweat and tears. One part of him was happy to be alive; the other sad that Anna and Alex had left him.

Anna Committed

Slowly, Piero and Assunta drove past stately homes toward Butler Hospital. Gloom hung over them like a black cloud.

Bogged down in juvenile court, besieged by psychiatrists,

psychologists, and social workers, and seen as objects of curiosity by their neighbors, they sold their house, packed up their belongings, and moved to Providence.

"Nothing in this world is as it seems, including myself," Piero said. Cars trying to pass honked. He made no effort to drive faster. "It just doesn't add up. No matter how you figure it," he said. Had Felicia read his letter? What had happened to her remained a mystery. The West Warwick police had focused on one suspect—Anna.

Assunta looked straight ahead, ignoring the irascible drivers honking behind. Piero worried her: no friends, no interests, his heartache over Felicia and Anna consumed him. Assunta's wound from Marco's untimely death had never healed; and now Felicia murdered and Anna confined.

The scene that had driven Piero to despair all these months shot through his mind: his mother getting the court order and wailing for hours, closed in her room. He had been listening to Richard Strauss's *Metamorphosen for Twenty-Three Strings.* The music merged in his heart with his grief. And, weeks later, when the social worker seemed to wrench Anna from his mother's arms, Assunta howled and passed out. Since then, Assunta cleaved to the church. But he found that world harder and harder to hold on to.

Now, without thinking, he turned onto Blackstone Boulevard. Drivers at last able to pass on a two-lane highway gave him dirty looks.

"One thing I've learned," Assunta said, "nothing comes easy in this world. Life's a mystery . . . a damned struggle too, if you ask me." After some time she said: "I don't know whether I'm coming or going these days." She tried to perk herself up. "Listen, Piero, we're Romans, aren't we? We'll survive."

"I used to pride myself," Piero said. "I thought I was made of courage—a Roman come to live among barbarians. The count and countess—"

"Please, Piero, let's not get on that topic again. Whew, thank God the Petrarcas are back in Rome!"

"Thank goodness the funds are flowing back again, from Rome to Providence—in the nick of time. There's no way we

could stay on Wakefield Lane. Sure, living in Providence, with
Anna at Butler, is costly. Driving back and forth to work is hard.
But getting away from small-town life is a blessing. Anyway,
we're close to Anna."

As he looked for the entrance to Butler, his thoughts went
back to Prospect Hill. He missed family life with Marco, Felicia,
and the kids; he missed the river flowing through the valley, the
south slopes, and the morning and evening bells ringing at Sacred
Heart. While it had its hills and beautiful houses, Providence
was a lonely place. Their life was sad and uprooted. "You know,
the count may be right—" he said when Assunta interrupted
him again.

"Look, Piero, we may be out of place here. But let's face it.
Anna and Alessandro are Americans first. And then, how can
Anna be rushed off to Rome, even if Alex can? God only knows
when she'll pull out of it."

"If Alex's to take on the title (and more than likely he will),
he'll have to take in Italian culture. And, as the count said, better
sooner than later. Our compromise, I think, is a fitting one—
surely, for Alex's sake."

"Let's wait and see. First things first. The Petrarcas are only
too happy to pay for private school for Alex, and Moses Brown
is the best prep school around. Poor Alex. Living and learning
among those snobs! But Anna—she's our big worry right now."
Assunta had no relief from the sharp pain in her chest. "If
everything goes right, *magari*, God grant," she hastened to make
the sign of the cross—"we'll carry out our end of the bargain:
we'll send Alex to Rome for his high school years. By then, Anna
should have finished eleventh grade. God willing."

Piero's thoughts crept back to his letter to Felicia. Never found.
And Anna had not spoken since Felicia's death. "Anna's been the
sole suspect. But my letter to Felicia is the key to finding the
killer. No forcible entry, no evidence of anyone coming in. Where
did it go?"

"Every inch of the house got turned upside down by the police.
They even sifted through our trash. What a muddle!"

"Now, another of these psychiatrists. One says this, another
says that. We get further and further from the truth all the time.

And the labels they put on Anna!"

They fell silent as Piero turned off Blackstone Boulevard onto a curving driveway that led to Butler Hospital. An immense, formidable compound greeted them with refined surroundings that resembled a ducal estate more than hospital grounds.

A receptionist ushered them into a large oak-paneled office in a grand nineteenth-century structure that put Assunta and Piero in mind of a palazzo. A tall heavy-set freckled-faced man with carrot-colored hair walked in and stood before a wall stacked with books from floor to ceiling. Huge well-shaped teeth made his big round face cherubic when he smiled. He struck Assunta as incongruous—such a husky body wrapped around such a young person—not more than thirty-five. An overgrown football player.

"I'm Dr. Leach," he said in a gentle voice, shaking first Assunta's hand, then Piero's. He moved a second chair in front of his desk. "Please," he said, pointing.

He took note of Assunta dressed in a tailored charcoal-gray suit with mink collar and a mink-trimmed pillbox hat. She seemed pretty fit for her early sixties. Her dark gray-speckled hair was pulled back in a twist, and her green-blue eyes looked sad and tired. Piero sat aloof in a blue sports jacket, white oxford shirt, and red-striped tie. Not at all what Dr. Leach expected to see from reading some of the court testimony.

"Would you like me to bring in some coffee, Dr. Leach?" the receptionist asked.

Dr. Leach turned to them. "Coffee? . . . tea?, Mrs. Benedicta . . . Mr. Benedicta."

They both declined and the receptionist left.

"Thank you for being patient and honoring my request to put off meeting for two weeks, to let me get to know Anna a bit. As you know, juvenile court put Anna in my care. I understand, Mr. Benedicta, the court appointed you her guardian," he said.

"Yes, my mother and me." Piero felt relieved that Dr. Leach didn't mention another option—Oaklawn School for Girls, if not committed to Butler Hospital. Piero and Assunta had seen that—a reform school—as a death sentence for Anna.

"Well, let's see," Dr. Leach went on. "I'd like to go over the investigating officer's report to juvenile court and the court's order to me. This may be wearisome, but bear with me for Anna's sake. We want to be clear about the evidence, and what happened to her. He read:

> . . . *the child may remain in the care of the family (in this case Mr. Benedicta and his mother Assunta) for at least six months under guidance of a court-appointed social worker to oversee the child's progress. Upon such terms as the court shall determine, the child may then be placed in the custody of other suitable persons, or in the custody of any of the agencies, societies or institutions under the control of or approved by the department of social welfare. In the case of Anna Maria Benedicta, it is determined that the child be placed in the care of Daniel Leach, M. D., Butler Hospital . . .*

He skipped the next paragraph about Oaklawn School.

Piero and Assunta exchanged glances, relieved.

Dr. Leach began shuffling sheets in a large file, searching for something. "I'm sorry to put you through this. In criminal acts involving a minor, the case is sent to juvenile court. As you know, the prosecutor's office does not figure in the court hearing; the prosecutor relinquishes all police and medical examiner's reports to juvenile court. Instead of trying a juvenile—in this case Anna—juvenile court makes her its ward and determines what's in her best interest. I'm sure you've heard this all before."

"Yes, yes, I understand," Piero said, his voice cracking. "The court clerk reviewed the options with us."

Assunta reached over and squeezed Piero's hand.

"Yes, for six months—to see whether, left to you and Mrs. Benedicta, she might pull out of the trauma," Dr. Leach said, looking at Piero. "Has she changed much during these months?"

"Not much. She hasn't spoken—been lethargic. Often she'd stand before her bed for hours, hardly moving. She's trying to deal with her grief, I believe . . . I hope." His voice trembled.

"Before going over the reports with you," Dr. Leach said, hesitating, "I want to . . . to . . . emphasize my approach." He groped for words to avoid the murder scene for the moment, turning pages in a thick folder. Their anguish struck a chord in him. He cleared his throat before continuing. "I'm concerned first and foremost with . . . with Anna's health . . . not taking anything for granted. Psychiatric and social worker reports— I'm putting them aside, I'm starting from scratch. 'What seems to be' and 'what really is' are often at odds with one another. We want to find out how Anna thinks, how she feels—her values, desires, goals. It'll be hard to help her if we condemn her in any way. Asking 'what's wrong with Anna?' or 'How did it happen?' or 'Who's to blame?' or 'How do we fix her?' are not, in my judgment, very helpful questions." He began shuffling pages again.

Assunta sensed gentleness in Dr. Leach and began to feel less anxious. Hope sprouted in her.

"Now, let's begin with the police report." Dr. Leach pulled out several pages from his folder and read:

> . . . *At 9 A.M. I was dispatched to 12 Wakefield Lane to investigate the death of a woman. Upon arrival, I was led to the second story to find the dead woman in blue cotton dress, lying on living room floor, feet extended out living room door into hallway, wounds on hand and shoulder, blood pooled on floor. Girl child in pink, bloodstained nightgown had a 10" knife lying in lap; she rocked back and forth in rocker, her hands clutching its arms. She said nothing, she looked straight ahead, her posture was rigid. The child's bed covering had bloodstains on it. Fingerprints were—*

"Before the police arrived," Piero interrupted, "Anna rocked, as the officer noted, but kept repeating: 'I want my mamma! I want my mamma!' over and over again. Once strangers came in she stopped talking. She hasn't spoken since." Bowing his head, Piero fought back tears.

Assunta looked down, cupped some loose hairs from the nape of her neck into her twist with her left hand, then fumbled around in her purse for a handkerchief.

"Yes, I recall reading—in the report," Dr. Leach said. "There's no evidence of forced entry or of fingerprints other than those of family members. The fingerprints on the knife are Anna's. Let's take a look at the medical examiner's report.

Monday, March 27, 1950:
35-year-old female, estimated time of death 1:30 A.M., March 25. Autopsy performed at 4 P.M., March 27, reveals superficial stab wound to the left shoulder, 1.5 cm inferior to the acromio-clavicular joint, without evidence of injury to underlying vasculature. Two superficial lacerations on the volar aspect of the right hand, measuring . . .

Dr. Leach looked up, "The cause of death is not the knife wounds."

. . . The superficial stab wound to left shoulder is consistent with a knife wound, which is not the cause of death. Lacerations on the right palm very likely related to victim attempting to fend off assailant's knife.

"What's the cause of death? It seems to have come from the fall—the young Mrs. Benedicta must've struck her head. The blow is what killed her." Maybe Anna and her mother had been fighting, Dr. Leach thought. Anna might have attacked her mother without intent to kill. "The court, given the medical examiner's report, ruled the death accidental." At home with the technical language, Dr. Leach continued:

An occipital laceration, measuring approximately 3 cm, is present. There is an underlying depressed fracture of the occipital bone ("the back part of the skull," Dr. Leach gestured, putting his hand to the back of his head to show them) *with extension of the fracture into the temporal bone and right mastoid sinus. A substantial epidural hematoma is noted overlying the occipitoparietal convexity with resultant transtentorial herniation. Hemorrhage is present in the anterior aspect of the right temporal lobe, consistent with a contrecoup injury. The cause of death is from a blow to back of head with a blunt object, resulting in herniation of the brain.*

"I'm sorry to put you through this, but I want to make clear that your daughter-in-law, Mrs. Benedicta, did not die from knife wounds but from her head hitting the table. It seems that a blow, here at the bottom of the skull" (he put his hand behind his head, again, to point it out), caused massive bleeding in the brain, forcing a displacement of the brain. This is the only logical explanation since no blunt instrument was found."

"That's the bang we heard from our downstairs bedrooms, Piero," Assunta said.

"I took it to be an upstairs shutter banging against the house. If only I'd gone to look . . ." Piero was racked by guilt.

"It wouldn't have saved her, Mr. Benedicta. Herniation— that is, the pushing on the brain by the hematoma, the internal bleeding—brings on death very quickly."

Assunta sobbed at the thought of Felicia's brutal end. Piero got up to comfort her and to hide his own tears.

Dr. Leach called for coffee over his intercom and excused himself to give them time to collect themselves.

"Piero, promise me—you must make a novena with me. For nine days we'll devote our prayers to Felicia and Anna."

"I will, Mamma, I will." Unlike his mother, he found no consolation in prayer. Yet, he mustn't thwart whatever solace faith granted her.

"I can't tell you how much Tuesday night Benediction eases my pain and gives me strength to go on."

"Yes, Mamma, yes, I know. We have to keep calm. It's so lonely with Alex away at school and Anna . . . we'll make it. We'll pull through."

Dr. Leach came back carrying a tray and poured some coffee.

"What do the psychological reports show, Doctor?" Piero asked, puzzled by the diagnoses submitted to the court.

"Have you seen the police reports about . . . about . . . your neighbors' claims? Some say your sister-in-law was pretty hard on Anna." Dr. Leach brought up the subject that concerned him most—Felicia's character and the slurs against the Benedicta family.

Neither Piero nor Assunta answered. The bizarre accusations brought against Felicia, Piero, and Anna had shocked them.

Initially the presiding judge was against releasing Anna to Assunta and Piero. The testimony of Lillian and her supporters, depicting the Benedictas as abusive and tyrannical, turned the judge against them. Mrs. Lambert proved pivotal in the court's decision. In her testimony, she gave a glowing account of the Benedicta family—their devotion to the children and the church. Mrs. Lambert disputed her daughter Lillian's version of things, saying that Lillian liked to meddle. During the hearing, only Mrs. Lambert, of all the neighbors, testified that she had visited the Benedicta home regularly. She alone knew the Benedictas intimately. The judge relied on her testimony, making Assunta and Piero Anna's legal guardians.

"Well, it seems that according to some neighbors, a boy by the name of Ralph Mullen said Felicia and Anna had quite a fight in the back yard on the evening of Friday, March 24."

"Ralph lived up the hill from us. He claimed he saw Felicia beat Anna," Piero said, sipping his coffee.

"I see. Is his testimony credible?"

"He's not too bright . . . honest, affectionate—a gentle person. Very fond of Anna—obsessed with her, really. Followed her every move and spied on her with binoculars. He's got a pretty good view of our yard from the top of the hill. Seeing clearly is another matter. That Anna and her mother fought outside that night is hard for me to believe. I would've heard it; they were never out of earshot. They might've argued upstairs; it's hard to hear from upstairs down."

"Listen, Dr. Leach. The truth is that my granddaughter Anna is one of those children born adjusted to the world from the first," Assunta said. Lillian's vicious stories angered her. "Alex, her brother—well, a different matter, a bit harder to handle. But Anna—I've taken care of since birth. She made our life a joy. She and Felicia walked about arm in arm that night under my very nose. Wouldn't I have heard?" Her eyes watered. "Excuse me, if I get emotional." She pulled a handkerchief out of her purse. "Anna got on with her mother like a sister—so close were they. It sounds too good to be true, I know." Her hands trembled as she reached for the cup of coffee.

"Then how do you account for the testimony of a Mrs. Lillian Pastori? Mrs. Pastori paints a different picture. Anna not allowed to play with other children; a mother too strict and harsh; a daughter in rebellion against this tyranny. The beatings Felicia gave Anna, she claims, are in keeping with your daughter-in-law's character—'cold, unfeeling, uncaring, and self-centered.'"

Her hands shaking, Assunta took a long sip of coffee as if trying to calm her anger. "Even Lillian's mother, Mrs. Lambert, said her daughter was a chatterbox who could be mean-spirited sometimes." Rage boiled up in Assunta. "That woman—that envious woman—tormenting poor Felicia for years! Her mother such a saint."

Dr. Leach looked away, flushed. He fingered the pages of the folder, pulling out several sheets. He said sheepishly: "Forgive me for prying, Mr. Benedicta, but the police reports—statements made in them and at juvenile court—say that something illicit was going on between you and your sister-in-law." Dr. Leach's reluctance to press Piero on this point did not keep him from looking Piero straight in the eye.

"I loved my sister-in-law dearly." Piero's heart pounded and his face turned crimson. "There's never been any impropriety in our relationship. I asked my sister-in-law to marry me that evening—in a letter. The police doubt my claim of a missing letter. They said any such 'missing letter, its existence unverified, cannot itself be *prima-facie* evidence of forcible entry by an outsider.'" Stamped in his memory, those harsh words meant one thing: the police had no intention of seriously pursuing other leads.

Piero's tone and manner put to rest Dr. Leach's questions about the Benedicta family. Piero didn't try to justify himself, Dr. Leach thought. Next he fixed on a scathing attack against Piero by a Miss Mildred Bergman of Prospect Hill. He read the following to himself:

. . . not a very nice man. He thinks because he's good looking he can charm any girl he wants and lead her on. Then he doesn't feel sorry for them when he doesn't keep his promises. He needs

*the attention of many girls to make him feel big. I don't think
he's very honest or very trusting. He led me on and never did say
he was sorry for all the trouble he caused me and my
family . . .*

Riveted to the testimony, Dr. Leach went on to read Lillian
Pastori's, forgetting for a moment Assunta and Piero sitting across
from him.

Piero and Assunta waited what seemed like an eternity, fearing
they'd have to defend themselves all over again. What humiliation
they had endured at juvenile court!

Gripped by Lillian's diatribe against the Benedictas, Dr. Leach
read it to the end:

*. . . little wonder this thing happened. What can you expect?
Anna, a sensitive child, punished by an unfeeling, self-centered
mother, the mistress of her brother-in-law. When the law is no
longer honored in your own home, you're bound to feel the lash
of suffering, which is nothing more than the wages of sin. May
God have mercy on them.*

He skipped over to the letter of a fourteen-year-old neighbor,
Paul Risch, and resumed reading to himself:

*. . . I can't believe that two of the nicest people on Prospect Hill,
Mr. Benedicta and his sister-in-law, got such bad things said
about them. Anna's uncle and mother are people I'm proud to
call my friends. Every time I have been with them, they have
been kind. I wish the people who don't have warmth and love,
as the Benedicta family have, were like them . . .*

He then skimmed through Mrs. Angela Risch Flynn's
remarks, trying to get a full view of the Benedictas:

*. . . Peter is a kind and intelligent man. Women are attracted to
his good looks and wit. He was not able to commit himself fully,
but I do feel he was sincere in his love for me at one time. Peter
is an honorable and responsible family man. He's like a father*

*to his sister-in-law's children. I will always value his friendship.
I'm sure I'm a better person for having known Peter, in spite of
the fact that he broke off our . . .*

Dr. Leach needed to weigh the reports in light of the
impression he got firsthand from talking to Anna's uncle and
grandmother. Before this, the reports had seemed a jumble of
names.

"I'm still interested in your diagnosis, Doctor? What do you
see as Anna's problem?" Piero asked.

Dr. Leach shuffled through the pages looking for the
psychiatric reports. "You'll have to give me more time, Mr.
Benedicta. Our talk today—yours and Mrs. Benedicta," he said,
turning to Assunta, "has been helpful. Ah, here we have a few
diagnoses—one by a psychiatrist and one by a social worker. Let
me see . . . I see . . . huh, hunh! . . . huh, hunh! . . . "Hmmm—
as I expected: a lot of technical terms. Give me another week or
so with Anna—"

"What are these syndromes or disorders they claim they've
found?"

"Well, Mr. Benedicta, sometimes it's better to say too little
than too much. What we've got here is technical language, pretty
harsh, probably of little value in helping Anna."

"It's like the blind leading the blind, if you ask me!" Assunta
blurted, giving vent to all her suffering—not only from the
nastiness of the townsfolk but from the folly of the professionals
who had handled Anna's case, including the police. "I couldn't
help thinking about a saying in our family about psychiatrists:
'If you can't separate yourself from the garbage, how are you
going to pull a pearl necklace out of it?' No offense intended,
Doctor."

Piero turned to his mother with arched eyebrows. What's got
hold of her? he wondered.

Dr. Leach's face flushed, camouflaging scores of freckles. "Yes,
Mrs. Benedicta, I understand." He smiled in admiration at
Assunta's blunt depiction of his profession.

"Are you saying these reports are useless?" Piero asked.

"No, we can't say that. Let's keep an open mind. Let me see," he said, as he went over a psychiatric report in silence:

> *Twelve-year-old girl, living with widowed mother, is unresponsive and presents with marked psychomotor disturbances accompanied by stupor and mutism. Diagnostic criteria such as bizarre delusions or auditory hallucination are absent. Schizophrenic disorder is ruled out in favor of separation anxiety disorder with violent behavior toward an individual forcing separation, in this case her mother, whom she is overconcerned about and fears separation from.*

He turned to a social worker's account and went on reading in silence:

> *. . . presents with a developmental problem stemming from unspecified emotional disorder representing outcome of family circumstances involving child abuse. The diagnosis is of a child maltreatment syndrome—abused child presents with traumas and aggressive, antisocial behavior.*

He looked at a third opinion by a psychologist:

> *. . . Because of lack of information about the mental life of the accused before the alleged crime, it is wise, in my judgment, to call her condition an X syndrome, on which later we will be able to project those attributes that gave rise to the violence.*

These reports may be harmful to Anna and her family, he thought. Possibly meaningless speculation. After some time he said, "Well, put in plain English, the first report says that Anna, worried about her mother's leaving her, feared being abandoned. This led Anna to violent acts against her mother. The second says that Anna, abused by her mother, assaulted her. The motivation for the violence is to some extent the opposite of the first. The third claims that, there being no solid evidence about Anna's behavior, the name of her condition should be left open."

"What do you think, Doctor?"

"I don't think we should prejudge Anna, Mr. Benedicta. She

comes to me emotionally distraught, in deep grief, regardless of how the tragedy happened." Dr. Leach stopped as though enough had been said.

Despite Dr. Leach's eagerness to end the meeting, Piero asked: "How do you intend to treat Anna? What approach do you use?"

"The best therapeutic tool is compassion. Meeting Anna empathically is, in my judgment, the most effective path to healing." He stood up. "I'm sorry," he said looking at his watch, "you'll have to postpone visiting Anna today; it's past visiting hours. If things go well during the month . . . you were told no one is allowed to go home for a weekend visit before a month's stay . . . as soon as Anna makes a breakthrough, we'll talk about home visits."

They thanked Dr. Leach, feeling encouraged by his concern and openness.

The Psychiatric Profession

On the way home, Piero and Assunta, feeling the first relief from months of grief-filled solitude, felt lighthearted.

"What's with this 'necklace-out-of-the-garbage' nonsense, Mamma? For a minute there I thought Dr. Leach might commit you to Butler, too."

Meeting with Dr. Leach unleashed legions of memories in Assunta. Vivid among them, long forgotten and little understood till now, was her father's obsession with the psychiatric profession—as far back as the '20s.

"Well?" Piero asked. He turned a corner and gunned the motor to make it up one of the steep hills of Providence.

"Do you remember Father D. telling us not to put much stock in psychiatric reports?"

"He ignored them, as I remember."

Assunta recalled their visit with Father D. several months back. "Please, Assunta, don't take those reports to heart," he had told her. "A lot in them is nonsense, childish. If you must know, they're nothing more than *post hoc, ergo propter hoc* thinking—that is, if something happens after something, then it happens because of it. A real fallacy in the profession, Assunta—thinking backwards.

"You see, Assunta," Father D. went on, "psychiatrists and psychologists have based their views not on knowing Anna but on the opinions of your neighbors. Now, tell me this: how sound can these reports on Anna's or Felicia's mental health be? Anna's alleged crime, they said, resulted from the 'abuse' suffered from her cold, hateful mother or the result of an 'emotional disorder' caused by her mother. Actually, Assunta, the psychiatrists and social workers didn't have any direct knowledge of Anna's family life. They read the neighbors' testimony. Felicia abused Anna, they had an awful row, the mother is unloving, and so forth. From this the psychiatrists and social workers came to believe that the murder resulted from a fight and the child abuse they read about. They reasoned backward: Anna became violent toward her mother because she had been maltreated, or she had an emotional disorder stemming from an abusive relationship that led to violence against her mother. Whether that is so or not cannot be known by thinking backwards, can it?"

Assunta turned to Piero. "You know Piero, Father D.'s views are not all that different from my father's, come to think of it. I remember how fascinated he became with this new field of medicine after his brother Domenico fell under its spell. Uncle Domenico, to be sure, was more than slightly nuts. My father often said his brother Domenico had a few screws loose."

"Who could forget Uncle Domenico—there were so many family jokes about him. What happened to him? Wasn't he a skirt chaser?"

"To put it mildly. He stalked *little* skirts—girls who were barely in their teens."

"No wonder the family was shocked." Piero blew his horn and swerved away from a car that had pulled out in front of him.

"Be careful, Piero, for goodness sake! Her body stiffened in panic. "Whew! You've got to watch these fools."

"I've got the car under control."

"Today, thinking of our poor Anna—of the syndromes these experts dredged up—I got my first glimpse of their silliness. Dr.

Leach brought to mind my father's fascination—his negative fascination—with psychiatry and psychology. He took to calling it 'the flatus of the modern mind.' He couldn't learn enough about it. One day he said, 'Since these modern doctors of the soul don't believe in any goodness, they don't understand that mental illness is not an illness at all. It comes from not thinking right and not living right.'

"I had the 'thinking backward' problem till today," Assunta said. "You see, when psychiatry first reared its head, the older intelligentsia didn't buy it as easily as we do today. Unlike us, they had many qualms about it. We Italians are a pretty rebellious lot—"

"A country of anarchists, if you ask me."

"Uncle Domenico's psychiatrist—if you can believe it— blamed Domenico's disorder on his parents. His pedophilia came after his upbringing, consequently it sprang from this upbringing. Do you see how simple-minded this thinking is?"

"Well, maybe," Piero said.

"Well, you see, they were blaming Domenico's lust for little girls on his father and mother—they didn't bring him up right. Many a young chicken got chased around the city (younger than his daughters, mind you!)—not to mention the suffering he caused their families and ours. Domenico's parents had psychologically crippled him, sabotaged his will, took away his power of choice. My father said this new science conjured up imaginary defects in upbringing. After all, none of the other boys in the family 'caught this crap in his soul,' as my father put it. He used to say 'who but God knows where these desires come from? We probably all have them. It's up to us to control them and, with the help of God, kill them.'"

"It seems to me this thinking backwards excused Uncle Domenico—"

"That's what got my father's goat. He kept babbling about the mis-science of the soul." Assunta's meeting with Dr. Leach and the memories of her talk with Father D. helped console her now. She became convinced that Anna's grief over her mother's death had little to do with the diagnoses presented to juvenile court. Something had gone awry the night of Felicia's death.

"By the way, what happened to Uncle Domenico?"

"He got caught seducing young girls—some the age of his daughters and younger, some his daughters' friends. His psychiatrist focused on its origin—not on means to get rid of it. As if something so complex can be easily passed off onto one's parents."

"Seems Grandpa didn't kowtow to the new profession."

"He was a Roman, wasn't he? Anger got the better of him. He told Domenico to get a grip on himself. He tried to knock some sense into his brother. So did our parish priest. When I think back, my father had a handle on this foolishness. He'd say: 'it brings about a society of whiners—looking to blame others—and at the same time a breed of prowlers indulging all kinds of shameful urges.'"

"But surely, Mamma, some people scarred in their upbringing need psychiatric help."

"Of course. Of course. Didn't you miss our street?"

"No, the turn off is coming up," he said, bearing right onto Angell Street.

"As Father D. said: 'the mind like the body may become so unbalanced you need these modern mechanics.' As I see it, when what you do is seen simply as the fault of your upbringing or the fault of your genes, or the fault of society you begin to feel sorry for yourself. Gradually, you give in to strong impulses harmful to others and to yourself. After all, you're not to blame. Others are: society, parents, genes, whatever. Imagine medicine practiced simply by focusing on the origin of a disease without treating the disease and its symptoms."

"Lillian had a real gossip mill going—" Piero said.

"Let's forget her, please—"

"How do you see the charming redhead? Does Doctor Leach pass the litmus test? Can he be counted among the human?"

"He's more than charming. He's *furbo*—clever."

"Yeah!"

"He was hanging on our every word—weighing Anna's family against the testimony given in the court hearing," Assunta said.

"You saw how he looked me in the eye—trying to gauge the 'Benedicta scandal'."

"Thank God he's not dogmatic and shallow. There's a human being lurking behind all that bulk," she said. "You know, psychiatry can be helpful, as our redhead suggested—if centered in compassion. Poor Anna, she needs a break."

"There's hope. Some lustful fantasies Lillian concocted."

"Her imagination got the better of her: Felicia had many lovers; you and Felicia lived in sin. To hell with Lillian. She's not worth thinking about."

"But the facts still don't square," he said, as they pulled into the driveway. "I've been thinking about a private eye. Clues may have been overlooked. Norman's alibi seems airtight. Who knows? Then the other characters hanging out at Lillian's—"

"You're grasping at straws. We'll see. It's time to think of our little *ragazzina*, Anna."

Lillian's Torment

Lillian set out to visit Rose Golanski, Ralph Mullen's sister, who lived a few blocks away. "Hello, Rose," Lillian yelled, as she passed through the opening in the high hedges forming an archway into the yard.

Rose, a heavy-set woman with puffy red cheeks, sat sorting papers in the gazebo attached to her house.

"Hello, Lillian. Come on up!" Rose moved a lawn chair next to hers.

"Spring cleaning in October?" Lillian handed Rose a package. "Sweets for you and Jim."

"Thanks, Lillian—nice of you. I'll throw on a pot of coffee." Rose hurried into the house.

Contrasting the Golanskis' manicured lawn with her overgrown, weed-infested plot, Lillian's chipper mood turned to self-pity. Her husband Frank, already off to the tavern to play the slot machine or to shoot craps with his cronies, galled her. He's on his regular Saturday bender—guzzling up a storm. Eddy, her older son unschooled and left behind, ended up as her charge. Frank, she felt, simply tolerated his family and took advantage of their home only when it pleased him. He felt that as long as he brought home the bacon he could do as he damn well pleased.

She was proud Tony and Cecilia were doing well at West Warwick Junior high: Tony in the ninth grade, Cecilia in the seventh. Frank had shirked his responsibilities.

Rose came back balancing a tray loaded with coffee, cake, cream, sugar, and cups. "All these boxes. What on earth are you and Jim up to?" Lillian asked.

"Got a mess on my hands, really." Rose managed to set the tray down. "Jim's finally laid down the law—get rid of all this rubbish. You know, Jim—disorder's a mortal sin."

Rose cut the cake and poured coffee. Lillian scanned the manicured lawn, the attractive red brick house, and the charming gardens. Unlike Frank, a slug around the house, Jim spent most of his free time working on the place, faithful to Rose and his family.

"You've got to give it to Jim: he works hard keeping up the yard," Lillian said.

"Landscaping's the love of his life." Rose handed Lillian a piece of cake and placed a cup of coffee on an end table next to her.

Lillian took a bite of cake. "Mmmm . . . Mmmm . . . delicious chocolate cake, Rose." She sighed and took another bite.

"When my brother Ralph died, we sold Mother's house and all the odds and ends ended up here." Rose took a sip of coffee. "We've had two tragedies in a row: first Mother, then Ralph a few months later." Her eyes teared.

"Poor Ralph," Lillian said, sipping her coffee.

"He seems to have gone to pieces after Mother died. But it began earlier, really. Late last spring he started to put on a lot of weight."

"Congenital heart defect, wasn't it? Poor Ralph, had more and more trouble making it up the hill."

"In spite of it, he kept up the house and yard. Sure, my brothers and sisters pitched in."

"He stopped coming to see Eddy months before he died."

"Gave up working at the church. He'd been so proud of working for Father D., you know. Living nearby, we became the dumping ground, taking in all this junk when Mother's house got sold. As they sipped their coffee and enjoyed the chocolate cake, Rose went on rummaging through a stack of boxes, discarding this and that and saving things she thought valuable.

"When did he stop working for Father D.?"

"Let's see—about the time of Felicia's death, I believe. Where does the time go?" Rose dumped a pile of old magazines into a trash burner and lifted out a cigar box. "The things Ralph and Mother saved! What's this . . . pictures . . . look familiar." Rose took two pictures out of Ralph's cigar box. "Isn't this Anna Benedicta?" She handed a photograph to Lillian.

"Sure is—looks about ten years old."

"That Ralph! So admired Anna." Rose smiled as she studied the photos.

"He loved to sit on the wall with Eddy; both of them had a regular afternoon ritual waiting for the kids to come home from school," Lillian said.

"The hill's never been the same since *it* happened."

"Lots happened since then—Mitri Mansour died . . . your mother and brother . . . the Benedictas left . . . so did Paul Risch and his family."

"How's Eddy these days?" Rose asked. "I seldom see him."

"Mopes much of the time—not interested in anything. You know, he and Ralph went around the neighborhood together, picked up odd jobs—kept them busy. Their friendship gave some meaning to their lives." Lillian looked away, pained.

"When Felicia died and Anna no longer came out, Ralph went through a time of terrible grief," Rose noted.

"It took a long time before he started dropping by again. Never quite himself—"

"He practically fell to pieces when he learned that Anna murdered her mother," Rose admitted. "That's what I think."

They went on to talk about Rose's children and what was going on in the neighborhood. Suddenly Rose picked up two stained and crumpled envelopes. "I wonder what . . . 'Piero' . . . 'Felicia'," she read. She flattened out the two envelopes: one, sealed, addressed to Piero; the other, opened, to Felicia. "What on earth are these doing in Ralph's cigar box?" She considered whether or not to take a look at them, then pulled out the letter from the envelope addressed to Felicia and began to read:

Cara Felicia,

Half from anguish, half from apprehension, my heart is bursting. Could I but go on, I would wish for an eternity of tomorrows as we are rather than lose you. It is not as in-laws that we have lived these nearly seven years. What have we been to one another, in honesty? Tell me you care as I do, as your every smile makes me hope. Since Marco died I have loved you: I suppressed it, denied it to myself. My love only grew stronger, till it consumes me . . .

She felt like a voyeur looking into Felicia's personal life. Finishing the letter in silence, she passed it on to Lillian and tore open the second one, itching to know Felicia's response.

Caro Piero,

Yes, my love. My heart is yours—forever. With everything wonderful there is always a condition, so let this be mine: you must grant us all, Mamma and the children, a honeymoon at the villa . . .

She handed it to Lillian who read it closely. Neither note was dated.

"What are they doing in Ralph's junk pile?" Rose posed the question as if talking to herself. Though the letters surprised her, her wonder soon flagged and her thoughts turned to other matters.

Lillian went from one letter to the other, reading and rereading them—trying to put them in the context of Felicia's murder as Rose continued to sort through Ralph's stuff. "Very strange! Strange indeed!" Lillian repeated several times.

"I can see Ralph getting Anna's photos . . . but the love letters—very odd," Rose said, putting them back into their envelopes and putting them and the pictures among the things she was saving. She turned to the topic of the Benedicta family. "Whatever happened to Anna after they moved?"

"No one seems to know. The Benedictas broke all ties with my mother. All she did for them—going out on a limb at juvenile court and all. Real appreciation."

The fact that Ralph had the letters baffled Lillian. There had been a big to-do about Piero's letter to Felicia during the police investigation. Many wondered what the letter had to do with Anna's murdering her mother. Lillian soon began feeling more and more uneasy. How had Ralph Mullen come by the letters? she asked herself. He had never opened the one addressed to Piero. And the brown stains—were they from blood?

A sally of thoughts about the evening of Anna's beating by her mother and Felicia's murder came to mind. Ralph had never been a suspect. It was not that Ralph might have done it that now set her on edge. How could she possibly know? No, it was her own nastiness toward Felicia that troubled her. Learning of Felicia's noble roots had shocked Lillian at the time, and her jealousy often filled her with shame. Then her riling poor Ralph—puffing up what he'd seen. Maybe he was mistaken. Paul thought so; so did Cecilia and Tony. There must be some explanation for Ralph's having the letters.

Ralph's make up—his gentleness, his love of neighbors, his faith in God, his humility—made it impossible to believe he was culpable. Yet an unusual emotion, something strange and foreboding, sprang up in her, and she began to feel faint. Felicia's bludgeoned body flashed before her—Ralph standing with a bloody knife in his hand. She couldn't shake the image from her mind.

Her heart beat so fast she felt it was about to burst. Life seemed to be turning upside down in her. She felt as though a membrane had ruptured within her as painful feelings and abhorrent thoughts came tumbling through. She clutched her breast. Guilt, like a serpent entwining her body, suffocated her. Suddenly she wrenched herself from the chair and stumbled down the gazebo stairs, fleeing toward home. She felt her insides quivering and tried to give voice to words. "Well, Rose, I better be off," she managed to say.

Before Rose could look up, Lillian was already down the gazebo stairs. "What's the rush?" Rose looked into Lillian's blanched face. "My God, Lillian, are you all right? What's come over you? I'll walk you home." She trailed after Lillian.

"No. No," Lillian said, flustered. She felt like screaming—let me be. She rushed out of the yard and toward the street, with Rose still tagging behind. "I'll be all right, Rose. Please." She gasped for breath.

"You don't look well."

"I just need a little rest," she said as calmly as she could. She was about to collapse.

With every step, she felt a weariness coming over her. Oh, my God. What's happening to me? What have those letters to do with me? she thought. As soon as she entered the house, she flopped down in a living-room chair, nearly delirious.

Eddy, in the den with the TV blaring, was oblivious to his mother's return.

Her thoughts went back to the night of the murder—to that Friday night and Saturday morning. Weeks had passed before Ralph came down and sat on the wall. When he did, he never mentioned Anna again. He began to get fat. The fatter he got, the more withdrawn he became. Could it be? How could Ralph have gotten into the Benedicta house? Where could he have gotten the letters? And even if he did break in, there was no evidence of it. How could so gentle a boy be capable of such evil? It's absurd, she told herself.

Memories of that evening tormented her: her viciousness, her gossip, her delight in being at the center of childish play. On and on she brooded about her feelings of inferiority, her meaningless marriage, her attraction to Piero.

No, Ralph Mullen could not have killed Felicia. It's impossible, she told herself. But her heart refused to listen. Poor Felicia. Poor Anna. Anxiety gave way to a morbid helplessness. Gradually she withdrew from the world in utter self-rejection.

Anna at Butler Hospital

Dr. Leach expected Anna at any moment. He pulled out his notes from his morning conference with the acute-ward staff— Anna's ward.

He was thinking of the commotion that had been going on when he entered the conference room. Everyone was huddled around two student nurses—Miss Miller and Miss DeCiantis. The staff was listening to them tell about morning break: a glass vase from the third floor had dropped onto the outside terrace, smashing near Anna and Mrs. Tuttle. The crash startled the patients and the student nurses. Hardly catching their breath, the student nurses were shocked to see Mrs. Tuttle lunge for a piece of broken glass and threaten to cut her wrists. Anna looked on frightened. Miss Miller and Miss DeCiantis rushed to dislodge the glass from Mrs. Tuttle's hand. She gave up the "weapon," willingly. It turned out to be all show—like a child drawing on the wall for attention.

Anna's weeks in therapy seemed fruitless. Following Dr. Leach's advice, the staff continued to give thumbs down to any form of physical or chemical therapy—whether electroshock or insulin—or the use of sodium pentothal, which some felt might get her to open up. An encouraging word filtered in now and then. A slight change in Anna's bearing became noticeable during occupational therapy: from the mute, frozen, human-sized toy, pulled and tugged here and there, to greater self-propulsion. The traumatized child within peered out now and again. Anna seemed to take some pleasure in creating animal figures out of clay.

There was a knocking at the door. "Come in," Dr. Leach called out.

"Hello, Dr. Leach," Miss Miller greeted him. Anna trailed behind. A nineteen-year-old student nurse in a white cap and starched pinafore over a light blue dress, Delia Miller stood in stark contrast to Anna. With clothes more draped on her than worn, Anna drooped, wafer thin and gaunt. Delia, vivacious and smiling, spoke warmly to Anna, who stared at the floor.

"Anna, say hello to Dr. Leach," Delia coaxed, tugging her into the office. "Anna and I have been building castles with a deck of cards. Later Anna's going with Peggy DeCiantis to occupational therapy. You love working with clay, don't you Anna?" Anna's body stiffened.

"Quite a commotion on the terrace this morning," Dr. Leach said, looking at Anna. "Anna, has Miss Miller told you? We'll be showing *Meet Me in St. Louis* Saturday night. I think you'll like it. Thank you, Miss Miller," Dr. Leach said, excusing her. He led Anna toward the brown leather couch facing a glass door looking onto a courtyard in its autumn splendor of bright orange, red, and brown leaves. Anna fell onto the couch.

Dr. Leach sat beside her, talking, hoping to form a bond with her, to build a bridge—an invisible link between their worlds. He spurned the cause-and-effect thinking given in the reports of the court-appointed experts. They relied too heavily on appearances and put too much trust in interpersonal relations and group interaction. He was sure something more profound and mysterious—something deeper, more complex and ineffable—takes place in human life. True, a good personal history and a good background knowledge of the patient are helpful. The psychiatric and psychological accounts may reflect what took place between Anna and her mother. Who knows? But how do past experiences relate to present reality? To Anna's inner life, *now?* A puzzle not easily pieced together. How does Anna see life after her traumatic experience? What are her expectations and feelings? In life, as in therapy, thinking in interpersonal terms alone is too shallow, too horizontal—it hides the full measure of the human being whose life has roots in the eternal and the infinite.

Yes, something deep within takes place in our life, buried beneath the flat, constrained habits of our thoughts. He needed to pierce Anna's defenses—to be let in. She must open her heart, the very thing she locked behind her sluggish body. No one, not even her grandmother and uncle, gained entry into her hidden depths. No doubt her world had been blown to bits on that night. To make a breakthrough, he had to win her trust. Then she'd make clear for him the way she sees reality. Only then would he be able to help her sort out her suffering and find a path out of darkness.

Day after day in hourlong sessions, Anna listened without saying a word. He told her stories about himself and his approach, as he sat next to her, often putting his arm around her shoulder. He talked about school, religion, and any topic he believed promising.

"As soon as you feel ready, we'll make a visit to my daughter

Sarah's school, not too far from your home. And you'll want to visit with your uncle and grandmother soon. Do you miss school?" Her progress did not warrant a weekend pass yet.

Anna looked vacantly at the bookshelves. Might she be allowed to have some books? she wondered. How could she go to school—to Sarah's school? She'd already missed many months of study. And her wickedness—she could never talk about that. She was ever mindful of the shame Dr. Leach's encouraging words stirred in her.

Seeing her stare at his books so often he said, "Anna, if there are any books you'd like to borrow, look around and please yourself. Take any you'd like. If you wish, you can have library privileges as soon as I can take you off the acute ward. I'm waiting on you. The library downstairs has many fine books. Miss DeCiantis and Miss Miller tell me you enjoy working with clay. When am I going to see some of your animals?" He was interrupted by a knock on the door. Peggy DeCiantis had come for her.

Peggy took Anna's hand to lead her back to the ward, but Anna pulled back, nearly losing her balance. Her body remained twisted like a cripple's, her eyes glued to the bookshelves. Peggy was baffled.

"Anna," Dr. Leach said, "it's time for Miss DeCiantis to take you back."

Anna pulled away from Peggy, thrusting her body toward the bookshelves, nearly falling over. She regained her balance and, as though sleepwalking, stumbled over to the books. Dr. Leach motioned to Peggy to let her be. Here and there Anna grabbed a book off the shelf till she had five books tucked between her left arm and breast. She turned back toward Peggy and took hold of her hand. Dr. Leach smiled.

Anna kept her self-imposed silence during the weeks that followed, absorbed in one book after another—from one subject to another. At first, reading helped block out her painful world; later she found it comforting.

Dr. Leach kept track of the books she read: poetry, literature, history, encyclopedias, and, when she discovered them, his children's old math and geometry books stored in his office for want of space at home.

Frank's Caper

"Amen!" . . . "Ah!" . . . "Oh!" . . . "Wow!" . . . "Me oh my!"
. . . "My god!" . . . "Jesus save me!" . . . "Amen, mamma!" . . .
"Give me more!" . . . "I'd like a piece of that!" . . .

All heads at Milner's Bar were bent, ogling bare bodies in
carnal contortions on a deck of playing cards that passed down
the long bar, over to the tables, and across to the booths. Frank
Pastori sat rammed up against Etta Boyer in a booth, running
his hand up her thighs.

Before Lillian had taken off for Rose Golanski's, Lillian's
husband Frank had gone to pick up Etta. They'd driven to
Milner's, about four miles from Prospect Hill. Frank had pleased
Etta mightily when he'd moved their long-time affair out of the
shadows into the light of day a few weeks back.

Her get-togethers with Frank had long been hidden, or so
she thought. Lately he told her all his cronies had known about
their affair for years. This pleased her even more. She was tired
of "happening" to meet him at Milner's, using eye contact and
the subtle language of lovers to get together clandestinely. She'd
laughed till her eyes teared over when Frank had told her, "It
took the skill of a damned priest who doesn't believe in God to
carry it off. But you can bet your ass it was worth it." This
would set him off laughing so hard he'd end in a fit of coughing.
No more pretense for Etta. She'd jumped for joy when Frank
told her, "The whole town can go to hell—the Lamberts
included."

During the past few weeks Milner's patrons got a real show
as Frank pawed her while he and she were dancing. She chuckled
when she'd heard that Jim Golanski had told his wife Rose that
Frank had trouble keeping his pants zipped up. She and Frank
were the talk of the town. Only Lillian, Etta thought, was in the
dark.

Frank said he wanted to end his twenty-four-year marriage.
Lillian, he told Etta, was to blame for having connived her way
into his life. Years before they'd courted, they'd meet in passing
to and from work at the Natick Mills. He found himself linked
to Lillian because he humored her when she flirted with him.

The fact was he found her short, dumpy, and unattractive. Encouraged by his friendliness, she found ways to run into him, to walk up the hill beside him, to confide in others his affection for her. Soon both sets of parents got wind of a budding romance and met to talk about a possible match.

The attempt by his and Lillian's parents to arrange a marriage he found laughable. A lure dangled before him gradually infected his judgment. The Lambert family, fairly well off, threw into the marriage bargain the Prospect Hill property—house, barn, and garage on a half-acre plot, plus a five-acre piece of land next to Indian Rock.

Frank's parents played up the advantages of marrying into a respected and prosperous family. Under pressure to consider the offer, Frank gave in to his parents' nagging and engaged himself to Lillian. Getting so much wealth in '29, on the eve of the great depression, crippled his will. His year-long courtship, in the presence of Lillian's parents or sisters and brothers, shielded rather than exposed her temperament. Often since, he had berated himself for his youthful folly. "If I'd've spent just one night alone with her, a thousand acres of land and a palace wouldn't have swayed me," he'd told Etta.

Etta was now floating on air after so many years—anticipating a fuller, more satisfying tie with Frank. A buxom brunette, thirty-five and well over the full flush of youth, she had, up to now, despaired of finding a husband. As Lillian's rival, she prided herself on being younger, less inhibited, more fun-loving, and more able to satisfy Frank's lust.

In Milner's Bar this Saturday afternoon no ordinary deck of playing cards sexually charged the patrons, and an erotic atmosphere infected the place. Sitting in a booth and a bit tipsy, Frank and Etta leered lustfully at images of well-formed bodies in sexual positions promising undreamed-of pleasure. Their eyes met in yearning. He ran his hand up her thighs, gently massaging her. An intense passion burned in them.

Etta looked at Frank and smiled. A balding, handsome man of forty-seven, Frank looked to her a good deal like Eisenhower in his prime. She was amused by his friends who called him "the cocksman on the prowl," a label he wallowed in. She knew she was by no means his only extra-marital partner but believed that would change now that their relationship promised to become stable. She was convinced she could satisfy his enormous craving. Long ago Lillian's family had heard of his adulteries but kept them under cover. They thought that with age he'd become more prudent.

Suddenly Frank got up, stumbled out of the booth, and staggered to the men's room, steadying himself on the walls. He came out with his fly unzipped and sauntered toward the bar. Frank put his hand into his pants and took it out. "How do you like the size of this?" Flashing it around, he challenged his pals to match him. "Come on, let's see you top it." He staggered, his belly laughs giving rise to another fit of coughing.

All eyes turned on Frank as laughter rippled through the barroom. Ray the bartender smiled and pretended to take part in the folly. He came out from behind the bar and, putting his arm around Frank's shoulders, tried steering him back to his booth. "Come on, Frank. Put it away before you lose it," he said.

"Whata you mean 'lose it,' Ray?" Frank pulled away, staggering. "Put up, or shut up."

Ray played along with Frank and, glancing over at Etta, motioned for her to come and help him out. "Let's get him home," he whispered, as Frank turned in a circle, daring the others. "He's already had enough—having a hard time standing."

Frank made a few more turns, proudly displaying his endowment. "Ain't a one of you bastards got such a tool," he boasted. He tried to force it back into his pants and zip up. Etta grabbed him as he tottered, about to fall. He put his arms around her, pulling her into a dance position while grabbing both cheeks of her buttocks. Laughter accompanied their gyrating motions as Frank, overpowering her, used his hands to move her hips and buttocks back and forth in rhythm with his. Helped by a few friends, Etta slowly guided him toward the back door, steadying him as he staggered out to the parking lot. Three men held up his sagging body, bending his bulky frame and pushing him into Etta's car.

Etta drove her trophy home, laughing all the way. Within

hours the townsfolk would be fascinated by Frank's caper at the bar (more than likely embellishing it!), she thought, while Frank'll be oblivious to his grand performance. As for her, Frank's family could go to hell. No longer would she badger him to break ties with Lillian. He'd laid the groundwork for that himself.

Lillian's Self-Condemnation

"Lillian," Frank yelled as he entered the kitchen. "Eddy, Eddy! Where the hell's your mother?" He had sobered up a bit at Etta's.

Eddy ignored him.

"What the hell's going on?" Frank stomped into the living room, to find Lillian staring into space. "Jesus Christ almighty. What the hell gives here?" He grabbed a vase and smashed it on the floor at Lillian's feet. "Where's my supper? A man works like a son of a bitch all week while his wife pisses away her time!"

Eddy rushed in to see what crashed. Seeing his mother slumped in the chair, he put his arm around her. "Ma, Ma! What's wrong?" He tried to shake her. She neither resisted nor spoke.

By this time Frank, noticing her trancelike state, feared the worst. "What's wrong, woman? What happened, Eddy?"

"Nuthin'."

"Did she go anywhere?"

"I think she went over to Rose's."

Frank quickly rang up his mother-in-law and took off to get Mrs. Lambert. Cecilia arrived shortly.

"Ma, what happened? Talk to me." Cecilia began picking up the pieces of the broken vase.

"I think Ralph did something bad," Lillian mumbled, staring at the wall.

"What are you talking about? Ralph's been dead for weeks."

"Anna's pictures . . . she's ten years old . . . love letters . . . two of them . . . Ralph's got a junk box."

"You're not making sense, Ma. What happened?"

Lillian began groaning.

"Please Ma, don't."

Lillian didn't know where the suffocating, choking feeling came from. Suddenly she slid off the chair onto the floor and drew her knees toward her chest, putting herself in a fetal position, trying to rid herself of pain.

Frank returned with Mrs. Lambert to find Cecilia and Eddy standing over Lillian. Mrs. Lambert knelt down and put her arms gently around Lillian's shoulders. "Lillian, where's the pain?" she asked firmly. "Answer me, Lillian! . . . Frank, better call Dr. Calci . . . Cecilia, a pillow for your mother's head . . . Eddy, a glass of water." Mrs. Lambert started to rub her daughter's back gently and to pat her head, as she put the pillow under it and coaxed her to take some water. "It's all right, dear, Dr. Calci will soon be here. Relax my dear."

"Oh, oh!" Lillian began wailing, taking deep breaths.

"Tell me. Where's the pain?"

"All over. Life's full of filth!"

"What filth? You'll be the death of me yet!"

"All over, can't you see it? All over, for God's sake, are you blind? It's all nonsense—all nonsense." She let out a piercing, unnerving laugh.

Mrs. Lambert put her palm to Lillian's forehead to see whether she was running a temperature. Could Lillian be delirious? "Relax, my dear," Mrs. Lambert said, realizing the futility of rebuking or reasoning with her daughter.

A short old man, Dr. Calci, soon came and found the four of them circling Lillian. Mrs. Lambert sat bent over, holding her daughter.

"Well, Lillian, let's have a look," Dr. Calci said, taking his stethoscope, blood pressure cuff, and thermometer out of his black satchel, while noting her bloated face, tired eyes, lack of focus. "Listen, Lillian, I want you to tell me what you're feeling. Where's the pain?"

"I don't know. All over. Can't you find it?" she asked childishly.

Adeptly, Dr. Calci set about taking her pulse, temperature, and blood pressure. They proved normal. "Can you tell me what happened today, Lillian? It's been quite a beautiful day, hasn't it?" He palpated her to find possible physical signs or symptoms.

"It's more than I can bear," Lillian said, letting out a pitiable laugh. Her body heaved with sobs. "I'm just a piece of shit!"

"Please, Lillian," Mrs. Lambert said in an authoritative but gentle voice. "Please, please, my dear."

Frank wished one thing at the moment—to escape to Etta. Cecilia and Eddy looked on, frightened.

Dr. Calci suspected a nervous disorder or a depression brought on by some incident, something fraught with guilt. "I'll give you something to lessen your pain, Lillian." He proceeded to give her a shot of morphine. "You'll soon feel a lot better."

"Listen, Florence . . . Frank," Dr. Calci turned to them in confidence. "Let's get her to bed. The sedative will soon be taking effect—unlikely she's had a fall or fractured anything—no danger in moving her."

Frank, Cecilia, and Eddy slowly eased Lillian up the stairs to her bedroom. By the time they came back down, Dr. Calci had written a prescription.

"She's not running a temperature . . . pulse and pressure normal . . . no irregularities in the heart or lungs . . . no sign of infection anywhere," he said.

"What is it, Doctor? What's wrong?" Frank asked.

"Contents of her speech are abnormal and her conversation full of pessimistic thoughts—fears, expressions of worthlessness, guilt. I think she's in depression; probably a reaction to some circumstance. Anything out of the ordinary happen today?"

"Not that I know. Seems she visited Rose Golanski, that's all," Frank said.

"I wasn't around," Cecilia noted.

Eddy shrugged.

Dr. Calci kept a close check on Lillian for the next few weeks. He cautioned Frank that the depression could last for months.

On one of his visits he told Frank: "She's helpless and disheartened. If it goes on, she's going to find it hard to concentrate or carry out routine tasks. Watch for signs of suicide. If it's a long-term bout, you'll have to think, Frank, of psychiatric treatment for her. You might notice a mood shift from depression to mania—she'll become upbeat and life will look all rosy, for a time. It may not last long: she might revert to depression."

Anna opens up

Anna showed interest in reading and in occupational therapy. Her bearing gradually improved but, after months of therapy, she still had not spoken.

One day, Dr. Leach talked to her about his crystal theory. "You know, Anna, every person is like a crystal—like a gem. Each has a mind made up of many facets, and each facet takes in the light of life as we take in the light of the sun. And this crystal bends the light coming into it into rays that shoot out from it like stars. You know, Anna, each person is unique. Each is like a special gem. No two people are born exactly alike. Yes, all of us are small universes with the light of life shining in us and, at the same time, giving off the light of life to the world."

"What if there's something black at the center of the crystal?" Anna asked in a scratchy voice. "The rays of life wouldn't come in and nothing would bend back." She'd talked. She felt relieved. There was so much she wanted to talk to Dr. Leach about.

He went on as if nothing had changed. "It's not possible, Anna. The crystal is transparent. Most remarkable of all: nothing can darken its center from the outside. Its facets, of course, may get grimed up, blocking some of life's rays."

Anna was silent for some time and then said morosely: "I've been hiding inside my crystal."

"I'm happy to see you bend back some of those rays of light. Tell me about your crystal self." He got up and pulled an armchair next to the couch to sit facing her. His heart nearly skipped several beats when he looked at her. Her rigid contorted body had come alive. She looked up at him with tears in her eyes. His face beamed when he saw a hint of a smile on her lips.

"I had a dream last night."

"Am I going to be lucky enough to hear about it?"

"You were in it," she said, looking up sheepishly to weigh his response. After months of being with him, she'd come to trust him. Every day she looked forward to his stories, to his kind efforts to amuse her. She didn't want to disappoint him.

"Well, you've got my undivided attention. Don't hold out on me." The psychological bridge had been partially built; he now hoped the healing could begin.

"You were a priest in gold and green brocade." She looked up at him, testing him.

"And what was I up to in my new calling?"

"You'll think I'm silly?"

"I'll think nothing of the sort."

"My grandmother used to help me make sense of my dreams."

"Yes, your grandmother's a fine woman. But this dream, you can't mean to keep it from me." He sensed her desire to confide in him.

"It was the happiest day of my life. My mother had made matching gowns—mine in green, hers in pink . . ." She became pensive.

"We must've been very colorful: you in green, your mother in pink, and me in green and gold. What were we doing?"

"We were walking toward you down a long aisle . . ." She took several deep breaths as if weighing the risk of going on. "My brother Alex was giving Mamma away in marriage to Uncle Peter. I walked behind as her maid of honor. Uncle Peter stood next to our neighbor Paul Risch, the best man. They walked out of the sacristy and stood next to you, waiting for us. The marriage was finally taking place and . . ." She stopped as though faced by a stone wall and sobbed, her body heaving as if to dispel the evil she bore within.

Dr. Leach moved back to the couch and drew her head to his shoulder, letting her cry. He reached over, took some tissues from his desk, and passed them to her.

"My mother seemed sad," she said sobbing. "You looked at her and said, 'Your daughter won't leave you, Demeter. Don't fret so!' Who's Demeter? I want my mamma! I want my mamma!" Tears streamed down her face.

"I know. I know. Let it out." Quickly he rifled through his mind, trying to hit upon the name Demeter. From deep in his memory from college days, he recalled the myth of the goddess, Demeter—the Greek goddess of agriculture and family life.

After some time had passed, he said, "Anna, I've been

thinking . . ."

"Yes, Doctor Leach?" She still sobbed.

"Would you like to visit your uncle Peter and your grandmother this weekend?"

"You mean it?"

"Would I say it if I didn't?"

"Will I meet Sarah sometime?" She remembered he'd promised to take her to Sarah's school.

"Should I call your grandmother for this weekend? We'll talk about Sarah's school later. When you get back. Okay?"

"Yes, I'd like it. Thank you."

He went to his bookshelf and grabbed Edith Hamilton's book, *Mythology: Timeless Tales of Gods and Heroes*. He thumbed through it to see whether there was anything on the goddess Demeter and her daughter Persephone. There were. He scanned the story:

> *Demeter had an only daughter, Persephone, who was the maiden of spring. Somehow she had been lost to her mother . . . the daughter was abducted by the ruler of the underworld, Hades, and taken to the underworld. The mother petitioned the great god Zeus to get her daughter back . . . Zeus, moved by compassion, pleaded with his brother Hermes, who was guide and protector of souls, to secure Persephone's release . . . The angry mother forsook heaven and dwelt on earth . . . The ruler of the underworld agreed to release the daughter on condition that she return to the home of the dead four months each year . . . During Persephone's absence, her mother, Demeter, and all mankind had to endure the death brought on by winter when the maiden of spring slipped back to Hades.*

Anna's working through her relations with her mother, he thought. What a dream. How had a child this age come across the name Demeter? He decided to hold off approaching this subject. He handed the book to her.

"I'd like to know what you think of the story about Demeter and her daughter, Persephone? Will you read it?" There was a knock on the door as Delia Miller came for Anna.

Lillian's Suffering

Father D. was putting some finishing touches on his Sunday sermon—"The Gift, Mystery, and Struggle of Life"—when his thoughts were interrupted by a knock on the door.

Lillian Pastori was ushered into the study by his housekeeper, Mrs. Sassi. He looked up to see Lillian thin, gaunt, and stooped over like a prisoner sent before the warden. She seemed confused and worried.

"Thank you, Mrs. Sassi," he said, getting up and approaching Lillian, who stood awkward and ill at ease. "Well, well, well, Lillian Pastori. Come, sit, please." He pulled a chair up beside his desk.

"Hello, Father," she said, looking down clutching her purse with both hands. Slowly she sat down, hardly moving her body. She stared at the floor.

For a woman in her early forties, she looked haggard, with dark circles around her eyes and a sagging chin. He knew that for months she'd been depressed. Frank consented to therapy for her, for involutional melancholia, a variant of manic-depression, against the wishes of Lillian's mother, who considered the treatment barbaric. According to Lillian's psychiatrist, an electric current through her temples—twenty treatments—would rid her of troubling memories, reduce her anxiety, and ready her for some form of talk therapy.

"How are you feeling? Good to see you in church last Sunday," Father D. said, dismayed by the change in her bearing.

Without raising her head, she stole a glance at him for a second and lowered her eyes. "I'm feeling better—somewhat."

"Healing takes time." He'd been in contact with Mrs. Lambert, who, after Lillian's discharge from the hospital, looked after her. Gradually Mrs. Lambert convinced her daughter of the healing power of prayer. A month after her release, Lillian, at the insistence of her mother, consented to meet with him. "Your mother's concerned about you."

"I don't know what I would've done without her," she said sadly.

"Your mother's pretty spry—she's getting on in years," Father

D. said, to make conversation. It was obvious Lillian hadn't come of her own volition.

"Sixty-six. She works circles around me."

"I hear Tony's doing well at West Warwick High." Her old exuberant self was gone—as if the gift of life had taken flight, he thought.

"He's keeping up with school work . . . loves sports." She fidgeted with her handbag and stared at the floor.

"Are you through with your treatments?"

"More like torture . . ." A trace of life seeped into her voice. Father D. waited. "They call it treatment—strange way to treat you . . ."

"What treatment? Electroshock?"

"More like electrocution." She glanced up at him. "I can't remember much—wonder where I am sometimes . . . what's going on . . . forgotten so many things . . ."

He'd heard one of the prevailing theories about electroconvulsive therapy: to erase recent memories close to the surface of consciousness and, following each treatment, to imprint happy or loving thoughts. All this, in the name of "curing" depression, he thought.

"Time's a good healer, Lillian. In a little time, you'll be back, fit as a fiddle."

"Yeah, hear that all the time. Got plenty of time, for sure. Life's pretty damn empty—excuse me, Father—lonely . . ." She eyed the large crucifix on the wall behind the desk.

"You used to be the life of the hill—lots of friends." He'd heard by now some of her gossip about Felicia Benedicta. "How are things going on the hill?"

"Dunno."

"What do you think happened, Lillian? What do you think brought this change in you?"

"Shame . . . guilt," she whispered.

"What did you say?"

"I dunno . . . I . . . I'm . . . full of guilt."

"Well, now, have you thought—guilt can be a good teacher for us, Lillian?" he said. She looked at him baffled. "Truly. For all of us. Goodness gracious, where would we be without guilt?

Do you know? Some people do wrong and don't feel guilt. Now, there's a real problem for you." He wanted to lighten her mood.

"What do you mean? Not feeling guilt is worse than feeling guilt?" Her eyes widened.

Lillian's passing through a crisis, he thought. Her trials and tribulations should help form and shape her spirit—should help her gain some sense about life. But, sadly, such suffering is often stillborn—it leaves little or no trace, like footprints in the sand blown away by the next storm. Surely her moral affliction can, with some reflection, afford her an opportunity for growth and understanding. But her mind, like most people's, may not stir despite acute suffering. This he found to be a disheartening part of his job. Too many lack introspection—gaining little from their daily struggles. Many become more impaired by them. Others, few though they may be, learn and grow spiritually. Could it be, he thought, that some people are given a gift or may be chosen to become enlightened? The question had always baffled him. Who could say at this point whether or not Lillian would profit from her plight?

"Good Lord, Lillian, if people felt guilt for their wrongdoing, there'd be a lot less suffering in this world." He didn't want to be flippant, but he needed to shake her up. "You see, when we do something wrong and don't feel guilty, we sort of build up toxins in our soul—we bottle and cork them up and they stew and brew. And what do these devilish toxins brew into? Well—loneliness, yearning, fears, anxieties, depression—all sorts of nasty feelings we can't quite understand or figure out. Now, when we do something wrong and we feel guilty—well, you see, you know where the pain is coming from. Uh, huh, we say. I know what provoked that nasty feeling. I did such and such. And darned if I'm going to do that again. No, siree, we say, I'm going to avoid that one. And, sure enough, we say an Act of Contrition and the Lord's Prayer, asking for forgiveness and for strength against temptations." Lillian perked up as if something had bounced off her head.

"When we suffer from guilt, Lillian, something is nudging us to learn something about ourselves—like a teacher who nags at us to read properly or do our math. Do you see? To be sure, not all guilt is healthy. But one thing is certain: we can't live in guilt. We ought not dwell on it. We have to rise above it—learn from it. What wrong did you do?" He sneaked the question in without warning. "Do you want to talk about it?"

"Envy, jealousy, I guess—led me to foolishness—to worse than foolishness," she mumbled almost inaudibly.

"Lord help us," he said smiling. "We all pass down that road once in a while, more often than is good for us. Well, let me tell you, Lillian Pastori, shame, guilt, envy, jealousy—these are all part of being human. There's a Latin saying that anybody who advances in wisdom knows and takes to heart—*nihil humanum me alienum:* nothing human is alien to me, or to you, or to each of us. Anyhow, in our emptiness we imagine that if we have what the person we envy has—we'll be fulfilled; if we get the love the person we are jealous of gets—we'll be happy."

Her jealousy of Felicia, he surmised, was nothing more than her loneliness—a lack of feeling loved; her envy—a repressed admiration for Felicia's more enlightened and fulfilled life.

"But you see, Lillian Pastori, envy and jealousy teach us about errors in our thinking and living." She didn't respond but she listened.

"It's not that we're bad. Dear Lord, the whole world would be bad if it were judged for its envy and jealousy. No. No. It's that we live in error. You're not condemned if you fall into error," he said. "After all, we are all connected to God, to the ground of life, whatever we might do in ignorance or in sin. Do you understand, Lillian?"

"No I don't, Father. Suppose you've done something bad?" She sat twisting the straps of her handbag.

"Well, you need to repent and to get absolution through confession, contrition, and prayer." He saw a spark of hope flicker in her face. He wished to drive the point home. He wanted to tell her about his God: about forgiveness and love, about being forgiven ad infinitum, about the power that re-virginizes and makes us whole and pure through faith and forgiveness.

"Shame, guilt, loneliness—these result from ignorance and sin and can be overcome, Lillian. They're not inborn, not part of our nature, but tendencies we all fall into when we're not careful. It's our job as human beings to struggle against them. You see, Lillian, if in cutting a piece of bread you hold the knife upside down and you cut your finger, it hurts. So, too, do we hurt from our sin—the pain of guilt, shame, emptiness for the bad we've done. Our soul, like our finger, needs to be healed."

"So people can do bad things without paying a price for it. Merely confess it and it's all over?"

"Good God, no. Not at all," he said, smiling at her innocence. "Oh, dear, please don't misunderstand me. Whenever we're in error there's always a price, whether we recognize it or not. Indeed, when we make mistakes we all pay a price. You see, in your envy and jealousy you probably hurt somebody. Right? And you're now paying a price." He didn't want to push her to see more clearly what her heart knew so well.

"What is the price, Father?"

"Why the things you've told me: emptiness, guilt, shame. But you know, Lillian, life's a gift given to us and a gift that's going to be taken away some day. It's a sin not to enjoy it. We must live lovingly—in our family and with our neighbors. *Nisi Dominus frusta.*"

"What's that, Father?"

"Unless God be with you, all is in vain. I mean that nothing, no thing in this world—whatever you were envious or jealous of—can satisfy you. Do you understand me? Only one thing can bring about well-being—can make us happy."

"What could that be?" she asked, aroused by the lure of happiness. Her body had straightened and life seemed to be flowing through again.

"Only one thing, for sure. Living in love, in the gratitude for the life given us, living in harmony with other human beings who make our life possible. Only a loving life can bring us peace and fulfillment. Envy and jealousy are like sicknesses. We must try to keep them under control and get rid of them—"

"I can't make sense of it."

He saw a glow in her eyes that told a different story. A dim awareness was taking hold. She was more relaxed.

She asked him to hear her confession and give her absolution for her sins.

Anna's Progress

Anna began going home on weekends. Yet it took several months before she opened up again. Dr. Leach held off setting a date for her to visit Classical High, where his daughter Sarah went. Piero and Assunta agreed to send her there when she was released from Butler. It depended on her recovery.

Anna set up a strict study routine for herself. She formed a friendship with Mrs. Tuttle, a former teacher married to a minister, not too much older than her mother. Afflicted with hebephrenia, a form of schizophrenia, Mrs. Tuttle—a minister's wife taking care of three sons—could not cope with the demands of the outside world. Hospitalized, she seemed more adjusted to life. Once discharged, her speech would become bizarre or incoherent, her behavior strange and silly: meaningless smiles, grimaces, childish giggles, and sudden fits of laughing. She'd lose all concern for her personal appearance and ignore basic rules of social conduct. Anna read to her every evening. Sometimes she just sat with Mrs. Tuttle and chatted.

Anna formed links with other patients and soon found herself at the beck and call of many. She suggested to Mrs. Tuttle that they set up an evening reading group to include Mrs. Adams and Mrs. Petrella. Mrs. Tuttle said no. "They'll disturb the reading."

"But Mrs. Tuttle," Anna argued gently, "they'd like to join us. You can still pick out the books. I know you'd like to hear *Silas Marner.* I promise that if they disturb us, I won't read to them."

"If you insist, Anna, but you'd better stick to your promise!"

Impressed by Anna's love of reading, Dr. Leach needed to draw her out. Could reading be an obsession? Was it an escape from reality? Her general appearance improved greatly—she looked wholesome and alive.

She came into the session in a well-fitting skirt and matching blouse, her hair nicely combed, her cheeks and lips slightly red. Was she responding to the staff's habitual encouragement to take an interest in "grooming"? Or was it her own natural color returning?

"Tell me about your group, Anna? What are you reading to Mrs. Tuttle and the others?"

"Mrs. Tuttle likes books by George Eliot. We're reading *Silas Marner.*"

"I see. Mrs. Petrella and Mrs. Adams have joined?"

"Yes. They hardly talk to one another, but they listen." She smiled.

"What are you yourself reading these days?" Dr. Leach kept tabs on her selections from his collection and from the library: Emily Brontë's *Wuthering Heights*, Charles Dickens's *David Copperfield*, Jane Austen's *Emma*, Nathaniel Hawthorne's *Scarlet Letter.* Not exactly kid stuff.

"*Jane Eyre.*"

"Have you always been interested in novels?"

"Yes, but I read mostly . . . well . . . stories friends were reading. Our sixth-grade teacher made us take out one book a week from the Natick Library.

"And now? What authors are you drawn to?"

"The Brontë sisters. I like *Jane Eyre*; *Wuthering Heights*—a frightening story, hard to understand . . . some Dickens. I keep wishing the poor could live the way the rich do," she said, frowning. Maybe she took these stories too seriously. These writers, didn't they tell us something about life? She asked, "Has it always been so, Dr. Leach? Some people seem to do all the work; others do all the living."

"What do you mean?"

"Well in Jane Eyre, Mr. Rochester is a good man and all, Jane is a good and honest woman. Yet the servants are pushed around as if . . . as if they're nobody—less than human."

"I think I see what you're getting at. But surely Mr. Rochester, a gentleman, suffers greatly. Doesn't he?"

"Yes, that's true," she admitted half-heartedly. Yet, something puzzled her. "Poor people suffer terrible accidents, just as Mr. Rochester did, but . . . but in his case he's wealthy. He gets lots of help. Jane goes back to him and marries him. The poor are left homeless, sick, starving. No one seems to care about them."

"Maybe Charlotte Brontë's trying to get us to see the unfairness many suffer."

"Well, it's just a story," she said, as if to lay the matter to rest.

"Stories may teach us about life and its meaning," Dr. Leach said to test her.

That's it—artists are teachers, kind of, she thought. George Eliot's *Middlemarch* came to mind. Timidly, she voiced a view she'd been mulling over for some time. "Wealthy parents—those with the best of everything—suffer from worrying about their children's marriages: getting more money and moving up in society. Love seems to be the least of it." She thought of her mother being disinherited because of marrying her father.

Anna's reading of literary works, and the depth of her insights, astonished Dr. Leach. Her interest in history, mathematics, and geometry, too. "Anna, tell me about math and geometry. Do you enjoy them as much as literature?"

"You'll think I'm silly . . ."

"Silly?"

"They tell me a story. History too." She looked at Dr. Leach to see if he'd ridicule her.

"A story? What about?"

"About how things . . . about how everything is made."

"How is that."

"Well, whatever I see . . . you know—buildings, cars, clothes, roads, things—I wonder how they got here," she said, feeling foolish expressing a thought hardly understandable.

"How does history and math fit in?"

"Well, this building—where are the people who made it? You can't see them even when you're living inside it."

"You mean this building has a history?"

"You could say that." Anna's faced reddened. "But more than a history, I think." She was mystified by her own remark. What could she mean? It had to do with an idea that had been forming in her mind for some time. "It's the living people I was thinking of—all those who planned and built this hospital. People with families, getting up every morning, coming to work. When we see this building, all we see stands without the life that made it—all those having thoughts and wishes and feelings, who laughed and cried, who rushed around." Wasn't this building once a thought in the mind of its architect? she asked herself.

Her own life tormented her. Her mother and father, her village of Natick, her friends Cecilia and Paul—all were lost to her. Yet her life could not be what it was without them. She had them in her, hidden. They formed a part of her, yet she stood apart from them—lost to them.

"I think I see," Dr. Leach said. "You mean this building is the residue of all the activity of living people—the architects, laborers, craftsmen—hidden from our view, their past activity is in the structure, a structure that could not exist without it." He saw what she meant. Written history reduces reality to words and ideas, but the living event itself—the actual thoughts and activities giving birth to reality—is visible only to the mind's eye. "How does math fit in?"

"Well, we can't see math either. Math and geometry in the building are invisible—just like all the workers and their thoughts that made it—no one sees them. These buildings couldn't have been made without math and geometry." She blushed. These ideas might sound absurd to Dr. Leach, she feared. "I wonder . . ."

"Wonder?"

"When we see this building, do we see reality? I mean—all of its reality?" Again Anna stopped, worried what Dr. Leach would think.

"What do you mean?"

"I'm afraid I get silly ideas." After some time, she went on. "You see, I got this idea—it sort of snuck into my mind—we only see a part of reality. We never see all of it."

"And which part is that? Which part do we see?"

Looking down, she smiled shyly. "Well . . . the end, I suppose—what comes from all the work people do and all the thoughts and ideas needed to do it." She didn't herself know exactly what she meant. Her mother's death convinced her that appearances are the outer face of some mysterious workings— not fully knowable.

"I see," Dr. Leach said pensively. "Behind everything there's something hidden. *Who* do the creating and *how* they do it can't be seen when we see the things created?"

Anna shook her head. It seemed like a muddle to her. Deep down, she knew this must be true of her own life and of her mother's death. Her thoughts went back to that dreadful night and she suddenly withdrew into herself.

He saw a look of fright on her face and didn't press her further. She'd been working out the mystery of her mother's death. Having suffered terrible grief and now freed from structured learning, she'd been searching on her own for answers. Not only did this draw her to novels touching on life's problems, but it moved a gifted child to look into the tragic nature of the human condition. He felt she would soon be ready to talk about her mother's murder.

Lillian and Frank

Soon after her visit with Fr. DiSanto, Lillian began to go to mass with her mother on holy days. Feeling more energetic one evening, she primped, made Frank's favorite meal, set the dining-room table with the best dishes, and sent Eddy off to Petrella's bakery for fresh bread.

"My God, Lillian, you outdid yourself," Frank said, happy to see the kindling of life in her. Since the day she visited Rose Golanski, he'd been walking on pins and needles. Mrs. Lambert had given him a good piece of her mind when she learned about the obscene romp at Milner's Bar.

"We have to celebrate once in a while, don't we?" Lillian grinned at him now.

"Well, what are we celebrating?" Frank asked in good humor, amused by her childlikeness.

"Living . . . life, I guess."

"Well, damn good that . . . yeah, let's celebrate life. I need me a few brews to make the celebration official!" he said.

It took many months for Lillian to have more and more days of sunshine and fewer and fewer days of darkness. Propped up by Father D. and her mother, she slowly joined the land of the living, but her will had been broken and her heart clung to the tree of ritual. Of religion's roots she was no more the wiser. Now under the guidance of an external authority she lost much of her need to rake others over the coals. She stayed at home more and was less inclined to feel envy and jealousy. In her former days she strove for the heights—for admiration, acceptance, and love. Now she settled for the plains: her hills and valleys had been levelled and she resigned herself to a routine life.

Frank went through a crisis of his own. He had told his mother-in-law several months back that he intended to leave Lillian. Mrs. Lambert warned him that that course would bring him grief. Frank soon came to see what she meant when he experienced his children's resentment and his friends' disapproval.

Once it leaked out that he wanted to leave Lillian for Etta, his friends seemed to shun him. He found that while they overlooked his promiscuity, they strongly disapproved of divorce. Their scorn soon forced him to accept the bitter dregs of those original vows—"for better or for worse."

He saw now that if he left Lillian, he'd cut himself off from his friends. Their will to ostracize him, he believed, came from their being trapped in their own loveless marriages. Lacking the courage to free themselves for a better life, they resented others doing so. His divorce would have threatened their own marriages. He felt locked in a social prison.

He and Etta drifted apart: he out of fear, she out of shame. Her "friends" no longer viewed her as fun-loving and out to have a good time, but as a home-wrecker. Both Frank and Etta learned that divorce was not a real option in a small town. Frank saw that he'd had the freedom to marry in youthful ignorance, but not the freedom to divorce in midlife disappointment.

Recalling the Tragedy

Dr. Leach could see Anna becoming more cheerful and blossoming into a gifted adolescent—a far cry from the haunted, frightened child of nearly a year earlier.

Several months had passed since her breakthrough. He'd been waiting for an opportunity to get back to her dream about the goddess Demeter, centered as it is on the relationship between mother and daughter. Suddenly it sprang up in the middle of a session.

". . . poor Demeter, she suffered so much when she lost her daughter, Persephone—four months every year at wintertime. But winter needn't be so sad."

His ears perked up. "True today. But in ancient times?"

She looked away pensively, ignoring his question. When she started to speak, it was as though she were trying to relate the story of Demeter and her daughter to her own plight—as if talking to herself. "Persephone, the maiden of spring, brought new life each spring. When she was away, her mother Demeter, the goddess of all living things, felt death in everything. But winter's a time for rest and closeness. I remember Christmas and winters, snug at home: warm and cozy during the long cold months."

"Anna, do you want to talk about *it?*" She's ready to take the plunge, he thought.

There was a long silence. Tears trickled down her cheeks; her eyes were glued to the floor. Pent-up emotions erupted in her. Could she bring herself to talk about that morning? Self-doubt clutched at her and she couldn't answer. How could she? What did she know? Fighting her darkest fears, she heard herself whispering, "Yes."

"Good."

After another long silence, she spoke in a whisper. "That night—the happiest in my life." Her voice trembled. All at once, like the bursting of a dam, a surge of suppressed memories streamed into consciousness. She forgot where she was. She was back home that horrible morning of March 25. Her body stiffened and her eyes glazed over.

"Anna, tell me—what's happening?" He saw fright come across her face.

Anna heard him. But images flashed through her like slides from a projector rushing by, making her dizzy. Then one stopped and, as a camera lens zoomed in, the image of her mother's bloody body on the floor enlarged in her mind, forcing out everything else. Grief shot through her as it had on that terrible morning.

"Anna! What's happening?"

"I was mean . . . my mother slapped me . . . I wouldn't disobey her. We hugged and kissed . . . I felt so sorry . . . But I didn't know my mother suffered—people gossiped about her," Anna said, her voice full of terror. "My mother tried to tell me why she was strict with me. I wasn't like Persephone. I wasn't going to be taken from her by the mean people who were hurting her. I wouldn't leave her . . . like . . ." She reached over for some tissues from Dr. Leach's desk.

"Leave her?"

"As she left her parents." She felt a slight relief coming over her. Slowly, she gained her composure and shifted back to the present, her face reshaping itself. She looked up at Dr. Leach. "We had a wonderful talk. Mamma explained many things to me—the nobility and her family. One thing I wanted to know: Was she going to marry Uncle Peter? I was sure they loved each other. I told her Uncle Peter loved her and she should marry him. Then she made me so happy when she smiled and called me a noseybody. I knew the answer by the sparkle in her eyes. I was happy for her and Uncle Peter."

"What happened to your uncle's letter?"

"I never saw or heard about the letter until later . . . after . . ."

"After?"

"That night . . ."

"What happened that night?"

"I went to bed happy and woke up to hear my brother Alex running downstairs, screaming—Mamma é morta! Mamma é morta! Mamma is dead!" Anna burst into tears.

"Let it all out, Anna. It's all right. Don't hold it in." He moved to the couch and drew her head to his shoulder.

Anna strained to get control of herself, to tell Dr. Leach about the shock of waking up and finding her mother's body. She needed to get rid of it—like nausea before throwing up. "In a daze, I woke up to find blood smeared on my bed. I was terrified." The words sprang from her in spurts between sobs. "I rushed into the hallway to see my mother's feet on the floor . . . coming out the living-room door . . . I saw her body . . . in a pool of blood . . . dried up . . . our bread knife was next to her . . . I lay down beside her and hugged her . . . her body was cold. I got up, picked up the knife, thinking I'd clean up the mess, and fell into a rocking chair . . . I seemed to fall into some sort of a trance."

Her body heaved with sobs, but he urged her to get the hidden memories out in the open, to bring them into the light of day. "That's all right. That's all right," he said, waiting for her to stop. "Now tell me, what do you mean—you fell into a trance?"

"Everything became unreal—like a movie going on before me. I could hear people talking, but I couldn't enter in. I couldn't answer. I wouldn't answer. I thought if I answered it might be true—my mother might be dead . . ."

"Yes?"

"Then a change came over me. I could hear people saying I did it. I was to blame. I had killed my mother. How could I do such a thing? No, it's a dream, I said to myself. I must wake up. I couldn't wake up. I felt frozen, watching a horror show going on before me . . ." She paused, her face contorted by pain.

"Please, go on."

"The hordes."

"What hordes?"

"Hordes of people trooping through our house, looking into everything . . . questioning me. Fingerprints . . . Where's Piero's letter? . . . Why'd you do it? I rocked back and forth, back and forth, fighting back the terrible thought. 'Maybe I did do it. In my sleep? Why?' As long as I rocked, just looking at them as though I were watching a movie, I thought I might be saved." Anna's sobbing kept her from going on.

Dr. Leach waited for her to calm down. "Couldn't you confide in your grandmother and uncle?"

"I was afraid to say anything. Maybe it's true, I thought. I had no father. Now I had no mother. I mustn't enter that world, ever. I prayed for help, and every time the thought crossed my mind—'I must've done it'—I prayed and prayed to be saved. And in my prayers I found comfort. No, I must not enter that awful world—ever again."

"Tell me more about this comfort?"

"My world had turned upside down—the inside became real, the outside, unreal. How could I enter into that moving picture? No more than you would think of being able to enter a movie projected onto a screen."

"The comforting?"

"My grandmother had taught me to say . . . to say . . ."

"To say?"

"A prayer—the Jesus Prayer. You see, pain seemed to eat into me—all over. How could I live without my mother? The Jesus Prayer gave me comfort."

"I see."

"My grandmother and her friend Florence Lambert are very religious—Mrs. Lambert, especially. Often they'd talk about prayer. Sometimes they'd talk about the dark night of the soul." A memory of Mrs. Lambert in her grandmother's kitchen reciting the Jesus Prayer flashed through her mind. She could see Mrs. Lambert's face full of love. "I was hurting so much. Mrs. Lambert told Nonna that saying the Jesus Prayer brings about the Holy presence of Our Lord and that saying His Holy Name makes you feel his divine energy inside."

"You felt the prayer helping you?"

"Every time I prayed, I felt . . . comforted. That's a word Mrs. Lambert used to use. Praying eased my pain. Cecilia, Mrs. Lambert's granddaughter, had told me that her grandmother said the rosary every day as she stood and faced a crucifix above her bed. I made a cross out of palm leaves Nonna got on Palm Sunday and stood in front of my bed every day and said the rosary. Praying kept the world outside from coming in and hurting me."

"How did your uncle and grandmother react to you, isolated in your sealed-off world?"

"I knew they worried . . . but I felt . . ."

"Yes?"

"Unworthy. I must've done something bad. But something deep inside told me that the people in the movie going on about me—these people were wrong. Why would I kill my mother?"

"Who could've done it?"

"I don't know. My mother was so beautiful and kind. I can't think anybody'd want to hurt her."

Gradually Anna calmed down, feeling better for having finally shared her dark secret.

He needed to probe a bit further. "You lived in your crystal self then. Tell me about your dream of Demeter?"

"It's a dream. That's all." She blushed.

"I know. But who is she?"

"My mother? My mother's worry—like Demeter's I think—came from her fear that I'd leave her, the way she left her parents. Her strictness with me and Alex—she was afraid we'd . . . or maybe we'd hear the gossip about her . . . I don't know."

"She left her parents?"

"I never heard much about it. It had to do with getting married to my father. He was a commoner. She's from the nobility."

Slowly Anna began to recover her composure. The glow on her face and the tenderness of her words gave her an air of a person far older than fourteen. Dr. Leach, seeing her strength return, asked about the redheaded priest in her dream.

"I don't know."

"You're holding out on me."

"It's his green and gold vestment . . ."

"Tell me about it."

"Well, I think . . . green stood for life, gold for truth?" This idea popped into her thoughts. "Yes," she smiled, pleased with herself, "you, in a priest's habit, could wash away the dirt on the crystal facets—then the truth of life could shine in." Anna laughed at herself. She felt a release from the pain of guilt which, like a toothache, had not left her since that dreadful day. In its place, she sensed something long absent—the surging of life within her.

Dr. Leach smiled at her intuition. "And, don't forget—shine out, too," he added of the crystal self.

Anna's Release

Anna found herself recovering more memories. In sharing her inner thoughts and emotions with Dr. Leach she grew stronger and more sure of herself.

She kept studying, preparing to return to school. Aptitude tests placed her in math, history, and literature at the eleventh-grade level; but Dr. Leach, in consultation with the school principal, decided she should be put in the tenth grade. In two years she'd have advanced from the sixth to the tenth.

Upon Dr. Leach's advice, Piero and Assunta sent Anna, under the name Mary Anne Benedict, to Classical High. He persuaded the family and juvenile court to be mindful of the need to safeguard her identity. Interest in her alleged crime, he warned, could once again catapult her into the limelight, and this, he said, should be avoided at all costs.

Anna didn't take lightly to changing her name. Dr. Leach convinced her that it reflected, less drastically, the change she'd undergone, and that she, like her name, retained her most significant part—her roots.

More than a year had passed since she entered Butler, and nearly two years since her mother's death. Patiently, she peered out the window waiting for Uncle Peter, Nonna, and Alex to take her home for good.

Dr. Leach sent a report to juvenile court:

Re: Anna Maria Benedicta, Butler Hospital
Committed by order of the Juvenile Court,
State of Rhode Island: September 1950.
Discharged: December 1951.

This is to inform the Rhode Island Juvenile Court that the above-named has been discharged from Butler Hospital into the care of Mrs. Assunta Benedicta, her grandmother, and Mr. Piero Benedicta, her uncle. She is attending Classical High School, having been enrolled, upon successful completion of achievement tests, as a sophomore. With the permission of the court clerk, she has been enrolled under the name Mary Anne Benedict, to protect her privacy.

Anna no longer suffers from severe depression exacerbated by profound grief over her mother's death. I am convinced, after months of seeing her in therapy, that she was not her mother's assailant in the early hours of March 25, 1950.

The prognosis for Anna is, I believe, very good. She has a firm religious and moral foundation and is a precocious adolescent. I am confident that she will excel academically.

Any further information warranted by the court will be supplied upon request.

Daniel Leach, M. D.

A few months later Dr. Leach dispatched a letter to Anna:

Dear Anna,

The court clerk informs me that the "Benedicta Case" has been closed and sealed at the time of your release from Butler. I am happy to tell you that any allegations brought against you or judgments rendered have been removed from your record and are not available to any court or police district in the land. According to the law, "Any evidence given in the court shall not be admissible as evidence against the child in any case or proceeding in any other court, nor shall such disposition or evidence operate to disqualify a child in any future civil service application, examination or appointment." In other words, you will have no legal record.

From a personal point of view, of course, you may not be fully satisfied without a full accounting of the tragedy. My advice to you is to put this terrible misfortune behind you. I am confident that, given your emotional, intellectual, and spiritual strength, you will direct your considerable talents toward a full and rewarding life. I hope that you will never forget that truth resides in the eyes of God, not in the imperfect judgment of the law.

If I can ever be of any help, please feel free to call on me.

Sincerely,
Daniel Leach, M. D.

5
Bewildered in
Providence and Rome

Much had changed on Prospect Hill in the seven years since Felicia's death.

Some families had moved away and others had come to live among us. People kept to themselves and fewer people visited me on my porch. I spent much of my time reading or visiting Father D., who shared his personal library with me.

Lillian and Frank Pastori still lived in the same house. The Mansours, who lived across from them, sold their property and moved to another village.

More wives on the hill began to work, and many folk took to feathering their nest as money became easier to get. Lillian herself took a part-time job as cashier at Natick Grocery and liked working to augment the family income.

The mills in the town had shut down—West Warwick no longer produced textiles. People now worked in many industries all over the state. The main shopping center, Arctic, had lost its prominence as many shopped in the new discount stores, to buy their clothes and household goods. Supermarkets sprang up all over and put most small family-run groceries out of business.

Paul Risch's family had moved to Providence not long after the Benedictas. Paul went to LaSalle High and then on to Brown

University, where he played varsity football and baseball.

Tony and Cecilia Pastori finished high school in West Warwick. Tony entered Brown University, and Cecilia Bryant College, where she struck up a close friendship with Rachel Mansour. Eddy Pastori hung around the house when not doing odd jobs for Louie's Tavern or for his parents. He became more and more withdrawn after Ralph Mullen died.

Rose and Jim Golanski, Ralph Mullen's sister and brother-in-law, still lived on one of the lanes off Prospect Hill.

Alberta, after she completed secretarial studies, became head secretary for the West Warwick Police. Dante Giorgio, a police officer who helped investigate Felicia's murder, still worked for the West Warwick Police.

After Anna finished Classical High, she left for Rome with her grandmother and uncle. Alex had gone to live with the count and countess the year before.

Paul's Predicament

Standing in line to register for classes, Paul and Tony argued, oblivious to others staring at them. Paul had suddenly decided to quit playing baseball. They'd been teammates since the fall of '54, freshman year.

"Come on, Paul—dropping out a month before practice begins. Geez, be reasonable. What a break for the Brown Bruins!"

Paul tried for nearly an hour to explain his reasons without making it clear what they were. Paul wasn't sure himself. "What can I say? I'm not up to it. Let's leave it at that." Tony was disappointed. "I'm up to my neck in coursework and medical school applications coming up . . . and . . ." Paul stopped as if he'd hit a wall.

"And what?"

"Nothing."

"How are you going to face the coach?"

"I'll deal with that when I come to it."

Paul was not being straight with him, Tony thought. How could Paul have changed overnight? Something had happened. But what? "Well, Paul," Tony said with a wry smile, "what about the limelight?—you'll miss all the fun traveling with the team."

"I'll have to give it up, won't I," Paul said, relieved.

"Hell, I'm just jealous. With you out of the way, the field will be open for us lesser mortals," Tony joked. "You know what they say about you, Paul? Girls are always shadowing you. And what do you do? Run like hell. And me? Coeds look past me like I'm a shadow. When I'm on the prowl . . . well, they run like hell." Tony laughed at his wisecrack. Paul laughed along with him.

"Poor Tony!" Cecilia had looked a lot like her brother in childhood. Tony had come to resemble the Pastori side of the family more—tall and dark-eyed. Cecilia took more after the Lamberts—light skin, hair that turned from sandy blond to light brown. She had become much prettier than she had been in elementary school, having learned to do her hair and make herself up to advantage.

"You know, you haven't gone out with Irene and me since your date with Penny, after the Harvard game," Tony noted. "You've become quite a loner."

"You keeping tabs on my love life?" Paul's face reddened. That was the football weekend Brown beat Harvard a whopping 33 to 6.

"Don't get defensive," Tony said, amused.

"Me, defensive? Man, I'm always on the offense." Paul had for some time puzzled his teammates with his spartan ways; the ascetic life he led was part of the team scuttlebutt. "Look, I've gotta run—talk to you later." Paul put on a smile as they parted.

Tony was right: how would Paul face the coach? He didn't know himself what was nagging him. Tony had hit on the very thing that had unsettled Paul—the Harvard weekend.

He thought back to the double date after the game. Tony was driving with his date, Irene, in the front and making his way through the traffic as Paul and Penny, in the back seat, went from casual talk to heavy petting. They soon got heated up, and their legs and arms entwined in a spiraling passion. Nature took charge, driving Paul on—urging him toward a need he could no more block than the need to breathe. Her hand, brushing him on that spot, brought about an eruption from the

depths against which his will had absolutely no say. He bolted
upright, shoving poor Penny against the front seat. He throbbed
from groin to throat. He froze, anticipating an embarrassment
the least of which was the puzzled look on Penny's face, as she
clutched her head. "I'm sorry," Paul mumbled, as his thoughts
rushed back to the problem at hand—the secretion was seeping
through to his trousers. In panic, he stripped off his jacket to
cover it up. This failed to mask the smell he imagined diffusing
itself throughout the car. Saying he felt hot, he rolled down the
back window. The cold blustery air blasted them. Tony and their
dates screamed and Paul hurried to close the window. A long,
awkward evening ensued. Paul was glad finally to see Penny
home. It was that night that the passion to find Anna invaded
his thoughts and raged in him ever since.

Paul had read the meager reports written about Felicia's
stabbing in the *Pawtuxet Valley Times* and the *Providence Journal*.
He knew Anna had moved to Providence—address unknown.
He heard that a private detective hired by the Benedictas found
no new evidence. Bogged down with study and sports, he'd
forgotten all about Anna. But, rising like the lost Atlantis from
the ocean depths, his concern for her surfaced during that
Harvard weekend. Now he had to face the coach!

"Have you ever heard of commitment, Risch?" the coach
asked when he learned he was about to lose his star pitcher.
"How about responsibility?" Paul didn't answer. The coach
looked at him, waiting for a reply. "For Pete's sake, Paul, think
of the team—the Bruins need you. Running out on us now
puts us in a terrible fix. Please, Paul, think it over," he pleaded,
looking into Paul's eyes and seeing something was amiss.

What could Paul say? Could he explain what was troubling
him when he himself didn't know.

"What on earth's going on with you, Paul?" the coach asked,
his face red. "Damn good thing you didn't pull this on us last
fall." Paul stood silent, trying to find something to say. "I suppose
we should be glad you didn't screw us up football season!" the
coach said. His rebuke saddened Paul, and he badly wanted to
mollify the coach, who searched Paul's face, expecting a reply.
Paul stared at the ground. The coach wrenched himself away.

For days Paul wallowed in guilt. He threw himself into study, trying to purge the coach's angry face from his thoughts. He scheduled his medical school interviews, was accepted at three universities, and chose the University of Michigan.

Slowly his guilt for deserting the team lessened as his urge to find Anna surged—till he could think of nothing else.

Where should he start? He pinned his hope on Father D., his old hometown priest. Surely he'd know. But would Father D. remember him?

Anna in Rome

Sitting at her mother's desk, Anna could feel her mother's presence. Everything in the suite of rooms had stayed fixed as her mother had left it in 1936: clothing, writing paper, personal journals on the bookshelves, even pens and pencils crammed into a stubby ceramic vase. She lived and breathed in her mother's aura and found herself struggling against the anguish of her mother's death.

It was her nineteenth birthday and Nonna Clara and Nonno Luigi had planned a party for that evening. More than three years in Rome. How time flew! She was already in her third year at the University of Rome.

When she arrived, Nonno insisted she take her mother's rooms on the third floor of the palazzo, as if to deny his daughter's tragic end. Anna gazed down at the traffic on the Lungotevere. She had hours yet to get ready for the party. Her thoughts crept back to her first day in Rome.

Alex had left the States a year before her and Nonna and Uncle Peter. She smiled remembering how happy she was to see him again. He and Antonio came to the airport to pick them up. It was Nonna's and Uncle Peter's first time back in twenty years.

Together they embraced Alex.

"Alex, you've grown. You look like a real count!" Anna kidded.

"Don't I now!" He laughed.

"You'd better stop growing," Piero said, mussing his hair as they kissed on both cheeks. "Getting too big and burly for the soccer team!"

"*Madonna mia*, Uncle, you're shrinking. Getting old or what?" Alex, now six feet tall, topped his uncle by an inch. "Didn't I tell you—I made first squad."

Nonna pulled his ear. "Are you behaving yourself? I've come home to bring some order into your life."

"How did you get Nonna away from her old cronies on Federal Hill, Uncle?" Alex teased.

"*Mamma mia!* What a mouth he's gotten since he came to Rome." Nonna pulled his other ear. "What do you expect? Living among the high and mighty!" At sixty-eight, Assunta, still as spunky as ever, had grayed considerably.

Alex put his arm around Anna as they walked to the car. "You're going to be a knockout in Rome, Sis. Nonno is rounding up every eligible bachelor on the social register. Poor you."

On the way home Alex asked Antonio to drive through the Campo to show Anna the statue of Giordano Bruno.

Antonio took a right off the Via Arenula onto the Via dei Giubbinari, slowly winding his way through the narrow street filled with small shops, sightseers, and shoppers. Passing behind the Palazzo Pio, the Campo opened to full view, and Giordano Bruno, with his ageless gaze, towered above the medieval piazza.

As they drove, Anna had been fighting back tears as Alex spoke the names of streets familiar to them since childhood. When she saw the statue of Bruno, she burst into tears.

Assunta took hold of her on one side and Piero the other. Alex, sitting in the front with Antonio, turned around. No one spoke. Anna's sorrow touched them.

They passed the Palazzo Farnese and were approaching the Via Giulia. "Antonio, please drive past the palazzo and turn around," Alex said.

Antonio went a few streets past the palazzo slowly circling around till he was sure they had regained their composure. He drove back, stopped, and got out to open the high steel gate hinged on heavy stone pillars that interrupted the eight-foot brick wall encircling the grounds. Anna got her first glimpse of the massive building and the flower beds set like jewels in the lush lawn.

She was soon embracing her grandparents, making every effort to smile and appear happy.

"How wonderful to have you home, mia cara," Nonna Clara said, drawing Anna tightly to her bosom. "Look at her, Luigi. The spitting image of her mother."

Anna felt that her grandparents were welcoming her mother home.

A sudden knocking on the door stirred Anna from her thoughts. Alex barged in.

"Francesca's making quite a fuss downstairs—wants everything perfect for tonight."

"Hi, Alex," Anna said, downcast.

"All this attention getting you down? Since you got here I've been shoved in the corner." He hoped to humor her.

"Alex, listen. I've made up my mind. I'm going back."

"To the States?"

"Yes. I—"

"You're out of your mind! If you haven't noticed, Italy's on the rise—rebuilding herself. Think of the opportunities. And you want to leave. It's going to be like nothing you can imagine. Already tourists are flocking to Rome. It's the treasure house of Europe." He jumped from one reason to another, sounding like an agent of the Italian Government Travel Office.

"That's not the point."

"What is the point?"

"Well, Anna," Piero said, popping his head in the doorway, "getting ready for the big night?"

"She's fed up with Rome!" Alex blurted.

"Just pre-party jitters. You'll be the belle of . . ." Piero, about to tease, saw the same telltale signs of anguish he'd seen in Felicia. He'd noticed it in Anna for some time. "Anna, please, don't dwell on the past. You know—the evidence and testimony were fine-combed. Nothing, absolutely nothing, turned up. Whether we like it or not, we've got to live with it."

"But how can we go on—as if nothing happened? Among the nobility . . ." She tried to hide her bitterness.

"Life's complex, messy. What do you expect?" He wanted to dispute the idealism of her youth, to get her to see life as it is—

good and bad intermingled.

"Dream and reality—worlds apart, I'm sure," she said indifferently.

"Look Anna, tonight's very special for Nonno and Nonna Clara. *Sta attenta!"* Alex cautioned. "Don't be too hard on them. They're old and you can't change them. And I don't want to hear any more foolishness about going back. *Basta!"*

"What—is the count-to-be taking himself seriously?"

"What's got into you two?" Piero looked from one to the other. "Enough bickering. Anna, listen. They mean well. Remember, your grandparents have suffered terribly, too. They're fixed on family lineage—a troubling matter, for sure." He turned to Alex. "Alessandro, please, be more understanding. Come you two, keep in mind, we can't always have things our own way— *pazienza, pazienza!"* He forced himself to smile as he put his arm around Alex and then around Anna, squeezing them both.

Soon after coming to Rome Anna found herself facing the same difficulty her mother had: her grandparents' preoccupation with marriage to this one or that. She felt she was reliving her mother's past. For months now she'd been thinking about going back to the States. Not only did she want more freedom, but the horror of her mother's death still haunted her. All she knew was that she yearned to go back. It was simply a matter of when.

"Zio, senti," she said, making every effort to compose herself. "Listen to what Mamma had to say before her break with Nonno." She opened one of her mother's journals and started to read without waiting for him to answer.

There is only one true *aristocracy and that is the aristocracy of the spirit. The true aristocrats, the best, are those who, in conquering their self-centeredness and in recognizing a higher reality, become enlightened. Inherited privilege is built on error and lies—it imprisons those it is bestowed on.*

True aristocrats are liberated from their false self. Pride—giving rise to resentments, ambitions, love of power, envy, jealousy— evaporates from their lives and allows a place for humility to flourish. They do not lust after power and fame; they are mercifully freed from resentment. The love of and gratitude for life inspire them to a devotion to truth.

Had Anna looked up, she would have seen Piero's pained expression. When Anna sought consolation, she had no idea how it distressed him to talk about Felicia. His life was filled with remorse. Had he proposed sooner, he believed, the tragedy might have been averted.

"Zio . . . I'm going to leave after I finish the exams for my *Laurea in Lettere,*" she said.

"Leave! Where to?"

"Give us a break!" Alex spurted out in anger.

"Please, Alex, not so fast—" Piero began saying.

"I've thought a great deal about it," Anna interrupted.

"She wants to go back to the States. As if she didn't have enough trouble there!" Alex said.

"You're doing so well—" Piero started saying, putting his arm around Alex to quiet him. Turning to her and about to continue, he felt her fingers across his lips.

"Shush, Zio. Please. I've decided to do graduate study in the States," she said.

"But your degree, *come prenderai la laurea?* You've got about seven or eight months before you finish your *laurea.*"

"I know. It won't be till August '58. I've already started my thesis—sent a draft to Professor Basanti."

"I understand . . . look, listen, cara," he said, winking at Alex. "When you finish classes, you, Alex, Mamma, and I," he said as cheerfully as he could, "let's invade the *castello* in Rignano. By then, you'll see things more clearly. Don't rush it."

"Who knows? By July you and Monica . . . maybe she'll come with us to Rignano," Anna said smiling. She saw her uncle's sadness and wanted to turn to more pleasant thoughts. Nonno had been trying to arrange a marriage between Piero and her mother's cousin, Monica. She believed her uncle liked Monica.

"Still the same busybody." Piero smiled.

"Maybe Carlo will come too," Alex said, wanting to make peace with his sister. The count and countess had talked up Carlo Orsini, one of Rome's most sought-after bachelors, as a suitor for her.

She smiled and gave Alex a push. Then she turned to Piero. "I'm just not interested in all these aristocrats Nonno digs up."

"Federico Colonna's pretty decent," Piero teased. "But then, you're only nineteen. You've got years ahead of you. Once married, it's forever."

"He's probably the best of the lot," she said.

"For sure! He looks a lot like a certain boy in West Warwick. Have you noticed, Uncle?" Alex meant this to be funny but, facing his uncle, he did not see Anna's pained look.

Anna's expression sent shivers up Piero's spine. He sensed a second reason for her going back. "Let's see your dress for tonight."

"You'll have to wait. You'll like it. My mother wore it at my age. Francesca had the seamstress shorten it. Will Nonno seat Monica next to you? Francesca's keeping it a big secret."

"You're determined to get this old bachelor married. Goodness, I'm over forty!"

"What a laugh," Alex said. "He's got those roving Roman eyes—sizing them up. He thinks I was born yesterday."

They laughed at Alex as he rolled his eyes. Still youthful, Piero was looked at as a good catch. The Count and Countess Petrarca treated him as a son. They set their minds to marrying him off to one of their nieces.

"*Mamma mia*, a man can't keep a secret around here with you brats," Piero said, happy to see Anna amused.

Meeting with Father D.

Paul drove onto Providence Street, toward the neighborhood of his youth. He pulled onto the driveway at Sacred Heart rectory and glanced at the grammar school across from the church—a stark rectangular building, with white clapboard and black trim. It looked more like a jail. Anxiety and ecstasy intermingled in him.

The stuccoed church stood like a citadel painted a light umber and trimmed in dark brown wood. He looked up at its high spire dwarfing the gabled rectory. Several flights of massive steps led into its sanctuary. It still enthralled him as it did in childhood; a sacredness emanated from within. About a hundred feet behind and soaring high above the steeple, the exposed face of a massive rock—"the mountain"—enshrined the church in a grotto-like setting. In its crevices, the mountain sprouted flowers and bushes here and there. Laurels, lilacs, and tall trees sat atop it like crown jewels. Paul remembered how he and his friends scaled the mountain to take a shortcut to Prospect Hill.

He climbed two flights of steps to the rectory and rang the doorbell. Mrs. Sassi, the plump old housekeeper still wearing her familiar gray dress and matching apron, greeted him as if he'd never left. "Fatah D. 'e's inah 'isah study, Paolo," she said in her thick Italian accent. "He's ahwaitah you." She accompanied him down the left hallway to the priest's study.

"How's Guido doing?" Paul asked. As long as he'd known her, she'd been a widow. Her son was a year older than Paul.

"Guido, she's ah finah."

Paul held back a chuckle as usual when talking to Mrs. Sassi. In all her years in this country she hadn't mastered English pronouns. Poor Guido—Paul remembered the terrible licking Norman gave him.

She knocked on Father D.'s door.

"Come in. Well, well, good to see you, Paul."

"Hello, Father," Paul said, walking into the study and shaking hands.

"I see you and Tony have done quite well—5 wins, 4 losses, same as last year," Father D. said of Brown's '57 football season, as Paul sat down across from him. "Too bad about the Columbia and Princeton games. Well, you can't win 'em all."

"So you keep an eye on the Ivy League, I see." Paul was on edge. Father D.'s delight in the success of his hometown boys surprised him. Except for balding a bit, he hadn't changed much.

"I hear you'll be off to medical school soon. Where?"

"University of Michigan."

Paul fidgeted in the chair and couldn't get comfortable. Very little the priest misses, he thought, raising his hope of getting news about Anna. Father D. indulged him in small talk. Paul waited for an opening, to come to the point. The spotless study looked like a room in a monastery: bare white walls, dark-stained moldings, hardwood floors. A large crucifix hung behind the desk. A soothing smell of incense permeated the place.

"How was your move to Providence?"

"Providence took a while getting used to. I missed my friends. But, you know, I never started high school here—went to La Salle after junior high." Paul wiggled about in the hard chair, trying to settle down. How could he bring up the subject of Anna?

"A wise choice of high school—high standards, good education."

"I've often thought, Father . . ." Paul started reluctantly, feeling foolish, but his need to know outweighed his sense of pride.

"Yes, Paul?" The priest pictured a personal problem of crisis proportions coming.

"Do you know what's become of the Benedictas? Have you seen them lately?"

"You know that Anna went to Classical, don't you?" Father D. said, relieved.

"I had no idea. It's not far from my house. In fact, if I hadn't gone to La Salle, I would've chosen Classical." Paul relaxed.

"Yes, it's in your neck of the woods. Piero came to me after Anna was discharged and asked me to support his request—"

"Discharged! Discharged from where?" Paul nearly jumped out of the chair. "Were those awful rumors true?"

"Perhaps, Paul, we ought to let the Benedictas . . . ought to forget the past . . . let them get on with their lives." Father D. caught a wild look in Paul's eyes.

"Was she sent to prison, Father? Anna could no more kill her mother than St. Francis betray Christ!"

"No, no, Paul, she was not imprisoned."

"What've they done with her, Father?"

"Alleged crimes by juveniles, you see, are handled differently from those of adults, Paul. She was discharged . . . I mean released into the hands of her uncle and her grandmother. They became her legal guardians under court order." Piero and Assunta had visited him after they moved to Providence. Father D. had learned that Anna got over her grief, was doing very well at Classical, and was viewed by her psychiatrist as an unlikely suspect in her mother's death.

"Well," Paul said, "I shouldn't have trouble finding her. She'd have graduated in the class of '56. Knowing the Benedictas, as I do, I just don't believe Anna was involved in Felicia's death."

"Piero asked me to support his request for a re-investigation. He hired a private eye, but nothing new turned up. As far as I know, the case is closed and Anna's getting on with her life."

"Where does she live?"

"I don't know. Most likely, Anna wishes to break with the past. Grief over her mother's death overwhelmed her."

"I understand. But don't you need to believe that justice is served? . . . and . . . you have a right to know about your friends? About Felicia's murder and the accusations against Anna? When a town's faced with such a catastrophe—one that makes no sense—far from the realm of possibility, knowing Anna . . . to be without facts that vindicate her . . . it's frightening. At least I find it so. It's as if part of your life has been ripped out . . . sure life goes on—in a crippled way. No one seems to care about the truth. I find it disturbing to hear Anna condemned—about no ordinary crime. No, it's impossible, absolutely impossible, I tell you, for someone so sensitive . . . it's unthinkable."

"You know, Paul, now that you're going on to medical school, keep in mind the divine mysteries and the need for prayer. *Si Deus nobiscum, quis contra nos?* Remember your Latin. If God be with us, who shall stand against us? Religion has deeper meaning than that given out in Sunday sermons. The parish priest speaks to his flock in the simplest terms."

"What do you mean, Father?" Paul was jarred by this sudden turn. "Don't your sermons deal with divine revelation—with absolutes?" What was the priest getting at? He's worried about me—thinks me mentally unbalanced, Paul thought.

"Of course, of course. *Nil desperandum*: there's no reason for despair. Sermons are given to a mass audience—the mysteries brought down to the lowest common level. This is troubling today: we're losing many of our professionals who, learned in the ways of the world, lose their faith and begin to question church dogma. They fall prey to worldly views that explain away divine truths."

Paul tried to follow the priest, puzzled that he was talking about issues having little to do with Anna. "How do they lose their faith, Father?"

"Well, as their education proceeds, their beliefs get tested by all sorts of tangled theories."

"What theories?"

"You know: evolutionism, materialism, reductionism, psychologism, scientism, and so forth. Now, tell me this. Can those of weak belief stand their ground against a world bogged down in such thinking? You know, Paul, as faith weakens, virtue declines. Many today think they see through their childhood beliefs—are liberated. They delude themselves. They merely trade one set of beliefs for another."

"I don't understand? You've always said that '*veritas prevalebit*'—truth will prevail. Won't the educated see the error of their way and return to faith?"

"Well, well, I see our catechism classes weren't lost on you." Father D. smiled. He went into a discourse on science and religion and finally said, "Keep in mind, truth will prevail in the long haul of history, Paul—after much suffering. Each of us is tested and many fall by the wayside. Remember: you must watch and pray—*vigila et ora*. Given the great arc of history, truth conquers all things—*vincit omnia veritas*."

Father D. looked at his watch. "I'm sorry to cut short our talk, Paul. It's time for me to meet with young couples for marriage instruction. When will you be leaving for Michigan?"

"Middle of August."

"Well, Paul, I wish you the best of luck. I hope to see you again."

"Thanks for your time, Father."

He walked Paul to the door and wished his family well. "Keep in mind: *Vigila et ora, vincit omnia veritas*, and—"

"And *Deo volente*—God willing," Paul said.

"*Deus vobiscum!*—God be with you," Father D. said smiling.

Anna's Party

The receiving line stood before the magnificent curving stairway. In the background a sixteenth-century fresco depicted Dante's *Purgatorio*. A mountain scene reaching from the floor to the vaulted ceiling above symbolized the long upward journey of those who enter the gates of purgatory and climb the steep slope to paradise. At the base Dante, the stains of Hell washed from his face, waits as the angel boatman ferries the souls of the elect from their gathering place at the mouth of the Tiber to the shores of Purgatory.

Francesca escorted the guests one by one to the receiving line: the count at the head, then the countess, followed by Alex, heir to the count's title, and Anna, next in line. Piero and Assunta stood next to Anna, representing the lost generation—Felicia and Marco.

Anna wore a blue velvet princess-style dress. She had a strand of pearls around her neck. Her dark wavy, shoulder-length hair was parted in the middle. In heels, she stood at eye level with her uncle and looked much older than nineteen.

"What a beauty! Anna, you look stunning. Wouldn't you say, Ida?" Carla hugged and kissed her niece on the cheek.

"Anna," said Ida, following on the heels of Carla, "you've grown since I saw you last. How adorable you look. How elegant." She embraced Anna.

Anna flushed, bowed graciously, and thanked them for coming.

Having welcomed her uncles and other guests, Anna heard Carlo Orsini laughing loudly with Alex, waiting to take her hand.

"Anna, you've been avoiding me—no answers to my notes. What am I to think? I'm glad the count thought to include me in your soirée," he said loudly, turning and smiling at the count. He kissed the back of her hand.

She had put him off during the past months at the university. "Carlo," she said a bit flustered, "with half the girls in Rome traipsing after you, I thought I might—"

"You flatter me. I'd be happy if one of them were the right one."

Anna blushed and waited politely for him to pass on. Nervously she said: "Professor Basanti's a slave driver—he's got me loaded down with work."

Federico Colonna pushed his way into the line, joining Anna and Carlo, then reached for Anna's hand.

"Ciao, Federico." Anna greeted him.

"Ciao, Anna. Ciao, Carlo." Federico kissed her hand. "Stay away from this flirt," he said, motioning to Carlo. "I hear Professor Basanti's giving you a hard time on your thesis. I know him like the back of my hand, Anna. He's marked you out as his pet."

"A real grapevine we've got going among Basanti's clique," Anna said. "If truth be told, Federico, he's quite unhappy with some of my ideas."

"Listen to him, Anna. Come on Federico," Carlo let out good-naturedly. "Loosen up." He and Federico, in their early twenties, were Rome's most eligible bachelors. The remnants of the old nobility, including Count Petrarca, competed for their favor for their daughters and granddaughters.

Anna's friend from the university, Stefania, came in just as the reception line broke up. Anna waved to her to come over.

"Ciao, Stefania." Anna took hold of her hands as they kissed each other on the cheek.

The guests were soon called and seated in the dining hall. The count sat at the head of the long table, flanked by Anna on his right and Piero across from her, the countess at the other end, with Alex on her right and Assunta across from him. Anna smiled to herself to see Carlo placed on her right and her cousin Monica on Piero's left. She was right: Nonno had picked out her mother's cousin Monica for Uncle Peter. So, she thought, Nonno favors Carlo Orsini over Federico Colonna. Little did Nonno know how little her heart inclined in either direction.

The servants started serving the antipasto, and the count stood up to make a toast. "We are grateful to have our friends and family with us tonight on the grand occasion of Anna's nineteenth birthday. She and Alessandro, our little Americans, have brought the countess and me great joy in our old age." He lifted his wine glass. "Clara and I wish to toast Anna and to wish her many wonderful years in our great city. Excuse an old man for bragging. Anna's a true flower of Rome who warms the hearts of her grandparents, if I may say so." He turned to her and bowed. "Of course, much of the credit for Anna's and Alessandro's upbringing goes to our dear Assunta and Piero Benedicta." He turned to each and bowed. "To Carla and Giuseppe and Ida and Maurizio our deepest gratitude for all you've done. We're happy to have with us my brother Alfonso, his wife Elvira, and their daughter, Monica. And of course, Anna, we are honored by Carlo, Federico, Stefania, and all the others here from Rome's new generation—the inheritors of Rome's glory. To Anna's health." They all stood and toasted her.

Anna thanked them and said she had spent many happy days in Rome.

"*Bon apetito* and may God watch over you all," the count added.

Conversation broke out around the table as the company turned to the lavish platters of the *antipasto all'Italiana*—thinly sliced Italian hams and olives with fresh-baked bread.

Beside Nonno sat Piero, Nonna Clara sat next to Assunta—people hardly welcomed in the palazzo in the '30s, Anna thought. The nobility now needed the bourgeoisie for its survival. Piero, on Alex's request, was made chief administrator—the count's right-hand man. Her poor father had been scorned by her grandparents and treated shabbily during her parents' courtship. What an irony! Nevertheless, she took consolation in the fact that family relations go a long way in tearing down class barriers. She suddenly realized that Carlo was addressing her.

". . . yet, Anna, it seems the general consensus that Americans have gained a reputation for being loud, uncouth, and spoiled by their wealth and prosperity. Do you hold to such views?"

"You might add a few more disparagements, probably little warranted, to that litany," Federico put in: "sloppily dressed, poorly educated, and philosophically naive."

Anna was about to answer when the count spoke passionately for the Americans. "How do we account for the Marshall Plan that helped rebuild all of Europe? An act of generosity after America sacrificed her brave sons to save us in two wars."

"True, Nonno, America is given short shrift and taken for granted," Anna said. She turned to Zia Carla, who had close contact with Americans at the embassy. "Surely, Zia Carla has an insider's view."

"Not really, Anna. Yet, I've learned, such commonplaces often contain a grain of truth," Carla said. "Most Americans I meet are well educated and represent the wealthier classes in America—not typical of the masses, for sure. What did you find, Anna?"

"Should Americans be lumped together?" Anna asked. "They're racially and ethnically diverse—a rich cultural mix quite foreign to Europeans. But if you're asking about the social character of Americans, Carlo, that's a different matter."

"Well," Carlo said, as a servant filled a bowl of *zuppa di asparagi* from a large tureen, placing it before him. The smell of the steaming soup with spears of asparagus floating on a bed of cream stirred his appetite. "What do you see as the major differences in character, Anna?"

"Tell them, Anna, how Americans see Italians," Alex said. "You'd be shocked, Carlo. A favorite joke goes something like this—'What's the difference between an elephant and an Italian grandmother?' The response—'A hundred pounds and a black cotton dress.' No offense intended to my Nonne." Alex turned toward Anna with a sly smile.

"Remember," Piero said, "Americans know next to nothing of Italians. They see mostly poorly educated immigrants from the *mezzogiorno.* Then, too, they distrust the old nobility of Europe."

"Yet, Piero," Assunta said, "how do you account for their fascination with royalty and their own uppercrust?"

"Yes, Mamma, a real irony," Piero said. "The masses seem to devour any word of the goings-on of socialites and celebrities. Haven't they always? In their heart of hearts, the masses revere the upper classes and, being proud of their egalitarian heritage, come to believe a lofty station can be gained by hard work alone."

The smell of mushrooms cooked in a cream sauce, wrapped in a crepe and baked with a cheese topping, wafted though the dining hall. The guests relished the dish, and their discussion momentarily languished as they complimented the countess.

"Anna, you haven't answered Carlo," the countess said. "How does the American character differ from the Italian?" Nearly a decade had passed since Felicia's death and Clara was still mystified. She and Luigi seldom spoke of it. When she saw how Felicia had lived among the working class in a small clapboard house, she was horrified at the poverty. Prospect Hill looked like the end of the earth.

"I suppose . . . their vision of progress and future perfectibility. Americans don't think they live in a class society. They go on as if there were no such thing in America. Everybody, it's believed, has an opportunity to advance to the highest social level and, even though Americans esteem the wealthy and powerful, they abhor inherited privilege."

"Surely, Anna," Federico said, "a classless society is an unattainable ideal."

"You'd be surprised, Federico, to see very bright children at public schools coming from all classes—some from very poor working-class families. Given the chance, some can and do jump social levels within a generation—"

"But, Anna," Alex disputed her, "many of these kids fall behind as they go on to higher grades—often dampened by their parents' doubt—thinking education a waste of time and effort."

A *contorni* of vegetables was being served with large platters of roast lamb and veal, encircled by roasted, seasoned potatoes. The wine kept flowing and the conversation became more jovial, many talking at once.

Anna became indifferent to the pretentious talk going on, and her thoughts roamed back to her childhood. Ralph Mullen was always an enigma to her: at times he had deep insights and a refreshing simplicity. Once he told her that many people on Prospect Hill were sick—they gossiped so much because of hungry souls and empty hearts stuffed with demons. He knew that many people lied, because he got a funny feeling inside when they did. She heard Federico addressing her.

"I'd like to hear how Italian-Americans characterize us, Anna," Federico said.

Anna laughed. "Come, now, Federico, we're dealing with a diverse people . . . it's hard to say."

"No, no, Anna," Federico said laughing, "you—how do you see us? After all, you're an Italian-American."

"What Federico wants to know, I think—correct me if I'm mistaken, Federico—is whether Italian-Americans assimilate so well into American society as to take on a prejudice toward Italians themselves," Carlo said. "As our dear Basanti would say, you're ambicultural. How's that for a fancy label?" He laughed.

"Hard to say," Anna said, amused. "But as Alessandro said, Americans don't take too kindly to Italians, who are often viewed as the bottom of the European ethnic barrel."

"Well, do second- and third-generation Italian-Americans assimilate in the U. S.?" Carlo asked.

"Some begin to believe in the stereotype—become ashamed of their origins. Things are changing quickly there. Americans, no doubt, are optimistic and give credence to man's perfectibility—the idea of the City on the Hill, a community of all ethnic groups and creeds intermingling."

"Between ideal and reality there's a big gap," Uncle Alfonso noted.

"I think you miss Anna's point, Alfonso," Piero said. "It's the vision America sets—yes, falling short, in practice. Yet, it's the first nation to achieve a unity on a vast scale of diverse racial and ethnic types and, in my view, greater by far than that achieved during the Roman Empire. It presents a model, on a smaller scale, of the goals of the United Nations."

During the salad, cheese, and fruit courses, a lot of bantering and chatting took place. The guests marveled at a colossal cake formed in the shape of a mountain and covered with whipped cream to resemble fallen snow. Carried around the table by two servants, the cake was offered to the guests, who cut a piece to their heart's content.

"If I may say, Clara," Assunta said, tasting the cake, "the *monte bianco* is exquisite. About Americans—Alfonso is right. Reality is a far cry from their ideals."

For Anna the conversation dragged on tediously. She was eager for the guests to finish their coffee and brandy so that she could talk more with Stefania and the other students who had hardly spoken a word all evening.

Paul visits Lillian

After leaving the rectory, Paul on the spur of the moment made up his mind to go up to Prospect Hill.

He turned onto Providence Street, driving along the same road Felicia and Marco had taken in 1936. The old Natick Mills lay in ruins, burned to the ground years ago. He climbed to the center of Natick and turned up the steep hill. He soon passed the lane where he used to live. This was his first time back in years, and his pulse quickened as he glanced at Anna's old house on Wakefield Lane. It looked like a mausoleum. Workmen moved in and out of the Mansours' house. He parked across from it in front of the Pastoris'.

Lillian's front steps lured him. Many happy days in his youth were spent there: playful and innocent, secure and trusting. The steps also revolted him. An odious primeval force seemed to emanate from them. Attracted and repelled at the same time, he knocked at the front door as the sun hid behind the clouds.

The door flung open and Lillian greeted him. "My goodness, Paul. What brings you from the big city? About time you paid us a visit. It's great to see you. Just a few days ago I asked Tony, 'Why doesn't Paul ever visit us?'"

"Hi, Lillian," Paul managed to slip in. She had lost some weight and was wearing slacks and a loose-fitting halter top. Her short permed hair, bleached blond, looked like a frizzed-up wig set on top of a beach ball. "Not much has changed on the hill."

"True, True. But you have—you've changed. Tony tells me you're quite a big man on campus. So, you've dropped out of baseball. By the way, congratulations on your acceptance to medical school. I always knew you'd make something of yourself. Too bad your family moved away—"

"Hi, Eddy!" Paul caught a glimpse of Eddy slouched in an overstuffed living-room chair. "Gosh, Lillian, you've changed the place." He marveled at the inner space of the house, now painted a pastel yellow. Wide arches replacing the old narrow doors made it spacious and light.

"What do you think of it?"

"Pretty nice. You painted over the wallpaper, I see. It's brightened up the rooms." The old dark victorian wallpaper had made the rooms look small and stuffy. He turned to Eddy, who hadn't answered. "Say Eddy, what're you doing these days?"

"Nuthin'."

She led Paul into the living room. "Paul, please sit down. Don't mind the mess. I just got back from Natick Grocery. You know I'm cashier there—part time, of course. I'll put some coffee on. Eddy, be a dear and take the package off the coffee table. Oh, Paul. It's so good of you to drop by. Cecilia, I know, would be delighted to see you. Eddy, be a dear and put the package on top of the piano, will you? Well, I'm off to get—" The phone rang.

"Yes, dear. You won't believe who dropped by—Paul Risch. He's a real doll . . ."

Paul tuned out and turned around to look out the living-room window toward his old house. He remembered his first kiss in the basement while looking at his trains with Cecilia. She eleven, he thirteen. Children are more precocious than adults want to believe, he thought. Playful experimenting between kids—boy-girl, or boy-boy, or girl-girl—happens in an erotic underworld hidden from others. It's easy to forget such things as you get older. You want to hide them from yourself.

Lillian was still talking on the phone. Paul thought of that first fooling around with Cecilia as the moment he gained insight into his own dark underworld—lust being one of its most powerful urges. He went up to Eddy, still slumped in his chair, and gave him an affectionate punch in the arm.

"Say, Eddy. How're things going?"

"Not good."

"What do you think of Tony's record this year—top end in the Ivy League. Pretty good, huh!"

"He'd go pro if he was smart."

"Pretty rough to break into professional ball. But he's being scouted, all right."

"What about you?"

"Ah, my football days are over, I'm afraid. Anyway, did Tony tell you? I'm off to medical school soon—probably flunk out my first year."

"Fat chance. You'll make it all right. Dartmouth gave you guys a real beatin'—0 to 35. But then, ya kicked the pants off Rhode Island—21 to 0." Eddy laughed.

"Well, what about Harvard and Colgate, huh? We gave them a good trouncing."

"Yeah, a good shellackin'," Eddy said and fell silent.

"For God's sake, Eddy!" With a tray in hand, Lillian looked for a place to set it down. "Couldn't you move the package?" Paul put the package on top of the piano. He helped her set the tray on the coffee table. "Thanks, Paul. Since Ralph died, Eddy's been moping around—won't do a thing."

"Talk about me . . . huh . . . what about you? You forget those years when you was sick," Eddy said. "Yeah, my ma had electricity sent through her head. Her brains got fried. She don't remember nuthin' no more—like what happened to Felicia."

"Too bad about Ralph." Paul rushed to change the subject. "Heart attack while walking up the hill, I heard."

"Yes, poor Ralph. He'd put on a lot of weight," she said flustered. "He had a congenital heart defect, I'm told. Died a few months after his mother. Rose—you remember Rose Golanski, his sister?—pretty much looked after him. Really, all his brothers and sisters pitched in and made sure he got along all right." She poured the coffee and offered Paul some cookies.

"You know what killed Ralph? I know. His heart was broken when they blamed poor Anna for killin' her mother. That sure was dumb. Anna kill her mother! What a laugh. Man, them police was stupid who said that. Norman and his gang did it. Who else? Ralph got fat like a pig, eatin' himself to death, tryin' to fill up his heart," Eddy yelled and turned back to the TV.

"That was Cecilia on the phone." Lillian's face turned scarlet. "Cecilia said to say hello."

"How does she like her job? She's with the Reid Legal Agency, Tony tells me."

"I've been after her to get her teacher's certificate. She did the secretarial program at Bryant College. Likes her job all right . . . I guess. Well, Paul, what brings you to our bailiwick after all these years, pray tell?"

"I stopped over to see Father D. I'm off to Michigan in about four months. Just thought I'd drop by."

"Well, I'm glad you did. All the way to Michigan—too bad Rhode Island's without a medical school. You know, I miss the old gang. The hill's not the same. Most of the kids have moved away. Mildred, you know, married and then divorced three years later—a painful separation. She's got a son, about three or four, I believe. Phyllis is now married. She's moved to Arctic. Alberta married a disc jockey; she's now head secretary for the West Warwick police. Gloria moved to Arctic. Helen Butler ran away from home—eloped. Did you hear? Her family hasn't heard from her since. You've no doubt heard—Norman ended up in the federal pen. Turned out a real crook. Nancy married and is living in Phenix—"

Paul had heard all this before from Tony. "What ever happened to Anna?" he asked.

"She went to Classical after she got out of Butler but I don't know for sure. You know, the whole thing was hushed up—"

"Butler! Butler Hospital for the insane? Are you sure? Tony never said a word about it. He never mentioned Classical, either." Though he and Tony rarely talked about Anna or about Felicia's death, they both wondered what had happened to the Benedictas.

Lillian saw distress written all over Paul. All this time she'd been dying to know the reason for his visit. "Tony couldn't have told you. I learned it quite recently from the DiPadua family— they lived down the hill, near the church. They bought the old Mansour house about six months ago—"

"I thought the Mancinis bought the Mansours'?"

"Yes, some time back—not too long after the Benedictas moved away. Six months ago the Mancinis sold to the DiPaduas. It turns out that Mary DiPadua has a friend working at Butler. She told Mary that Anna Benedicta was committed to Butler shortly after her mother's death, and she went on to Classical High when she was discharged."

"How's that possible? She must've been in the hospital for years to transfer to a high school. It doesn't make sense."

"That's all I can tell you."

Bewildered, Paul got up and glanced out the window at the

Mansour house. "What are they doing?"

"Remodeling the place from top to bottom—for the past few months. Pretty nice job—gonna be beautiful."

"When did Mrs. DiPadua tell you about Anna?"

"Two days ago, to be exact. Quite by accident. She called and asked me about the Mansours. Do I see them since they left the hill? I told her Cecilia had gotten to be friends with Rachel Mansour. Rachel, you know, goes to Bryant College, where Cecilia went. Some books were found in the upstairs bedrooms and Mary DiPadua asked if I knew where the Mansours lived. They moved to Wescott but are away visiting their family in Lebanon. Rachel is staying with her married brother. Anyway, Mary sent over the package—the one you put on the piano. It's been sitting here for Rachel to pick up. I told Mary the Benedicta place had changed a lot since Assunta and Peter left. She said: 'Did you know Anna was at Butler?' I was shocked, of course. Poor Anna—must've had a rough time."

Paul sat down. "Where is she now?"

"No one seems to know. Assunta never contacted my mother after they moved from the hill. Surprising, to say the least— they were so close." Another one bitten by the charm of the Benedictas, Lillian thought.

Paul turned inward, reflecting on Father D.'s slip—"after she was discharged." He covered up Anna's psychiatric history. A priest protecting his flock!

"Well, Lillian, thanks for your hospitality," Paul said abruptly. "Say hello to Cecilia for me, please." He was anxious to leave. "Bye, Eddy. Take care." Eddy, too engrossed in TV, didn't answer.

"Don't be such a stranger, do you hear?" Lillian said as cheerfully as she could. Envy of Felicia, long gone and forgotten, flared up in her. "Come visit us more often," she said, sad that Cecilia was not at home.

Paul got in his car, turned it around, and drove past his old house. He thought of Cecilia and the trains—a memory he had long forgotten until today. He was reminded of his sociology class last year when his teacher, Prof. Davis, had been talking about *Brave New World*—about the path of least resistance to a new enslavement. Prof. Davis was a short woman with a widow's peak and as dogmatic a teacher as you'd ever want to meet. Her sarcasm could cut you to the quick. She was always harping on the child's social womb. As long as the family, church, and school—the child's social womb, as she'd often say—are united to confine physical intimacy within marriage, most kids cease experimenting sexually by the time they are fifteen or sixteen. Sex gets routed down accepted channels. But if stirred by external stimuli in the absence of moral restraint so intense a passion could give rise to widespread promiscuity. "Only a human being can say no!" Professor Davis would say with such zeal spit would spew from her lips. "No other creature on the planet," she'd say, banging her palm on the podium, "has the power to inhibit, to stall, or, in some cases, to triumph over impulses. Think about it!"

He thought about it. He was at the bottom of Prospect Hill, and he turned toward Providence.

Anna's Thesis

"Whew! I'm glad that's over," Stefania sighed. "I enjoyed the food immensely, Anna, but I'm dying to find out if it's true." The students had retreated to a quiet corner of the great hall.

"If what's true?"

"Come on, Anna," Carlo said, "don't play the fool with us. It's out in the open."

"A misunderstanding," Federico assured them. "Professor Basanti does it to all his favorites. Believe me, when I tell you— it's his métier."

"I'm not so convinced," Anna replied.

"He can be insensitive . . . arrogant," Stefania said. "What happened? 'Fess up, Anna."

"It's nothing really."

"What do you mean, nothing? Carlo questioned. "I'd like to give Basanti a good piece of my mind."

"Look, Basanti pushes his top pupils pretty hard," Federico said, a bit more sanguine. "He's hooked on the draft of your thesis, Anna. Did you know? He read excerpts from it to one of his classes."

"*Anna!*" Stefania said.

Anna did not want to discuss her ideas about motherhood in earlier societies—the topic of her thesis. Professor Basanti, her major professor, had taken her to task when she differed from him and a highly respected thinker—a nineteenth-century Swiss writer, Johann Jakob Bachofen, who studied the role of women in the ancient world. Recently, she'd found herself drawn to the question of the role of the mother in past civilizations. She fell upon Bachofen's writings by chance. Her friends knew nothing of her mother's death or of her subsequent mental breakdown. As for her family, everyone went on as if nothing happened.

Hoping to put the matter to rest, she said: "Professor Basanti had a fit when he saw the preliminary draft of my thesis. That's all."

"Basanti, the eminent scholar, shaken up? You must have challenged him. Out with it."

"You flatter me, Stefania."

"Let's not beat about the bush, Anna. What's going on between you and Basanti?"

"I take it," Federico said, sensing Anna's reluctance, "you accept Bachofen's view that some pre-Hellenic and pre-Roman civilizations were dominated by women. Professor Basanti holds the same views."

Anna heard him, but her thoughts were back at Sacred Heart with Father D. in catechism class, discussing marriage as a vocation. "Marriage is not unlike the vocation of a priest," she recalled him saying; "it's another path to salvation—another calling." The idea astonished her. A calling to the priesthood compared to marriage! Paul sat at the end of the pew across the aisle. As if drawn by an irresistible force, she turned and looked at him. Their eyes met for a moment. A delightful feeling suffused her.

"Yes, Federico, women may once have been dominant. My research bears this out."

"Well, Anna," Stefania said, "if you agree with Professor Basanti, where's the problem?"

"If you must know," she said, wishing she could avoid getting deeper into it, "I set forth the view in my draft that patriarchy, male-dominance since ancient times, is a passing phase in human evolution. Like matriarchy, female-dominance, which preceded it, patriarchy too will pass away. This seems to have rankled him."

"Well, it might," Carlo chuckled, thinking of Anna facing up to Marco Basanti, revered by Rome's brightest history students. Carlo loved Anna's spunk, but he wasn't going to let her off the hook. "Patriarchy replaced by what?"

"That's the rub, Carlo. I haven't thought it out too well yet." Anna smiled, remembering Professor Basanti's face when he called her in.

"Now I see," Federico said. "The good Professor Basanti regards male-dominant civilizations to be superior to female-dominant ones. If my memory serves me, he sees male dominance as the final stage in a long evolutionary process going back to the neolithic revolution—some ten thousand years."

"Exactly," Anna said. "I've disputed Basanti's views, I suppose."

"How so?" Stefania asked.

"In my draft I suggest that a just society is only possible with full equality of men and women." Talking about motherhood brought back the grief over the loss of her mother and her father, and she found it hard to concentrate. Theirs was a union based on equality. Then she remembered that Father D. had set forth the possibility of a new social order—beyond both matriarchy and patriarchy.

"Equality of men and women. Poppycock!" Carlo scoffed. "What did our scholarly wizard, Basanti, say to that? Can you imagine paunchy Basanti, normally flocked by his adoring students, being assailed by St. Anna!" They all laughed.

"What do you think?" Anna laughed, recalling Basanti's reply. "In his arrogant voice, he bellowed—'Proof, PROOF, **P R O O F**, Miss Benedicta!' Instead of citing some of the studies I'd use to make my case, I jumped onto my hobby horse: 'We're already at the end of patriarchy!' I declared. His face reddened. He let me go on. 'The killings in the twentieth century alone—a century of murder and mayhem—reveal the end of male rule, the end of over five thousand years of male dominance.

Upwards of one hundred seventy-five millions killed already in wars, revolutions, and prisons this century. It's the sign of the times—' He interrupted me and said, 'Miss Benedicta this is a university, not a sect for divas and diviners. Here, take your draft. Off with you now. Come back when you're ready.'"

Picturing Professor Basanti—his unkempt goatee and spectacles hanging from his long nose—shooing Anna out of his office, they all broke out laughing once more.

"Well, for my part," Carlo said seriously, "you're barking up the wrong intellectual tree, Anna. I, for one, am not inclined to accept Basanti's views at all. I do not believe there were significant societies in which women dominated. I can't fathom such a thing. And then, to posit a new civilization based on equality of men and women beyond patriarchy! Sorry, Anna, to throw cold water on your thesis."

"There we go, Anna," Stefania said. "Carlo, you miss the point. The question is not whether you agree with it or not, but whether it is historically valid. Societies have been discovered, you know, where children took their mother's name, not their father's?"

"What's the basis of Basanti's claim to 'mother right'—to female-dominant civilizations?" Federico asked. He never had grasped Basanti's position.

"Professor Basanti, following Bachofen, contends that in pre-Hellenic civilizations the mother ruled over the father, and the daughter stood before the son in inheritance," Anna said.

"Did marriage evolve in human societies at the behest of women, then?" Carlo asked. "Surely men played a role in these early civilizations."

"Yes, of course. But marriage has a distinct dynamic in human life, Carlo," Anna said, despite herself. "Without marriage, men tend to abuse women more. Unbridled lust on the part of men gives rise to promiscuity. Fathers exercise little responsibility for the children they spawn. Actually, it's hard to tell who the father is. Then, some women left to raise children alone become belligerent toward men—they seek revenge for their suffering. In turn, men react against women—"

"Basanti's argument—God only knows how many times I've

heard him preach it," Carlo said with an air of disbelief, "goes something like this: Two extremes—unbridled sexuality (on the part of self-indulgent men) and unbridled hostility (on the part of strong women, those Bachofen calls Amazons, after female warriors of Greek mythology)—set the stage for marriage as an institution in the evolutionary process. Marriage, if you take him seriously, is matriarchal at the beginning. That is, women hold the power in the community. Poppycock!"

"Well, it's a bit more complicated, Carlo," Anna said, weary of talking about something she hadn't worked out yet. She remembered how many men lorded it over their wives and went out drinking night after night with their buddies on Prospect Hill. Louie's Tavern filled with men almost every night, many going home to their wives and children in a stupor. Yet, many men still kowtowed to their wives in the family setting, having become dependent on them. What happens when there is no marriage arrangement? When women and men interact indiscriminately? "You see, Carlo, women are pretty badly abused by men in promiscuous relations. And with hostile women who try to put men down, men react hostilely. Given the superior strength of men, women come in for some pretty rough treatment. So the horror is that, in promiscuous relations, most women suffer. This suffering gives rise to a marriage structure—the only means by which most women will ever have peace in their lives. And men too, for that matter. In marriage the man's sexual appetite is tethered as he bonds to his offspring."

"So, Basanti's saying . . ." Stefania groped for words.

"That marriage alone is woman's salvation—her only way to peace," Anna said.

"So civilization begins through the action of women, then?" Stefania asked.

"Yes, but with the cooperation of men: the majority of women are looking for a solution to their torment from promiscuity—to indiscriminate sexual relations—and, to get it, they need the help of men to bring about a civil structure. Civilization cannot endure with either widespread promiscuity or the outright hostility of women toward men."

"Marriage, you're saying, evolves to bring order into the lives of human beings. So?" Carlo said.

"Keep in mind," Anna said, "the enormous value of marriage. Men, once bonded to their children and to their wives, are diverted from lust—more or less. It's given up for the ends of family, community, higher human attainment—men and women working together for higher social ends."

"Marriage, I take it," Federico said, "is nothing more than a choice human beings make. You seem to be saying that there's nothing absolute about it. Is that Basanti's position, Anna?"

"Not at all—"

Stefania interrupted. "I get it, Federico. It's the discovery of a principle underlying human life: the knowledge of how society and civilization evolve." They laughed at her exuberance.

"So?" Carlo said, once more.

"Let me put it this way, Carlo. As human beings discovered mathematics to help create all kinds of things, so human beings discovered marriage as the base of civilization." Stefania thought she had said it all.

"What are you talking about? You're mixing oranges and apples and getting mush," Carlo said.

"Look, Carlo, as mathematics is real, so is the knowledge of the need for marriage to establish civilization. Losing our understanding of mathematics, we risk the loss of technological civilization," Stefania said. "Losing knowledge of the proper relations among men, woman, and their offspring, we risk the loss of human communities and descend into the war between the sexes."

"*Brava*, Stefania, you hit the nail on the head. Human beings discovered the absolute underlying marriage," Anna praised her. "Motherhood is sacred—it's holy. When motherhood is violated, civilization declines. A threat to motherhood and marriage is a blow to the very foundation of civilization and a relapse to a promiscuous life and the tyranny of men over women and the reaction of women against men—"

"What about fatherhood?" Federico frowned.

"Fatherhood too—fatherhood is correlative to motherhood . . . I mean . . ." But she couldn't go on. Suddenly she felt a sharp pain in her chest, and an image of her mother's body wrenched itself from her depths. She could barely breathe. Excusing herself, she hastened from the room. Alone, she could think of one thing—prayer—her sole consolation against the inner wound she feared she would carry to her grave. Gradually she began to breathe easier and to feel a clearing of her mind.

"Listen, Anna, Carla wants to talk to you before she leaves," Piero said, grabbing Anna's arm as she came back into the room. "You didn't tell me—you've begun applying . . ."

"I haven't, yet."

"Carla tells me she's—"

"I'm sorry, Uncle Peter. I thought you might try to talk me out of it. It's a decision I've got to make on my own. I thought Zia Carla might get some information for me at the embassy to help—"

"I think I've found a way," Carla said, overhearing part of their conversation.

"Can it be done?" Anna asked eagerly. How much easier, she thought, to go back to the States with her identity masked.

"Instead of a change in name on your passport used primarily for purposes of international travel, why not have your university transcripts sent out with your name as you wish it to appear in the States?" Carla advised.

"How's that possible?" Anna's face lit up.

"Well, you're enrolled as Anna Maria Margarita Petrarca Benedicta. You want to suppress the Anna Maria and the Benedicta in favor of 'Margarita' and 'Petrarca'. Why not use the anglicized equivalents—Margaret and Petrarch? You could apply to American universities as Margaret Petrarch."

Glancing at her uncle, Anna thought he looked offended.

"It retains the names on your maternal side and skirts the paternal," Carla said.

"Is it hard to do?" Anna couldn't bring herself to look at Piero.

"Not if you don't ask for a passport change."

"What's to be done?"

"Apply for advanced study under the new name. Advise the university here you want your name anglicized as such-and-such when sending out your transcripts. Then maybe you should approach each of your major professors to let them know."

"More than likely," Piero said, "your new name will appear on your transcripts, along with your official one."

"If that's the case," Carla said, "there's no problem. You may even decide to change your name legally in the States—it's a simple court procedure."

Piero saw a tranquil look come over Anna's troubled face. "Have you discussed this with Nonno?" he asked.

"He won't be too happy about his 'second Felicia' going abroad."

An alarm bell went off in Piero—Anna's assuming her mother's identity!

Paul visits Classical High

On his way back to Providence, Paul stopped off at Classical High, not far from his home. He figured Anna had had to be either in the class of '56 or '57. If at Butler for a short while, she would have had to go on to junior high first. A long stay at Butler would place her in a later class.

He introduced himself to the secretary in the principal's office as a student from Brown. "I'm looking for a former friend from West Warwick who graduated from Classical. I lost touch with her and I'd like to know her address."

"Her name and class?" she asked brusquely.

"Anna Maria Benedicta, '56."

She opened a file drawer and pulled out a manila folder. She looked down the page. "No one here by that name in '56." You sure about the year?"

"Sorry. It must've been the class of '57 then."

She went back, stuffed the folder in the file, and yanked out the drawer for 1957. Again, she looked down the list. "No one by that name in '57. Do you think you've got the right school? Look, I'm pretty busy. Why don't you check our yearbooks in the library. Her picture would be in one of them. If you don't know her class, you might be smart enough to recognize her face."

A student standing at the counter caught Paul's eye and made a gesture as if to say, ain't she a beaut?

Paul was unnerved, but he persisted. "If her name isn't listed, how would her picture be in the yearbook?"

"Of course it wouldn't. How could it? The lists I have are of all the graduates for that year. The yearbooks might be missing some photographs, but they contain a complete list of graduates. Do you get it?" She rolled her eyes upward as if talking to a dodo bird.

The student looked over at Paul and the secretary and walked out.

"Maybe she's in this year's graduating class—'58. I might be off two years," he said, ignoring her incivility.

"This year's class—there's no one here by that name. I can assure you." As if to prove a point, she stomped back and banged the drawers about, snatching two folders: one for the class of '58 and the other the class of '55. Slapping them down on the counter she said, "Let's hope we don't have to go back to the American revolution!"

She looked at both lists and Anna Benedicta was on neither. "If you ask me, you've got the wrong school. How old is she, anyway?"

"She's either 18 or 19."

"Should've been in the class of '56 or '57. Exactly where we started." She looked up at Paul and saw distress and disappointment. "I'm sorry I can't help you." A trace of kindness crept into her voice.

"Thanks for your trouble," Paul managed to say. Father D. and Lillian must be mistaken.

Paul visits Dante

Could Dante Giorgio help him? Hope sprang anew, and Paul rushed ten miles back to West Warwick, dodging the late afternoon traffic.

Ten years older, Dante had lived next to Louie's Tavern. Surely, he'd have a lead on Anna; he'd been on the police force at the time of Felicia's death.

Paul saw Dante coming out the rear door of the police station as he pulled into the parking lot. "Hey, Dante, got a few minutes?"

he yelled.

"Paul! How the hell are you?" A burly six-footer with a bulky head, greasy black hair, and an arching paunch, Dante walked toward Paul's car and shook hands vigorously.

Dante looked at his watch. "Yeah, I got a few to spare," he said, turned around, and followed Paul into the station. "What's this I hear—bugged out on the Bruins. No wonder they're doing so lousy—without their top pitcher—downed by Yale, Army, Harvard. And Navy coming up next week."

"Don't remind me. I'm public enemy number one at the fieldhouse." He felt like a pariah on campus.

"What's on your mind?"

"Trying to track down Anna Benedicta. Seems she went to Classical—no record of her there."

"Well, my boy," Dante said slapping him on the back, "it'll be easier for you to get info on the goings-on in the governor's office than on a juvenile accused of a crime."

"You've got her record on file. I'd just like to get her address. That's all."

"File or no file, that's not the point. Man, juvenile cases are held in strict confidence. They're out of bounds, even to police districts in the state. Would you believe—even our own. Now if Anna had committed a crime as an adult, I'd have the court records at my finger tips."

"Must be *some* place I can get it." Paul found himself against another wall. Imagine, a simple thing like an address. He was mystified.

"The clerk at juvenile court must have her address. But forget that. The West Warwick police would not be privy to those files unless they originated here. Of course, when necessary, we can get around the law. That's off the record, you understand." Dante smiled. "No way you can get a handle on what happened in juvenile court, or since. Come on in." They'd been talking in the corridor.

"But you were in on the case—doing the investigation, weren't you?"

"Alberta, pull the file on Anna Benedicta," Dante said on the intercom. He looked up at Paul, "Was it '50 or '51?"

"Spring of '50."

"Nineteen-fifty. Thanks. We did a thorough job of compiling evidence, Paul. Of course we have a copy of the report we sent to juvenile court. My second year on the force, as a matter of fact. But the short and the long of it is that we are mandated by law to keep our files under wraps. If new evidence surfaced, we'd be called in to ascertain its bearing on the case before forwarding it to the juvenile court clerk." He pulled a large tome from his desk drawer.

"Pretty complicated."

"Sure is. But it protects juveniles. It gives them a chance to straighten up and fly right under the eyes of the court and, of course, a cadre of social workers snooping on them," he explained, flipping through the pages of *The Proceedings In Juvenile Court and An Act Creating A Juvenile Court For The State Of Rhode Island.* "Listen.

> . . . *Said court shall be a court of record. . . . No provision of this act shall be construed to require the taking of stenographic notes or other transcripts of the hearing held by said court.*

"The judge, you see, is charged with complete discretion in conducting hearings. Listen to this.

> . . . *In the hearing of any case the general public shall be excluded; only an attorney, selected by the parents or guardian of a child, to represent such child, may attend, and such persons shall be admitted as have a direct interest in the case, and as the judge may direct. . . . The court shall, except as herein otherwise specifically provided, hear and determine all cases within its jurisdiction without a jury.*

"Even our office," Dante said, "doesn't know exactly what happened after our investigation of the murder led us to petition the juvenile court for a hearing about Anna. Of course, social workers, psychologists, and psychiatrists called in to help Anna are given access to pertinent documents collected by the judge."

"I find it hard to believe," Paul said.

"That's the truth. Here's the law:

> *The records of the juvenile court shall not be available for public inspection. Said records shall be available for inspection by persons having a justifiable ground for inquiry, and only upon the written order of a judge of the juvenile court, and by no other person.*

Paul sighed just as Alberta came in, carrying a thick manila folder. She glanced at him. "Here they are, Dante. My goodness. Paul! Paul Risch—the twins' little cousin. My oh my, you've grown up."

"Hi, Alberta." Paul stood up and walked toward the door to talk to her, away from Dante, who'd already started leafing through the file. Alberta used to live on a street to the north of his, a cul-de-sac that ended on the edge of the forest near the mountaintop. A pretty brunette, six years older than he and full of life, she had been a friend of his cousins Angela and Lenora. All the boys on the hill had a crush on Alberta at one time or another. Still a knockout, as Tony would say.

"You're not so little now, huh Paul? God, you were a scrawny kid!" Paul blushed. "Darn, I should've waited for you to grow up. Ha ha!"

Though Alberta appeared to be a flirt (when she was not with her husband Gene, that is) she was, Angela said, the most decent of all her friends. Paul glanced over at Dante, who was still immersed in Anna's file. With her husband Gene, a tall thin handsome guy who struck Paul as humorless, Alberta put on a sophisticated pose. As Gene Johnson, disc jockey, he could be funny and endearing, and his commentaries filled with wit. Here were two people, Paul thought, who have dual personalities: a lovely spontaneous woman full of life who plays a dour role beside her husband; and he, a straight-laced somber husband, channeling his humor to an anonymous audience. He'd go into cardiac arrest if he saw how Alberta was with other people.

"How's Gene? I hear him every now and then on WPRO."

"You mean my tall stick-in-the-mud? Goodness, he's such a bore. But, you know, he's great on the air waves," she said proudly.

"I'll have to tell Angela and Lenora to bring you around. Ha ha! I see you still blush a lot," she said as she left Dante's office.

"Very interesting case, indeed." Dante finally pulled his head out of the folder. "I can tell you this much, Paul: no one ever requested us to do a follow-up on Anna. No new evidence turned up." He went on thumbing through the file. "Nothing new. That's all I can tell you—nothing more. Of course you know—don't you?—she moved away to Providence some months after we investigated. But where to? I don't know. That information was filed with juvenile court." He knew he could get his hands on it but thought better of delving into a matter that might spell trouble for him.

"Nothing in there about a forced entry the night of the crime?" Paul asked.

"Fingerprint evidence pretty contaminated by the time we got there—no evidence of forced entry. Of course, we can't preclude the possibility."

"Was Anna ever committed to Butler?"

"I don't know. But, you know Paul, if I did—which I don't— I wouldn't be able to tell you." Dante sensed an unhealthy fixation in Paul. "Look, Paul, forget it. It's all in the past."

At every turn Paul found an impasse. He'd become a prisoner to his longing for Anna, and it was getting worse. He knew he ought to give up and get on with his life. But something urged him on.

"What's it all about?" Dante asked, seeing Paul's sudden withdrawal. "It happened nearly eight years ago, for goodness sake."

"I dunno . . . just feel like something was . . . just curious . . . can't believe Anna could do such a thing."

"I really never knew her. She was a bit behind me in school," Dante said. "In fact, I remember when she and Alex were born; even earlier, when the Benedictas came to live on the hill. I'd already started grammar school. I'd see Anna pass my house on her way home from school once in a while—"

"Well, Dante, thanks a lot for your time. Sorry to hold you up," Paul said abruptly.

Anna and Alex

Anna went back to her study, feeling a sense of relief she'd not known for years. She took one of her mother's journals from the bookshelf. She'd put a gold book marker where she'd left off some days before. She curled up on the sofa and, still fresh in the early hours of the morning, began to read:

February 1936

. . . Despite the tyrannies plaguing Europe—perhaps because of them—I believe I will see in my lifetime a general enlightenment of mankind, a quantum leap forward in human consciousness, which is bound up with marriage and the family.

Since ancient times all religions have broken into the mystery of marriage and the family, to a greater or lesser degree. In various symbolic-mythological systems of thought, world religions have laid bare the hidden, sacred dynamics of sex and marriage. The present system—a system of power and authority dominant for six millennia or more—may be nearing its end.

Starting with the war of 1914, the twentieth century has been imbued with secular attempts to prop up civilization—all doomed to collapse by the end of this century (whether communist, fascist, or capitalist) from exhaustion, chaos, and madness. For long, postmodern civilizations—torn from their ancient and medieval moorings—have gotten out of control. Even the religious humanism of the fourteenth and fifteenth centuries has been lost. Today's secular endeavors to organize the world are grounded in materialism, evolutionism, and nationalism. These attempts will one day fail and their failure will stand as testimony that civilization, unlike its material structures, cannot be rooted fully in time and in history. Civilization has a deeper mathematics—a sacred geometry— from which, if civilization is cut off, it withers and dies. The dynamic underlying civilization, for lack of a better term, let me call the mathematics of marriage.

The mathematics . . .

There was a knocking at her door.

"I saw your lights on. Can I come in?" Alex asked.

"Come. Sit down," she said, patting the plush sofa to get him to sit next to her, as she slid over. She was glad to see him.

"You seem pretty chipper," he said. "Back to Mamma's journals, I see."

"You've no doubt heard—"

"I'll be sorry to see you go. Our lives are one of continual loss." He thought better of getting trapped in another fight with her and started chuckling. "I don't like the ring of it— Margaret Petrarch. The change from an 'a' to an 'h' in Petrarca—it's so artificial. Sounds like Italian translated to English. And you, will you turn into a Yank?"

"Not on your life. Not with you hounding me," she said, delighted, putting her arms around him and kissing his cheek. "Thanks, Alex, for understanding. Don't look so glum. It's months away, assuming I get admitted to a graduate program somewhere. Nonno will have you married off by then."

"Hey, give me a break—at seventeen! I need some time to fill out my shoes," he said laughing. "Federico's already trying to rope me in with his sister. But I know his real motive and it's sure as hell's not me. He doesn't see too straight when you're around." She flushed.

"To be truthful, I look forward to Rignano and the Tuscan Hills." He got up to leave. "Hurry up with your studies, especially *la tua tesi di laurea*—your damnable thesis—so we can be off. *Buona notte!*" he said as he closed the door behind him.

The short talk with Alex took a load off her mind. She opened the journal to read on from where she'd left off.

The mathematics of marriage is the foundation of civilization, as the mathematics of engineering is the foundation of material structures. The latter is taught in all schools; the former remains shrouded in mythology and symbols. The collapse of the modern world may expedite the learning of the mathematics of marriage—of union in love.

The root of the mathematics of marriage lies in the sacrament of love. Neither in the sexual act nor in perpetuating the species lies a true union. The new life, the eternal life, lies in marriage founded in love. And in marriage there is true vocation; there is predestination.

Here are some correspondences that need to be worked out:

MATHEMATICS	SOCIAL MATHEMATICS
ENGINEERING	MARRIAGE
PHYSICAL REALITY:	CIVILIZED REALITY:

Things	Humans
Physicochemical	Psychological
Energy	Consciousness
Intellect	Spirit
Quantity	Quality
Principles:	Virtues:
Addition	Temperance
Subtraction	Courage
Multiplication	Wisdom
Division	Justice
Infinity	Eternity
Unity	God . . .

Anna let the journal fall to the floor, for the present.

Paul visits Butler

Driving home Paul hit upon another possibility—Butler Hospital. All else had failed him: Father D., Lillian, high school records, police reports. Following Lillian's lead, he thought it time to look into the psychiatric hospital. Had Anna been treated there?

How to get in? That was the question on his mind as he frantically sped back to Providence, hardly knowing how he got there. For the rest of the night he tried to figure out a strategy.

To pry into Anna's case would be no easy task, assuming she'd been committed. He would find himself head on against another wall of secrecy. Psychiatrists were as tight-lipped as priests hearing confessions. Yet the urge grew so strong in him that he was willing to use deceit, and to justify it to himself. To his surprise the next morning a phone call as a Brown pre-med student got him an afternoon appointment. He said nothing of his real intent.

On his way there he ran into Tony. "Your name's mud at the fieldhouse," Tony said bitterly. "Bugging out on us—"

"Things would've been far worse if I'd played the season. I'm in no shape to pitch."

Tony sensed Paul's wish to flee from him. Lillian had told Tony about Paul's visit and how Paul "had it bad for Anna." Tony knew something was amiss. "Boy, you sure made an impression on my mother yesterday."

"Strange to be back on the hill after all these years. Look, I gotta run." Paul put on a smile.

When they parted, Paul began to have second thoughts about visiting Butler on a false pretext. Looking into psychiatry as a medical field, something he might eventually do, in no way pressed upon him now. But it was his only excuse.

He went into the stately administrative building in the large compound and told the receptionist he wanted to talk to someone about psychiatry and also inquire about a former patient, Anna Benedicta.

"Are you a family member?"

"A friend."

"Unlikely a patient at Butler would be discussed with anyone but family," she said emphatically.

As if he didn't know. He saw her thumb through several files and heard her speak to a Dr. Leach.

"Dr. Leach will see you, Mr. Risch," she announced.

Paul was escorted to Dr. Leach's office after a short wait and soon found himself talking to a bulky man with red hair and scores of freckles on his face. He was surrounded by books and talked like a scholar.

Paul only half listened to Dr. Leach's little lecture about the various fields of medicine. Paul's thoughts began to spin out of control. Should he abandon his attempt to find out about Anna? The only decent thing to do. What would Dr. Leach think of him? But this might be his last chance. What difference would it make what Dr. Leach might think? He had compromised himself already. If he let the moment slip, he might never find

Anna. Besides, Dr. Leach might let him off with a moral slap on the wrist. A moral whiplashing more likely! If Dr. Leach had not treated Anna, what harm could asking do her? What risk would Paul be taking? Certainly none. And the doctor? What possible harm could it do him? Certainly none. This inner chatter went on while Dr. Leach outlined the different fields of medicine and where psychiatry fit in.

" . . . it's a matter, Mr. Risch, of interests and talents but mostly, I'm inclined to believe, of whether your interests are more priestly or scientific."

"Priestly or scientific!"

"Well, to be quite frank, Mr. Risch, there's a great confusion about psychiatry. For one thing, the notion that mental illness is like a sickness in the body may be inappropriate, if not harmful. Can therapy be done on the mind?"

"I've never thought about it." Paul felt shipwrecked without a lifeboat.

"Well, let's think about it, Mr. Risch. What's the pathology— what's the disease, or more accurately, the disease entity in mental illness? Surely, in bodily diseases there are problems due to biological and physicochemical processes that medical science can study and find cures for. But is there in mental illness a biological entity that is infected or disordered? Or is the trouble coming from conflicting personal needs, opinions, values, and social aspirations. Suppose somebody believes he's Franklin Roosevelt or that his internal organs are disintegrating? Is this explainable by a disease in the nervous system? In so-called mental illness, I believe, the explanation must be sought along different lines. Wouldn't you say?"

Paul's strategy to find out about Anna was backfiring. "What about a nervous breakdown—isn't this a condition of the nerves, synapses, and the brain?" he asked.

"Well, it depends on what we mean by nervous breakdown. If the breakdown comes from some organic condition of the nerves and brain—and some breakdowns can be traced to an organic condition—then it is a neurological problem and should be treated by a neurologist not a psychiatrist. The sickness we'd say is biological and medical, as opposed to moral. It has little to do with the way a person lives and functions as a human being."

"I see," Paul said half-heartedly. This seemed to wind Dr. Leach up.

"Our society today, with its materialist view of reality, has handed over the priestly function of dealing with moral problems to the medical profession—psychiatric branch. But mental illness has to do with misperceptions about what is good, what is true, what is valid in life. Medicine is ill-equipped to deal with or heal that kind of suffering."

Paul nodded as if he understood. He wondered how he was going to get to Anna.

"In previous centuries novelists like Dostoevsky and Tolstoy and philosophers like Pascal and Kierkegaard wrote about the functioning of the soul and the conflict between the unconscious and conscious mind of the afflicted. Unlike psychiatry today, such thinkers advanced the notion of a superconscious mind—"

"Superconscious mind!"

"Well, what we'd call the enlightened or spiritually awakened state of consciousness—beyond the conscious and unconscious—"

"But surely psychiatry sees mental problems coming from . . . uh, disorders in the brain and nervous system. Don't they? Research focuses in, if I'm not mistaken, on . . . uh, such things as chemical imbalances and biological disorders treatable by biochemicals. Are they all on the wrong track?"

"An important reason for locating psychiatry in medicine is to be able to sound out the causes of any so-called mental ailment. We need to distinguish problems that are organic (that is, bodily or medical) from functional (that is, psychological or moral) and then to treat each of them accordingly. The psychiatrist would take on those cases needing a priestly type and shift the others over to physicians in the specialties called for."

"And how do you handle . . . care for individuals in a priestly role?"

"Not by probing the patient's past per se but allowing the patient to reveal it in the course of therapy—gaining some insight into how he lives and deals with life. I've found that we get well not so much *because* we remember as that we remember because we are getting well. Many people live routine, preconceived lives based on what should or should not be, with little thought about

what's true and real—that is, without knowing how to bring
their life into harmony with the fundamental order of existence.
Psychiatry, as well as psychology, has made great strides in the
workings of the unconscious and the conscious minds. But both
have little or no notion of the superconscious—that is, of the
enlightened mind. As Pascal once put it: there's the order of
bodies or matter, the order of the mind or the intellect, and the
order of the spirit—the superconscious. Pascal believed that an
infinite qualitative distance separates the order of the intellect
from that of matter; but an infinitely greater distance separates
the order of spirit from that of the intellect. And this reality,
called the spiritual, is what I call the superconscious: it goes
beyond the darkness of the unconscious and the semi-darkness
of the conscious mind. These problems take us way beyond your
interest in psychiatry, I'm afraid."

After this last assault, Paul thought better of asking any more
questions, even though some popped into his mind. He was in
no mood for more talk that had nothing to do with Anna.

An embarrassing silence ensued. "I guess we're stuck in a
mind-body divide," Paul said, to fill the void.

"Precisely," Dr. Leach said, smiling.

It's time to spring Anna's case on Dr. Leach, Paul thought.
He had to act and to act fast and to act without tact. "Did you
know Anna Benedicta? Was Anna a patient here?" He turned
red as a beet.

"So . . . I see . . . Mr. Risch . . . huh hunh, . . . you had
another reason . . . on your mind."

"No . . . yes . . . I'm sorry, Dr. Leach. I knew the Benedicta
family well—they lived next door. I'll be leaving the state soon.
I've never been able to accept what happened to Anna—the
accusations brought against her. I can't believe she'd . . ." He
heard himself going on and on, stammering, justifying himself.

"On that account I'm afraid I can't help you, Mr. Risch."

Dr. Leach's response had revealed an important fact—Anna
had been treated at Butler. Having gotten this far, Paul persisted.
"I heard Anna had been treated at Butler and then went on to
Classical. I checked there. They've no record of her. This is my
last resort, Dr. Leach, and I beg you to honor my good intentions

toward Anna and her family."

"How did you learn that Anna was a patient here?" Dr. Leach asked amiably.

"From a former neighbor living in West Warwick," Paul said, encouraged.

"Well, Mr. Risch, I wish you every success in your medical studies." Dr. Leach got up and rang for someone to show Paul out.

Paul was bewildered by his abrupt dismissal.

Dr. Leach shook Paul's hand in parting and said, "Well, Mr. Risch, I shouldn't gratify you. You weren't straight with me."

"I hope I made my intentions clear—"

"All I can tell you is that Anna pulled out of her grief wonderfully and left for Italy some time ago. Goodbye, Mr. Risch."

"Thanks," Paul said as an attendant rushed Paul from the room. He learned finally that Anna was all right. She'd survived the tragedy. He was relieved and sad. She was gone.

The Charge of Manslaughter

The Mansours returned from their trip to Lebanon in November 1958 and found a piece of evidence that fingered the dead Ralph Mullen in the death of Felicia. The evidence was in Mitri's diary, and dated March 24, 1950.

Mitri, who'd met his end the day after Felicia's when his car careened into the Pawtuxet River, had kept his diaries under a floorboard. Sam and Irma Mansour sold the house on Prospect Hill, unaware of them. The house, sold a second time, underwent a renovation and several of his diaries surfaced. The books had been wrapped in brown paper and sent across to Lillian's. The new owners had never met the Mansours and had learned that Lillian could get in touch with them. The Mansours at the time were out of the country, visiting relatives. The package sat on Lillian's coffee table and then on top of her piano for weeks, waiting for Rachel Mansour to pick it up.

Rachel retrieved it finally and, being a college student buried in assigned readings, was loathe to open a package containing more books. So, when Sam and Irma Mansour got back from Lebanon in the fall of 1958, they found themselves in possession of Mitri's diaries and were grateful for the precious gift left behind. At the same time they had reservations about prying into his personal life and private thoughts. Would decency forbid them to read his writings?

After thoughtful consideration, they decided to read his last entry. This would settle the matter: if they found it too intimate, they would honor Mitri's memory by putting the diaries away unread.

His last entry, of March 24, 1950, the day before he died, was amusing, full of wit, and sensitive to the world about him. His final remark, simple and baffling, had no relevance to anything else written that day.

Looks like Ralph Mullen at Assunta's west door. He turned, stooped in the flowerbed to pick flowers, then took off toward the hill—strange! (2 A.M.).

Sam and Irma Mansour read it over several times, trying to decipher it. Anna's terrible ordeal came to mind—her hearing before the juvenile court. They wondered what Ralph Mullen could have been doing at Assunta's back door that night. Mitri placed Ralph outside the west door that opened into a stairway leading upstairs to Felicia's apartment, at 2 A.M. Since the words were inserted at the end of the March 24 account, the Mansours understood the 2 A.M. to refer to the early hours of March 25, rather than March 24. Could Ralph have had a hand in Felicia's death? It seemed preposterous. But so did Anna's assault on her mother. They contacted the West Warwick police.

Several weeks later, the West Warwick Police petitioned the Rhode Island Juvenile Court for permission to re-open the Benedicta case, got approval a month later, and set out to examine the new evidence.

Dante Giorgio, involved in the original inquiry, headed the investigation. Without any urgency, the hearing dragged on for weeks. Alberta obtained the addresses of the Mullen family members and scheduled Rose and Jim Golanski as the first to be interviewed.

When confronted by the entry in Mitri's diary placing Ralph at Assunta's door in the early morning hours of March 25, Rose found it very strange. "Lord," she said, "that was more than eight years ago, Dante. My brother died not long after Felicia. What can I add? If he was there at that hour, as strange as it seems, he was there."

Dante asked her whether Ralph ever mentioned anything about the Benedictas that might shed some light. Did he leave anything behind? Mention anything about what happened that night?

A memory of Lillian visiting Rose weeks after her brother died sprang to mind. She remembered the photos and the letters among Ralph's junk. Rose became uneasy.

Dante saw a pained expression on her face. "What is it, Rose?"

"Years ago, shortly after Ralph died, I found two letters stashed away in a cigar box found in Ralph's closet. I think I may still have them."

"What letters?"

Horrified beyond belief at the thought of Ralph being a suspect, Rose recounted the story about how she found the letters and the photos and how they meant nothing to her at the time.

Dante waited while she went down to the basement to retrieve them. After some time she came back up and handed him the letters and photos.

It didn't take Dante long to recognize that he had the missing link—Piero's letter—which put Ralph inside the Benedicta home in the early hours of March 25, 1950. He explained to Rose the significance of Piero's letter for solving the mystery of Felicia's death.

With a heavy heart Rose again went over how the photos and the letters had puzzled her at the time, but not for a moment had she suspected Ralph of having anything to do with the murder. Ralph, she reminded Dante, was always so kind and gentle and had so much love for his neighbors. She could not imagine him capable of violence. It seemed not his nature. "No, Dante," she said mournfully, "the thought of Ralph doing it had never crossed my mind. How could it?"

Dante took possession of the letters and photos. "Piero had

made a general nuisance of himself during the police investigation, insisting his letter to Felicia was the key to unravelling the mystery. The second letter, never mentioned, must have been written shortly—just hours, or even minutes— before Felicia's death."

By now, Dante surmised that Ralph's forced entry into Felicia's apartment had come on the evening she had received Peter's letter and after she had written her reply to him. Peter couldn't have known of her letter, as it must have been taken from her when she met her death. Dante assumed that the stains on the envelopes were Felicia's blood. The two letters, probably in her hand or in her dress pocket when Ralph stabbed her, he had taken on impulse. The only factor missing was a motive.

"Why would Ralph have broken into the Benedicta house, Rose? Why would he hurt Felicia?"

Rose was stumped. Both she and Dante knew that violence of any kind did not square with Ralph's character. The neighbors all agreed that he was simple-minded and loveable. He remembered the birthdates of all on the hill and, if they had a phone, called them to sing happy birthday. If they didn't, he'd visit their houses and sing to them. Though generally a busybody, he displayed an uncanny sensitivity in settling differences among neighbors and in allaying animosity.

Dante spent several weeks tracking down those present at Lillian's steps the evening of March 24. A key witness, Lillian was again tormented by the investigation. For years after electroshock, she'd forgotten all about the letters, Ralph's implication in the death, and her lack of discretion on that night. Little by little, from one lead to another—from Phyllis and Gloria, from Cecilia and Mildred, from Dom and Nancy, and so on—Dante pieced together a mosaic of the circumstantial evidence and submitted a report to the Rhode Island Juvenile Court. It read, in part:

> . . . *At the time of the death of the victim, Mrs. Felicia Benedicta,*
> *12 Wakefield Lane, Natick, in the town of West Warwick, the*
> *suspect Ralph Mullen, a mentally limited adolescent of sixteen,*
> *of Fiume Lane, Natick, showed an abnormal attachment to*

Anna Maria Benedicta, the victim's daughter, then twelve. Mullen, having claimed to witness the victim harm her daughter and, being prone to accept the neighbors' gossip depicting the victim as wicked, broke into her house to assure himself that Anna Benedicta had not been harmed by her mother. Evidence is abundant that Mullen spied on the Benedicta family.

According to the testimony of various witnesses present at a gathering in front of the Pastori house the evening of March 24, 1950, rumors circulated to the effect that the victim, Mrs. Benedicta, abused her daughter Anna. It is presumed that the rumors adversely stirred the mind and emotions of the suspect. Believing Anna to have been severely beaten by her mother, he feared for her safety. The intention in breaking into and entering the Benedicta home, it is contended, was not murder—the knife used to slash the victim was one found on the premises, not one taken there by the suspect with the intent to do harm.

Forced entry without injury to the premises, it is presumed, was possible because the suspect had knowledge of the whereabouts of a key. This conclusion is plausible if information is considered from the diary entry of Mitri Mansour, a neighbor living to the north of the Benedicta residence, who places the suspect outside the Benedictas' west door at about 2 A.M. (shortly after the estimated time of death of the victim), stooping in the flowerbed—the place the Benedictas hid a house key.

It is contended that the victim's death was manslaughter. The suspect, now deceased, was overwrought by the malicious gossip of neighbors, and his mental condition urged him to enter the premises to discern the condition of the girl—Anna Maria Benedicta. Possibly confronted by Mrs. Benedicta, he grabbed a knife from the kitchen out of fear, to ward her off, believing her to be vicious. Mrs. Benedicta, slashed on her hands and shoulder, must have stepped backwards to avoid being further wounded, and tripped, falling through the living-room door, and hitting her head on an end table beside the sofa.

The suspect, it is further assumed, must have entered the bedroom of the daughter, Anna, to see for himself that she was safe, and must have placed the bloody knife on her comforter.

Going back to look at the victim, he then put the knife down next to her and, on impulse, took from her pocket or hand the letters later found among his belongings . . .

May 9, 1959

6
The Professional World

In August 1958, several months after Paul visited Butler Hospital, Anna had called Dr. Leach to let him know she was back in the States, studying at Yale under the name Margaret Petrarch. To her questions about any new development in her case, he told her that her records were closed to any public or private scrutiny and, if she chose, she could use her birth name without fear of reprisal or reproach. Juvenile court had fully protected her from disclosure, from any allegation of crime, or from any written record of criminal behavior. She was free to lead a life unfettered by the past. He took down her address and invited her to visit him, should she feel the need.

I come now to one of those sad facts that reality flings into our faces from time to time—the disposition of the police report sent to the juvenile court. Whether it was an upshot of a court overly protective of youth or a court burdened with other cases or an incompetent court clerk—maybe all of the above—who knows? But the fact is that the police report bringing to light new evidence and a new suspect in Felicia's death sat on the clerk's desk for weeks before being put into a dormant file. The new information just did not become public.

The Benedictas had returned to Rome years before, Ralph Mullen (at the time of the crime, a juvenile) was dead, some who had given testimony no longer lived on the hill or in the state, Paul Risch's parents had moved from Rhode Island. Father D., his thoughts and efforts on the immediate needs of his parish, was busying himself with the youth in the church.

When I look back on the summer of 1959, I think of Father D.'s morbid words. "We can hear the rumblings of a social earthquake coming, Pasqualina," he told me. "It's not only a crisis in humanism—of man supplanting God—we now face. No, it's far more insidious. For humanists, who try to do God's work while denying God, are still hopeful and still in the grips of doing good. It's a crisis in humanity itself that worries me, Pasqualina. Human life is being threatened by weapons with the power to destroy the planet. Then, we're developing biochemicals to control and sedate the mind and soul. As if those two were not enough, we've brought on a revolution that uproots and warps human consciousness—the radio, the television, the tabloids, and so on. Sorry, to say, Pasqualina, mankind has gotten itself in a terrible fix."

Whenever Father D. talked about these crises with me, which was often, he always made clear to me that a crisis is an opportunity for growth, for personal and social progress. "Remember, Pasqualina," he'd say, "we also have the possibility of an apocalypse—a revelation of the truth—of a new spiritual epoch." He never gave in to either pessimism or optimism and expressed a deep belief and trust in mankind and the power of the divine working in human life.

So, it seems to me that many things conspired against Anna's learning about Mitri Mansour's diary, about the allegations brought against Ralph Mullen, and about her possible exoneration. By the autumn of 1965, Anna still carried the dreadful moral burden of the unsolved crime within her.

On receiving her Ph.D. in psychology from Yale and, after several visits back to Rome, she took a teaching position at Michigan State University.

Anna talks to professionals

Anna sat nervously next to the podium.

The chatter in the large auditorium at Wayne State University grew louder as people filed in. Why in the world had she submitted a paper to be read at *The Mental Health Symposium of*

1965? she thought. To top it off, her paper was selected as the keynote address.

The moderator had not yet arrived and already several hundred people were seated or milling around. Teaching had come easily to her. She felt comfortable with students, even as her classes grew in size. But a talk to so many professionals made her heart pound and her stomach knot up.

She now lived in Indian Hills, a suburb of East Lansing with old oaks and rolling hills sloping down to the Red Cedar River— a world far removed from her former life on Prospect Hill, or Providence, or Rome. She glanced at the program as if she were reading about someone else: 'Mental Health 2015: A New Renaissance,' Margaret Petrarch, Assistant Professor of Psychology, Michigan State University." Strange, she thought. She'd become a multiple personality. Anna Maria Benedicta who had lived as Mary Anne Benedict reading about Margaret Petrarch. She smiled to herself.

Her earlier years—filled with joy and suffering, love and heartache—ended in the loss of her parents and in terrible grief. Her mother's death and Butler Hospital, though present to her thoughts, were thankfully hidden from view. Natick, so imprinted in her mind's eye, scrolled before her: Wakefield Lane, Providence Street Grammar, Sacred Heart, Cecilia and Paul. Some of her best and worst years were spent in Natick. She could picture the Natick Bridge spanning the river on Providence Street, high above the dark deep water that gushed over the falls toward the old Natick Mills.

She lived alone now, her family an ocean away. At Classical High, Mary Anne Benedict had hid Anna Maria Benedicta behind an identity that gave her the chance to grow safe from scandal. Dr. Leach had been wise to petition the court for a name change to preserve her privacy. Rome, a place of great learning, often saddened her. She saw the ascendant class firsthand—fixed on itself and unmindful of the laboring masses. She had longed to come back to the New World, the land of her birth. Is it possible, she thought, that suffering and grace are mysteriously bound together in the inner depths of your soul? That suffering and sacrifice produce, by an inner contortion of the spirit, an ecstasy you yearn for? Her trust in the goodness of life came from her faith in the primacy of her spiritual over her lower nature. Nonna had often said that faith, above all, spins a web of love and peace around you and shelters you from the frailty and turbulence of the world.

Despite the din in the auditorium, she tuned in to two people talking in the doorway directly behind her.

"Did you see what that cursed Harpo did to my pants, Yarda? Take a look." The man was sounding a bit peeved at, perhaps, finding a rip on his pants cuff.

"*Himmel*, Paul! One wonders how you get on—letting Harpo rankle you. He's taken to you, you know. Yes, he has. Leave it to a psychiatrist to confuse affection and aggression." The woman laughed her hearty laugh.

"His nips are signs of affection! The little beast's got a sadistic streak."

Anna detected some playfulness in the man's words.

"Maybe you'd like to take us both on as patients. How about group therapy? You can shrink our lives and shape us into servants." The woman laughed heartily again. Anna couldn't help smiling. She wondered what the couple looked like but resisted the desire to turn around.

"You internists get a kick poking fun at us shrinks. Watch out for those myths infecting medicine."

Given his tone of voice, Anna imagined the man smiling.

"*Milda makter!* I've no idea what you're talking about."

"Huh, hunh . . . exactly what we shrinks expect—repression rooted in resistance and denial. The myopia of internal medicine—the body can be healed without touching the heart." The man gave a chuckle.

"And who do you think props up the broad field of medicine, if not the internist?"

"So, Harpo's antics are mere attachment to me—that straight from Wayne State's gifted internist!"

"Thanks for the compliment. Admit it. He's a little dear, isn't he?"

"Jumping on the table and stealing my spaghetti! And just who had to clean up the mess? The little dear's got the manners of a piglet."

"He did look like such a little darling, didn't he? His whiskers all orange. Your life's so dull, Paul, I'd never see you if it weren't for Harpo."

"More to the point—I'm favored with your Swedish treats as a quid pro quo to walk the little beast. Did you hear him growl at me while I cleaned him up? You might think I was punishing him."

"Ah, Paul and my little bichon—"

"Bichon, all right. He looks like a white puff that couldn't make up its mind whether to be a terrier or a poodle."

"Look, Paul. There's Helen Anne and Tom—still empty seats next to them."

Anna saw the man and woman walk in front of the podium. A tall blond man with horned-rim glasses and a vivacious full-bodied blond woman, both in their early thirties. He yelled, "Hold three seats for us," and motioned to the others, holding up three fingers.

"Go on up, Yarda. I'll wait for Lucky. Oh, tell Helen Anne that Lucky'll be coming along tonight." Paul went back to the door behind Anna.

Anna listened as Paul greeted Lucky. She watched them climb the stairs and seat themselves next to Yarda. Lucky was slightly shorter and stockier than Paul and about the same age.

The moderator finally came rushing in and, while quickly peeling off his coat and introducing himself to Anna, shook her hand warmly. "Sorry to be so late," he said, puffing. Of short and stocky build, he had a gentle face and twinkling blue eyes. She liked him at once.

Hardly catching his breath, he turned to the audience. "Ladies and gentlemen! Ladies and gentlemen, may I have your attention, please?" He hastened to open the Symposium. "I'm Dr. Danova, your moderator for the next few days. Before I introduce our speaker this morning, I want to call your attention to . . ." John Danova, head of psychiatry at Wayne, addressed the nearly full auditorium with the self-confidence of a man accustomed to lead. He went on about the various afternoon sessions, the agenda to be followed, and the topics to be covered.

"I'm proud to introduce our keynote speaker, Professor Margaret Petrarch, who hails from one of our sister institutions— Michigan State. A graduate of Yale, Professor Petrarch has distinguished herself in a new field coming into prominence— humanistic psychology." He praised Margaret's research, her knowledge of various approaches to healing, and her idea of tailoring the form of therapy to the personal history and temperament of the patient . . .

During this time, Paul had introduced Luke (Lucky) Evans, assistant dean at the medical school being set up at Michigan State, to his friend, Yarda Andersson, an attending physician at Wayne State. Luke knew Thomas James who, with big blue eyes and youthful face, could pass for a college freshman, and Helen Anne Danova, a pretty, cheerful intern in radiology at Wayne, the daughter of Dr. Danova, the moderator. Yarda and Helen (as everyone but her family called her) and Tom came to the symposium as Paul's guests. A radiologist, Tom shared with Paul an interest in many of the symposium's topics.

A competent physician turned administrator, Luke Evans preferred to be called Lucky. He'd be presenting the major address the following morning. Always on the run (he had just gotten back from D.C.), he seemed tired and listless. A workaholic with ample stature in the medical profession, he managed to find time to keep up many friendships and had a reputation as a generous man. Once seated, he relaxed and began to look forward to the opening address. He had heard a good deal about Yarda from Paul but had never met her. During the moderator's lengthy speech, Luke glanced at Yarda numerous times.

As Dr. Danova went on and on in praise of the speaker, Tom turned to Helen and whispered, "Your old man's sure long-winded today. I've got to give it to him—that's the longest I've seen him keep a straight face." Outside of class, John Danova, known for his keen wit, rarely talked about his work.

"He's Janus-faced, you know," Helen said. "He's more comfortable as an entertainer than an academic!"

Tom nodded.

The audience began clapping as Anna took the podium. "Thank you, Dr. Danova, for your close attention to my writings." Anna turned to him and smiled. "I'm honored. I hope to live up to your tribute to my studies still in the early stage and needing much work . . ." She welcomed the various groups at the symposium and mentioned the need to summarize a lot of her ideas for so short a talk.

Paul put on his glasses to get a better look at the speaker and saw a woman in her twenties with dark hair softly covering her ears and gently drawn back into a twist. She wore a burgundy suit and white blouse. Her pleasant voice complemented her beauty.

". . . In trying to envisage the future we must keep in mind that history teaches us two paradoxical things. All cultural achievements, regardless of their greatness, contain seeds of their own decay. All attempts to bring about an abundant and harmonious life have ended in tragedy.

"During the decline of civilizations—as was the case in Babylon, ancient Greece, ancient Rome, the theocracy of the Middle Ages—new forces eventually rose out of their ashes, inspiring the human spirit to bring forth new social forms. History reminds us that progress—a direct line of human evolution—does not bear serious examination. Life evolves in a cycle of ups and downs, of flourishings and declines, of decreasing and increasing suffering . . ."

"Paul, Paul," Yarda whispered, nudging to stir him. She saw her name being written on the blackboard beside the podium—a request that she respond to a call from Good Samaritan Hospital. "I've got to call in," she said, getting up and quickly filing out of the cramped row.

" . . . We human beings are both blessed and cursed by the wondrous gift of freedom that, like the weather, can be creative as well as destructive—a power for both good and evil. In fact, our lives are rooted in freedom. Among all our fellow earth-dwellers, we alone are born incomplete and must create a social and cultural womb to grow and shape our lives in. Our destiny springs from freedom. Ignoring this, many mental health professionals and social scientists mistakenly regard human beings as mere biological machines or mere instinctual animals. But doesn't history tell us a different story about human greatness— tragic as it may be? Aren't we alone, among all creatures, equipped to transform the planet, taking part in our own destiny?"

"What happened?" Yarda's hand was shaking.

"He was wild—" Shannon sobbed.

"Get hold of yourself, Shannon."

"He invited me over last night—a party for first-year interns, he said."

"Well?"

"When I got to his apartment, no one was there but him."

"*Himmel!* Why didn't you leave?"

"He said he was waiting for the others . . . crowded me up against the couch arm."

"Oh, no!" Yarda said, thinking about the ugly stuffed pea-green couch in Charlie Martin's apartment. Everything in the place—rug, walls, ceilings—was a sickening pea green. "Listen, Shannon. Take the day off. I'll get a sub for you."

"I'll be all right."

"Did you bop him a good one?"

" . . . pinned me down—I couldn't move. Thank goodness the phone rang!"

Yarda pictured the petite bubbly brunette manhandled by Charlie Martin who, during the last few weeks, had become unkempt and bloated. Before then, he had won over the hearts and minds of Wayne's interns and residents in medicine, been appointed chief resident, and was thought of as an exceptional internist. Yarda, like many others, had seen a swift swing in Charlie. Too fast for her to react to him. All she needed now was a rape charge! Charlie was out of control.

"You're sure you're up to it?" Yarda asked.

"Yeah."

"I'll be back in touch." Yarda rang Martin. No answer. She

tried the hospital—nowhere to be found. Where *was* he? About to start back, she turned around and called the ward again. "Tell Martin to call me at Wayne as soon as possible." She walked back to the auditorium exasperated, not only with Martin but with herself.

" . . . The question is this: what will life be like in fifty years—in 2015? What will mental health practices be?

"Let us assume that we avert a nuclear holocaust in the next fifty years. The most plausible prediction is this: There will be no end of chaos during the rest of this century. We will live more and more in a shattered world, feel less and less safe, and dream hopefully of repairing communal life. As for 2015, we can only hazard a guess about our civilization from the vantage point of 1965—"

"What a mess!" Yarda whispered, slipping back into her seat.
"Mess?"
"Charlie Martin."
"Not again!"
"I'm going to can him!"
"About time. He's been nothing but trouble . . ."
"Hard to believe—his credentials and past performance. We worked really well together."
"From the U. of M., no less. What's he up to?"
"Damn near raped a first-year resident last night. I couldn't reach him."
"Good God!"

" . . . most important of all will be the collapse of both superpowers now aligned against one another. Both are founded on falsehoods. Hard as it is to admit, our plight today resembles that of a party of ignorant travelers who find themselves on a bus launched at reckless speed, driverless, rushing headlong down a hilly terrain strewn with rocks and trees. When the communist bloc and the capitalist bloc will smash up, nobody knows. It may be decades, perhaps the next century.

"My guess is that the communist world, where the disdain

for truth is greater, will fall first. In these empires the will to power is more and more set against truth. The will to power more and more thrives on falsehood—till we come to believe that falsehood should be embraced for the sake of defending our way of life.

"Revolutions now breaking out all over will change mankind little, if at all. We've learned that no political change in itself, no matter how important, can make a human being out of an ape! . . ."

Shannon Sherman, taking a break alone in the doctors' lounge at Samaritan, froze when Charlie Martin walked in. His savage look sent shivers up her spine. He's gone over the edge, she thought. His tight, wrinkled lab coat, stretched over his protruding stomach, was splotched with old blood and yellow stains.

Shannon wished for one thing at the moment—to flee. Why hadn't she taken the day off?

"Get your ass in gear, Sherman," he barked. "We've got an emergency in 225."

What could she do? What should she do? Adrenalin coursed through her body readying her for flight. But her training—years of obedience—immobilized her.

"Do you hear me, Sherman—get your ass moving! *Now!*"

Down the long corridor she tagged behind at breakneck speed in the wake of anger and bitterness that trailed after him.

"You're going to see, Sherman"—he turned round to make sure she followed—"I'm going to teach you to cure a comatose old wreck—an up-to-date, one step, quick fix."

How am I going to get out of this? she thought. Her head was swiveling—right . . . forward . . . left, right . . . forward . . . left—scanning the long hall, hoping to find a staff physician. No one around. Her heart was pounding and she felt like crying. She followed Charlie into room 225. Old Mary Miller lay comatose, barely breathing.

"This is not only a comatose," Charlie ranted. "What we got here is an old wreck kept alive too long by medical technology. Worthless . . . time consuming . . . useless! Watch and learn the marvels of modern medicine." Shannon could feel the deep anger spewing out of his corpulent face. "I'm sick of being screwed over," he muttered, pulling a bottle from his pocket.

"The poor old lady—why take your frustration out on her?" What's Charlie up to, she wondered. For some time now she'd suspected that he was losing it. Why hadn't Yarda done anything about it?

"Out of my way, Sherman. Overworked, underpaid, castrated—turned into a . . . Andersson can go to hell, too."

"Charlie, you're overwrought. For God's sake!" she screamed, seeing him get a hypodermic ready.

"No psychological bullshit!"

"What are you doing, Charlie?" she yelled as she saw him draw a large amount of KCL into the syringe. "Are you out of your mind? Potassium chloride! Charlie, listen to me. Stop it—*Now!*" Oh dear God, she thought, he's going to kill her. He's lost his mind.

"Out of my way, bitch!" He shoved her aside. "This modern medicine works wonders—watch and see. Oh, how effective we can be—one, two, three."

Looking at the dark circles under his glassy eyes, she knew he was mad. She saw him feel around Mary Miller's atrophied arm. *"Help! Help!"* she began screaming at the top of her lungs, pulling frantically at his arm. "Don't do it! You're going to kill her, you idiot . . . *Don't do it!*"

The needle pierced the flaccid flesh, shooting fluid into the old woman's skeletal body as a whole cadre of nurses and aides stormed into the room. Shannon, wailing and pulling frantically at Charlie's coat sleeve, slumped to the floor. Charlie kicked her aside.

"Everything's fine. Get on with your work."

"Everything's not fine!" a stout nurse fired back. "Dr. Andersson has called and—" Charlie bolted from the room.

Shannon sobbed uncontrollably. Two nurses took hold of her, pulling her crumpled body up, trying to steady her. With their arms around her, they gently ushered her toward the nurses' station. As she left the room, she looked back at the lifeless body.

". . . What will the general pattern of life be like by century's end? Human beings will still be worshiping the ideal of productivity and be valued as units of production. Increased wealth will be seen as man's salvation. Everywhere, ambition for material success and power will result in a merciless attitude toward the weak and the less talented. Competitiveness and crude individualism will breed nonconformity, cynicism, rage, and criminality. Once the two superpowers break down, the splintering of civilization will quicken. Without fear of an enemy to make citizens susceptible to governmental manipulation, society, rife with injustices, will decline ever faster. As civilized life is collapsing, human beings will take it upon themselves to congratulate one another on being the crowning jewel of evolution. Pride and arrogance will spark an absolute relativism— anything goes. Human beings will see no limits, no meaning, no purpose in life save boosting pleasure. Those in authority, infected with such passions themselves, will be powerless to stem the decline . . ."

Yarda was tense. She had difficulty focusing on Margaret's talk, her thoughts kept running back to Shannon. Just then, Yarda saw her name being written on the blackboard, again. It must be Charlie Martin! She was going to light into him. Disrupting those seated next to her, she rushed off to call.

". . . are two signs of the twilight of civilization. The first is the breakdown of the family and the brushing-off of marriage as a sacrament. As tidal waves on a coastal town in a hurricane rip away houses—the sturdy alone endure the pounding force of wind and water—so does the collapse of marriage assail a decaying culture. Only firm families can hold fast against the animal urges let loose as divorce, broken homes, promiscuity take their toll. Marriage becomes an unwelcome burden; many eager to be foot-loose and fancy free, grope their way along the slippery slope of narcissism and self-indulgence.

"The second sign is pride amid the rubble. Many take themselves to be the center of a godless universe—free of a higher good at last. Pride reigns, and so do disorder, anarchy, and ignorance . . ."

Shaken, Yarda put the receiver back. Charlie Martin had cracked. Her anger turned on herself. His use of crude language, his weight gain, his recklessness, tardiness—and, yes, his recent incompetence—were signs for anyone to see. She wasn't blind. But something came to mind, something she'd forgotten: Martin's mother had died recently after a long terminal illness. That's why she'd been so easy on him, even though his behavior was becoming erratic. She believed that so capable and committed a doctor deserved a chance to pull himself together. True. But how could she explain her oversight—not seeing the signs of his mental breakdown? She could not avoid admitting that she too was responsible for Mary Miller's death. She'd let Martin off the hook when he'd begun to fall apart. Her neglect shook her self-confidence. She dreaded the thought of the legal charges that would be levied against the hospital. She'd be right in the center.

". . . Moral degeneration will give rise to hedonism, cynicism, amorality, immorality, irrationality, nihilism, and insanity.

"A new epoch, a new Renaissance, if mankind survives, may be wrought out of the anarchy let loose. This is our hope and trust in the freedom of mankind: out of terrible suffering a new flourishing—a new Renaissance—may be born from the dying culture. There is no guarantee. We could face a long period of decay—a new Dark Age.

"Where does hope spring for a positive vision for the twenty-first century? This is the vital issue for mental health experts today.

"Remember our bus rushing down the hill strewn with obstacles without a driver. When it crashes, a need to heal the sick and dying will scream out to the world. Revolutionaries, lusting after power and prone to violence, fail to grasp the engine of history. Needed is a creative minority, the morally and spiritually transformed, who will become a core the masses will rally around. Tuned to the march of history, the creative minority alone may see the path out of the moral morass."

Paul became uneasy. Yarda had been away for some time. Luke inquired into the nature of the problem at Samaritan. Paul, saying nothing about Shannon, merely assured Lucky that Yarda had things under control.

". . . A new Renaissance—what will it be like? Among old and young, men and women, educated and uneducated, and from all races and creeds—leaders will spring forth. Carrying within themselves the truth of past traditions, they will crystallize into a nucleus to instruct and lead the masses. Bit by bit the scales will fall from the eyes of the many. Their barbarism, standing naked before them, will shock them. They'd mistaken licentiousness for freedom; violated nature's limits; founded their lives on disinformation, propaganda, public relations, miseducation, scientism, and news media based on falsehood and illusion . . ."

"What's going on?" Paul asked, as Yarda slipped into her seat.

"I'm in a God-awful fix."

"What now?"

"Can you run me back to my apartment for my car? You can come back to the afternoon sessions. I'll fill you in on the way."

"Can I help?"

"Advice . . . maybe more."

Paul looked at his watch—six or seven minutes remained. "Let me catch Professor Petrarch's summary . . ."

"A few minutes more hardly matters. The damage's done!"

" . . . As for mental health in the new Renaissance, human beings will march to a different drumbeat. Man's spiritual nature will have primacy over his material. Yet, the spiritual and material will be seen as two parts of a whole. Unlike the Middle Ages, when the primacy of the spiritual crushed and subdued the material, or the twentieth century, when the material crushed and subdued the spiritual, the new Renaissance will unite these facets of reality.

"A new consciousness will emerge—the *'go-beyond.'* Psychologists must *go beyond* psychology—beyond the soul to its spiritual ground. Psychiatrists must *go beyond* psychiatry—

beyond the biological to the unitive power of life, its ordering principle. Students must *go beyond* education—to contribute their learning to the life of the community. People must *go beyond* the church—seeking to live in union with goodness, truth, and beauty. The state must *go beyond* authority and power—to serve the weaker against the rapacious nature of the stronger. Family members must *go beyond* the family—to contribute to the larger community. Business must *go beyond* profits—to serve the community and uphold the dignity of labor, recognizing labor to be of central importance. One of the greatest evils, the exploitation of labor, will gradually lessen. The mass media must *go beyond* mass appeal—to communicate responsibly rather than pander to man's base urges. The greatest of all evils since the sacrifice of children to the gods is the harming of the spirit of our children. No longer will our children's hearts and minds be polluted, whether for profits or for power.

"The new Renaissance will not be a movement into a Golden Age but the flourishing of a new epoch, subject to the ravages of time. During its upward phase, mankind will become more firm in faith and steadfast in hope, striving with zeal for a healthier life. Taking up the shield of truth and casting off the stubbornness of pride and arrogance, men and women will carry their burden of freedom with joy and good hope. Accountability will replace blame; spontaneous use of intelligence will replace conformity and nonconformity; justice will replace self-aggrandizement; at-one-ness will replace the yearning for power and status.

"A new epoch stems from the human will and freedom and, should it be realized, will give way in time to evil, suffering, and disruption. History teaches us this: human freedom embodies the potential for both good and evil. Human creativity is finite and though intertwined with the infinite . . ."

Yarda grew more and more impatient. She pulled at Paul's sleeve to follow. She got up to leave; Paul followed.

The Party

Anna was exhausted. Questions had been flying left and right during the afternoon sessions. She meant to spark debate and discussion, and had done so. Now, eager to get away, she happily accepted John Danova's invitation to a party at his house in Grosse Pointe Farms.

She rushed back to her hotel, showered, took a short nap, and was dressed and ready when John came by to pick her up.

Controversy over her talk seemed to follow her to the Danovas', as she sat sipping a glass of wine and relishing the *hors d'oeuvres*. "Goodness, I'm glad to see idealism's not fully dead, but . . ." "What a wonderful idea—a new Renaissance. Rather an extravagant view of us mortals!" "Surely, Dr. Petrarch, you expect a tad much of us!" So it went: some thought her too cynical ("much too jaundiced a view of the world") and others mocked her ("Indeed, Professor Petrarch, one wonders, unjustly perhaps, whether the problem lies with the world or with the stance you take!").

Several groups clustered here and there in the crowded living room, spilling out into the dining room, library, and foyer. Anna saw John Danova approach her. "Margaret, here are two fans of yours," he said with a twinkle in his eyes. "This is Luke Evans, assistant dean of medicine at Michigan State." Margaret shook hands with Luke. She remembered him as the dark-haired man who passed by her that morning. "And this is Paul—" John was interrupted by Helen Anne calling from another room, just as Margaret and Paul shook hands.

"Paul, Paul! Telephone! It's Yarda—urgent."

"I'm coming," Paul yelled, staring into Anna's green eyes. "Excuse me, please," he said, bewildered, withdrawing his hand before John could say another word.

Anna recognized him as the blond man who had been waiting for Luke Evans. When she looked into his face, an intense emotion of delight unsettled her. Her thoughts spun back to Prospect Hill and to Paul Risch. She listened to Luke saying to John, ". . . must be trying for Yarda to go through. I've been impressed, John, with your new program—psychiatric staff put at the service of medical students, interns, and residents. It diffuses potential problems. Any warning signs that Charlie Martin was headed for trouble?"

John was distressed that Luke would make reference to Martin publicly. Hospital administrators at the moment were in turmoil; their lawyers had asked everyone to exercise discretion if the topic came up. John turned to Margaret. "One of our residents giving Dr. Andersson trouble," he said softly.

"Well Lucky, about our psychiatric staff—keep in mind it's a two-way street. You know yourself, there's a lot of self-denial . . . what I mean is your psychiatric staff's available, but can you make your students and staff take advantage of it? That's the dilemma we face. Those most in need are often last to seek help."

"Similar to the situation at Lakeside a few months back?" Luke asked.

"In some ways the opposite," John said, annoyed at Luke. John looked around and practically whispered: "The resident at Lakeside attempted suicide, turning his rage onto himself— masochistic. In the case at Samaritan rage was turned outward—sadistic," John spoke so softly that Anna, standing right next to him, hardly made out his words.

"The Lakeside resident—still in a coma?" Luke whispered, getting the point.

"Overdosed on insulin. Enough to render him comatose. Actually he and the present case share one thing—both were exceptional physicians showing little sign of sickness—"

"Has Paul decided to take the position at Wayne?"

Up to this point Anna half listened, not being able to make sense of their conversation—what little she did hear.

"Paul's staying on at the U. of M.," John answered, breathing a sigh of relief that they had turned to a safer topic. "Be nice for us and for Yarda, of course, if Paul came on board at Wayne."

John, Anna could see, was unhappy about Paul's decision. But Luke's face lit up. She suspected Paul had a competitor for Yarda's affections.

Anna's attention turned to a young man in a wheelchair with a girl about seven or eight on his lap making his way toward them. "Dad, Mother wants you in the kitchen!" she announced.

"Okay, Sarah. Excuse me, Lucky . . . Margaret," John nodded as he took leave.

"Have you met Sarah and Jeff, yet?" Luke asked. Margaret shook her head. "This is Sarah, the boss of the Danova household, and Jeff, her brother."

"Me, the boss? Lucky Evans, you're a fibber," Sarah said. "Do you like it?" Sarah showed off to Margaret and others the bracelet Luke had given her. "Thanks, Lucky."

"*Dr.* Evans to you, Runty," Jeff scolded.

"So, *Dr.* Evans, you see how I'm treated," Sarah said. "Jeff makes me out to be the runt of the litter. Oh, oh! Being the baby of the family, the bane of my life." They all laughed.

Seeing Helen Anne come into the room, Lucky excused himself and went over to her.

"Are you a doctor?" Sarah asked Margaret.

"Yes."

"A real doctor?"

"Are there unreal ones?"

"Touché, Runty!" Jeff teased.

"Watch out Jeff, or I won't lend you my eyes. You know, like my father's a real doctor."

"And what's an unreal one?" Margaret asked.

"Like professors—they're called doctors. They can't help sick people."

"I must be half real, then," Margaret answered, smiling.

"What do you mean?"

"Well, I teach and I try to help people, too."

"You give them pills to cure them?"

"Well, yes. Medicine for their mind."

"What's a mind?"

"Enough, Sarah, enough," Jeff said. "We haven't had a proper introduction to Dr. Petrarch, have we Runty?"

"No," Sarah said, pleased.

As Anna was to learn later, Jeff was nearly blind and saw faces and bodies in blurred images. Sarah helped him to get a closer look through a game they made up. Two years earlier, Jeff had played varsity basketball and drums in the high school band. He had looked forward to college, planning to follow in his father's footsteps. Quite suddenly his vision worsened and he lost his balance as neurofibromas—"benign" tumors—sprang up randomly, impairing both his sight and his hearing. He had to withdraw from Michigan State after his first year.

"Jeff's got to guess who you look like," Sarah said, delighted. "Dr. Petrarch has dark, wavy hair and she's very pretty."

"Ginger Rogers," he said, straightfaced.

"No, you ninny!" she said, giggling. "Come on now, think. Dr. Petrarch is tall with sparkling green eyes."

"Doris Day!"

"No. Doris Day is Yarda, don't you remember—blond hair and blue eyes." She laughed and squirmed on his knees.

"No, No, Runty! We agreed Yarda is half Ginger and half Doris. Did you forget? Well, go on, Runty."

"She's got on a black velvet top with a crew neck and a white-and-black-print skirt that flares out. Now think, I'm shifting gears, Jeffrey—nose and mouth of *Father of the Bride* and *National Velvet*."

"Gotcha—Phyllis Diller."

"Ha, ha! No, you goose! One more try or—"

"Elizabeth Taylor. Whew!"

"You got it. Sometimes he can be so slow. Now, listen, Jeff: voice, and hairdo—a French twist—as in *My Fair Lady*."

"Ah . . . that's got to be *Roman Holiday*."

"Ha! You're cheating, you're supposed to play by the rules— name please?" Sarah giggled. "You forgot her name?"

"Oh! Runty, how could I forget Audrey Hepburn. Wow!" Jeff exclaimed. "A Taylor-Hepburn hybrid. This must be some charming woman."

Sarah amused the guests and loved being the center of attention. "My sister Helen Anne says Harpo's Paul's bane. Have you seen Harpo, Dr. Petrarch?"

"No. Some ferocious beast?"

"Oh, no! He's a cute white bitchowin—"

"No, Sarah, bichon," Jeff corrected her.

"Bichon or whatever. He's playful and likes Paul but chews up his clothes. I think he's jealous of Paul."

"My, you're quite a psychologist!" Margaret joked.

"I'm gonna be a psychiatrist like my dad and Dr. Risch," Sarah said.

Anna's heart quickened at the mention of "Dr. Risch." Paul Risch! Could Paul possibly be Paul Risch? Yes, those eyes and that face. She hadn't recognized him. It must be fourteen years, at least. Things immediately took on a new meaning for her. She wished for a moment to be alone and to collect her thoughts about him, since she'd heard him speaking to Yarda that morning in the auditorium.

"What's all the noise in this corner about?" Helen Anne asked, making her way toward her brother and sister. "Sarah, Mother needs you in the kitchen, pronto. On the double."

"It's Runty telling tales out of school again—Helen Anne says this, Helen Anne says that—"

"Watch yourself, Jeffrey Danova. I've got half a mind to tell everyone your middle name, Jeffrey Eelrebo Danova—heavy on the *Eel!*" Sarah laughed, bouncing off Jeff's knees and making a face at him as he tried to slap her bottom. She skipped off.

"Poor, Yarda," Tom said, joining them. "Paul just called. He doubts they'll be back tonight. He's staying at Samaritan to help Yarda straighten things out."

"What's going on at Samaritan, Tom? I keep hearing about some murder and mayhem."

"Dad's trying to hush it up," Helen Anne said, looking around to see whether anyone picked up Jeff's remark. "It's the topic of conversation all over! Has Jeff asked you about your talk, Dr. Petrarch?"

Anna's mind was on Paul. "Margaret—please call me Margaret," she said flushing. "No. Sarah's been entertaining us. You were at the talk this morning, Jeff?"

"Dad told me about parts of your paper. Your ideas impressed him," Jeff was saying as Mrs. Danova called the guests to the buffet.

Anna on edge

Anna roamed among the guests, avoiding small talk when possible and affecting civility when not.

She'd found Paul. Yet she felt uneasy. Her identity would surely bring out all the old unsettled questions about her mother's death long buried among the debris of her former life. No, better to keep herself hidden. Suppose Paul recognized her? Thank goodness her name cloaked her real identity. Proving agile of mind and holding her heart at bay, she'd be able to keep up her disguise.

How might they meet again and what would she say to him? Lost in such thoughts she pricked up her ears for any word about him or Yarda. Paul was unlikely to return to the Danovas' that evening. She could relax till tomorrow. Maybe she should cut short her stay in Detroit. But she hated to leave the symposium she'd so much looked forward to. So many people and so many different sessions the next two days—her path and Paul's might not cross again. She noticed Jeff drawing near. Sitting at the end of the divan she turned to face him.

"You must think I'm childish—Sarah and I!" He backed his wheelchair beside her.

"Your teasing Sarah reminded me of my brother. He could be a royal pain sometimes, needling me no end." Memories of life on Prospect Hill in the forties forced themselves on her— the years after her father's death. Life then was in stark contrast to the wealth and freedom of the present.

"Dad said your talk went well this morning," Jeff said. "Seems MSU students are getting a bit stirred up over the war—"

"Well, we're in for a cultural bump—a jarring of values— probably aggravated by the controversy over the Vietnam War. The war, as I see it, is more a result than a cause of changing values," she was saying as she tuned into two women nearby. ". . . Yarda, I'm sure, is just wasting her time, if you ask me," one was saying. "She's in for a letdown—like all the others!" The other replied: "Paul's a pretty decent guy—not about to string anyone along."

". . . see as the difference between conservatives and liberals?"

Jeff was asking.

"Well, lets see . . . well," Anna stammered, trying to focus on Jeff's question. "Conservatives seem to see the golden age in the past, liberals in the future. Don't you think?"

"In ways I'm conservative—in others, I'm liberal."

"Well, conservatives are a bit nostalgic about the past— liberals, too optimistic about the future."

"Where do you come down?"

She thought about the stubbornness of her paternal grandparents. They'd disinherited their only daughter and demeaned her father. Tradition, valued higher than love and life, brought great suffering to her mother. Goodness and love should be put above abstract traditions—especially decadent ones as there were among the privileged. Out of the love of an idea, people may end up torturing others. No! Tradition must always be weighed in the balance of good and evil. But she feared liberals, too; many naively take history to be redemptive. How could material changes in the world alone bring harmony, love, and justice?

"I listen to both sides—to the dialogue between conservatives and liberals," she said, "bearing in mind the problem of time."

"Problem of time?"

"Well, you see, past and future live in the present moment. See what I mean? We can't cast our lot fully with either conservatives or liberals, traditionalists or progressives. The present is tethered to the past and evolving into the future— liberals and conservatives alike embody part of the truth. Liberals are too fixed on the future; conservatives too wedded to the past. I'm afraid neither group embraces the whole of truth. Truth lies deeper—beyond time."

"Can't pin a label on you. You're pretty slippery—elusive!" Jeff said, laughing.

"Jeff!" Helen Anne called out, "Phone! Wanna take it?"

"Be there in a sec. Excuse me, Margaret, I've been expecting— something I need to attend to. You won't run off on me, leaving me in ignorance, will you?" he asked, rolling out of the room before she could reply.

A joyful feeling awakened Anna to thoughts of Paul when

she heard Yarda's name mentioned. Helen, Tom, and Luke had moved closer to her and were talking about events at Wayne.

"If Yarda tries to cover it up, she'd be guilty as an accessory to the crime," Tom warned. "Believe me, there's no way it's going to be covered up. And what about Shannon?"

"You're right, Tom," Lucky said. "I know John thinks the case at Lakeside and this one are not connected, but the media sure as hell will play up the similarities—more noise about the way residents are overworked and underpaid. In the suicide attempt at Lakeside, the director of the residency program had to run for cover: the residents had long hours and little sleep." He glanced at his watch. "Look, it's getting late. I've got to be off—get ready for tomorrow's talk." Paul and Yarda walked in just as he was about to leave.

The guests started moving into the foyer, getting ready to leave. Mrs. Danova stood in the center saying her goodbyes as the guests thanked her.

Helen Anne remembered that her father had told her to be sure Margaret got a ride back to her hotel if he didn't get back from Wayne in time. Yarda said she'd drive Margaret back. Paul invited Luke to stay at his place in Ann Arbor—a good forty-mile drive.

As they entered the foyer, Jeff rolled in. "Caught you running out on me," he said to Margaret. "Just a minute."

"Yes?"

"Helen Anne, how about arranging a dinner party tomorrow night at Mario's—you, Tom, Lucky, Paul, Yarda? We'll tempt Margaret to join us," Jeff said.

"Ah, such a temptation!" Anna said.

"How about Dr. Andersson convincing you of our good company and Mario's fine food?"

"Settled," Yarda said. "I'll do my best."

"Dr. Petrarch, Dr. Petrarch, don't forget me!" Sarah practically slid down the banister.

"Runty, what are you doing up so late?" Jeff scolded.

"Hush, Eelrebo, you're not my dad!" She made a face at him. "Is it okay, Mother, to say goodbye to Dr. Petrarch?"

"Yes, dear. But little girls should be sound asleep by now!"

Sarah hugged Margaret. "Lucky Evans," she said, "you—"

"*Dr.* Evans, do I have to remind you?" Mrs. Danova told her.

"*Dr.* Evans, you better not fib about me anymore." She hugged Luke. "Goodbye, Paul . . . uh . . . Dr. Risch and Dr. Andersson. When will I see Harpo again? Is he still biting Paul's pants and eating his spaghetti?"

"You'd better be on guard when you meet that little monster," Paul said, laughing. "I'm gonna hang him up by his whiskers if he steals my spaghetti again."

"Don't you dare, Paul Risch! Yarda'll take a stick to you."

Busy filing out, saying her goodbyes, and getting into Yarda's car, Anna did not get a good look at Paul.

Paul and Luke

Someone (was it Shannon Sherman?) kept screaming at the top of her lungs as some brute was raping her. How could Paul help? A wire fence barred him. The gruesome scene changed and Shannon's face turned into that of Anna the last time he saw her. She was gaunt and cadaverous, riding down Prospect Hill in Piero's car. Anna's arms stretched out imploring him. Paul's eyes met hers across the fence and then in a flash her face turned into Margaret's. As their eyes met, an explosion went off in him. Thrashing about in bed, Paul woke up with a start, in a sweat. Reality slowly trickled back into him.

He heard Lucky rattling around in the kitchen, and smelled the smell of freshly brewed coffee drifting into the room. Paul lay still in his warm bed, happy to be alive. Rolling over, he folded his arms behind his head and stared up at the ceiling.

His dream life had a world all its own. It struggled and wrestled in the night, often taking him on a voyage to hell. Some other intelligence seemed to take hold of him. What was it trying to tell him?

His body too was a mystery, a wonder! It digested food, breathed, pumped his heart, rushed blood through the network of his arteries and veins. Always at work changing food and oxygen into energy—into himself—all without the effort of his will.

Awake, we're half asleep playing roles—multiple personalities, that's what we humans are, he thought. Living mechanically, we take ourselves to be masters of our own destiny. Think again. Fear, anxiety, dread, jealousy, anger, vexation, lust, despair—our heart testifies to our madness and suffering. The dark drama at night is telling. When awake we live on the threshold between dream and reality, floundering about in the bedlam of changing fads and fashions.

He showered, freed himself of morbid thoughts, and joined Lucky, who put a cup of coffee in front of him.

"Paul, I want you to know," Lucky said, weighing his words carefully, "in what I'm about to say . . . ah . . . my intentions are not altogether honorable."

Paul saw the sparkle in Lucky's eyes. "Not honorable? You, Lucky!"

"Things are not always what they seem."

"Well, out with it!" Paul saw a sly smile on Lucky's face.

"Something I need to talk to you about, Paul—something, I'm sorry to say, I can't resist. No. Something I don't want to resist—have no intention of resisting."

"Can it be so serious?"

Luke laughed nervously. "I mean . . . I . . . I want you to know . . . ah . . . I intend to marry Yarda Andersson."

Lucky's boldness astounded Paul. It didn't seem to suit Luke. "What are you talking about?"

"It's not a 'what,' Paul, but a 'when!'" Lucky grinned.

Paul fell silent. Over the past year, he had confided in Luke the nature of his relationship with Yarda. Luke knew, as did she, that Paul was not ready for a deeper commitment. Yarda enjoyed Paul's company, and both he and she felt comfortable in their friendship.

"Well?"

"What can I say? Affairs of the heart are made in heaven." Oddly, Lucky's forthrightness did not faze Paul. In fact, it made him lighthearted. This troubled Paul a little. Had his relationship with Yarda run its course?

"Come on, Paul, don't be coy with me."

Paul felt embarrassed not for Luke but for himself. No matter how he answered, it would be an insult to Yarda, whom he loved dearly. Yet he wasn't in love with her. Luke's bluntness didn't offend Paul. His heart had its own agenda and, till now, he didn't seem to be in on it. He found serenity—insofar as he did—in trusting fate to throw into his path the woman he'd eventually wed. What could he say to Luke? Any consent would be a sort of slight to Yarda. He stood by the golden rule—to remain silent. "What would you have me say, Lucky?"

"Think about it, Paul!"

"Listen, it's getting late. Let's shoot over to Zingerman's for breakfast before we take off for Detroit." Paul saw a wide grin break out on Lucky's face. Paul's few words evidently conveyed his deepest sentiments. He had given Luke an indirect answer— without demeaning Yarda. He hoped.

Dinner at Mario's

Anna felt like an outsider. The intimate talk around the table was a manifestation of friendships forged in the crucible of time.

They were at Mario's, Jeff's favorite Italian restaurant. Luke sat at one end of a rectangular table, and Jeff in his wheelchair at the other. Paul and Yarda sat to Luke's left, and Helen, Tom, and Anna shared the side to his right. Anna sat across from Paul.

The red-and-white checkered tablecloths blended in with the decor. Waiters in black suits bussed big trays of food. Anna savored the marvelous smells mixed with smoke and laughter as they drank chianti and waited for the *antipasto*.

Anna's thoughts wandered. Her heart and her head spoke to one another. Each person sitting around the table was also in an internal dialogue while talking to others. The loftiness of a human being is this power of consciousness—inner discourses going on in a rich internal brew, unseen. Isn't everyone shrouded in mystery—worlds within worlds? And what of hers, stocked with memories: didn't she carry around one big riddle of her mother's death? She'd long become wary of taking what she saw or heard as reality.

They'd just finished a toast to Lucky, commending him on

his morning talk: *"The Discovery of the Lost Atlantis: Public Health 2015, a Fifty-Year Perspective."*

"A toast to Yarda, too," Lucky said, turning to Yarda. "She made it through yesterday's ordeal—kept the media at bay."

"Let's not push our luck," Yarda said. "Lord, it's bound to jump in our faces in tomorrow's news. It's a mercy that Charlie Martin's homicide hasn't leaked to the press—so far." Anna sensed that Yarda hid even from Paul the strain of the terrible guilt she carried.

As for Paul, Anna felt deceitful and troubled. Would she or wouldn't she reveal herself? Should she or shouldn't she? Could she bear opening up the wound of her childhood? So far, no opportunity offered itself. Paul hardly noticed her, and not once did they chance to meet alone. As for Yarda, any man would be happy to have such a fiancée.

"Yes, Lucky," Paul said. "Yarda handled it like a pro. She's now become a legal tactician."

They all raised their glasses—"To the legal tactician!"

"Don't be so modest, Paul. You and John deserve most of the credit." Paul shook his head. "No, Paul, that's the truth," Yarda said. "Besides, the Detroit police kept to their bargain and didn't leak to the press. We lucked out . . ."

Paul's thoughts turned to Lucky and Yarda. How did Lucky interpret Paul's response to Lucky's infatuation with Yarda? How would Lucky act on it? How would Yarda respond? He wanted to stare at Margaret across the table—to take in her full beauty. How did she fit into his dream last night? Having forgotten Anna for years, why did her face fade into Margaret's like a film changing scenes? Since he'd first laid eyes on her, his memories of Prospect Hill had invaded his thoughts. He hadn't been down in that psychic cellar in years.

"The prosecutor's office promised to keep the murder charge quiet for the moment—for our cooperation, of course," Yarda said. "We've made a deal." She paused for a few minutes and Anna could see pain written in her face. "Oh, to be back to the simple life of Tustin up north, roaming around the eighty acres, living in the old cottage, seeing the old Swedes there." She fought back tears.

"Come now, Yarda," Paul said. "Don't take it to heart. Who of us foresees these messes life flings in our path."

"Given your report, Paul, and the backing by another psychiatrist, the charge against Charlie is likely to be dismissed with a plea of temporary insanity," she said. *"Milda makter!* Charlie's going to lose his license and be put on probation with lots of community service. What a mess. Poor Charlie." Tears trickled down her cheeks.

"You . . . we . . . all did our best," Paul said, filling her wine glass. "Medicine's a pretty tricky business—split-second decisions, not to mention the heavy hospital load. Besides, Detroit's a dispiriting place—a merry-go-round of drugs and crime. It wears down the stamina of geniuses and saints."

"I can't condone euthanasia," Yarda said, still puzzled by Charlie Martin's crime, "and Charlie's terrible treatment of Shannon! Yet, he's done a lot of good. I know it doesn't excuse him. Did you know, Paul, his mother died recently, after a long terminal illness?" Paul nodded.

Helen, feeling Yarda's distress, was reminded of Luke's talk that morning—*Discovery of the Lost Atlantis*. "I think your metaphor was intriguing, Lucky. The meaning of suffering, you say, is being lost, going underground, and becoming the lost Atlantis of our psyches. Something of an original idea. As the use of more and more drugs lessen pain, the tragic sense of life will diminish as people are narcotized—a sort of Brave New World in the making!"

"We forget that suffering—not a good in itself—is a force for mental and physical health. It flags the disease—it's a marker of error and of disharmony," Luke said.

Anna, enjoying her calamari, put down her fork and looked up at Lucky. "Your position, Lucky, brings to mind our parish priest who loved to spark up his teachings with Latin tags . . ." My God, she thought, Paul would know who she's talking about. She paused.

"Yes?" Luke waited.

"This priest was always throwing out Latin sayings—one was *nil nisi cruce*, no dependence but on the Cross. His view, Lucky, was something like yours: an important pathway to spiritual health is through suffering." Try as she might, she could not resist glancing at Paul for a second and saw a flicker in his eyes.

"Dependence on the cross, Margaret? My position?"

"Well, the priest put it in . . . in . . . paradoxical terms. His view, as far as I could figure it out, was that as Christ suffered on the cross and was resurrected in body and soul, so can we be, if we freely take up the cross to triumph over suffering." They ate in silence for a few seconds. Had she broken some unwritten code of etiquette?

Astonished to hear something out of Father D.'s own bag of tricks, Paul felt even more drawn to Margaret. It brought to mind another idea Father D. bandied about—*noli fronti credere*, trust not to appearances. Our words are like invisible missiles fired into the inner arena of others, Paul thought. They can implode into joy or fear or horror or anger; they can land in deserts. One cannot tell from outside what goes on in the inner sanctum of another.

"Mmmm . . . my roast veal—it must be seasoned with rosemary and sage and wine—is tops," Luke said. Looking up at Margaret, he asked: "Do you really believe, Margaret, that we should revert to religious symbols?"

"Oh, no, no. It's not a matter of belief or religion I'm getting at but a matter of paradox." Anna felt her face flush. "The point is, I think, . . . ah . . . suffering does not always make you better—improve you morally. A weak person not developed in character, you see, can be crippled by suffering, turning masochistic or sadistic—sometimes both. Those of strong character . . . it's different—there's hope suffering might have a positive effect, as you say. But there's no guarantee."

"But you yourself argued," Jeff said, "that we must go beyond religion. You called it the 'go-beyond,' a major value of the new age coming."

"Yes, Jeff. Suffering I believe can help us toward virtue—the true and only nobility, as the Romans put it. But the paradox of the cross—the priest meant, I think—the paradox turns our attention to the need for inner transformation, an inner change. Well, you see, putting it paradoxically saves us from being trapped in partial truths." Anna felt she was maundering and she hoped she hadn't given offense to Lucky's world view.

"How do we go beyond religion, then?" Jeff asked.

"We must not be merely believers or affirmers of our faith—we must live it. There's a new movement afoot: a return to a childlike, literal view of religion," she said, though afraid of getting herself further mired. "Naturally, children in their tender years should be introduced to religion literally. But don't you think many adults who take religious mythology and symbols literally suppose themselves converted? They call their conversion a rebirth. It's nothing more than a sideways shift from one dogmatic outlook to its opposite—from secular to religious beliefs. It's not a rebirth in the sense of awakening to conscience. It's merely a shift from belief in materialism to belief in religious dogma. A new belief is not necessarily a spiritual awakening." Anna began eating again, hoping she'd said her last words.

All this time Tom had been listening closely. "This sea squab is the best I've had," he said.

The talk momentarily languished as they talked about the Danova children—Sarah, Jeff, and Helen Anne—and how they got on so well with their father, whose sense of humor seemed to have been passed on to Sarah.

"Sarah's precocious all right," Tom observed. "A wonder she doesn't drive Jeff round the bend! But back to this business of religion. It troubles me. Whenever I point out the perversions of religion, my dad, a humanistic psychologist, too (excuse me, Margaret, no offense intended!) tells me, *ad nauseam*, that I've thrown the baby out with the bath since I began studying medicine. You've got to separate the truth, he lectures, from the church—the earthen vessel that carries it. To me *faith* is a very private thing. Ritual control of the masses, which I associate with *religion,* is frightening because . . . well, it tends, you see, to turn people either into swine or sheep. Either people give in to terrible crimes—like the Inquisition or the lynching of blacks and the gassing of Jews—or are utterly submissive and forfeit their freedom to those in authority. When I think of *religion,* I think of Dostoevsky's Grand Inquisitor."

"I understand your misgivings, Tom," Paul said. "But Margaret's idea of going beyond religion, as I understand it, is for the responsible practice of one's faith."

"Look here, Paul, the church has always justified compulsion in questions of faith, used fear, inhibited freedom of conscience. God, Paul, how many heretics have been punished, their ideas later grabbed on to by the church? Think of Giordano Bruno! And need we say what the general outcome has been? The Inquisition! I tell you, Christendom has run amuck. Extreme forms of violence have been used in the name of the religion of love and freedom."

Tom let out this blast with a passion that surprised only Anna. She saw the others smiling, amused at Tom and Paul at it again.

"No doubt the history of Christianity is jam-packed with acts of violence," Paul conceded. "But we must take care in our thinking, Tom, be more careful in our charges. We've got to distinguish the history of Christendom from the truth of Christianity. Really, Tom. Do acts of violence carried out by people of power in the Church have anything to do with the spiritual order itself—with the truth itself? Be reasonable. Violence belongs to the social activity of humans and comes from the desire for power and success in the world."

Paul was as passionate as Tom. Anna got so drawn into their arguments that she failed to see the others looking at each other, arching their eyebrows, waiting patiently for the two of them to talk themselves out.

"Your distinctions trifle with the facts, Paul—with what history teaches us. My goodness, the religion of love and freedom is a history of fanaticism and the imprisoning of the human spirit!"

"The same case surely can be made for higher education and for science," Paul said. "The path they've traveled ends in atomic warfare and potential world destruction. Would we deny mathematical truth, given the service mathematics has been put to? No, Tom, think about it. We can no more deny the need for religion than we can the need for higher education. The evils done in the name of religion can no more serve as an argument to deny the truth of a spiritual reality than the evils done in the name of higher education can serve to deny the existence of mathematics and the physical sciences."

Their waiter came over to see whether these talkers wanted
dessert and coffee. They ordered espressos.

"What are you talking about, Paul? There's a world of
difference between religion and education," Tom said. "I'm not
ready to buy your argument. Education seeks to free us from
intolerance; religion rides roughshod over freedom—breeds
intolerance."

Paul motioned to the waiter. "A round of brandies, too, please.
Your best." The women demurred. Paul insisted. "It'll go well
with the story I'm going to tell." They laughed and went along.

"You promise to roll me home if you put me to sleep?" Jeff
said.

"You'll be all ears."

"Is it an exposé?" Yarda asked.

"You bet," Paul said. "I've never told anyone before—a deep
dark secret of my youth." He winked at Yarda.

They started on their coffee as the brandies were being passed
around. Paul took a sip.

"You see," he said, "I come from a small milltown straddling
hills and valleys along a winding river. Among its second- and
third-generation working-class immigrants, there was a family
from Rome who came to live there about the time I was born,
next door to my parents'. They stood out like jewels in a junk
heap and turned their house and land into a charming place.
They had two children—a pretty daughter two years younger
than I, and a brother two years younger than she. An aura about
this family, including a grandmother and uncle, set them off
from the other families on the hill. The way they dressed and
talked: they were highly educated, especially the talented and
beautiful mother. Something happened to destroy their lives.
An unspeakable crime took place in this family, shocking
everyone. All evidence pointed to the daughter—a girl of twelve.
Living next door, I got to know and respect them. After their
misfortune, not one school chum or neighbor was allowed to
see the girl or her brother. No one knew until the murder that
the family came from the nobility. They soon moved away from
the hill. I was fourteen and horrified by the allegations brought
against the daughter. I refused absolutely to believe them. I

blocked the whole thing from my mind."

They all sipped brandy, absorbed in the story. Anna sat trembling. Her heart pumped so fast she had trouble breathing. She folded her hands tightly on her lap to keep them from shaking. She would always be remembered for that unspeakable crime. Paul's story convinced her that she would never reveal her identity to him or anyone else.

"In my last year at Brown, after I'd about finished my B.S. and been accepted at the U. of M., I became obsessed with finding her. In a frenzy, I followed every possible avenue: going to the police, to the gossip in our village, to the local priest, even to the psychiatrist called in to help her. Every path led to a dead end—as if she'd vanished into thin air. Seeing my frantic state, the priest took it upon himself to counsel me—"

"I knew Paul would lead us back to religion with this story," Tom yelled out. "'Unspeakable crime'! A crime that can't speak its name—'*the* crime that can't speak its name,' Paul?"

"Well, take it as you will but hear me out. The brandy will help with the digestion, Tom," Paul said. Anna saw them all smiling at one another.

"It'll give us the courage to weather this journey into fantasyland!" Tom laughed.

"A fantasy all right. It'll dredge up truth locked up in the secret recesses of your soul," Paul said.

"Good God, psychiatry lost its soul a long time ago." Tom laughed heartily.

"Some one give Jeff a poke, I think the brandy's got to him," Paul said.

"I'm all ears. Get on with your priest."

"When the priest saw me so distraught, he had to say some words of wisdom. He was afraid I'd lost my mental balance or, more likely, lost my beliefs—maybe both. He told me I should rise above the authoritarian form of religion as preached to a congregation and open myself up to the meaning of dogma— mysteries revealed only in our inner life. The real authority of the church is invisible, he told me. Its seat is not in the Church but in our hearts and can only be demonstrated in faith and in freedom. He warned me that there can be no compelling material proofs of religious truths—the criteria reside in ourselves. Growth in the sciences without a parallel growth in spiritual knowledge produces slaves who squander their lives. Freedom stands above authority—whether the authority of the church or the state. But he made it clear that spiritual growth requires participation in the community—to grow spiritually is more than a personal and individual matter. At the time, of course, his words, though branded in my memory, were hardly burnished in my mind—"

"You lost me a while back—" Jeff interjected.

Tom interrupted. "Lost indeed! Did you expect Paul to lead you along the pathway of beautiful scenery congenial to the mind's eye instead of into a dark, damp jungle, jumbled with thorny philosophical issues to weary the mind?" Tom laughed heartily.

"Maybe the priest was mad," Paul said.

"What's gotten into you, Tom?" Jeff asked, chuckling. "Don't let the brandy go to your brain. What I wanted to know, Paul, is what your priest meant by 'the criteria are in ourselves'?"

"I think he was referring to our spiritual power—our mind's ability to discover meaning—the mental equivalent of phenomena, the things we sense. This is the greatest mystery of human life, he said. We have the power to discover reality and to know it—validating it in ourselves. He said the true rebirth in our lives takes place when our awareness shifts from the authority of the Church and Scriptures or from the authority of the state and society to the inner arena where grace and freedom dwell. He called this the Second Coming—"

"Well, Paul, be proud of yourself," Tom put in. "I feel the slings and arrows of your message all right! So, nailing my skepticism to the cross is your idea of fun. Let me tell you, I take your good padre to be another figment of your imagination. The priests *I've* known have been too mentally—or should I say, spiritually—constipated to be able to distinguish freedom from authority!"

"My goodness, Tom," Jeff laughed, "don't take it so personally."

Paul winked at Helen.

Anna had been listening very closely. A nagging uneasiness

clung to her and pangs of shame tore through her. She wanted
to flee from them, but her body felt paralyzed. They'd be mortified
to know that the girl in Paul's story sat at their very table. How
strange to hear her own story from his lips.

A spark of joy broke through her pain. Paul had come to the
same position as she. We must pass beyond authoritarianisms of
all forms—for apart from freedom there is no spirit, and apart
from spirit there is no freedom. She called it the "go-beyond" of
the next epoch. Unlike Tom, she knew what priest Paul referred
to. Some of these ideas came from their Confirmation classes!
Whether Paul ever visited Father D. or not she had no idea. She
had found Paul but had also lost him. He must never know who
she was. Her shame would be unbearable. And yet Paul never
believed she committed the crime. This heartened her in her
sorrow.

"Thanks for the compliment, Tom," Paul laughed. "Really.
Nailing your skepticism to the cross! But, Tom, you shall know
the truth and the truth shall set you free."

"Have it your way, buddy. You're a perfervid plagiarizer." Tom
stretched his arm across the table and patted his friend on the
shoulder. "A hell of a good yarn—unspeakable crime!" he
guffawed. "Imagine what vile reality I'm bound to invest that
generic nomenclature with."

Soon they trotted out into the darkness of a Detroit night,
tired and, save for Anna, emotionally refreshed from their revelry.

7
Longings

.

Anna and David

Sitting on the edge of the wooded bank of the Red Cedar River not far from her office, Anna gazed at the ducks bobbing in the foamy rapids in the warm glow of the afternoon sunlight.

Hiding from Paul had not eased her yearning. Days dragged into weeks and she looked to time to lessen her longings.

Success, power, wealth, youth, comeliness—all these could not shield you from suffering, she thought. Suffering's the lot of us all. Hadn't her life—not to mention the life of the privileged in Rome—been a testimony to that? Those set on changing society alone, to rout suffering, soon learn that it cannot be easily done. Is there anything that can deliver us from inner bondage or banish cruelty in our heart? No. The overcoming of hunger, sickness, injustice, and illiteracy is, in itself, a goal we must work endlessly for. Yet solutions to social problems, necessary as they are, cannot in themselves satisfy the longings of the heart.

Human dignity, she told herself, lies in our being able to rise above distress. Nonna often cautioned her to fend off petty worries, for "grace is given to him who returns thanks, and what is wont to be given to the humble will be taken away from the

proud." Absent-mindedly, she took Alex's letter from her
briefcase, and re-read it.

> *. . . Nonno has died. We were taken by surprise. He had been in*
> *the best of health, or so we thought. He complained of chest*
> *pains and minutes later keeled over—a heart attack. Fortunately,*
> *he suffered little. Nonna Clara is inconsolable. Wish you were*
> *here . . .*

Mamma would have been thrilled, Anna thought, to see how
Nonna Assunta's and Nonna Clara's friendship had blossomed
after Assunta returned to Rome. How the deepest joys sometimes
rose from the deepest sorrows! She must stand firm and let fate
settle her dilemma. To expect calm within this world is to delude
yourself. Gradually her brooding thoughts began to lift as she
took joy in the serene beauty of the floating ducks in the rapids.

She fished for her mother's leatherbound journal in her
briefcase, flipped through its well-worn pages, and fell on a
passage—January 1936:

> *I shudder at the sight of people racing everywhere toward a*
> *totalitarianism that usurps life in all spheres, including thought,*
> *emotion, and sensation. More and more the axis of family, school,*
> *church, business, and morality falls under the sway of the state.*
> *Frightening still is the subordination of economic to military*
> *interests.*
>
> *Nothing but cooperation by all can halt the momentum of the*
> *state machine rushing headlong toward centralization till it*
> *suddenly jams and bursts to bits. Large, complex organizations*
> *spawn human cogs compelled to slough off their humanity. Yet,*
> *human beings are charged, despite their limited freedom, to*
> *bring about a balance between centralization and*
> *decentralization, between order and freedom, between efficiency*
> *and innovation, between administration and entrepreneurship.*
>
> *Budding professionalism, bureaucratism, and materialism are*
> *relegating the untutored aristocracy to the dustbin of history.*
> *The eternal principle of democracy, founded on the fundamental*
> *rights of the human personality, must be cultivated among the*

*mass of humanity: the freedom of spiritual life, of conscience, of
thought, of speech, and of creativity. We must take every
opportunity to encourage freedom, in the economic realm, too.
A democratic state must encourage democracy in business—a
democratic government shanghaied by the ownership class is
simply a sham democracy.*

*Yes, we must bring workers into management decisions and
ownership, bind businesses to local communities, safeguard
workers from absentee owners purloining unearned profits,
protect the workers from a new form of enslavement in a world
in perpetual motion.*

*Infantilized, proletarianized, and wrenched from community
life, a frightened people breeds disorder, disorder breeds suffering,
and suffering breeds the centralization of life under the power
of the state. Government commandeered by a dominant class
may operate under the guise of liberal democracy, but in reality
it will be a bureaucratized state, a "corporatized" state, if I
must coin that word.*

"Hello, Margaret. Thought I'd find you here." A familiar
voice intruded on her solitude.

She looked up. "David . . . glad to see you . . . back?"

David sat down beside her. "I returned a month ago by way
of Japan. You'd already gone off to the Wayne symposium."

"But . . . but, your last letter—I didn't think you'd be back
till winter term. Nearly a month on campus . . . not a note . . ."

"I poked into my office for a few hours and ran off to New
York," he said, delighted that his absence mattered. "Racing to
get my research in top form before the term begins."

"Grandpa's been pretty good to you." She relaxed, recalling
that David's grandfather had footed the bill for his stay in Asia,
to his parents' chagrin.

"You bet. My mother and father, I can tell you, are not
thrilled—Gramps coughing up a pile for their renegade son.
But he's tickled pink to be dishing it out to the black sheep of
the family."

David Letzow had shocked his parents by switching his major
from pre-med to philosophy, a subject and a degree they saw as

next to useless. Then his father, a lawyer standing high on the corporate ladder, despaired when David showed an interest in theology. Both his father and his mother, secular humanists from liberal Jewish families, took his dabbling in religion as a sign of mental derangement.

"Your grandfather seems to get your parents' dander up," Anna said, amused by the intergenerational friction. She'd met David at a faculty seminar shortly after coming to M.S.U.; they shared an interest in philosophy and history. "Still, it's nice to know you're loved even if the love's misguided." She lowered her head, gripped by sadness at the thought of her mother treated so shabbily by her Petrarca grandparents.

"Some people, you know, live in a world of folly—think themselves in possession of ultimate truth. My father, sorry to say, is one of them. That's why Gramps irks him. Gramps believes the young need time to think, to be free from formal learning for short spells, to have some intellectual fresh air—to grow and find their way in the world. When I quit school to go to Israel for a year, my parents thought I was . . . well, how shall I put it, emotionally unbalanced."

"It turned out well. You're successful in medicine, after all. Didn't that please them?"

"They see me as a religious fanatic. I see religion as an important grounding for the moral order."

"A religious fanatic!" Margaret laughed. "I would've thought you a physician tinkering in philosophy. But, your medical degree—?"

"While finishing philosophy, I prepared for the medical school exams."

"You haven't asked me about the Wayne symposium. I got trounced a bit. But I managed to stay alive."

"I wouldn't have known." He laughed. "Well, aren't you glad we'll be working together?"

"Together?"

"Didn't you get Lucky Evans's letter?"

"No, but I talked to him."

"I got a letter of confirmation this morning. Yours must be in your mailbox."

She sifted through the sheaf of mail stuffed into her briefcase. Seeing the logo of the College of Human Medicine, she pulled it out.

"That's it. How about picking you up for breakfast before the meeting?"

Luke had phoned and invited her to meet with him to sign a contract as a paid consultant on a research project in psychoneuroimmunology—a holistic approach to medicine. The letter confirmed the telephone conversation. She had no idea David would be working with Luke, too. Paul's name at the bottom of the letter set her trembling.

CC: *David Letzow, M.D., Asst. Professor,*
              Dept. of Internal Medicine, MSU
        Margaret Petrarch, Ph.D., Asst. Prof.,
              Dept. of Psychology, MSU
        Paul Risch, M.D., Dept. of Psychiatry, U-M

"What do you say?"

"About what?"

"Breakfast. You're coming to the meeting tomorrow, aren't you?"

"Yes."

"Well?"

"Yes, I'll be there."

"And breakfast?"

"Why not?" she said, her thoughts riveted to Paul.

"Is something wrong, Margaret?"

"I learned this afternoon that my grandfather died." She dismissed the other thing troubling her. He offered his condolences. "But, you haven't . . . ah, haven't mentioned your odyssey to the East," she made an effort to say, putting her journal and letter back into her briefcase, as if shutting away her personal life.

"I missed you, you know." Sadness in his eyes and on his lips spoiled his good looks.

"Well, think of me. Without our literary chitchats and having to muse over the state of the world by myself, my students found

me moribund for lack of intellectual stimulation," she said
flippantly. Though she loved him dearly as a friend, she had
kept a certain distance. And now, Paul had come back into the
picture.

"So I prop up your classes!" he said. He turned and glanced
at the floating ducks. After a short silence he said, "The East I
found waking from its slumber and getting ready to walk onto
the world stage."

"I look forward to your paper. Do you focus on the medical
or—" she said, full of compassion for him.

"Neither medical nor philosophical—more cultural and
historical—in line with my interests outside medicine. I've got
together a rough draft of my findings. I'll share it with you if
you promise not to be too critical."

"Hardly likely. I plead ignorance," she said.

"Asia seems to be entering the torrent of history once more.
The union of East and West will help European culture rise
above its limits, or that's what I believe. The East, you know,
carries the principle much in need of nurturing in the materialist
West—man's contemplative nature."

"What do you mean? Contemplation's no stranger to the
West."

"But it's buried under the dirt of materialism. The East will
spark traditional values and the contemplative science long
forsaken here."

"No doubt our inner life has weakened—"

"We're being swallowed up by external stimuli. Eastern
thought will help mobilize us against modern forms of idolatry
such as materialism and consumerism."

They got into a long discussion about the differences between
Western civilization, on the one hand, and Eastern culture, on
the other. David suggested that the world, in a state of confusion,
was getting out of control.

"More like going mad," Anna declared. She pulled out a
notebook into which she had jotted some ideas from one of her
favorite philosophers. "Listen to this:

We live in an insane world and fail to see that man has become insane. Man has lost his mental balance and thirsts for life. Fascism and communism were a warning that the human being slides back either to animalism or gets caught in a mechanism— becoming either a beast or a disposable cog in the social machine.

What is needed is a new piety—a calling to our creative role *in the world.*

As for the old piety, love of God often meant the lack of love for man and the renunciation and denunciation of the natural order. But the New Christian does not curse the world nor condemn idolaters. No! The New Christian must share the suffering of the world, must bear in himself the tragedy of man, striving to bring the spiritual element into the totality of human life.

Indeed, the New Piety, the new reverence for life, is the path not only from man to God, but the path from God to man: the descent as well as the ascent . . ."

"Who's the author?"

"Nicholas Berdyaev, a Russian philosopher." She put her notebook back into her briefcase. They fell silent for a few moments. She stood up, brushed her skirt off, and readied herself to leave.

"By the way, do you know the psychiatrist from the U. of M. that we'll be working with—Risch?" David got up and followed her.

As they walked toward the parking lot, Anna filled him in on what little she knew of Paul's professional life.

First meeting

Paul rushed the seventy-mile drive from Ann Arbor to East Lansing to be at Lucky's office a half hour early. This was his and Lucky's first meeting since the symposium.

Luke wanted to make sure there were no wrinkles in their friendship. During the past month he and Yarda had begun seeing each other. Paul had visited Yarda twice since then; they were good friends still.

"Pretty chipper this morning, Paul," Luke said, taking in Paul's mood.

"I see you've taken a shine to Detroit these days, Lucky." Paul hoped to put his friend at ease.

Luke smiled. They shook hands. Nothing more needed to be said.

"So you plan to extend our research, I see," Paul said, his thoughts turning to the meeting. "What role will the professor of internal medicine play?"

"You'll like David Letzow. Just returned from a while in India and Japan—broadly educated, has a lot of ideas beyond medicine. I'm bringing him on board—a good resource person in his own right—to help in the selection of faculty and in the enrollment of the first class of medical students at MSU. Pretty exciting being on the ground floor and getting the College of Human Medicine off to a good start! We want to integrate psychology, psychiatry, and neurology, as you know, with immunology and endocrinology. Ah, here they come!" he broke off to greet Margaret and David.

Paul shook hands with Margaret, looking into her green eyes. She was more beautiful than he had remembered. He marveled that he had so much of her in himself. His whole youth tumbled into consciousness at the sight of her. He was ecstatic. Her beauty seemed both to penetrate him and to be projected out of him. Few words had passed between them at the symposium. Not once did they talk alone face to face.

David turned out to be a tall, spirited man of thirty-five with friendly brown eyes, well-groomed beard, and brown curly hair. It didn't take Paul long to see that Margaret and David shared more than admiration for each other. Gradually through the course of the morning, Paul felt his joy turn sour. By midmorning his blood seemed to drain from his body. Pangs of jealousy ripped through him for the first time in years. Margaret's affection seemed to be well fixed to David.

He half listened to Lucky's summary of research in progress and the need for preventive medicine. Paul's own presentation, a report on holistic medicine, lacked enthusiasm. A vacuum seemed to grow in him and displace his internal organs. The pain was unbearable.

About to take off at coffee break, he fell into talking medicine with David. To Paul's dismay, he found David likeable, friendly, and well informed. Paul understood Margaret's attraction to him.

"How's Yarda?" Margaret asked. Her cheeks flushed.

"To tell the truth, I haven't seen much of her lately," Paul said.

"And the outcome of her problems at Samaritan?"

"Ah, Martin. You remember Charlie Martin?" She nodded.

"Well, Yarda, as usual, had it right. Martin pleaded temporary insanity, lost his license, and was put on probation for five years. She's taking it pretty badly—blames herself."

"Did things work out for Shannon Sherman?"

"Yes," Paul said, surprised at her interest.

"And the Danovas? Precocious Sarah, wise beyond her years, and her patient brother Jeff? And lovely Helen Anne?"

David's eyes darted back and forth from one to the other, listening to their somehow intimate chat in wonder.

"The Danovas—quite a family. Actually, I haven't visited them since the symposium. I've thought about Mario's, though, and about your priest and his Latin saying, *nil nisis cruce*. The pastor in my hometown was fond of quoting it. What a coincidence!"

"Yes." Her faced turned scarlet. "Please excuse me."

Paul hardly had time to respond before she charged out of the room. He looked at David, who was frowning. "Well, David," Paul said, baffled, "we'll be seeing a lot of each other."

"Right! I look forward to it and I'm sure Margaret does, too."

In the second half of the meeting, Margaret was aloof and cold. Paul was wounded. It would be four weeks till he'd see her again.

Paul and Tom

"Good God, Paul, get hold of yourself!" Tom said as he and Paul walked along a path of the arboretum beside the Huron River, close by the hospital.

Paul stared into space. One week had passed since he had seen Margaret, and he was beside himself.

Tom had heard about Paul's heartache, more amused than shocked. "You expect too much of life," Tom said as Paul stared at the dirty water flowing by. "As for me," Tom went on, glancing furtively at Paul to make sure he was not too downcast, "I've resigned myself to the fact that life's sorrows can't be overcome— even by joy. Joy and sorrow get tangled up with one another. But joy is fleeting."

"No doubt. But my feelings seem to go deeper than sorrow; deeper than sadness—more like despair. Something I've not known before," Paul confessed.

They veered off the road down to the riverbank beside a small rapids where the riverbed dipped slightly.

"Tell me about her dashing suitor," Tom said playfully.

"David's the kind of guy you'd choose for your own sister: full of life, charming, refined, interesting, intellectually and morally alive."

"Reading John Keats's *Ode to a Nightingale* last night, I see Keats wished to throw his consciousness to the wind, to feel the immortal longing of his heart, and to let his poetic imagination stream forth," Tom said, hoping to engage Paul. "We've all gone down that route some time or other. But Keats knew all too well that love and beauty give way to misery." Tom went on to quote a stanza.

> *Where youth grows pale, and specter-thin, and dies;*
> *Where but to think is to be full of sorrow*
> *And leaden-eyed despairs,*
> *Where Beauty cannot keep her lustrous eyes,*
> *Or new Love pine at them beyond to-morrow."*

"Well, I think Keats missed the boat. I believe deeply that somehow the eternal ground of life seeps into our world of time and transfigures us."

"I'll stick with Keats: life is tragic and the perfection of art alone can bring us moments of bliss. Perfection and wholeness ever elude us. Of course, I know what boat you'd jump into—

one that's springing leaks all over." Tom nearly laughed out loud.

"What boat's that?"

"Religion, what else?"

"Well theology's got a hell of a lot more to say than Keats and the romantics. If we've learned anything from medicine, Tom, we've learned that there's a positive facet to suffering. It tells us something's wrong—something's to be dealt with. For the past week, I've had these terrible nightmares."

Tom took a long twig and held it in the rapids, feeling in his hand and arm the force of the flowing water. He had wrenched Paul's thoughts loose from Margaret for the moment. "I believe we've been duped and swindled by religion for the most part."

"That's too easy—all too easy, Tom. You're parroting conventional wisdom. But this dream . . ." he said, considering whether to discuss it with Tom. He lapsed into silence.

"What dream?"

"I've attained this magical power to fly and soar miles above the earth—a blissful power to navigate the heavens. In my all-too-happy joy, I look back to see the earth in flames. I stare in panic, stranded in the abyss above. I watch the blazing world slowly turn into a burning cross. Inscribed at the center is the word MATRICIDE glaring in scarlet, with blood-curdling screams coming from it. MATRICIDE on the burning cross turns into the face of Felicia, a woman I once knew who was found murdered in her home. Then, Felicia's face changes to Anna's, her daughter's, then to Margaret's."

"Physician heal thyself!"

"Remember the story I told at Mario's about an unspeakable crime?"

"Rather childish of you."

"I couldn't bring myself to name it at the time."

"You're scaring me, Paul. Not brain fever I'm seeing here?"

"You can bet on it." Paul smiled. "This I do know: the night before Mario's I had my first nightmare. There've been several since. In most of them Anna's face turns into Margaret's."

"Who's Anna?"

"That's what I'm trying to tell you. She's the girl accused of matricide—the unmentionable crime."

"Well, what possible connection can there be?"

"I haven't the slightest. I'm drawn to Margaret as I was to Anna."

"Does Margaret resemble Anna?"

"Yes, especially her eyes."

"Big problem! Your unconscious connects one to the other. Unconsciously you fear Margaret's not all she's cracked up to be. Beneath the veneer she's matricidal." Tom laughed.

"As all men are patricidal." Paul chuckled. "I never did believe Anna killed her mother, you see. Not for a moment."

"Ah, but your unconscious exposes you. Deep down you accuse her like everybody else. Now you meet Margaret. The resemblance is striking: she too must carry around a secret of 'unspeakable' evil." They laughed.

"Why I bother to indulge a radiologist is beyond me!"

"Why? Because we alone possess X-ray vision. Look, I'm starving. Let's get over to Zingerman's before it's too late."

"No doubt! You've used up all that mental energy."

On their walk to the delicatessen Tom felt relieved as they talked about other things. They put in their order and hunted for a table in the crowded place.

Paul had been pensive for some time. "Did you know St. Paul was blinded at the moment of his conversion?"

"Noooo! What got you off on that tack?" Tom asked as their names were called out.

"It reminds me—there's something I'm not seeing in my attraction to Margaret. Something doesn't fit. I'm missing something," Paul said, stumbling behind Tom, who was hurrying to the counter to pick up his food.

"I'm missing your whole point," Tom said, hurrying back to the table, his hunger getting the better of him. "Precisely what is it you're not seeing?" Tom began chomping on his five-inch-high beef-ham-salami-cheese sub before Paul could answer. "Zingerman's can sure throw together one fantastic sub!" Tom mumbled, mouth full.

"If I could see it, I'd know."

"Funny!"

"I'm not seeing the connection between Anna and Margaret."

Paul bit into his enormous hot pastrami on rye.

"Geez, I thought I worked that out for you—nothing but a resemblance backed up by hidden guilt for condemning an innocent child accused of matricide."

"How comforting to have a radiologist-cum-psychologist for a friend. Thank you for your official diagnosis. Pure malarkey."

"How's this for a bitter twist? Deep in the well-spring of the unconscious—"

"Every freshman that's ever heard of Freud harps on—"

"Hear me out, will you? As I was saying, there's a dark side to what's going on here," Tom said. "In the dark depths (how's that for a bit of poesy!) stands a beautiful blond (don't take this personally!) mourning her lover chasing after a new—"

"Rot!"

". . . chasing after a new beauty. The foothold the blond beauty has in his unconscious strums on the old conscience (what did Freud call it?—the superego, part of our mental apparatus!). Lover boy pursues the new, forsakes the old, and *ipso facto*—horrible guilt, burning earths, flying in the sky, transforming faces."

"Too simple—too sophomoric."

"Yeah, shrink, what's your view? You haven't come up with better."

"You want to hear?"

"Do I have to? I'm about to be pulled hither and yon in a world wrapped in enigmas and bound in riddles. Please don't blow any fuses in my mind. I'm on call tomorrow."

"When I mentioned to Margaret last week that our priest used the same Latin saying as hers did, she didn't reply. She bolted from the room as though I'd offended her."

"There's your connection, for goodness sake. She's probably from the same town."

"Hardly. I knew everybody her age in our town. There was nobody by that name. I'm sure of that. And why would she want to conceal it from me? Doesn't make sense."

"How about a piece of cheesecake or carrot cake? I'll get both and we'll split." Tom jumped up to put in the order without waiting for Paul to answer.

"Get us some coffee, too," Paul yelled after him.

Paul's thoughts fixed on Father D. He thought of Anna and how their eyes met when Father D. talked about the vocation of marriage. That was one time the priest was so far over Paul's head that he felt he missed the point utterly. Marriage, Father D. had told them, was a vocation as important as the calling to the priesthood. "Marriage is one of the sacraments of the Church given by God. It's a path by which each spouse helps the other climb the ladder from the fallen to the resurrected state." Paul could remember the words, but it still made little sense to him.

He remembered once Father D. talked about sex and marriage. "Sex is not only given to us for the end of bearing children," Father D. said, "it's a gift from God to be kept pure and to help bring about a true union between man and wife." Nervous laughter, giggling, and chatter reverberated in the nave. Father D. seemed unaffected by the childish response and went right on.

"What does Holy Mother Church mean by a true union in the holy bonds of matrimony?" he asked. After an embarrassed silence, he answered his own question. "A true union in marriage is the freely given love of husband and wife, each helping the other move upward toward God."

"At last," Paul said to Tom, who was trying to balance the coffee and cakes on the tray.

"Busy night."

"I've been thinking of our parish priest." Tom started to cut the desserts in half. "He'd say some pretty weird things as if we could understand him. He'd point to his heart and say, 'What's the name of our church?' All the kids would yell out: 'The Sacred Heart.' Then he'd point to his temple, implying crazy people, and say: "*Nomina stultorum parietibus haerent.*" And we were told to answer: 'Fool's names are stuck upon the walls.' Then he'd smile and say: 'Get it and keep it!' No one, of course, knew what the joke was about. When asked to explain it, he'd merely smile slyly."

"Pretty heady stuff for kids. He must've been some rebel in the church."

"His view, I believe, was to instill the idea in an impressionable mind. When ready, the adult would find it stashed away there."

"I thought you were going to get me beyond my sophomoric psychology."

"If you must know, my suffering is charging me to do something."

"To do what?"

"To search for the Holy Grail, I suppose." Paul laughed. "All these dreams and this terrible jealousy of David, this longing to see Margaret whom I hardly know—they're all new to me. It all started when Margaret entered the picture. That's why I think it has little to do with Yarda."

"Lucky's been sending her a dozen roses a week. He's practically made Detroit his home."

"It's a good match. I respect and admire them both."

"No misgivings?"

"No."

"Yarda's some catch. I hope you won't regret it. Your nightmare—what's it about?"

"I'm being called to carry out some deed and it's tied to Margaret in some way. As for my dreams, my unconscious has forged certain links I can't home in on. I know that the matricide is at the center of it. Somehow both Anna and Margaret are entangled in it."

"Yes, but your dream of the burning earth may be symbolic? Could be worries about mother earth."

"Possible. All dreams are actions given in symbols, more or less. But dreams also relate to one's daily life. I'm called to help someone. Who? Why? I'm mystified!"

"I know you're joking about the Holy Grail—"

"One has to be pure for . . . only the most perfect, the most pure, could—"

"I'm not so sure you . . . By the way, whatever happened to this girl, this Anna the matricide?"

"She disappeared—left our town. I never tracked her down. I even conned my way into her psychiatrist's office and made a fool of myself there. Evidently she pulled out of the shock of her mother's death and went to live in Italy with her grandparents."

"You could always use the power of your office to see whether

her psychiatrist might give you a lead. You're an honorable member of the profession now."

"What do you mean?"

"Why not call as 'Dr. Risch, psychiatrist, U. of M.,' and see whether her psychiatrist might open up about her? Argue for professional confidentiality. I don't see how it might help, but you never know unless you give it a shot."

"I don't see the point of it. Thanks for your listening ear and your sophomoric diagnosis. I enjoyed every minute of it."

"Laughing at me?"

"Well, if it makes you feel any better I admit to feeling a hell of a lot better myself, having roped you into my *affaire du coeur*."

"Wait till you get my bill!"

The Police Report

Paul, trying to hold onto the bundle of mail he picked up from his mailbox, dropped his briefcase on the floor. He still had a few hours of work to do. Tomorrow he'd be meeting with Luke, Margaret, and David and he'd promised to have a draft of his study ready for them.

He'd been waiting several weeks for a report on Anna Benedicta from Dante Giorgio. A few days after his talk with Tom, he telephoned Dante at the West Warwick Police station and discovered that Anna had been cleared of suspicion of manslaughter as far back as 1959. Dante briefed him and promised to send a copy of the report.

Paul spotted a big manila envelope—West Warwick Police Department. He dropped the rest of the mail and tore it open.

In part, Dante's letter read:

> . . . in that Anna at the time of the alleged crime was twelve the files were sealed by order of juvenile court. Fortunately, having been absolved of any wrongdoing, she is not in a position to be harmed civilly or morally by the release of our police reports to you. To date, no request by her or her family has been made. Neither the court clerk nor the West Warwick Police have made the outcome of our second investigation public (herein enclosed)

owing to the law that forbids any public disclosure of hearings
in cases involving juveniles. As for Ralph Mullen, the suspect in
the death of Felicia, he died before the new evidence came to
light, as I told you in our phone conversation . . .

Dante had included the whole police file going back to March
1950. The juvenile court hearing before a judge, of course, was
not and never would be made available, by state law. Paul read
the details of the police investigation: the stabbing of Felicia
and the probable cause of death—a fall resulting in an occipital
fracture, epidural hematoma, and herniation of the brain. As he
read about Anna's confinement at Butler, he pictured her sitting
in the back seat of Piero's car going down Prospect Hill. The
juvenile court did notify the West Warwick police of its order
remanding Anna from the custody of Peter and Assunta to the
custody of Dr. Leach at Butler Hospital or Oaklawn School for
Girls—"if her mental derangement persists." This told Paul
much about how Anna had landed in Butler.

Poor Anna. What torment she must've endured: she awakens
to find her mother dead and then is suspected of manslaughter.
A wonder she pulled out of it.

Still no letter from Dr. Leach, who'd been on leave when
Paul called Butler. Paul followed up the telephone call with a
letter requesting any information that might shed light on Anna's
whereabouts. He also mentioned that he'd been in touch with
the West Warwick Police and was happy to learn that Anna had
been cleared.

Paul got a black pressure binder from his desk and put the
pages in order. He made a title page—*THE EXONERATION*
OF ANNA MARIA BENEDICTA: THE INNOCENT LAMB.
He read Dante's report (the second police investigation), the
two love letters (Piero's and Felicia's), and the diary entry of
Mitri Mansour. He grieved the ill-fated Mitri, drowned in the
Pawtuxet River the day after Felicia's death. He read Lillian's
testimony and that of others during the police investigation.
What an impact their spite must have had on Ralph Mullen!
Lillian had had a breakdown herself shortly after Felicia's death.
Paul recalled visiting Lillian in his last year at Brown and hearing

Eddy Pastori refer to his mother's shock treatments—something about "electricity shot through her brains." Her depression, probably linked to Felicia's death, must have been treated with electroshock, which tends to erase memories.

By some mental contortion, Paul began to reflect on the Vietnam War. Is there some likeness between what happened to Felicia and the violence of war? Are innocent and ignorant people, not too much brighter than Ralph, made to sanction and commit odious violence by propaganda (a nation's false gossip) about the affairs of others? Are the sheep being led to slaughter in Vietnam? Are the enemy being demonized by accusations and misinformation about the complex interplay of forces in Vietnam—our one-time ally and a poor former colony of France? He remembered going to the movies as a kid where he and the other kids were moved deeply by black-and-white moral distinctions in movies portraying good and evil. In gearing up a nation for war, the stakes are power and resources. In Felicia's death, envy and jealousy had triggered Ralph's fears about Anna's safety. He shut the black binder, sick to death of the suffering of the Benedicta family and of Ralph, caught in a spider's web.

A passage in II Corinthians came to mind: "We are afflicted in every way, but not crushed; perplexed, but not driven to despair; persecuted, but not forsaken; struck down, but not destroyed." Yes, Anna had made it out of madness. He realized from Piero's and Felicia's letters that Piero Benedicta had also been cheated out of love.

He grabbed some stationery from his desk, stuffed it into a small leather briefcase, and set out for the arboretum. Until the symposium he thought he'd escaped the anguish of his youth. He'd been in denial all along. Those early years on Prospect Hill—he'd always come back to them.

He sat beside the flowing water, and his thoughts leaped back in time to the violent rapids of the Pawtuxet River some fifty feet below the Natick Bridge where Mitri plunged to his death. How tame the Huron River in Ann Arbor seemed, compared to the deep dark Pawtuxet River flowing through Natick.

Furiously he wrote to Fr. DiSanto, thanking him for his words of wisdom both in catechism classes and in talks at the rectory. As he wrote, a vitality seeped into him and suffused the sinews of his body. He told about Anna and his grief and about meeting Margaret. When he finished, he felt refreshed, alive, liberated— as if a demon, long hidden in his depths, had been dispelled.

When he got home, he put the black binder away. His past must be put to rest, too. Remembering, not forgetting, is a healing balm!

Slowly an idea took form in him. He must visit the priest. The more he thought about it, the more convinced he became. He would ask for a week off. Weeks of vacation were due him. Would he get it on short notice? With the joyful thought of going back to West Warwick, he set about putting the final touch on the draft of his study, for his meeting in East Lansing with Luke.

He ripped up the letter to Fr. DiSanto and planned the trip for the following week.

Back to Sacred Heart

When he arrived at the rectory on Providence Street, Mrs. Sassi, now old and frail, showed him to Father D.'s library, at the end of a long dark corridor in a spartan room. Paul waited for the priest. On the north wall two chairs stood next to a table and lamp. The smell of incense suffused the room, mixing with the musty smell of old books.

He took stock of the priest's library: Greeks, Romans, medievalists, moderns, contemporaries. Not a classic wanting. As if sparked by the titles of the books, his thoughts flitted helter-skelter.

Margaret had given him conflicting messages on Saturday morning: one of some deep sympathy with him, the other of not being accessible. He got the idea she was not in love with David.

He felt alienated from his hometown. The mills had shut down and, left to decay, scarred the landscape. The Pawtuxet River had lost its use as the source of power, and the Pawtuxet Valley its importance as an industrial center. Arctic, the shopping

district, had lost its vitality. Houses and businesses sprouted
everywhere, a hodgepodge bereft of beauty. Ugly buildings
mushroomed alongside the church, crowding it out. Most of
the Italian, French, and Portuguese bakeries had disappeared.
Prospect Hill looked deserted. The gentle fertile slope down to
the river had been plotted into streets and dinky lots by a land
developer.

Lillian and Frank still lived in the old white house with the
concrete steps. Paul had an eerie feeling looking at the old Risch
houses standing side by side east of the Benedictas' house. The
houses stood lost amid the clutter of little cardboard boxes
surrounding them. Tony, now married, had moved to Worcester,
Massachusetts; Cecilia, with five children, to South Carolina.

"Hello Paul," came the forceful voice of Father D.

Paul turned, shook hands, and found a short dark man staring
up at him with large, protuberant eyes.

"Thanks for seeing me," Paul said.

"The pleasure's all mine. It's been a long time." He sat down
and motioned to Paul to take the seat across the table. "Every
now and then I receive an unexpected but gratifying visit from
one of our old catechists."

"I've lost touch with my old friends from West Warwick."

The priest shared bits of news he had about some of Paul's
classmates. But Paul could see that the war in Vietnam was deeply
troubling Father D. As he got off on "the mess in Vietnam,"
the priest seemed to age before Paul's eyes. It had already touched
many families and their children in his parish, and this weighed
heavily on him.

"*Vis consili expers mole ruit sua.* Yes, strength without judgment
falls by its own might," he said. "Unfortunately, we've taken a
bad turn. You know the old adage, Paul: *Virtuti, non armis,
fidimus*—we should be putting our trust in virtue not weapons.
If this war expands and gets out of hand, it will have a terrible
impact on future generations. I shudder to think what it'll do to
authority, over the long haul."

As if Paul had come to hear a lecture, Father D. went on. "As
you know, Paul, there are endless examples of ignorance in the
world—from individuals all the way up to nations. The evil of

the Vietnam War is a clear indication of ignorance acting itself out on an international scale. No doubt this tragedy infects all the pores and spores of our institutions. *Bella! horrida bella! Wars! Horrid wars!*"

Looking at Paul and catching himself, the priest collected himself and readjusted his face. A peacefulness radiated from his eyes.

"I see you're quite a scholar," Paul said, glancing at the bookshelves. "Quite a library you've got."

"One of the privileges of the religious life—time to study. What brings you back?"

"I wish I knew. I wanted to thank you, and then I . . . I just got hold of the police reports on Anna Benedicta from Dante Giorgio." How much easier it would have been to send the letter instead, he thought. "A few months ago I began having nightmares about Anna and Felicia. For years, I thought I was free of them. Then . . ."

"Yes?"

"At a symposium in September I met a psychologist who teaches at Michigan State. She reminds me of Anna. That's when the dreams began. I'm sorry to bring it up," Paul said with finality.

"Sorry to bring it up? My son, love is the cornerstone, the foundation of life. One of the things I was always going on about in catechism classes."

He went to his bookshelf and pulled out two books. He opened to the title page and wrote a note in the first, *The Meaning of Love*, by Vladimir Solovyev:

Best wishes to Paul in the vocation of marriage—the path toward the reunion of Adam and Eve. Affectionately, Fr. Angelo DiSanto.

In the second, *The Meaning of the Creative Act*, by Nicholas Berdyaev, he wrote:

Dip deeply into the mystery—the union of Adam and Eve as the restoration of wholeness, harmony, wisdom. Love is fallen man's ascent toward the likeness of God—the final conquest of decadence and strife.

He handed them to Paul. "Take these and let them speak to your heart."

Paul thanked him. He opened the books, read the inscriptions, and shuddered.

"What a consolation to know that God has put into every soul his calling card—our longing for reunion with Him. Yes, Paul, God descends and works in us through His grace. He has also put in us a craving for Him. In our ignorance and sinfulness—in our suffering—we long for something, are restless, and look to the world. But no thing satisfies."

Paul looked at the priest speechless. He imagined himself back in catechism classes, confused.

"In our heart God has left two gifts, Paul, the yearning for eternity and the power to seek after wisdom. These gifts are the ladder for our search for Him—to end our longing."

"Descent and ascent!" Paul exclaimed. He had not counted on any long-drawn-out discourse. Why had he visited the priest, anyhow? "Love the cornerstone?" Paul said.

"Each of us must sacrifice our egoism—we must give it up freely. The power of love, especially love between man and woman in life-commitment, can strike a blow to egoism—the living death. Giving up egoism cannot be something we do in thought; it must be lived through in truth. So long as the living force of egoism does not encounter another living force opposed to it, knowledge of the truth about egoism—death that saps our life— remains superficial, untested, an external illumination not yet verified. Now, the *beloved* is a living force to oppose egoism."

"I'm sorry—the meaning of love?" Paul asked.

"Love helps us ascend, to rise above false consciousness— helps us become whole human beings."

"To rise above . . . ?"

"Arriving at the truth of ourselves—who we are—is a long hard struggle. Certain things help ease this struggle."

"What things?"

"Why, matricide, for one."

Paul looked aghast. He felt giddy and laughed out loud.

"Excuse me, Father." After all, he was a practicing psychiatrist.

"Of course I'm speaking figuratively—symbolically," Father D. said, aware he'd startled Paul. "Matricide, the killing of the mother, is the precondition of a new birth, of a new woman to fit our changing times. Most necessary for both the mother and her children, and the welfare of the family. Motherhood, the most precious underpinning of civilization—must be redefined in our swiftly changing times. You see, Paul, when the mother sacrifices herself totally for her children, she gives up her life for her children. But her children, living in another generation, have new and independent interests and problems. A sad fact of life is that the mother wrapped up in her children alone often sacrifices her individuality—her personality. But matricide may be botched!"

First matricide! Now it may be botched? Has Father D. . . . ? Maybe I ought to humor him, Paul thought. "Botched? How so?"

"You're distrustful of these ideas, I see," Father D. replied kindly.

"I'm sorry, Father." Pangs of embarrassment shot through Paul.

"To kill the mother means to help deliver her from her sacrificial life in order to lead a fuller and more meaningful life— to allow her to achieve her humanity. But if it is not to be botched, the others—children and spouse—must come freely to share in her 'mother' work. They must take on a responsibility that helps them grow to maturity, too. This means that patricide is also necessary."

Now patricide. "I'm not sure I grasp your idea of botching matricide."

"Well, matricide must *not* mean an end to motherhood and marriage, but a *spiritual* rebirth. Central to the life of the child is mother love, unconditioned love, that sets a model for the ascent of every human being. Matricide means an end to an undue reliance on one to do all the sacrificing and the others to depend on it, irresponsibly."

"And patricide?" Paul asked, his mind in disarray. He thought he'd be able, as a professional, to talk to Father D. on a level of equality. Instead, he felt like a child.

"Patricide—killing the father to transfer authority to the other members of the family and the community—means sharing the responsibility invested in an extreme form in the father in past epochs. As children grow up, they must with increased freedom take on authority for themselves and responsibility for their actions. And both mothers and fathers should share the responsibility. Patricide too can be botched."

"How so?" Paul asked, getting some inkling of Father D.'s metaphors.

"Well, I see you're a bit more trusting after the initial shock." Father D. smiled. Botching patricide is the fouling up of authority like the mess in Vietnam: authority breaks down, responsibility withers and gives rise to greater chaos. In other words death without rebirth—an end without an awakening. Will there be a fitting response on the part of the next generation to greater freedom? Will greater freedom bring greater responsibility?"

"To be truthful," Paul said, "I can't imagine 'matricide' and 'patricide,' to use your metaphors, to lead anywhere but to a mess!"

"Believe me, Paul, they are taking place at an ever faster pace despite our wishes, or learning, for that matter. At the end of time matricide and patricide are the signs of the time, if you take my meaning."

"When did it start?"

There was a knock on the door and Mrs. Sassi shuffled in with some refreshments. "Thank you, Mrs. Sassi," Father D. said as she put a tray on the table, nodded, and left. "When did what start?"

"Matricide," Paul answered. Father D. poured two cups of tea and offered Paul some cookies.

"Matricide and patricide are vital to our growing into a full human being. Surely, sacrificial love and self-rule blooming freely among our citizens—young and old, men and women—we must pray for. As a social phenomenon, matricide got its foothold with World War II and the enormous wealth and economic change following it: married women leaving home in droves to enter the work force, discovering talents, abilities, interests—

able to contribute more fully to their families and the larger society."

"And you think matricide and patricide can be directed effectively?"

"By honoring love in marriage. No other love has as great a power to shatter our enslavement to egoism, pride, narcissism, and crude individualism. If marriage breaks down generally, men and women will seek to advance and advantage themselves egoistically. Civilization will be ruptured and will crumble. Please, help yourself," Father D. said.

"I must say," Paul said sheepishly, taking another cookie.

"Yes?"

"Such thinking—wouldn't it be reactionary today? Marriage is already being scoffed at. Many people are choosing just to live together instead of taking vows."

"But we mustn't fear speaking the truth. Remember, *suppressio veri, suggestio falsi*—a suppression of the truth is the suggestion of a falsehood. *Venite summae dies et ineluctabile tempus*—the last day has come, and the inevitable doom. But death is the gate of life—*mors janua vitae!*"

They talked on and on about the state of the world. Paul looked at his watch, feeling he had taxed the priest's patience.

"When will you be going back to Michigan?"

"Fairly soon—perhaps tomorrow. May I use your phone?"

The priest led Paul to his study and left him. Paul stared up at the large crucifix behind Father D.'s desk as he rang Dr. Leach's office. Still not available. The secretary, recognizing Paul's name, told him Dr. Leach had already posted a letter to him.

When they parted, Father D. blessed him and wished him well in his career and in his personal life. Paul looked forward to getting home to the open spaces of the Midwest and to finding out what Dr. Leach had to tell him.

Discovery

Paul headed for the Department of Psychiatry the minute he got back to Ann Arbor, having driven straight through from Providence. Would the letter from Dr. Leach be there? What news would it bring? Would Dr. Leach hold back about Anna?

Paul searched through his mail for the letter, spotted it, and slit the envelope. He read the paragraph congratulating him on his successful completion of medical study and residency. It continued:

> *I am sorry to say I have lost track of Anna Benedicta. More accurately, she has chosen to cut all ties. As you may know, she went to Classical High and graduated in the class of 1954 (being advanced two years after her stay at Butler) under the name of Mary Anne Benedict. She was the valedictorian in her class. After that, she left for Rome with her grandmother and her uncle. She did her undergraduate studies at the University of Rome, returning to the States to do graduate work in psychology at Yale University. She took an English version of her mother's maiden name—Margaret Petrarch.*

Like the wind, Paul blew out of the hospital to pick up the black binder at home (removing the title page and the early reports of the crime), and putting in it the police report of 1959 clearing Anna. He drove full tilt to East Lansing. Everything seemed more beautiful—a transfiguration was happening before his eyes. He crossed the bridge over the Red Cedar River into Indian Hills. He drove south up a winding road, Nakoma Drive, that hugged and wound itself up the gentle hill studded with old oak trees. He spotted the small stone house with flowerbeds in the front yard. Its stone-framed door and picturesque dormers fit its surroundings: it looked as if it had been set down by a supernatural power. He had staked it out on his last visit to East Lansing. Thinking it Margaret Petrarch's, he had failed to see its Benedicta aura.

As he pulled up to the curb, he saw Anna coming out of the house with David. He watched them get into David's car in the driveway. They were talking and laughing like two lovers oblivious to everything around them. As David backed his car out of the driveway, Paul slumped in his seat to hide himself. He felt cheap and ashamed.

His heart turned upside down. How different everything had looked moments earlier: the blue sky, fresh air, oak-lined drive up Indian Hills. Everything now seemed inhospitable and he felt like an intruder in a world lost to him.

Their car passed by so close he could see Anna and David chatting gaily as he peered out the corner of the car-door window. Mindlessly, he started his car and drove at a safe distance behind them. Some irresistible force seemed to beckon him.

The sun was sinking and it was beginning to get dark. The couple's car turned toward the campus. Paul, hopeless on Mount Hope Road, kept his eyes on them through every stoplight, every crossroad. On campus they passed Spartan Stadium and parked south of the Red Cedar River. He watched them walk over the bridge to the woods across the river. Ducks floated and bobbed in the foamy water of the rapids. Hidden from view, he looked down at them from the far bank of the river, too far to hear but close enough to see.

They sat on a bench facing the river. Anna took out a book from her large handbag and a brown paper bag. David took the bag from her and pulled out something—snacks?—that they shared and a big chunk of bread they broke into pieces and threw to the ducks. Shortly, Anna began reading aloud from her book in spurts, interrupting herself to talk with David. This though the sky had darkened, and it was getting harder and harder to see.

Paul felt as though his world had collapsed. Guilt, shame, and jealousy commingled in him.

He knew he must leave, go back to Ann Arbor. He lacked the will to move. He hadn't eaten all day and hunger began to gnaw at him. It got colder and he began to shiver.

An idea bloomed in him: you have to fight for what you want—for what you yearn for. A ray of hope shot through him. He wouldn't come unannounced again. He'd write Anna first. She must invite him; she must consent to meet with him.

On the drive back to Ann Arbor, he explored various strategies. The more he thought, the more hopeful he became. His yearning buoyed his spirit and put him in a fighting mood. He must create the condition to resolve his longing.

Coming Home

When he got home, he gorged himself with leftovers, taking little stock of what he put in his mouth. With his mind focused on strategies for winning Anna, he fell asleep.

He found himself at the Brown University fieldhouse, alone and naked, cleaning toilets. How had he gotten here and what had happened to him?

From one end of a long corridor he heard the voices of screaming fans. He knew that if he walked out toward the football field, he could dress in his uniform—his locker was just outside the door. On the other side of the men's room, a long dark corridor housing the offices of the coach and his staff opened to the street. Anna was beckoning him. But he was naked. There were no lockers down that corridor. He had no idea where his clothes had gone.

He didn't know how he knew, but he knew for sure he had a choice: either go toward Anna naked, or take the field dressed in his football uniform. He also knew that if he took his place on the field, he would find adulation and success. To follow after Anna he would be walking naked into the street with no assurance of acceptance or success. He had time to think for he could not make a choice until the long rows of toilets were scrubbed and scoured.

When they were scrubbed and scoured, he was compelled to choose. He looked around for a towel or something to cover himself with. Nothing. His yearning for Anna conflicted with his longing for worldly success. He was ashamed of his nakedness. Time was running out. Fixed to a spot between the two doors leading to the two corridors, he spun first toward one, then toward the other. He knew which he'd choose, which he needed, but his nakedness stymied him. Finally, he willed with all his might to break out of the whirling motion and pulled toward Anna. In terrible fear, he ran naked through the door into the dark corridor.

Suddenly bright lights flashed all the way down the hallway that in a wink turned into a wind tunnel. The wind hurled his body hundreds of feet at frightening speed. He found himself fully dressed. He had no idea how it happened. He saw Anna speeding toward him. No power on earth could prevent a collision and save him. At the point of impact Anna gently converged with him and he fell to the ground outside the fieldhouse— whole, purified, full of love.

He awoke and found himself far from naked—he had fallen asleep without taking off his clothes. Love swelled within him. He knew, yes he knew without doubt, that he would win Anna. No, he knew he had to win her.

One more day of vacation remained. His appointments scheduled for the first day back to work would be heavy. He hurried to get a letter out.

Dear Margaret,

Yesterday I returned to Ann Arbor after being away for a few days. I need to see you before our next scheduled meeting. It is urgent—of the utmost importance.

Please let me know when I can see you.

Yours,

Paul

He knew she had both his telephone numbers—home and work. These had been supplied by Luke when she and David joined the team. Moreover, if she'd misplaced them, she could get them easily enough. And his address was on the letter.

Three days later he found a telephone message in his office mailbox:

Dr. Margaret Petrarch called at 9 A.M.

Will be available to meet with you at her home any evening from Monday through Saturday after 7. Please confirm.

Paul checked his schedule and found the earliest he could make a trip to East Lansing was on Friday, three days away. His secretary called Margaret's office and left a message. Paul did not hear further.

On Friday he left his office earlier than usual, making sure he'd be at her house on time. He thought about her all week and became surer of winning her. Something new and deep was taking root in him—a foresight. He knew what was going to happen. Anticipation grew in him day by day.

When he arrived at her house, he strode up to the front door, the black binder firmly in his hand, his heart pounding. Looking at his watch, he knocked boldly; it was nearly seven o'clock. It was getting dark and he waited what seemed like an eternity. No answer. He walked around to the back. Her yard sloped down to the Red Cedar River and to a path on its bank circling around the foot of Indian Hills. He sat down beside the flowing water and turned to look up at the house, the flowerbeds, the garden.

The house, unlit, reminded him of the abandoned Benedicta place on Prospect Hill after Felicia's death. Fear gripped him. Restless, he got up and roamed down the path that followed the river. He felt a touch of the same peacefulness that he used to feel when walking on the banks of the Pawtuxet River on the Lambert farm where he, Tony, Cecilia, Anna, and Alex used to play.

When he got back to the house, it was seven fifteen. He hurried round to the front door and knocked loudly. He made out footsteps within coming toward him.

The door opened into a world his heart yearned for. "Hello, Paul."

His whole being trembled and he had trouble sounding her name. "Anna!" He hardly recognized his own voice. He looked into her eyes to behold himself—the mirror image of his soul staring back at him. He pushed his way into the foyer, thrusting the binder toward her.

She took it, smiled, and without a word invited him into the living room.

He advanced toward her, the black binder pressed between them. Overcome with emotion, he said, "It's all over. I'm home."

"Yes," she sighed, "you're home."

He kissed her, and her body gently gave in to his embrace.

She took his hand and led him into her study. On the wall behind her desk stood a large oil painting of her mother, with several smaller portraits arranged in the form of a cross, Felicia's at the center. His eyes were drawn to Assunta, Marco, and Piero, set in a straight line on the left, and Anna, Alessandro, and himself, set on the far right. Below the portrait of Felicia was a remarkable painting of Pasqualina Penta, and above was a painting of Father D. Between Pasqualina and the priest was Anna's grandfather Luigi and grandmother Clara.

Paul studied each portrait, as if coming home to his true family. In his own portrait, next to Anna's, he saw himself leaping out to show himself to himself. In the corner he saw the initials—A.M.B., 1965.

Silently, they stared for some time at the paintings.

"Ralph Mullen did it," Paul whispered without turning to her. He felt her hand tighten its grip on his.

Tears ran down her cheeks. Paul drew her head to his shoulder, stroked her hair, and wept with her. "It's all over. It's all over."

Out Your Backdoor Press Catalog of Books

Topics

- **Outdoor Culture:**
  Momentum: Chasing the Olympic Dream—Pete Vordenberg
  A Dirt Road Rider's Trek Epic—Victor Vincente of America
  The Cross Country Look, Cook & Pleasure Book—Hal Painter
  The Captain Nemo Cookbook Papers—Hal Painter
- **Fiction**—Jack Saunders, Blackolive and **Potluck** *by Jack Rudloe*
- **Philosophy (Fifth Way Press)**—R. Puhek, V. Lombardi
- **Local Culture Ruminations**—Jeff Potter
- **OYB Anthologies Vols. I/II**—*The Magazine of Cultural Rescue, Modern Folkways and Homemade Adventure (OYB #1-8; #9)*

How to Order

Publisher: Jeff Potter
Mail: OYB Press, 4686 Meridian Rd., Williamston MI 48895
Email: jp@outyourbackdoor.com
Most books $15. Send cash, check, or MO. Shipping included.
Order with a credit card from the OYB Bookstore at OutYourBackdoor.com
All titles available via Amazon, Barnes&Noble, and Borders, who take more than
half the proceeds. Best to order from me directly! All titles in 'Books In Print.'

What is OYB?

What is OYB? It's a resource for otherwise unobtainable books which are at a high
level of cultural development. These titles have an integrity which is hard to find
these days. As a result, perhaps you'll be inspired to set aside any subject biases. If you
don't like bike books, novels, or religion books, don't fret. These ain't like that. OYB
books are cross-training for the brain, often in multi-genre format. Even when they're
about specific topics, they're general interest because they build from the roots of life,
working against fragmentation and alienation. I've read most of what's been done in
these areas, found something lacking, backtracked to the writer who fills that need
(often unknown or out-of-print)...and now publish them for you. A few years ago
this could *not* have happened. Thank you, Internet, for breaking down barriers set
up by the bookstore and publishing establishment. Thank you, DocuTec and recent
short-run printing innovations. Get your hands on an OYB First Edition and you
know you have something worth reading. Be the first on your block. And if you
know of similar topics or books that need help, feel free to let me know. —*Jeff Potter*

Outdoor Culture

Momentum: Chasing the Olympic Dream

AUTHOR: Pete Vordenberg ISBN:1892590565 PAGES: 200 LISTPRICE: $17.95 DESCRIPTION: An inside look into life as an elite XC skier. Vordenberg is a 2X-Olympian, Natl Champ and a current US Team Coach. The most interesting picture to date on what it's like to ski...and live...really fast. (With dozens of black&white photos.) Vordenberg says: "We have seen the Olympics through the filter of mass media. But at the edge of the screen there is another figure. When the camera zooms out you can see him, almost too small to recognize. This is the story of the figure at the edge of your screen. It's a voyage following the pursuit of my dream to win an Olympic gold medal. It travels the world, crossing from childhood to the precipitous edge of adulthood. It shares the quixotic humor, excitement, and poignancy inherent in the pursuit of dreams. It is not a retelling of the little engine that could. Rather, it is about why the little engine even tried." REVIEW: "The marvel of Vordenberg's book is that it appeals to the non-skier as well as to ski racers past and present. Healthy doses of self-revelation, touches of *On The Road*, and remarkable insights make this a unique book. It's supposedly about skiing—but it's more about life and seizing it." —Bob Woodward, veteran XC ski journalist.

The Recumbent Bicycle

AUTHOR: Gunnar Fehlau ISBN:1892590530 PAGES: 180 LISTPRICE: $22.95 DESCRIPTION: There haven't been any general books about a whole amazing, creative side of bicycling: recumbents and HPVs. Finally, here's one! Enjoy. This book covers History, Racing, Touring, Construction and much more, as regards the colorful, diverse world of recumbents and HPVs. Many great black&white photos, full color 12-pg center spread. REVIEWS: 5-star ratings at Amazon.com. "A most informative Recumbenteer's handbook. Its coverage from grass roots right up to current standards is a "must" for anyone interested in building or improving a recumbent."—L. Morse. "This is a fantastic history of recumbents, along with lots of technical information. It has everything you need to know to get started, if you're thinking about buying a recumbent. If you're experienced with recumbents, it has a lot to offer as well."—a reader "No other book that I know of deals with recumbent bicycles in this breadth and depth. It also helps that it is extremely readable and full of cool pictures. Lots of interesting stuff here, from the history of these odd vehicles to the latest speed records and excellent tips on how to get one for yourself. Very well written and well-suited to anyone who might be interested in these bikes, even if they have no previous knowledge. A bargain at twice the price."—P. Pancella.

A Dirt Road Rider's Trek Epic

AUTHOR: Victor Vicente of America ISBN:1892590506 PAGES: 100 LISTPRICE: $15 DESCRIPTION: If you're a bike buff, you know how rare bike literature is. Here's a bit of story-telling to savor, *A Dirt Road Rider's Trek Epic* by Victor Vincente of America, a bike cult guru hero. This book presents the many media offerings of a unique *victor*. The *Epic* is showcased in this volume along with media reprints from VVA's heyday as first US road racing champion, first modern-era Euro winner, first ultra-distance record holder, and early mountain-bike innovator, dirt guru, events host and then some. Illustrated with his own art from many projects, including bike-making, coin art, posters, and stamps. Sports today seem one-dimensional: why? Here's a fantastically different take: the world of a champ who explores widely. Among many surprises, you'll find that offroad riding offers a treasure of lore and insight. Our author has mined a wondrous chunk of life. His notorious So. Calif. newsletter was the first home of his prose-poem about days and nights in the natural and cultural outback.

Fold-It! —The World of the Folding Bicycle

AUTHOR: Gunnar Fehlau ISBN:1892590573 PAGES: 150 LISTPRICE: $21.95 DESCRIPTION: The world's only book with everything you need to know about folding bikes. Covers history, development, features and the various models offered, with pro's and con's. With so much new technology readily available, the scene is booming, and the future of the folding bike never looked better! Elegant established models are still inspiring and holding their own, while gorgeous new models are coming out to challenge rigid bikes in every way—but especially in convenience! Find out for yourself. *(Due to be released April, 2003.)*

DreamBoats: A Look at Small Boats in the Heritage of Seafaring Peoples

Memories, Explanation and Innovation with Coastal Craft, Junks, Dhows, Outriggers & More...in the eyes of an old salt. AUTHOR: Richard Carsen ISBN:1892590549 PAGES: 80 LISTPRICE: $10 DESCRIPTION: There aren't any books about the exotic sailboats of sea-faring peoples for the lay reader. And there sure aren't any on how and why they do what they do and how their methods might help the average backyard boater. 3rd World sailing: who'da thunk it? Richard Carsen did. He's 83 and traveled the world. He writes up his experiences with indigenous boats and rigs in the magazine *Messing About in Boats.* This book is a compilation of Carsen's columns as they appeared in *MAIB*. The anthropology of boats is fascinating and relevant: Western boating developed with expendable crews for maximum profit; 3rd World boating is about sustainability, family, and bringing 'em back alive with enough to live on. It still works this way. Whose heritage or reality seems better to you?

The Cross Country Ski, Cook, Look & Pleasure Book

(Out of Print: some dealer copies available.) AUTHOR: Hal Painter ISBN:1892590514 EDITION: 2 PAGES: 154 LISTPRICE: $20 DESCRIPTION: Reprints and originals available of this 60's-style classic. A unique literary art book on cross country skiing capturing the spirit of the outdoor culture heyday in the US. Zen and the art of skiing. An antidote to consumerism in skiing and an energetic attempt to reconnect skiing with its roots in fluidity, friendship and just plain fun.

The Captain Nemo Cookbook Papers

Everyone's Guide to Zen and the Art of Boating in Hard Times Illustrated, A Nautical Fantasy (Out of Print: some dealer copies available.) AUTHOR: Hal Painter ISBN:18925905522 PAGES: 135 LISTPRICE: $20 DESCRIPTION: Reprints and originals available of this comic 60's look at boating through the eyes of a variety of escapees from the rat race. Zen nuggets, marina etiquette, boat fixer-uppers and an appearance by a wildly mythic hero of boating all combine for a rare literary addition to the boating bookshelf. A great period piece that offers wit and antidotes to the consumerism that's overwhelming modern boating.

Fiction: The Novels of Jack Saunders

General Description of Jack's Style...

In no-holds-barred "Florida writer" tradition, Jack Saunders writes stories about publishing, academia and everyday life, about what it's like to work and succeed while being true to oneself and one's family and culture. He writes honestly and creatively, and that's the understatement of the year--yet it's accessible, fits like a shoe. Tastes like coffee (being an acquired taste, a step up). He writes with encyclopedic insight about how this effort relates to the world around him, other authors, books, movies, music, Florida, cooking, his life, work, business, progress. In folk vernacular with local color that won't quit. Jack names names, uses cultural artifacts in his poetry so superbly you'll be spurred to rent movies, read books, listen to music that you never would've otherwise. Heck, you'll get new appreciation for boxing and baseball..and everything else. (Sailing? Farming?) Folky yet also a linguistic eye-opener. It's that big. It's all about someone trying to do their best in the modern world, to write honestly. Give it a try and see where it gets you, is one of his motifs. Each book is a slice of a larger ouevre (ahem, can you say forklift pallet?)--with letters, memoir, poetry and essay all playing off each other. In the end, though, "it's just stories." Jazz and the blues. In the mainstream of American outsiders: Whitman, Melville, Faulkner, Kerouac, Miller, Algren, Thompson, Bukowski, MacDonald, Willeford, Burke, Hiassen and Finster. As he says, the Cracker spirit lives on and a country boy will make do. Except for insiders, he is entirely unknown. But he's been working close, prolific and giving it his all for 25 years now. Why haven't you heard of him? Find out...

General Reviews of Jack's Books...

In Jack Saunders our generation is extremely lucky to have a powerful and determined writer, an honest writer. A Diogenes not merely of words, but of provocative thoughts. From his hideaway in Florida, like a super-energized lobster, Saunders lashes out at the sickening hypocrisy which is deadening our senses and rotting our souls. It is Saunders' adamant, boneheaded, determined persistence that is his great strength, his great gift to a society staggering in its own materialistic greed. Saunders is America at its best. He spells out what spirit is all about. And humanity. How do we live? When do we really come

ALIVE? As we should? And deserve? America needs writers with such strength and ferocity and independence and integrity, not all those greedy little wordmongers contemplating their private parts on every supermarket shelf. Saunders is more than a literary volcano. He is a live, writhing, crackling wire. Spewing sparks in all directions. Creating and developing a brighter, newer world. *--Raymond Barrio*

As exasperating and slippery a "read" as they come. This work is totally unpretentious (and thus honest) and yet its theme is the total unrelenting pretension of a life. That life is excruciating and unavoidable, unedited and ambiguous, squalling and scrawling, elegant and vulgar, ordinary and completely out of the ordinary. Read it; you'll never forget it. *--John M. Bennett*

I have a hunch your stuff is wild and terrific and keeps going off the rails. I have no better explanation for why you don't find publishers, since you certainly write well enough sentence for sentence and paragraph for paragraph. *-Norman Mailer*

This is some very clever writing...rings true to my own wars with the publishers--good luck! *--Theodore Roszak*

All fine hard hitting work. The works of Jack Saunders give us hope. Hope that our lives won't be horrible wasted foolishness. Even when it seems that hope is all we have left, if you feel you can live a fuller life and spend your days in a more profitable way for yourself AND MANKIND you should read Jack Saunders for a ray of hope and a great deal of enjoyment and amusement. OK it rings so true that you'll forget you're reading & think you're talking to yourself. *--Larry Schlueter*

Hey it broke me up--I imagined someone calling here and asking what I was crying about. I was not crying, kid. I was laughing at Jack Saunders' new movie. *--David Zack*

Nothing studied about this one. He just knows. And does. It hangs together, flows together, makes a lot of sense. Cooking like a Tasmanian Dervish. All I can do is tip my hat. *--Carl Weissner*

Jack Saunders is an American original and his life is an open book. His dedication and commitment are evident throughout, and his abundant energy enlivens every page. *--Lawrence Block*

Screed

AUTHOR:Saunders,Jack,L ISBN: 0912824247 LISTPRICE: $15 DESCRIPTION: Stories about life and dealings with the fine arts scene, as world literature. REVIEWS: Thanks for the copy of Screed. I liked it very much. In fact, I've been reading it aloud to my wife in bed at night. You write in a kind of natural, organic, free-flowing and perfectly lucid style that I much admire. *--Edward Abbey* Dear Jack: Thanks for Screed. It's good diatribe. The reason I know is that diatribe makes me feel better. And I felt better reading it. *--Walker Percy* Thanks for Screed. Nicely done. He rolls on. *--Charles Bukowski*

Evil Genius

AUTHOR: Saunders, Jack L. ISBN: 1892590298 PAGES: 277 LISTPRICE: $15 DESCRIPTION: Mortgages house and gives self Evil Genius Award, first prize ever won. Many cultural reviews. Stories of his days in archeology and grad school, fun with The System, as world literature. REVIEWS: In my library the novels of Jack Saunders go right next to MOBY DICK, ISLANDIA, and THE RECOGNITIONS. EVIL GENIUS is an astonishing feat--like watching a man lay eight hundred miles of track single-handed, without ever once stopping, or faltering, or resorting to adjectives. *--Dr. Al Ackerman* Thank you for sending me EVIL GENIUS, which I read last night. I didn't really want to stay up so late, but the book moved forward with a momentum that was overpowering and almost tragic. Your fiction can also be very annoying-- which is a virtue, I think. *--Richard Grayson* I am very pleased at the way you handled the tale of your life in EVIL GENIUS. It owes something to Henry Miller, but every writer owes a debt to those before them and those in turn were helped by their predecessors. No one is an absolute original, but you come close. *-- William Eastlake* Words for Evil Genius? I took nearly a year out of my own writing time to work on SCREED, on its production, what more need to be said for how I feel about your worth? You're a diamond in the rough, Jack. You've got an intrinsic worth worth more than the realized worth of about 99% of the writers in this country lumped together. If you feel in your heart of hearts that what you're doing is what you must do, then that's settled. Settled with nothing further implied. I'd say your chances of being treated with any sort of kindness, your chances of being recognized for your intrinsic worth, are worse than mine, and mine are Virginia slim. *--John Bennett*

Open Book
AUTHOR: Saunders, Jack L. ISBN: 1892590301 PAGES: 250 LISTPRICE: $15 DESCRIPTION: Covers what happened to Evil Genius, how he goes from bad to worse: who would follow up EG with another book? None but a blockhead. Stories about working life after college, as world literature. REVIEW: Thanks for Evil Genius and Open Book; I enjoyed both of them, and asked my publisher to send you my new book, Sideswipe, when it comes out in Feb. In 1957, Theodore Pratt told me that Delray Beach was a better town than N. Y. for a writer. "If you stay in Florida," he told me, "you'll never run out of things to write about." He was right, of course; I never have, and you won't either. My most productive years were from age 50 to 55, and I'm sure that yours will be too. *--Charles Willeford*

Forty
AUTHOR:Saunders,Jack,L ISBN: 0945209010 LISTPRICE: $15 DESCRIPTION: Stories about Jack's efforts to enter "Stage 4" of writing, to give it up, then see what happens. Plenty of culture and bluegrass reviews and overview of life on the edge, with kids, as world literature.

Common Sense
AUTHOR: Saunders, Jack L. ISBN: 1892590263 PAGES: 137 LISTPRICE: $15 DESCRIPTION: Part 1 of a 2-part series, Jack Saunders writes stories about his efforts to acculturize IBM during the early days of the PC so they wouldn't get left behind by a competitor more in tune with the times...it didn't work. ("Full Plate", book 2.) An open discussion with his superiors asking how a committee system which rewards buck-passing could ever recognize innovation. "This is the only treaty I will make." World literature.

Full Plate

AUTHOR: Saunders, Jack L. ISBN: 1892590271 PAGES: 76 LISTPRICE: $15 DESCRIPTION: Part 2 of a 2-part series, Jack Saunders writes stories about his efforts to acculturize IBM during the early days of the PC so they wouldn't get left behind by a competitor more in tune with the times...it didn't work. ("Common Sense", book 1.) "A Contract between Dem and I'Ashola." World literature.

Blue Darter

AUTHOR: Saunders, Jack L. ISBN: 1892590255 PAGES: 85 LISTPRICE: $15 DESCRIPTION: An aggressive, tricky fast pitch: "Rare back and hurl your blue darter at their ear." Stories from Jack's youth. World literature.

Lost Writings

AUTHOR: Saunders, Jack L. ISBN: 189259028X PAGES: 158 LISTPRICE: $15 DESCRIPTION: "Minor chord: Bigfoot sidles into the shadows." Fiesty writings, as world literature.

Other Fiction

Potluck

AUTHOR: Rudloe, Jack ISBN: 1892590375 PAGES: 264 LISTPRICE: $14.95 DESCRIPTION: Hard times and opportunity collide on the high seas. *Potluck* is a page-turning thriller about a decent captain who decides, in extremity, to take a big risk. It's the only realistic picture of small family commercial fishing on the Gulf Coast of Florida and the problems and temptations that confront it. Corrupt forces on all sides are pushing this stalwart breed of Americans into desperation or extinction. But they still do their best to feed us. If you've ever wondered what the lives are like behind the few fishing boats you still see along the coast, look no further. A rare look at the broad and surprising impacts of drug smuggling, mis-guided regulation and realtor greed along the coast. Author Rudloe is the pre-eminent conservationist of the Florida Gulf Coast, author of highly regarded naturalist books, and operator of the only independent (and thus frequently bureaucratically besieged) marine institute in the region. REVIEW: "Jack Rudloe's non-fiction account of living on the Gulf Coast, *The Living Dock at Panacea*, is a Florida classic that ranks with *Cross Creek*. In *Potluck*, Rudloe proves he can handle fiction with the same energy and insightful style."—Randy Wayne White (*Shark River*, *Sanibel Flats*)

Tales From the Texas Gang

AUTHOR: Blackolive, Bill ISBN: 1892590387 PAGES: 339 LISTPRICE: $19.95 DESCRIPTION: Wild Bill's writing is in the tradition of Melville...and Keroauc and Castenada and Abbey. It's a bit like Cormac McCarthy as well, only more realistic, authentic and candid. If you like the thrust of those other writers, you'll be thankful for *Tales From the Texas Gang*. It's one of the rare significant additions to American literature. And it's based on real life, and a real life gang. It's set in the late 1800's. It's an outlaw gang gunfighter novel...but so much more. (*Due out Fall, 2003.*)

The Emeryville War

AUTHOR: Blackolive, Bill ISBN: 1892590395 PAGES: 109 LISTPRICE: $12.95 DESCRIPTION: If you liked *Confederacy of Dunces*, you'll like this. Only, remember, it's real. Life in the fringey, unhip edge of Berkeley in the 60's. You've never seen neighbors, cops and city officials like these, nor an observer like Wild Bill—dogs, barbels, wrecked cars and all. (*Due out Fall, 2003.*)

Philosophy: Fifth Way Press

Author: Ron Puhek

Fifth Way Press is an imprint of OYB. It is sponsored by the MIEM, the Michigan Institute of Educational Metapsychology—a fancy way to say "workable religion, philosophy and psychology for living today, inspired by the best of the past". The institute has been represented for 30 years by weekly meetings of quiet, polite folk. Typically these have been people from the 'helping' professions who themselves see that their ways need help. Are in desparate straits. Due to modernism. The 'Fifth Way' concept comes from 'the fourth way' of Ouspensky and Gurdjieff. The previous three ways to attain contact with reality were: the emotional way of the monk, the intellectual way of the yogi, and the physical way of the fakir. These were unified and superceded by the fourth way of the householder, who lives normally in everyday life. The Fifth Way takes the best of all ways without leaving any behind, transcending them all: count your fingers: thumbs up!

If you like Simone Weil, St. Theresa and St. John of the Cross, you'll like Puhek. It's plainly written but maximumly intense philosophy for a modern age. His reflections integrate and build on many works, especially Plato, Sartre, Jung and Freud.

Analects of Wisdom

SERIES: The Art of Living, Book 1 AUTHOR: Puhek, Ronald E. ISBN: 1892590123 PAGES: 118 LISTPRICE: $15 DESCRIPTION: Analects are, literally, "cut readings." In this collection of verses and commentaries, not just the verses but even the commentaries are brief. They all use two devices of higher knowledge: *paradoxical logic* and experiential thinking. Representing the first phase of the soul's transformation in this life, the *Analects* provide instruction in how to live. They establish "rules" whose truth can be tested even by the mind still held captive by the senses. Anyone can understand them without a great development of faith. These stirrings of other-worldly wisdom can work effectively in guiding life in this world. We are of the opinion that the verses themselves may have had more than one author. This is almost certainly true of the commentaries. *Analects of Wisdom* is the first volume of the trilogy, *The Art of Living*. This trilogy is companion to its predecessor, *The*

Science of Life, and it is recommended that each volume be read in tandem with its parallel in the other trilogy.

Descent into the World

SERIES: The Art of Living, Book 2 AUTHOR: Puhek, Ronald E. ISBN: 189259014X PAGES: 175 LISTPRICE: $15 DESCRIPTION: As the middle book of the *Art of Living* trilogy, *Descent into the World* deals with the second phase of development. It is the one hardest to pass through. In the first phase as we launch on our inner journey, hope sustains our spirits. In the third phase, as we draw closer to our destination, we see it distinctly ahead and the joy of anticipation arises. The second phase, however, requires that we return to face the world where we will do our final work. The *Descent* describes this harshest and driest time. Now the comforts of inward meditation leave us. We meditate but return to the world where we must overcome severe tests and avoid deep traps if we are to find in the end the redemption of love.

The Redemption of Love

SERIES: The Art of Living, Book 3 AUTHOR: Puhek, Ronald E. ISBN: 1892590158 PAGES: 209 LISTPRICE: $15 DESCRIPTION: Love is the greatest, most enduring, most divine blessing on earth. But love is also suffering, and much of what is done in its name makes it appear to be a curse. The Greeks celebrated love in the form of gods such as Aphrodite and Eros; the ancient Christians said, "God is love." As both indicate, love is a powerful spiritual principle in our lives, but any spiritual principle can be corrupted and its power transformed into a malignant force. *The Redemption of Love* seeks to answer how love gets corrupted and how it can be purified and freed to serve its natural function of rescuing human life and redeeming the world.

<u>Note:</u> *The Redemption of Love* stands on its own but is also the last book in a trilogy called *"The Art of Living,"* which further interacts with another trilogy called *"The Science of Life."* Each of the three volumes in the two trilogies describes development in qualities of soul called hope, faith, and love. The first volume in each trilogy focuses on the inner and outer growth of hope; the second in each, on faith; and the third in each, on love. The twin trilogies are distinct in as much as one (*"The Science of Life"*) deals with the three-step movement to integrity in life by means of an upward and inward journey to knowledge of the integrating good that alone makes a life of integrity possible while the other (*"The Art of Living"*) deals with how actually to live in the world with integrity and meaning. Each volume in the *"Science"* trilogy parallels its like number in the *"Art"* trilogy. This is because the first volume in each represents the principle of *hope*. Hope is the virtue of memory. The first volume of each trilogy represents how human, not individual, memory stimulates and guides hope's development first upward through group study under rules where the group represents human or universal wisdom and then downward through insightful sayings of inherited wisdom guiding life. The second volume in each trilogy represents the subsequent movement of *faith*. Similarly, this involves first an upward direction by losing illusory beliefs in the realm of visible goods and attending to the timeless or eternal good and then a downward direction

in the practical world. Finally, the third volumes represent the movement in *love* upward to the ultimately indefinable Good and downward to living divine love in the world. While each volume stands on its own and can be read independently, there are two additional reading strategies. First, the reader might follow the movement of understanding from one book to the next in the "Science" trilogy and then the movement of life in the world in the "Art" trilogy. Alternatively, the reader might even better follow the path of hope upward in the first book of "Science" and downward in the first book of "Art," then the path of faith upward and downward in the second books of each trilogy, and finally the path of love upward and downward in the third books.

A Guide to the Nature & Practice of Seminars in Integrative Studies

SERIES: The Science of Life, Book 1 AUTHOR: Puhek, Ronald E. ISBN: 1892590093 PAGES: 145 LISTPRICE: $15 DESCRIPTION:"Seminars in Integrative Studies" is written to serve a distinct and special kind of learning. Integrative studies focus on searching for a principle of unity or integrity to hold together our knowledge and our life. These studies concern themselves with consciousness and conscience. Consciousness and conscience are different from mere knowledge and value judgments. Consciousness and conscience are comprehensive and integrating instead of single, narrow and analytical. Consciousness integrates your understanding and conscience integrates your sense of the good. We concentrate here not on offering a preliminary and superficial "exposure" to the concept and practice of integrated knowledge. Instead, we address those with a serious commitment to integrative research and to those working together as a permanent community dedicated to integrative studies. Thus, the idea of "seminars" in integrative studies refers not to classes in any ordinary sense of external enrollment but to personal intention, interest, and involvement. Seminars are regular gatherings of those devoted to pursuing integration in knowledge and life. These seminars have formal and informal rules. They require an inner commitment and a desire to grow to knowledge of life through investigating the nature of life using the only concrete and direct perspective we have: our own existence.

Spiritual Meditations

SERIES: The Science of Life, Book 2 AUTHOR: Puhek, Ronald E. ISBN: 1892590107 PAGES: 166 LISTPRICE: $15 DESCRIPTION: Spiritual Meditations, the second book in the trilogy The Science of Life, is an excursion into the second stage of human spiritual development. Its primary focus is on the practices that will allow us to elevate our understanding so we might better perceive the standard of value that can inwardly bring us peace and outwardly guide us to the best life possible. Integrative knowledge is essential to both and methods of pursuing such knowledge are essential if we are to gain it and live fuller, less violent, and more harmonious lives. None of the methods prevailing today is adequate to the task of arriving at integrative knowledge. This book presents part of the process of an effective response to life.

The Spirit of Contemplation

SERIES: The Science of Life, Book 3 AUTHOR: Puhek, Ronald E. ISBN:

1892590115 PAGES: 175 LISTPRICE: $15 DESCRIPTION: *The Spirit of Contemplation* is the final book in the trilogy *The Science of Life*. It explores the culminating phase of spiritual development and what needs to happen after the completion of the spiritual exercises associated with meditation. Meditation takes us out of the world; contemplation returns us to it. Meditation renders us unable to live in reality; contemplation realizes the redemption of reality. It is the highest peak of the mountain of spritual growth. The entire trilogy, however, is only the first of two. *The Science of Life* concentrates on the development of spiritual understanding; the second trilogy, *The Art of Living*, will focus on the transformation of life.

Meaning & Creativity

SERIES: Blue Trilogy, Book 1 AUTHOR: Puhek, Ronald E. ISBN: 1892590069 PAGES: 118 LISTPRICE: $15 DESCRIPTION: Meaning and Creativity, first book of the Blue Trilogy, explores the illusions of meaning that dominate life today and how to break out of their chains-a vital first step in the process of reality. Life is not worth living if it is not meaningful. Most of the strategies for living today are, however, merely methods of enabling us to endure frightful meaninglessness. They are all mechanical and operate by encouraging us to flee from one meaningless activity as soon as we catch the scent of its decaying character and race to another, equally meaningless. Life becomes a continuous merry-go-round. We move in circles, getting nowhere, but are lost in the illusion that we are moving along a straight path to greater good-even when we try to use methods that are thought to counteract this. So long have we lived like this that if we would wake up and see our true state, we would be shattered. Nihilism would be our fate. To avoid this catastrophe, we need to prepare ourselves with some understanding of how to live a life of meaning. The only meaningful life is a creative life. This is easy to see once we realize what "creativity" consists of.

The Abyss Absolute

SUBTITLE: *The Autobiography of a Suicide* SERIES: Blue Trilogy, Book 2 AUTHOR: Puhek, Ronald E. ISBN: 1892590077 PAGES: 146 LISTPRICE: $15 DESCRIPTION: The Abyss Absolute is the second book of the Blue Trilogy. It is the heart and soul of this series. Realizing the meaning-lessness of most of contemporary life and even understanding how we must live if we are to find meaning are not enough. By themselves, these achievements may end in nothing but disillusion-disillusion of the meaninglessness and disillusion with the prospects of finding an alternative-even among those approaches typically thought to bring hope. This is because before we can find a way upward we must first allow ourselves to fall into an abyss so profound that it feels as if it will annihilate us. Courage to enter this abyss is the only hope of escaping the emptiness of contemporary life, but there are dangerous traps along the way.

Killer Competitiveness

SERIES: Blue Trilogy, Book 3 AUTHOR: Puhek, Ronald E. ISBN: 1892590085 PAGES: 130 LISTPRICE: $15 DESCRIPTION:Killer Competitiveness is the third and last book of the Blue Trilogy. We explored the meaninglessness that dominates life today in Meaning and Creativity, the first book of the series. Then we face a great challenge when we take up a path to meaning in the second book, The Abyss Absolute. This last book accounts for how it is possible for us today to exist so long under meaningless conditions without realizing it. So empty is life without meaning that it could continue only with the help of an extremely powerful illusion. This compelling illusion is generated by competitiveness in nearly everything we do-even in our supposed efforts to cooperate or function independently. Competitiveness generates the illusion of value. Therefore, we do not see the valuelessness of our lives even as we suffer from it.

Mind, Soul & Spirit

An Inquiry into the Spiritual Derailments of Modern Life AUTHOR: Puhek, Ronald E. ISBN: 1892590026 PAGES: 148 LISTPRICE: $15 DESCRIPTION:The prevailing styles of living today require the "derailment" of our energies. The spirit or energy that life grants us to fulfill our destiny is seized, imprisoned, and then turned away from its natural direction, usually to be amplified for ulterior motives. The various derailments of spirit operate unconsciously upon their victims. We today are particularly vulnerable to blindness here because of our ignorance of the dynamics of spiritual life-even as many of us pretend to spirituality and feel energy which we trust to be helpful. Spiritual knowledge is almost completely absent in all contemporary education, and, as a society, we are nearly bankrupt spiritually. This book maps out the many ways our spirit gets diverted without our knowing it. We must take back our spiritual birthright.

The Powers of Knowledge

SERIES: The Crisis in Modern Culture: Book 1 AUTHOR: Puhek, Ronald E. ISBN: 1892590042 PAGES: 83 LISTPRICE: $15 DESCRIPTION: Modern culture is the source of a crisis in civilization. This now world-wide culture is generating increasingly intolerable conditions of human life mostly because of the faulty assumptions built into it that concern our powers of knowledge. Because of these assumptions, we fail today to develop and use the whole range of our powers. Consequently, we find ourselves increasingly unable to perceive, let alone understand, the forces flowing into and out of our lives. We can see that things are bad but not why they are so. We do not see this because the very tools of perception we use are the flawed victims of a culture that renders them inadequate. The Powers of Knowledge (Book I of The Crisis of Modern Culture) explores our powers of knowledge-both those we only partly or wrongly develop and those we entirely neglect. It shows how we may expand our awareness by actualizing all of them in a more integrated way. It illustrates how we can turn aside the forces of destruction that today are reaching critical mass everywhere, even in places we thought were protected.

Violence

SERIES: The Crisis in Modern Culture: Book 2 AUTHOR: Puhek, Ronald E. ISBN: 1892590050 PAGES: 82 LISTPRICE: $15 DESCRIPTION:This book (Book II of The Crisis of Modern Culture) presents an approach to understanding the specific forms of violence particularly appropriate to contemporary life. It illustrates that most violence today is completely invisible both to those who do it and to those who suffer it. This is because the prevailing concept of violence is inadequate. If our concept of violence encompasses only its physical or sensible forms, we will not see it when it operates even when we think we fight against it in its emotional and especially in spiritual forms. Today the dominant form of violence is spiritual. Today we can even love violence because we suffer from it in ways we do not see. Today there is violence in our acts of love. We must be concerned, therefore, both about our love of violence and the violence of our love.

Stephen of the Holy Mountain

AUTHOR: Puhek, Ronald E. ISBN: 1892590018 PAGES: 94 LISTPRICE: $15 DESCRIPTION: An inner journey, outwardly masking itself as a sojourn up the side of a high mountain, Stephen of the Holy Mountain seeks answers to the most perplexing questions that come to those who have awakened from the sleep of ordinary existence. The mysterious figure of Stephen acts as a guide both to the author and to many others who climb Stephen's mountain to find him. His advice is often too harsh for many who think they seek it. Unfailingly kind, however, Stephen does his best to aid all who come to him.

The Metaphysical Imperative

A Critique of the Modern Approach to Science AUTHOR: Puhek, Ronald E. ISBN: 1892590034 PAGES: 135 LISTPRICE: $15 DESCRIPTION: Metaphysical assumptions are and have always been a necessary and unavoidable part of human life. Unfortunately, today we have fallen into the catastrophic belief that our basic perceptions of reality do not rest on metaphysical judgments but are purely "physical." If we use the term "metaphysics" at all, it is only to refer to abstract philosophical ideas or, worse, to half-crazed religious attitudes. Consequently, we have rendered ourselves unable to distinguish between the metaphysical and non-metaphysical aspects of any knowledge and are still less able to judge whether our hidden or flaunted metaphysical assumptions are faulty and, if so, how they might be corrected. The Metaphysical Imperative explores the nature of metaphysical assumptions, how they are all-pervasive, which ones dominate our attitudes today, what their flaws are, and how we might improve them.

Social Consciousness

Renewed Theory in the Social Sciences AUTHOR: Puhek, Ronald E. ISBN: 189259000X PAGES: 202 LISTPRICE: $15 DESCRIPTION:This is a unique study of the theoretical foundations of social science. In particular, it criticizes the practice of applying the methods of the physical sciences to the study of human life. Methods very appropriate to the study of "things" or objects are not appropriate to the study of the human self. When we use such inappropriate methods, we end in making the human self into a thing, and all the knowledge we gain affords us only more power to dominate and suppress the human. These methods violate human freedom and dignity in any use, let alone in their application in fields like psychology, advertising and politics. This study concludes by developing an alternative approach to explanation.

Matricide

AUTHOR: Lombardi, Vincent L. ISBN: 189259031X PAGES: 287 LISTPRICE: $15 DESCRIPTION: A novel about a crime that shook a small town and hurled a 12-year-old girl into the bizarre world of court-appointed professionals. As she grows up, she's driven to madness, torn between cultures, struggling at the crossroads of what comes next—will it be Brave New World or a new Renaissance?

Local Culture Ruminations

Growing Up in Freeway Exitville: Making Somewhere from Nowhere

AUTHOR: Potter, Jeff PAGES: 100 LISTPRICE: $15 DESCRIPTION: Contemporary essays written about the author's hometown—a faceless suburb of professors, professionals, mall-rats, and mini-malls. A rare look at 'here,' but perhaps it's important to break the aversion to looking at what's closest to home since everywhere is starting to look like 'here.' —It's a traffic-packed sector smashed out of the rural countryside in the last 30 years. But it's also a place with hidden natural and cultural distinctions. How can it survive the onslaught of speculation? That's the drama of it. Potter writes about Place versus Noplace and offers practical methods which can be used to rebuild somewhere out of the nowhere created by our best and brightest. A candid, polite, unpublishable point of view unseen before (the average view) intended to raise the level of discussion by taking it away from experts, specialists and those who hope to separate people from each other for their advantage.

"Out Your Backdoor" Zine Anthology, Vols. 1 & 2

OYB: the Magazine of Cultural Rescue, Modern Folkways and Homemade Adventure (*OYB* Issues #1-8 & #9)

OYB has been covering the neglected aspects of modern folk culture since 1990. The latest issue is the Vol. 2 anthology; earlier issues form Vol.1.

OYB is the back porch of culture, where people hang out helping each other find the nifty things that people really do. (The front door being for salesmen and authorities.) *OYB* revives the jaded, helps those who've 'been there, done that' to get to the next level. *OYB* is for all-rounders and generalists, like most people are. It works against the alienating specialties that society uses to split us from ourselves and each other. It creatively explores all sorts of things, including: biking, books, boats, movies, zines, religion, skiing, fishing, hunting, garage sales, getting by, making do. Get the picture? (Big website at www.outyourbackdoor.com.)